Jenny

Margaret Alty

Published 2010 by arima publishing
www.arimapublishing.com

ISBN 978 1 84549 442 1
© Margaret Alty 2010

Printed and bound in the United Kingdom

Typeset in Garamond 11/14

Swirl is an imprint of arima publishing.

arima publishing
ASK House, Northgate Avenue
Bury St Edmunds, Suffolk IP32 6BB
t: (+44) 01284 700321
www.arimapublishing.com

Chapter One
SOUTH OF FRANCE

They had driven south from Calais early in the morning as soon as the ferry had docked, stopping briefly half-way for something to eat: freshly baked baguettes still warm from the oven, filled with thick slices of camembert and it was late afternoon by the time they arrived in Villefranche-sur-Mer. It had been an easy journey; no problems, but mile after mile on the toll roads had been tedious, therefore, once they were on the coast road, with the incredible blue of the sea on their right and following them for the rest of the way, their flagging spirits began to dissipate.

'Wow!' Jenny exclaimed, leaning forward in her seat, 'This is brilliant! So much colour! It reminds me of one of those old movies when you expect to see Grace Kelly zooming past in an open-top sports car!'

'Good, eh?' James smiled at her, taking his eyes away from the road for a second.

'Okay. Okay,' she laughed, 'I'm behaving like a complete moron, but I've never been here before, remember?'

'I know, Jenny,' he said, 'so forgive me if I sound blasé. I don't mean to be, you know.'

'You're so lucky, James,' Caroline said from the back seat, 'to have parents who actually *own* a property here! Don't you think so, Paul?' she nudged the man sitting next to her.

'She's right,' Paul answered, having for the last fifty kilometres or so been drifting in and out of sleep, and pulling himself upright, 'it's a totally different world, isn't it?'

'Yes,' James agreed, changing gear as they entered the town and pulling up at the first set of traffic lights, 'but don't forget it is all a bit artificial; not quite real.'

'James!' Jenny exclaimed, turning sideways to look at him, a look of indignation on her face, 'At times you are such a cynic. Don't spoil it for us; let us just enjoy.'

The villa; one of several on the high ground overlooking the sea, had a sleepy afternoon look, with all its wooden shutters firmly closed. The building was on two storeys, a stone parapet running along the entire length of it; a curtain of blue and purple wisteria clinging to the window frames and drifting down on to the paved terrace below; enormous Matisse-blue pots; an identical shade to the shutters and filled to overflowing with geraniums: a riot of red, pink and white flowers, adding further splashes of dramatic colour. James drove up the steep drive, stopping in front of the garage and the four of them clambered out from the car.

'You *have* got a pool, I hope?' Caroline asked, running her fingers through her blonde curls, damp from too many hours of being confined inside the car which didn't have the luxury of air conditioning.

'Of course,' he grinned, 'it's at the back; we have to go through the house though.' he added, handing her a bunch of keys.

'Great,' she enthused, 'this I must see!'

'More than that,' Jenny put in, 'before I do anything else I'm going in!'

'Hey, you two,' James called to them, hauling out luggage from the boot, 'give us a hand with these! After all, most of this stuff is yours! Paul and I travel light.'

'Later,' Jenny laughed, 'I only need my bikini anyway, so I'll take this one.' she said, grabbing one of the smaller bags from him and following Caroline inside.

Most of the ground floor was open-plan; spacious, cool and uncluttered; pine-stripped flooring; cream-painted walls; rattan sofas and chairs with patterned linen cushions in pale lilac and lemon-green; a long glass-topped table and high-backed pine chairs. The girls threw back the shutters, immediately filling the room with light; softer now than the glaring brightness of earlier in the day. Sliding glass doors ran the length of one wall and opened out on to a stone-flagged terrace to face the swimming pool: a perfectly shaped oval, the water crystal clear and sparkling.

'I do believe,' Jenny said, looking at Caroline, her eyes bright with excitement, 'we are going to have a fantastic holiday!'

They were not disappointed. The days passed quickly; far too quickly, spent mostly during the first week swimming, sunbathing, idling away the hours of Mediterranean sunshine and waking up each morning to another hot day. They ate out each evening; much later than they did in London, waiting until almost eight to stroll down to the town and on to the quayside; their only decision being which restaurant to choose. It was in the one specialising in sea food and where they had been to a couple of times, when they met Ben Standish for the first time. They had noticed him before; he was never on his own, always with at least half a dozen other people. He had masses of confidence; handsome in a sleek Italian sort of way; dark hair worn slightly longer than the average Englishman, his clothes also: a fine cotton open-necked pink shirt, cream linen trousers and loafers. They had been quick to suss out he wasn't Italian at all, but English, with a slight London accent, also that he was quite a bit older than any of them; at least in his thirties and to them that was old.

That evening, he had looked across, only half-listening to what the woman sitting next to him was saying and, raising his glass, smiled at them.

'Cheeky sod!' James muttered under his breath.

'Sssh,' Jenny warned him, 'he's only being friendly.'

'I wonder who he is,' Caroline said, 'someone pretty important, I would say.'

'There you go again, Caroline,' Paul smiled at her, 'dramatising everyone you see. You've been doing it ever since we landed on French soil this morning!'

'Well,' she grinned back at him, 'I *am* an actress, so you should find it in your heart to forgive me!'

They were about to leave the restaurant when the man they had been watching stood up and walked over to their table.

'Hi, there.'

'Hi.' Caroline said.

'Ben Standish,' he said, shaking hands with her, 'you're staying in one of the Ridge villas, aren't you?'

'Observant.' James muttered again, ignoring the dig in the ribs from Jenny.

'We are, yes,' Caroline said, 'how did you know?'

'Easy,' he smiled, 'Villefranche, in case you haven't had time to realise it yet, is very much a village and two of my very good friends,' he went on, pointing back to his table, 'Diana and Stephan; they're neighbours of yours.'

'Really?'

'Yes and new arrivals here are like the proverbial breath of fresh air.'

'The villa we're staying in,' Jenny put in, 'belongs to James' parents.'

'I know.'

'Well,' James spoke for the first time, 'this is all very interesting and it's good to meet you – Ben,' he hesitated slightly over the name, 'but it's getting late and we must get back.'

'The night is young,' Ben smiled, 'why don't you join us? Believe me,' he added, 'it isn't often we have anyone new around here.'

And this is how it all started: the four of them; James and Paul with reluctance going along with the girls and joining the party at Ben Standish's table. It was late when they finally left the restaurant, and as they walked back up to the villa none of them were too sure what to make of him. He was charming, there was no doubt about that; he had an air of sophistication which they had never so far experienced, but he was fun, flattering and good company. His friends, while politely making room for them, displayed little interest which merely served as a reminder they could never be considered to be part of their clique and merely tolerated because Ben Standish had asked them. It was so completely different to what they were used to in London: impromptu parties, not much spare cash, but enough to buy a couple of litres of cheap red wine, sitting cross-legged in James' apartment and listening to rock music and sometimes for some nostalgia, John Lennon's 'Imagine' and Chris de Borg's 'Lady in Red'. They knew where they were; no-one was pretending to be someone else, not like this crowd. Even Jenny, who prided herself on being cosmopolitan and open-minded, did admit, albeit reluctantly, the falseness of it all, but it didn't prevent her from enjoying herself. Caroline also gave every appearance of accepting these new people; at least she never said anything to the contrary. Paul was the same, a laid-back kind of guy who could go through life without getting too rattled, but neither would he be blind to any pretentiousness and certainly Ben Standish and his entourage veered close to that. James was different; he had been brought up during school holidays and later university breaks, living cheek-by-jowl with those on-the-surface characters, although probably not all so unique in that part of Europe; the Côte d'Azur, where money appeared to be in plentiful supply and where only the rich and beautiful were treated with indulgence.

From that first evening, Ben was always around. He didn't seem to work and none of them felt the need to ask him and why should they? He told them he had a villa in Cap d'Ail, further along the coast on Monaco's doorstep and where they spent much of their time at the end of each day; the same crowd would be there, most of them Italian. There was always plenty of food set out for them on the terrace; a vast choice of dishes and more wine than they had ever known in their lives before. Ben also owned a yacht which he kept anchored off Cannes where they had enjoyed a few evenings, which stretched into the early hours; dancing and drinking and revelling in an extravagant lifestyle but, at the same time, having the sense to realise they would probably never experience again and they made the most of it.

'I've been thinking,' James said towards the end of their three weeks and they were all satiated by the sun, too much wine from the night before and spread out on loungers at the edge of his pool, 'about our friend, Ben.'

'What about him?' Caroline asked lazily, on the edge of sleep.

'He reminds me of someone.'

'Someone you've met?'

'No, at least I don't think so,' he answered slowly, his eyes narrowing with the effort of trying to remember, 'but he looks familiar; it could have been a photograph in a magazine or a newspaper. Oh, I don't know.' he said, giving up.

'Apparently,' Jenny remarked, 'everyone has a double.'

'Do they?' he grinned at her.

'What's so funny?'

'I was just imagining two like you, that's all.'

'Cheeky!' she laughed, 'I do have a sister, you know.'

'And I bet she isn't like you at all.'

'Well, not really,' she admitted, 'she's far more serious.'

'There you are then!'

'Going back to Ben, though,' Paul put in, 'James is right. I'm sure I've seen a photograph of him somewhere; at least it looked very much like him. I'm trying to remember the name, but I'm sure it wasn't Standish.'

'Perhaps he changed it.' Caroline suggested.

'He could have, I suppose,' James said, taking her seriously, 'people do.'

'Come on, you lot,' Jenny laughed, 'get real! Ben's okay, a bit of a smoothie, I'll admit, but you can't fault his generosity.'

Two nights before they were due to leave Ben threw another party on his yacht and, as previously, they were taken out on the speedboat to where he had it moored. The music was loud and Ben was in good form, greeting them effusively and telling them how sorry he was they would be going soon. Jenny and Caroline had dressed up especially: both in long white cotton shifts which accentuated their suntan, with scarlet and royal blue sashes tied around their waists. The boys in white denim, and pale blue and white striped muslin shirts they'd bought in the market the week before when they had spent the day in Antibes.

It was a warm balmy evening; too hot to stay inside, and they had stepped out on to the deck, taking their glasses of wine with them, to stand against the rail; each of them thinking that their holiday, which had been perfect, was almost at an end: Jenny and Caroline to their repertory company in Guildford; James to his accountancy firm and Paul back to being a club reporter for his newspaper in London's Fleet Street.

'I wish I could stay here forever.' Jenny sighed, leaning over the rail and staring out towards the lights stretched along the shore.

'What about your dreams?' James asked, putting an arm around her.

'My dreams?'

'Yes, Sarah Bernhardt.'

'Very funny,' she smiled up at him, 'but I could get work here in one of the theatres.'

'I don't think so.' Caroline said.

'Why not?'

'For the simple reason, Jenny Graham, we are in France and in case you hadn't noticed they speak French here!'

'Alright,' Jenny sighed again and took a long sip from her glass, 'but one day I will live in the sun. I mean it!' she added, throwing a defiant look up at James.

Light banter and that was all it was, neither of them really meant what they were saying; they were merely enjoying the moment and wanting it to last. When raised voices reached them from further along the deck, they each reacted in the same way; shocked that anything could disturb such tranquillity. They didn't say anything, but turned to face from where the voices were coming. Ben had come out on deck with two men; they were standing against the rail and one of them; they had seen him a number of times before; he was often in their company, took a sudden step forward and pushed Ben in the chest. Although they were shouting, they couldn't make out what they were saying; they were too far away, also the music was too loud, but they were arguing, that was obvious, and the four of them stood transfixed, waiting to see what would happen next. They didn't have long to wait. Ben moved to one side and made to walk away, but one of them was too quick for him: with a single movement he pinned Ben hard up against the rail, raising his feet from the deck while the other man, taller and more heavily built, shouted something and ran at him, instantly winding him and before they had time to grasp what was happening Ben was over the rail and into the sea. Simultaneously, they heard a gun being fired, but later, much later; they could never be certain, because someone inside had turned up the volume of the music.

'What the hell!' James yelled and started to run over to where the two men were now standing.

'James,' Jenny called out, dragging him back, 'don't interfere, they're armed!'

'My God!' Caroline gasped, ashen-faced as she stared at the spot where they had seen Ben going overboard. 'They've killed him!'

'Let go, Jenny,' James said, pushing her hand away, 'I'm going over there.'

'Not a good idea, James.' Paul said, 'I mean it; better not.'

'We can't just stand here,' he protested, 'and pretend nothing has happened!'

The men, perhaps for the first time noticing they had an audience, moved away from the rail and walked over towards them.

'What the hell is going on?' James demanded.

'That, young man is none of your business.' the thick-set man said to him, moving closer.

'That's where you are wrong.' James retaliated, 'we just saw what happened to Ben.'

By this time, the other man had joined them and with a smooth belligerent expression on his handsome face; the white of his dinner jacket shining beneath the lanterns above their heads, said: 'If you know what's good for you,' and making a point of looking at James directly, 'you will, all of you in fact, forget what you've seen.'

'You shot him, didn't you?' James insisted.

'Only a flesh wound, nothing more serious than that,' the man replied with an elegant shrug, 'he's probably swum ashore by now.'

'Flesh wound, my bloody foot!' James muttered under his breath.

'James, please,' Jenny pulled him back again, taking one of his hands, 'drop it.'

'Sensible lady.' The man said, his dark eyes appraising her, undisguised lust in his expression.

'Okay.' James said, raising his hands in mock surrender. He may have noticed the way the man was looking at her, but even if he hadn't he knew when he was losing. Who would believe them anyway; four young holidaymakers, guests on board one of the local resident's private yacht reporting a fight? A killing? He had spent enough time in that part of France to recognise the mafia when he met them and had heard enough stories and that was not to become involved, at any price.

In the short time left in Villefranche each of them continued to hope Ben may get in touch, not wanting to believe he may be dead and lying at the bottom of the Mediterranean, but he didn't. They did try to contact him, but his housekeeper; a woman they had seen a number of times but who couldn't speak one word of English, conveyed to them when they called at his villa, that Monsieur Standish was not there. And with that somewhat ambiguous explanation, they had no alternative but to accept they wouldn't be seeing him again and the following morning they closed up the villa where, for the most part of their holiday had been idyllic, and drove back up to Calais.

Neither of them forgot the incident; at least not for some time and James, in particular, couldn't prevent considering himself to be something of a wimp. He should have reported it, but to whom? The police? What could he tell them; that he had witnessed a fight on board a private yacht and the owner had been shot and thrown overboard? Who would believe him? He was pretty sure that the four of them hadn't been the only ones to see what had happened, but given the sort of people they were, they would hardly admit it. To do so would destroy their fun-loving existence he had concluded cynically.

It was several months later when James received a call from Paul telling him he had remembered where he had seen a photograph of Ben Standish. By now, rapidly losing interest in the whole business, James reluctantly listened to him.

'It was in one of the Sunday supplements,' Paul went on, 'an article about people who had succeeded in avoiding arrest. It was Ben Standish alright; there's no mistake, a different name naturally, but it was him.'

'And what was he supposed to have done, then?'

'In these days, nothing original,' Paul said, 'but apparently this was about four years ago; he had been working as an inside trader for one of the major European banks and managed to siphon off a vast sum of money. Falsifying accounts, you know, that kind of thing.'

'Clever. And then disappeared?'

'Yep, and if we are right and it was Ben, he's certainly built up for himself a rather lavish lifestyle on the proceeds.'

'*If* we are right,' James emphasised, 'also, *if* he's still alive!'

Chapter Two
ENGLAND

Tuesday, 14th June, Ten Years Later

Annette Graham, tired and stressed out from the long flight from San Francisco which had been over two hours late arriving at Heathrow, let herself into her apartment and as she always did when she had been away, walked over towards the ceiling-high plate glass windows. Centre stage: Chelsea Bridge. To see the myriad of lights illuminating the embankment along the stretch of the Thames was all she needed to remind her she was back home and as she stood there, looking over to what she always thought of as her part of London, gave a deep sigh of pleasure before turning away.

The green light was blinking on the answering machine and shrugging off her jacket and tossing it on to the sofa, she flicked the switch: two messages and both from David Grech asking her to call him. He didn't say urgently, but he didn't need to. She was swearing under her breath as she dialled his number. Why had she not told Jenny she was going to be away? Normally, Annette was meticulous about keeping in touch with her, although it was very much one-sided: Jenny was not into communicating, at least not on any regular basis, but it didn't make any difference; she still felt guilty. Her trip to the associate publishers in Oakland had been a last-minute decision. The problems over there had been simmering for some time and when Quenton had said jump that was what she had done. As always, but it was still no excuse; to have called her would only have taken minutes.

It was some time before David answered; his voice croaky as if he had a cold, but perhaps the call had woken him. She hadn't realised how late it was and with the one hour difference between England and Malta it would be well after midnight with him.

'Annette!' he said, 'I've been trying to call you!'

'I'm sorry,' she said, 'I really am, David, but I've been in the States and I've only just got back. What's wrong? It's Jenny, isn't it?'

'She's missing –'

'– Missing? What do you mean?'

She realised as soon as she uttered the words how banal they must sound. She also knew her reaction was irrational, but she was unable to take in what he had said and suddenly a wave of tiredness washed over her; the long flight fast catching up.

'It was on Friday morning,' he went on, his words sounding stilted as though he had said them many times before, 'I had an early appointment and left home shortly after seven. I thought Jenny was still asleep, but she couldn't have been, because someone, a man walking his dog along the edge of the water in Saint Paul's Bay, noticed that the door of my boat-shed was wide open and the boat wasn't in there. This was at eight-thirty,' he added, pausing for a fraction of a second, 'we'd had a storm the night before and there is always a swell around the north of the island afterwards and that –' he hesitated and this time she was too afraid to interrupt him, '– that,' he repeated, 'was where the boat was found; on the rocks, close to the hotel in Golden Bay.'

'And Jenny?' her name came out as a whisper.

'There was no sign of her, Annette. The police –'

'– police?'

'I had to call them.'

'Of course, I'm sorry, I'm being obtuse, but I want to know everything,' she insisted, 'What are they saying?'

'That it was a boating accident.'

Annette allowed his words to sink in, to penetrate the mounting fatigue and with a tremendous effort she tried to pull back from the weakening and enveloping despair which threatened to engulf her. Jenny; her sister. What he'd been telling her did not make any sense; no sense at all.

'And what do you think, David?'

She waited for him to answer, holding her breath, dreading what he was going to say next, but the need to know was far stronger.

'Oh, Annette,' he said at last, 'I honestly don't know what to think. I warned her not to take the boat out. She knew how treacherous these waters can be, but you know Jenny?'

'We're talking about my sister here, David,' Annette said sharply, immediately annoyed at the implication, 'Jenny is not reckless. Both of us were taught to respect the sea. I don't know whether she told you or not, but as children we spent most summers with our grandparents in Scotland; on the east coast, and we were well accustomed to changing conditions. Along that stretch of coastline the sea mist, or haar as it is described locally, could come in without any warning, so both of us developed an extra sense, also, our grandfather was an extremely hard task-master.'

'I know, Annette, I know,' he said and she realised he was trying to calm her down, 'but,' he went on, the sadness in his voice reaching out to her, 'what else can I think? They found the boat late on Friday –' this time his voice broke.

'- and still nothing?' she finished for him.

'Nothing.'

'David,' she persisted, 'you say the police have reached their decision, does this mean they have stopped looking for her?'

'I'm afraid so,' he answered, 'as far as they are concerned the incident is closed.'

'This is not an – an incident! My sister has disappeared! Perhaps at sea, but how do we know? Is this the best they can come up with – a boating accident! How can they be so certain? Are they not asking any questions; did anyone actually see her take the boat out that morning? Surely there must have been some-one?'

'I don't know what the police have been doing, Annette. If they were asking any questions, how do I know they were the right ones?'

'David,' she said, 'I just do not understand any of this. I'm trying to get my head around what you've told me, but all I know is that Jenny can't be found. They've got the boat, but –' she floundered.

'I feel exactly the same way, you know.' he said, 'Would it be possible for you to fly out? I feel that between us we could – oh, I don't know –'

'- David,-' she interrupted, 'you shouldn't need to ask. Of course I'll come. I *have* to find out what has happened.'

'Thank you, Annette.'

They rang off, with Annette promising to get the next available flight to Malta. First, she would have to clear it with Quenton, but that could wait until the morning. He was not going to be happy, but this time she decided it was just too bad. Even although she'd had no time off for over a year, it wouldn't make any difference to him. Quenton Barton was a tough employer and she had learned, provided she was always available and more than willing to dance to his particular tune, their working relationship would continue smoothly. She wasn't looking forward to the confrontation and already in her head beginning to write the script. But first, sleep. She turned off the lights in the lounge and prepared for bed, setting the alarm for seven. As she pulled the duvet over her shoulders and closed her eyes, willing herself to blot out at least for a few hours her worst imaginings, one thought predominated. She did not believe Jenny had gone; it was not possible. She had poured a generous measure of whisky into a mug of hot chocolate and the concoction worked, although she awoke long before the alarm went off, reluctantly opening her eyes, staring into the darkness and wishing it was time to get up.

Annette lay quite still and permitted herself to think about Jenny; her thoughts and memories moving backwards over the years. Jenny, her little sister, five years younger and even when they were still children, Annette had always felt responsible for her. Their mother had instilled in her this sense of responsibility, making it clear as she was the elder she had to look after her, ensuring she didn't come to any harm. They had been total opposites; she, the quiet one, content to spend hours on her own, curled up in front of the log fire in winter with a book and during the long summer months sitting below the trailing branches of the oak tree in their garden, sometimes reading, but more often than not, dreaming. Later, in their teens, when they spent their holidays up north, she would enjoy the swimming, remembering how the sea never got really warm, also the happy hours they spent out on their grandfather's boat, but she would always find time to wander off on her own. Jenny had been different. She would seldom sit still; always on the go and surrounded by friends. Wherever she went she seemed to collect them effortlessly, nothing worried her and, later, when they started having boyfriends, Jenny, quick to become bored, would flit from one boy to the next with never a backward glance or regret that she may have hurt his feelings. Acting, therefore, was probably the only profession she could have excelled in, which she did. Her natural spontaneity and her ability to skilfully absorb her personality into each of the roles she played, made her a joy to watch.

And, Annette sighed, where was she now? She hadn't seen her for almost a year; it had been a couple of days before she had left for Malta on holiday and then followed a week later by the excited phone call to say she would be staying on there and joining a new theatre on the island. Since then, there had been a few calls, not many, and letters were even more scarce. Annette remembered the last one she had received and throwing back the duvet and reaching for her wrap, padded barefoot across the bedroom to where she had left her bag.

The letter had arrived on the same morning, a week ago, when she was leaving for the States and she hadn't had time to reply to it. Taking it out and unfolding it, she read again what Jenny had written in her spidery scroll, in particular the part which had puzzled her at the time, although not unduly. Jenny was inclined to over-dramatise and Annette had learned not to pay too much attention to what often appeared to be ramblings and this one was no exception: "...... something rather strange happened the other night," her practically indecipherable words meandered and spread across the page, "so odd in fact, I can't be absolutely sure it was the same person. But it was the voice really. You know, Annette, when you think you recognise someone you once knew even although they actually look quite different? He could, I suppose, have a double! But, if I am right, well it's far too serious to jump to conclusions. I have to be sure, so I'm going back to the casino and see if he is there again. He might be and if so, I will know whether I am imagining things or not ......"

How like Jenny. She would begin a tale and you were even more confused when she reached the end, which was always as obscure and frustrating as when she started. Thoughtfully, Annette placed the letter back into her bag, wondering whether she should attach any importance to it. The ringing of the alarm made her jump, running over to the bedside to turn it off; the interruption acting as a signal.

Up to that moment she had not thought of any specific plan when she arrived in Malta, just to get there as soon as possible. She must talk to David again and to Jenny's friends and somehow try to piece together what she had been doing in the days leading up to her disappearance. She refused to believe she would have taken the boat out if there had been the remotest sign of any danger. Beyond that, she forced herself not to speculate; there was time enough for that, but first things first; the call to the travel agency before phoning Quenton. That way, with her flight booked it would, she hoped, be a *fait accompli*.

She was in luck; there had been a cancellation on the late afternoon's flight from Heathrow. The call to Quenton was not so straightforward, not that she expected anything else. Annette had not worked for him for the last ten years without understanding him and learning how to ride out the ebb and flow of his quick temper.

'I don't believe this, Annette!' was his first reaction, explosive but predictable. 'What do you think you'll achieve by flying off to that god-forsaken place. Looking for your sister, you say,' he went on and she could visualise his expression: the normally pallid complexion would be flushed and the wispy red-blond hair standing on end where he had run his fingers through it, 'that's the actress one, isn't it?'

'Quenton, I only have one sister and you're right, I don't know whether I will achieve anything, but I have to try.'

'What about my report?' Jenny now forgotten, he continued, true to form. 'You've just spent the last seven days in Oakland, Annette! We're talking about crucial company decisions here!'

'You'll get your report, Quenton;' she replied, a lot calmer than she felt. It wasn't often he managed to get to her, but he was succeeding that morning which only showed how fragile her nerves were, 'it's almost completed, anyway.' she went on, wondering if he would recognise the exasperation in her voice, 'I wasn't exactly idle on the flight back last night.'

'You do surprise me.' he retorted, the sarcasm apparent in every syllable, again predictable. It was the way he was; larger than life and equally as difficult.

'Quenton,' she began, keeping her tone level when all she wanted to do was yell at him, tell him for once in his life to consider other people and not always his publishing business.

'I'll fax it to you later this morning, around lunchtime. I'm not leaving until five.'

'So, you've booked your flight?' belligerent now, but she didn't respond. It hardly merited a response in any case she decided, realising she may say something she would later regret. Quenton was after all the person who authorised her monthly pay cheque.

'I have to do this, Quenton.'

'Okay. Okay. I am not completely insensitive, you know.' he said, quieter now, You are good at your job, Annette, very good; I shouldn't need to tell you that, but with you away it's not only going to be bloody inconvenient, it also means you won't be able to follow up on the Oakland business. The problem out there is going to worsen and you are the only person who has the ability to accurately assess the situation and tell me precisely what those idiots are playing at. I can rely on you handling it, Annette, and not to fill your report with a load of bullshit, like some of these still wet-behind-the-ears ex-graduates we have the dubious pleasure of having on our payroll!'

Flattery indeed, she thought cynically, not that he intended it as such. That wasn't his way, although she did sense a slight softening in his manner, but didn't allow herself to be seduced; he wasn't finished yet. Stifling a sigh, she waited.

'Look, Annette,' he said with well-practised persuasion in his voice. She had heard it often enough before with recalcitrant and unbending authors, and printers demanding payment, but it was there all the same and this time, for a change, she was at the receiving end. 'as you know, I have to be in Rome this weekend, why don't I break my journey on the way back and stop off in Malta. I might be able to help.' She was appalled, not expecting him to come from this angle. The last thing she wanted was for him bulldozing his way into whatever it was she was trying to achieve. It would be a disaster.

'I know what you're thinking, Annette,' he went on, jovial now; well into the second part of his placating act, 'I do know Malta pretty well which may come as a surprise to you and I wouldn't get in the way, step on anyone's toes; I'd keep in the background.'

An impossible promise! If the whole situation wasn't so dire, she would have laughed.

'I never —' Annette started to protest, politely, but having no idea how she could tell him he wouldn't be welcome and perhaps it was just as well he didn't give her the chance.

'Hush,' he interrupted, 'let's leave it like this, shall we? You go off to Malta, see what you can do to find that sister of yours. And for God's sake, keep in touch with the office. I'll phone you from Rome on Friday night and see how things are going. Okay?'

'Okay,' Annette agreed, 'and, Quenton, thank you. I know it's inconvenient for me being away at this time, but I am worried about her.'

It was with relief when she at last could replace the receiver. At least, she thought, they had reached a compromise; of a sort. There was no one else she needed to ring. Her friends were used to her flitting between London and the States and wouldn't be too concerned if they didn't hear from her for a few more days. Their parents were both in Australia on a six months' trip and she was reluctant to get in touch with them. Not yet. First, she must find out more.

Settling down at her desk, a mug of freshly made coffee in front of her, Annette reflected, but not for long, on how her life had changed; had moved back into the comfortable and relatively easy groove to how it had been before she had met Steve. They had spent three years together, but almost from the beginning of their relationship, it was apparent they would find it difficult to juggle their careers, and her frequent absences to America had not helped. Those days of being involved solely with one person seemed to her a lifetime away and with that prosaic thought she opened the file containing Quenton's report and began to pick up from where she had left off the night before.

Chapter Three
MALTA

The plane touched down at Luqa Airport at ten. Annette felt, as she stepped on to the tarmac, she had been travelling for days, which in a way she supposed she had been. This wasn't the first time she had visited Malta, but it had been some years ago and she had forgotten how stiflingly hot it could be, even so late at night; the way, during those first few seconds, it was necessary to catch one's breath, to adjust to the change of air. She missed the warm dry Californian climate, especially those evenings when, as soon as dusk fell, there would be a cool freshness.

Everything in Arrivals was exactly as she remembered it; little had changed. The straggle of coach drivers at the end of the barrier, each holding up the name of the tour group they were meeting; the loud voices echoing from the high ceilings; the sudden burst of laughter from the taxi drivers at the exit as they waited for their fares; even the passengers, most of them tourists at that time of the year, looked the same to her: tired and harassed parents pushing trolleys piled high with luggage and the children; so many of them, weaving in and out of the crowd, getting in everyone's way, squealing with delight after being confined for what must have seemed to them an incredibly long time on the flight over.

Annette had already reserved a room at the Holiday Inn Crowne Plaza in Sliema, choosing that one for the simple reason it was where she had stayed before. David had suggested she could stay with him in Balluta Bay, but she had tactfully declined, wanting to retain her independence, to come and go as she pleased and while she realised his villa would no doubt be luxurious from what Jenny had told her, it could create drawbacks. Also, never having met him, she was yet to get to know him and wanted to avoid any awkwardness.

Jenny's letter was beginning to disturb her now she'd had some time to think over what she had written. She hadn't mentioned it to David, mainly because she had no idea how serious he viewed their relationship. That would have to wait until she finally met him. If what Jenny had obliquely indicated in the letter was right, and it wasn't just another of her wild imaginings, she would be the last person to suggest to him there could be another man in Jenny's life. As things were at the moment, it would be too unkind. Perhaps, Annette thought, it was merely another example of Jenny being Jenny. She could hear Quenton's voice: "Well, she is an actress after all, what the hell do you expect!" She really must wean herself away from his influence she decided, as her taxi pulled up outside the hotel. Such thoughts continued to run disjointedly through her mind minutes later as she let herself into her hotel room and automatically going through the motions of unpacking the few clothes she had brought with her.

Her window overlooked Sliema Creek; quieter now, except for the occasional headlights from the traffic driving along the Strand and, leaving the curtains open, she poured herself a gin and tonic from the mini-bar. Although tired, Annette wasn't ready to go to bed. Weariness had begun to set in during the last hour of the flight when there was little to occupy her. She had read the in-flight magazine from cover to cover; picked disinterestedly, lacking any appetite, at the cold chicken and stared out at the dense blackness of the sky, waiting for the lights of Malta to appear and for the journey to end.

Sipping her drink, she flicked through the channels in an effort to find a programme which would occupy her thoughts and finally induce sleep, but most of them were either mindless game shows or movies she had seen at home or in impersonal hotel rooms in California. Exasperated, she switched off the television and once again took Jenny's letter from her bag. She had lost count of the times she had read it now, but it had become compulsive. She almost knew all the words off by heart, but some of them refused to budge and she found herself going over them again and again, trying and failing to find any meaning: " ...... But if I am right, well it's far too serious to jump to conclusions ...... so I'm going back to the casino ...... so I'm going back to the casino ......"

At that point she must have drifted off to sleep, awaking around five, the bedside lamp still on, the pages of the letter scattered on the pillow and her drink barely touched. Something had woken her, a small indistinct sound; a door or a window closing perhaps, not important she thought and, too tired to care, she closed her eyes and gave herself up to the welcome return of the oblivion of sleep.

*

Brilliant sunlight finally woke her before seven. She had forgotten to close the curtains and there was no relief from the penetrating heat which spread across to where she was lying, having thrown off the sheet sometime during the night. Threads of tiredness persisted, but she knew further sleep would be impossible. Sliding glass doors led out to the balcony and even so early in the morning the marble tiles felt warm underfoot. If only circumstances had been different she thought sadly, leaning against the rail and trying to appreciate the beauty of it all: the sparkling water in the creek, a vivid peacock-blue; a matching sky with no clouds to mar the expanse of blue; the shimmering flat roofs with already lines of washing hanging limply in the still air and, in the distance, the spires and orange domes of the churches. But, it was all wasted on her that morning; Jenny was on her mind and she struggled to come to terms with the unreality of what she had been told. Jenny was out there; somewhere. She *was* still alive and she would never give up until she knew the truth of what had happened. Annette remained standing there, scarcely aware of the day unfolding on the street below and felt for the first time since she had spoken to David, her strength and resolve returning. She was determined to find her and until she did she would, she decided, not leave the island. Quenton would have to go along with this decision, even if it meant losing her job. There would be other jobs, but she only had one sister. Brave thoughts, but they described exactly how she was feeling.

David called her when she was in the shower; the high pitched shrill of the telephone reaching her as she turned off the water.

'I hope I didn't wake you, Annette?' were his first words and tying the belt of the towelling robe, she assured him she had been up for hours which was almost true, not that it mattered; she had to see him. Already, too much time had been wasted.

'Listen,' he said, reminding her of how the Maltese would often start their sentences, 'can we meet this morning? For coffee?'

'Of course.'

'I'm afraid it will have to be in Valletta; I have an appointment there with some prospective clients in about half an hour.'

'That's alright, David.' she was quick to agree, thinking it would give her time to collect her thoughts, try to formulate some kind of plan. Obviously, David was her first line of contact and perhaps afterwards she could go along to the theatre; speak to people there, also the police. She felt quite within her rights as Jenny's sister to ask them about their search although realising in advance she wouldn't be all that welcome.

They agreed to meet at the 'Cordina'; one of the three cafés in Republic Square at eleven and it wasn't until after they had rung off it occurred to her she may not recognise him. She only had one photograph which Jenny had sent to her shortly after one of her rare telephone calls telling her about the new man in her life and she had assumed David had been in the group of people taken on a sunny afternoon; all of them standing against the wrought- iron railings of a balcony overlooking the water of what could be Balluta Bay. In the forefront of the picture; Jenny, the cat-like smile in place and looking directly at the camera, her arm draped possessively around the shoulders of the man next to her. He must be David, Annette had assumed at the time, although there was very little to distinguish him from any of the other three men in the photograph. All of them slim, dark-haired, casually dressed in open-necked shirts and jeans. Annette had no idea what her reactions would be when she finally came face to face with him: the man Jenny had insisted was *the one*! The person with whom she had stressed emphatically she wanted to spend the rest of her life. But over the years Annette had grown cynical as far as her sister was concerned and was accustomed to the pendulum swing of her emotions when falling in and out of love with helter-skelter regularity was the norm. She seriously wondered whether now at almost thirty, Jenny had changed all that much and more importantly, and this was the worrying part, if her choice of man was more reliable. These troubled thoughts were coursing through her brain as she prepared to meet David Grech.

Annette didn't notice the slip of paper until she was about to leave the room. It was lying on the floor by the door, and remembering the noise which had disturbed her earlier, she picked it up. There were only a few words in large childish hand-writing from someone called Angela saying she wanted to tell herself something and to meet her at 'Tony's' in Sliema at five that afternoon. "I can't make it before then because I will be working." she had added. Immediately she thought of Jenny; could this have anything to do with her she wondered. She shouldn't jump to conclusions like this, but what else was she meant to think; a scribbled message on a scrap of paper from a woman calling herself Angela?

Annette knew where 'Tony's' was; one of the many cafés in the Strand; she would, she decided, go along there and meet her and put the note in her bag along with Jenny's letter. Whatever she had to say could be relevant or it may turn out to be someone's idea of a joke. If that was the case, this Angela had a very peculiar sense of humour she concluded.

She already knew where to wait for the bus into Valletta and a good half an hour before she needed to leave the hotel, wanting to get there before him, she made her way down towards the Strand to queue with the rest of the people for the first bus which came along; all of them heading for the capital. This had been a mistake she thought; she should have taken a taxi, but it was too late now as the yellow and orange bus lumbered up and came to a juddering halt. She edged forward, aware of the impatient people pushing behind her, forcing her to hurry and climb up the rickety steps of what must be one of the oldest buses on the island. She managed to find a seat; squashed against a dust-smeared window, her knees almost reaching up to her chin, being unfortunate enough to have one above the wheel. With a grinding of gears they set off, stopping at every single bus stop until they reached the terminus in Valletta, but it didn't appear to have any effect on those already strap-hanging, when the driver having turned up the volume on his radio, the ear-shattering dulcet tones of Tom Jones adding to the decibels, continued to allow more and more passengers on board.

By the time she had clambered down from the bus, struggled through the mass of people in Republic Street, all of whom appeared to be going in the opposite direction, she felt she had emerged from a very warm bath. Her linen dress was even more creased than would be considered stylish and her feet ached in quite the wrong kind of shoes for the uneven pavements of Valletta. She did not feel her best and again wished she'd had the sense to either take a taxi or to hire a car, even if it would have meant trying to find a parking space which she remembered were at a premium in the city.

David was already there; sitting at one of the front tables facing the road with his head half-turned away from her, but Annette recognised him. He must have sensed, rather than having heard her, for he looked round, immediately jumping to his feet and taking both her hands in his.

'Annette,' he said, 'you have no idea how glad I am to see you! I would know you anywhere.' he added with a smile which lit up his gaunt features for a second as he pulled out a chair for her, waving over to attract the attention of one of the waiters.

'I'm not sure I should feel all that flattered,' she found herself smiling also, 'I must look a complete wreck. That bus journey!'

'They are dreadful.' he was quick to sympathise.

Of course, she thought, he probably hadn't been on a bus since his school days and perhaps not even then. David Grech exuded a privileged background and while there was no side to him, she felt he had never known what it was like to be short of money: to worry whether his cash card would work or not, but he had humility, a rarity, and she liked that.

'And,' he was still smiling, 'you don't look a wreck; far from it. In fact,' he added, 'you look like a lady who is in need of a long cool drink.'

The drink; a Kinnie, Malta's popular thirst-quencher, helped, although she would have preferred something less sweet, but too polite to mention what was a relatively trivial matter. David, giving her the necessary time to relax, silently sipped his coffee.

Annette was only half aware of her surroundings, but enough to register the rise and fall of voices; a predominant mixture of Maltese and Italian, with smatterings of English, German, Dutch and Spanish. This was Republic Square; the hub and central point of the Maltese capital, where locals and tourists congregated each morning, whether seeking quick refreshment from their constant and exhaustive walks around the capital, or office workers and lawyers and barristers taking a coffee break from the law courts further along the road. A classical guitarist began to play. He wasn't Maltese; he could be from one of the war-torn countries, Bosnia or Serbia perhaps and, unable to gain a work permit had chosen to scratch a living on the island, but many of them, like this young man, talented. The ancient and haunting melody of 'Green Sleeves' drifted over from where he was sitting outside the 'Cordina'; a portable amplifier on the pavement beside him, adding emphasis and cadence to each note. And in the centre of the square, where she had been for more years than anyone there could remember: a permanently silent and disapproving

Queen Victoria; her stone effigy encrusted not only with years of wear, but as a landing pad for generations of pigeons. They tip-toed delicately around the tables and chairs, reminding Annette with distaste from previous visits how they would swoop, without any warning, above everyone's heads and nose-dive, single-mindedly intent on picking up dropped crumbs; the normal debris left lying and thrown down for them throughout the day. She had always had a secret dread of these birds, comparing them unfavourably with the much larger species: the seagulls in Scotland and the vicious air fights they used to have.

'Better now?' David asked her.

She nodded, aware he must have been watching her for several minutes, 'Sorry, I was miles away.'

'I know,' he said slowly, his expression sad, 'Jenny used to do that –'

'– you believe she's dead, don't you?' Annette interrupted.

'Annette,' he leaned towards her, 'I don't know. I desperately want to believe she is alright and that nothing has happened to her, but I can't help thinking the worse.'

'I know you've already told me about that morning,' she prompted and feeling if she wasn't more positive, their conversation was in danger of going around in circles, 'but could you tell me again, please; perhaps from a day or two before. What had she been like? Did she seem worried, pre-occupied? I can understand, David, how fed up you must be having to go over the same ground again.'

He smiled, but this time instead of it lightening his expression as it had done before, it merely accentuated the tiredness. There were deep lines around his mouth which she felt sure hadn't been there before. Everything about him showed the strain he was under: from the tense set of his shoulders to the dark shadows beneath the brown, deep-set eyes. She rather suspected he'd had little sleep since Jenny had gone, but even now, when she could read the despair in his face, she refused to accept what may in the end prove inevitable.

'First, though,' he said, 'would you like something else to drink? I don't think you thought much of our Kinnie.'

'Was it so obvious?' she could not help but warm to him. This man of Jenny's had charm, but it was still too soon to entirely trust him. She didn't know why she had used that word; it implied something sinister and she was reluctant to think along those lines.

'Well,' David said, once the coffees had been brought to their table, 'I've spent hours going over and over in my mind just exactly how Jenny had been, like the day before for example; even several days before, but unless my memory is playing tricks, she seemed exactly the same. Perhaps a little bit more nervy than usual, but then she was often like that before a new production. She was heavily committed to the theatre, you know, Annette.'

Once again he had used the past tense, but this time she chose to ignore it. Also, she didn't want to interrupt him. He appeared to find it difficult to talk about her and the smallest distraction could very well prevent him altogether.

'There really isn't a lot more to say,' he went on, his eyes slightly unfocused as though he was trying to remember, 'the evening before; the night of the storm, Jenny got back home earlier than she usually did, so we were able to have a drink together before Marianne and her husband arrived for dinner.'

'Marianne?' Annette asked, trying to remember whether Jenny had ever mentioned the name to her.

'Yes, my sister.'

'Of course,' she nodded, 'Jenny did tell me about her. She's in partnership with you, isn't she?'

'That's right.'

'She might have been in a photograph Jenny sent to me, two or three months ago, but I'm not sure.'

'She was, yes; that would have been the one taken outside Moira

Refalo's villa. She is my nearest neighbour,' David added, 'I'm sure you will like her. Jenny did; in spite of the age difference they spent a lot of time together.'

'Is she Maltese?'

'No,' another quick smile, 'she's Scottish and was married to Julian Refalo. He was a great guy. Sadly, he died a couple of years ago; she then formed the New Theatre in Sliema.'

'You were saying, David,' Annette prompted him again, 'how Marianne and her husband spent the evening with you and Jenny.'

'Yes,' he answered, 'Moira was there also and one of my old tutors from university, Edward Coppini. The evening was very much like all the others we have had,' he went on, 'except for the wind which at times made conversation difficult, but everything was fine. Frank was niggling Marianne, as he has been doing for quite a while now, trying to persuade her to take some time off. I'm afraid he doesn't appreciate how impossible this would be at the moment. The development of new property on the island has accelerated at an incredible rate which has meant both Marianne and I have to work longer hours to keep in front of our competitors. Property investment companies have been sprouting up like mushrooms; there is absolutely no way either of us can take a break.'

Annette decided she had to do more than the gentle probing if she was going to get any further and wondering if he was always like this: reflective, his words lacking direction, but perhaps noticing her growing impatience, he smiled at her.

'Sorry, Annette. It's not easy; remembering and having no idea then it would be the last evening Jenny and I would be spending together. She was everything to me.' he said, the deep sadness in his eyes making her feel mean in being so persistent, but she had to.

'I believe that, David,' she said softly, taking a sip of the now lukewarm coffee, 'but if I am to be any help I do need to have a clear picture of what everything was like, especially that evening. It could be important.'

'Could it?'

'Well, yes,' she answered, 'whether she took the boat out the following morning or not, she went somewhere, didn't she?'

'Yes,' he agreed slowly, his reluctance to consider another possibility apparent in his expression.

'And,' Annette went on, 'she didn't tell you. Jenny is not the sort of person to get up early, unless it is absolutely essential, so I can't help thinking that wherever she was going must have been important to her.'

'Do you know,' he said, 'that hadn't occurred to me. I assumed it was a spur of the moment decision. Jenny could be like that sometimes.'

'Yes, but not first thing in the morning,' she stressed, wanting him to see her point, 'Jenny is a night-owl, David.'

'Well,' he began, but this time there was a small change in his manner; he had lost some of his dreadful air of despondency, 'to get back to that evening. Frank continued to nag away at Marianne, trying to wear her down, but she wasn't paying much attention to him. Anyway,' he continued, 'it was before the telephone rang when he gave up and turned his attentions towards Edward and started asking him about the Seychelles. Edward had recently returned from there.' he explained.

'The phone call, David? Who was it for?'

'Oh,' he answered quickly, appearing surprised by the question, 'for Jenny; someone from the theatre.'

'Did she tell you who it was?' she was pressing him, but had come to the realisation it was the only way with him and he didn't seem to object.

'No – no,' he admitted, 'she didn't, but then she often received calls from either Adam, he's their director or, if not him, his assistant, Linda. With the new production about to take off, there is a lot happening.'

'And how was she, after the call, I mean?'

'No different; she was just the same.'

There was something here she thought which wasn't exactly gelling, and as they both sat there; the square becoming more crowded with the approach of lunchtime, she couldn't work it out. On the face of things, what he had told her appeared to have been an ordinary and much-repeated dinner party with people who knew each other well. But did they?

There had been five of them there that Thursday evening and she ran through in her mind what David had told her. Somehow, she was finding it difficult to fit Jenny into their midst. Except for her friendship with Moira Refalo, Annette couldn't imagine what she could have in common with the other guests; certainly not Marianne and her husband. Annette had already gathered that David's sister was first and foremost a businesswoman, putting her career before everything else in her life, including it would seem that of her husband. As for Frank, he was definitely not Jenny's type. She was beginning now to remember what Jenny had mentioned about him; only that he owned a car rental business, but Annette got the impression she didn't think much of him. And what about Edward Coppini; this was the first time she had heard his name mentioned. Where did he fit in she wondered.

'Listen, Annette,' David broke into her thoughts, glancing at his watch, 'I'd like to take you for lunch, but I'm afraid I have to go. Another meeting,' he added, 'but this evening, please come for dinner.'

'I'd like that.'

'Good, I'll pick you up at your hotel.'

'There's no need,' she protested, 'I can easily get a taxi.'

'No, I insist. About seven, okay?'

*

The young woman sitting outside 'Tony's' had to be Angela. As soon as Annette walked towards her she looked up nervously, almost upsetting the glass on the table beside her as she half-rose from her chair.

'Annette?' she said her name softly, 'Annette Graham?'

'Yes, that's right,' Annette said, pulling out a chair and sitting down, 'you are Angela?'

The woman nodded and sat down again. She certainly didn't look like a practical joker Annette thought, looking closely at her, taking in the lank hair tied back from a thin, pale face, the bright pink lipstick doing little to disguise her plainness.

'I'm going to have a coffee,' Annette said, catching the eye of one of the waiters hovering in the open doorway of the café, 'what would you like?'

'Nothing, thank you, I'm fine.'

'If you're sure?'

'Yes, I'm sure.' Again, her voice came out not much more than a whisper, as if she didn't want anyone to hear her, 'I have to get back to work soon.'

'And where do you work, Angela?'

'At the Crowne Plaza.' she answered, making a poor attempt to smile.

'I see,' Annette said, not returning her smile; she had no intention of making it easy for her, 'and your note, what was it all about?'

'It was about your sister.'

Annette took a deep, painful breath and waited. Whatever this woman was about to tell her could be a complete fabrication; she hadn't even tried to fathom out why, but sufficient to know she had to remain calm, not to reveal how her words had affected her. And they had; of course they had.

'I didn't know Miss Graham,' she went on, 'but I had seen her many times and I knew who she was.'

'Yes.'

'And,' she hesitated; if anything, more nervous than she had been before, 'when I heard about the accident I wanted to say something, but- '

'- but?'

'I couldn't.'

'Why?'

'It's like this,' she said and Annette had to lean forward to hear her, 'on the news they said she must have gone out in the boat before eight-thirty in the morning, but she couldn't have.'

'Why?' Annette repeated, holding her breath.

'Because I saw her around that time; I was standing at the window inside the theatre when she drove up in front of the main door.'

'Go on.'

'She came in; not to where I was, I think she must have gone upstairs to the main part of the theatre,' she went on, her dark eyes looking directly at her.'

'Yes.'

'It was unusual for anyone to be there so early; the office hadn't opened yet and I knew they didn't start rehearsals until much later.'

'Let's get this straight, Angela,' Annette said, impatient and wanting her to get to the point. What was wrong with these people she wondered; they seemed to be intent in hovering around and leaving you completely in the air. She was no different from David Grech, 'you were there; at the theatre and you saw my sister?'

'Yes.' she nodded.

'Are you absolutely certain it was her?'

'Oh yes, it was Miss Graham alright. Also,' she added, 'there was another car parked there before she arrived and just as I was leaving I saw her get into it.'

'I thought you said there was no-one in the theatre, except for you and your sister.'

'I know, but people often park there; I've seen them and they have nothing to do with the theatre.'

'I see. Why didn't you tell this to the police, Angela?'

'I couldn't.'

'Why?'

'Well, I shouldn't have been at the theatre, but some mornings I help my sister. She cleans there and I give her a hand. If I had, she might have got into trouble and lost her job.'

'This car,' Annette asked, stifling her frustration and trying to curb the rising excitement which was very close to panic as she absorbed what the woman was telling her, 'did you happen to notice the make, or the number?' she added, but without much hope. She didn't think for one minute that people like Angela ever noticed car numbers, far less memorise them.

'All I know,' Angela said, 'it was a Renault. I'm certain about that because my uncle has one, but his is dark blue and the one I saw was silver grey.'

'Silver grey,' Annette repeated, 'and the driver, what did he look like?'

'He wasn't there.'

'Wasn't there? You're telling me my sister arrived at the theatre, parked her own car and then got into another one and there was no-one else in it?'

'Yes, I think she must have been waiting for him.'

'Why did you think that?'

'Well, she was sitting in the passenger seat, that's why.'

This needed some thinking through Annette thought and as she sat facing the woman she had no idea where she should start. But, if what she had heard was true, it did prove something. Jenny hadn't gone to Saint Paul's Bay; she hadn't taken the boat out, but where had she gone?

'I should have told the police, shouldn't I?' Angela said, her eyes brimming with tears.

'Perhaps, Angela,' Annette said, wanting in some way to put her at her ease. She understood the woman's dilemma; she hadn't wanted to make difficulties for her sister. That was understandable, but now she had passed on this shattering piece of evidence over to her, it had now become her problem, 'but you didn't.'

'Are you going to tell them?'

'Why did you tell me, Angela?' Annette asked, evading her question.

'I felt guilty. Also, I really admired Miss Graham. I had seen her on the stage and she was wonderful.'

How could she answer that she thought. She knew she had to do something with all of this, but watching the way Angela nervously clenched and unclenched her hands; red and work-worn, she realised for the moment she would keep the information to herself.

Chapter Four

The telephone rang as Annette pulled her dress over her head, groaning as her arms became entangled in the lace sleeves. Although a day earlier than he had said he would phone her, this was bound to be Quenton she thought and sighing, she picked up the receiver, bracing herself for the verbal bombardment.

'Hi, you're Annette, aren't you? Jenny's sister?' the voice, breathless and one she didn't recognise, continued quickly, giving her no time to answer, 'I'm sorry to phone you like this, but I have to see you! This evening!'

'I'm afraid that won't be possible,' Annette managed to get the few words in, 'but as I haven't a clue who you are –'

'How rude of me! What must you be thinking? I'm Caroline; Caroline Johnson from the theatre.'

'You're a friend of Jenny's?'

'Yes,' she went on, more slowly this time and lowering her voice as if something or someone had distracted her. 'I've been away, you see,' she went on, 'and only got back this afternoon and I've just heard about Jenny –' she faltered, apparently running out of steam.

'Yes?' Annette prompted, wishing she would come to the point. For a girl who started her conversations at great speed she was just as rapidly slowing down; her voice now practically inaudible.

' – Well,' she went on, 'I really need to talk to you. It's important; something isn't right. Can we meet; here, at the theatre?'

Annette explained she wouldn't be able to see her until the following morning and this appeared to satisfy her. She then went on to give her directions on how to find the theatre, telling her she would be in the Green Room.

Annette thoughtfully replaced the receiver, trying to remember whether Jenny had ever mentioned her name. She may have done; it was vaguely familiar but she didn't think it had been recently. How did the girl know she was here? And, come to that, how did Angela know? News certainly spread quickly on this island she thought, putting the finishing touches to her make-up and standing back from the mirror for a critical last-minute inspection before going down to reception to wait for David Grech.

*

David's villa in Balluta looked over the bay and out towards the Mediterranean. Beyond Balluta, the promenade swept around the bay and on towards Saint Julian's, the centre of Malta's nightlife. The drive from the hotel had taken them fifteen minutes and would have been even less if there hadn't been so much traffic: at its peak at that time in the early evening when shops and offices were closing and it would appear most of the island's inhabitants were on the move.

'Is it always like this?' Annette asked, wincing as another vehicle screeched past them and, like many of them, exceeding the speed limit.

'Always,' David said, 'but you get used to it.'

'I don't think I would.'

'You would, Annette. You might not think so, but believe me as soon as you were behind the wheel you would be like everyone else.'

'Does Jenny drive here?'

'Yes, of course.'

'I was wondering about that actually.' she went on, hoping he wouldn't realise what she was getting at. 'How she got to Saint Paul's Bay, I mean.'

'Were you?' he asked, taking his eyes off the road for a fraction of a second to look at her.

'Well, yes, I was. It's just that you hadn't mentioned it.'

'Sorry, Annette, I realise you want to know everything you can about that morning, but Jenny took her own car and left it where she always parked when she went there; at the side of the road above the boat-sheds. It was there when I drove along later. You see, when I tried to phone her during the morning and couldn't get hold of her and my housekeeper had told me she hadn't been at the villa when she arrived for work, I began to worry. She hadn't been in touch with the theatre either and that was unusual, so I got the idea into my head she may have decided to take the boat out.'

'I see,' Annette said trying to slot together the pieces of information she had managed to glean so far. Who had driven the car there? Not Jenny, if what Angela had told her was right. She couldn't have taken the boat out, but she had gone somewhere, whether willingly or not. There was much more to all of this and she was now eager to hear what Caroline Johnson would have to say, but it was pointless to imagine and speculate. She would have to wait until the morning.

They had now driven up the steep incline to the row of villas, David pulling up outside the first one: a tall stone-faced building with the obligatory balcony on the first floor and the windows with the rolled-up slatted blinds she had only ever seen in Malta. The sloping area in front of the villa was more rock than grass; clumps of scarlet perennials gainfully struggling for survival in the dry soil.

'Marianne and Frank are already here I see.' he said, pointing to the bright red Peugeot Cabriolet parked in front of them.

'Nice car.'

'Frank's.' he explained, giving her an inscrutable smile which told her quite a lot about his brother-in-law.

Marianne; a tall, heavily built woman; black hair cut short and brushed severely back from her face, did not resemble David in the least. She was some years older than him, Annette decided, perhaps by five or six years and was the type of woman who invariably made her feel uncomfortable and as she saw the way she was being closely scrutinised she wasn't about to change her mind. David introduced them and her hand felt cold in hers: mirroring what Annette could only describe as the icy expression in the dark, slightly hooded eyes; no wonder Jenny hadn't bothered to tell her about the woman. Jenny only liked what she described as 'sunny people'; those to whom she could immediately warm and relate to and without a doubt Marianne would not have fallen into that category.

Frank, although standing deferentially behind her, a full glass of whisky in his hand, did not give the impression he was in the least subservient. He was shorter than his wife, but what he lacked in stature Annette guessed he made up for in other ways. He positively oozed confidence; a bold, mocking smile hovering on his lips and Annette's immediate reaction was that she did not like him one little bit. A phrase her father would often use and one which in this instance was quite apt, came into her mind: "Would you buy a used car from a man like that?"

'A drink, Annette?' David asked her, once the introductions had been made, 'Wine or would you prefer something else?'

'Wine, please.' she answered; glad of the interruption and wondering how the rest of the evening would go.

'You don't look like Jenny.' Marianne said, although it sounded more like an accusation to Annette's over-sensitive ears.

'Oh, I don't know,' Frank drawled, giving Annette an exaggerated wink, 'she has the same beautiful eyes. Very few Maltese have blue eyes, you know.' he added informatively and totally unnecessarily.

'You're older than her, aren't you?' Marianne persisted and Annette couldn't believe how anyone could be so rude, but she had already made up her mind she wouldn't let her annoy her, sensing this would be the first of many little jibes.

'I am, yes.' Annette forced a smile, accepting a chilled glass of wine from David. She didn't know what Marianne was going to say next because they were interrupted by voices in the hall; one of them instantly transporting her back to her childhood; the soft lilting Scottish accent she hadn't heard for so long. Perhaps the evening wouldn't turn out to be such a trial after all she thought, turning round to face the open door, but not before she heard Marianne mutter under her breath, something which sounded very much like, 'there is no show without punch'!

'This is Moira Refalo, Annette,' David said, his arm around the shoulders of the woman beside him, 'and my oldest and dearest friend, Edward Coppini.'

'Less of the old, David, if you don't mind!'

'Sorry,' David smiled, 'but you know what I mean.'

'Of course I do, dear boy.'

'And you are Annette.' Moira Refalo smiled, surprising Annette by kissing her on both cheeks, 'I feel I know you already, my dear, although Jenny neglected to tell me how pretty you are.'

'Thank you,' Annette smiled, immediately warming to her, but it wasn't only because of the compliment; perhaps she was biased because she was from Scotland and reminded her of when Jenny and she had been girls, revelling in the freedom they had always enjoyed during those perfect holidays, but her reaction had been instant and she knew that here was a person she could talk to. Moira, many years older than Marianne, had lost none of her youthfulness. She must be in her sixties, Annette guessed, but there was nothing set or rigid about her and she had one of the sweetest expressions Annette had ever seen. She was diminutive compared to Marianne and even to herself: slender; elfin-featured with a mass of soft curling grey hair piled high on top of her head where already loose tendrils had escaped from the silver clasp. Annette found her enchanting and could well understand how Jenny and she must have built up a rapport. She could quite easily imagine in the years to come Jenny could look very much like her; they shared something similar: they embraced life, looked at you directly and had no time for those they considered false. Annette didn't understand how she could so quickly have reached such a decision about a woman she had only just met and so far had exchanged the briefest of words, but that had been her immediate impression and hoped David would place her next to her at the dinner table and far enough away as possible from either Marianne or her husband.

She need not have worried. She had been seated with Moira Refalo on her left and Edward Coppini on her other side; opposite were Marianne and Frank, with David on his own at the end of the table. She tried not to think how it should have been or how it had been when Jenny had been there; it was pointless to torment herself in this way, time enough later when she was back in the privacy of her hotel room.

The meal was excellent, far surpassing any Annette had eaten for a long time: crunchy deep-fried *noisettes* of goats' cheese; sizzling hot rack of lamb with mint sauce; small cubes of roasted potatoes and Gozo-grown vegetables: sprigs of broccoli and courgettes in a cream sauce and finally, before the cheese platter, individual mouth-sized apple tartlets topped with double cream and the wine, a perfect choice; Marsovin 'Special Reserve', Malta's own product.

Did they eat like this every evening, Annette wondered as one course followed another and although the portions could not be described as over-facing, it still amounted to a lot of food. Apart from Moira Refalo, whom Annette noticed ate very little, everyone else did the meal full justice. Watching them, she could not imagine Jenny enjoying such an obviously well-practiced and formal routine, preferring a more relaxed way of eating; usually around the kitchen table as she had done in her London flat, late at night after a performance along with her fellow actors and eating thick slices of pizza bought from their local take-away. This was not her scene at all, Annette decided.

'Well, Annette,' Marianne looked across at her, delicately wiping the corners of her mouth with her napkin, 'what exactly do you hope to achieve by coming to Malta?'

'I thought that might have been obvious, Marianne,' Annette replied, unable to keep the sharpness from her voice in spite of her earlier resolve not to allow herself to be irritated by her, 'I'm here to find Jenny.' There, she had said her name and the first time it had been mentioned that evening.

'I really think you will have to face the fact, Annette, your sister drowned. Sad, I know, but –' she didn't finish her sentence, looking instead towards David as though expecting his support. Who could tell what was in her mind, except to reinforce her assertiveness. Marianne, Annette was rapidly beginning to realise, was always right and was not accustomed to being contradicted and she wondered what she and David were like during their business hours. Was she the self-appointed leader there also?

'I'm afraid what Marianne is saying must be true, Annette.' Edward said, at the same time nodding his acceptance as David offered to top up his glass, 'A dreadful accident. Dreadful.'

'Was it, though? An accident?'

'Of course it was, Annette,' Frank put in quickly, 'what else?'

'Exactly!' Marianne's agreement sounding triumphant, 'Jenny unwisely, and to her cost, took it upon herself to take the boat out, in spite of being warned how treacherous these waters can be. Apparently,' she added, her eyes piercing in their intensity as she looked at each person in turn, no doubt to make sure she had their full attention, 'the storm the night before was the worst we have had on the island ever since records began.'

'The police have reached their conclusions, I understand,' Edward said, a sad smile on his round face, the lights from the candelabra glinting off the frames of his spectacles, 'the verdict being death by misadventure.'

Death by misadventure; the three words echoed and re-echoed in Annette's brain, but they were not true. Everybody it would seem, including the police, is assuming. Assuming Jenny went to Saint Paul's Bay. Assuming she took the boat out. Assuming she got into difficulties and because the boat was found smashed up on the rocks, again assuming she had drowned. She remembered her father repeatedly telling them:

"Girls," he would say, with one of his infrequent stern expressions, "you should never assume; to do so is dangerous. I want you both to remember that". And she had. She looked at David who, so far, had said nothing, not joining in their conversation and she wondered what he was thinking. Perhaps she had sown a tiny seed of doubt in his mind earlier, but if she had it could be no consolation to him. Nothing could alter the fact that Jenny had gone. The verdict, while difficult and painful for him to accept and come to terms with, would she felt sure, be less devastating than the alternative; that Jenny had decided to leave him, but Jenny was not a coward. If she wanted to end their relationship she would have come out with it and said so.

'Yes, well,' Marianne said quickly, 'whatever. Don't you think, David, it's time you sorted out Jenny's things. Now that Annette is here, I would think this was an excellent opportunity, wouldn't you?'

Annette, shocked, stared at her. How crass! And judging by the expressions on the other faces, she wasn't the only one who thought so. Even Frank, his glass suspended half-way to his mouth, looked momentarily stunned. Moira, turning slightly round in her chair, gave her a small smile of sympathy, but said nothing.

'Marianne,' David said smoothly, 'I appreciate your concern, but this is neither the time nor the place to speak about this sort of thing. It is personal and one which will only be discussed between Annette and myself. When we are alone.' he added firmly.

So, he can assert himself after all, Annette thought, relieved. She hadn't relished the idea of having continual battles of will with her during the time she spent on the island. Nothing, she was certain, would ever be gained by that.

'As you wish, David.' Marianne said at last, every line of her body rigid with indignation, 'Far be it for me to interfere. It is after all none of my business but, perhaps next time,' she went on spitefully, 'you should find a girl who is more down to earth!'

'Marianne, dear,' Frank was forced to interrupt her flow, 'don't you think you should drop it?'

'Drop it, Frank! You should know me better than that! She wasn't David's type; I told you at the time when we first met her, but then of course, she was an actress and you know what actresses are like!'

There was a unanimous gasp around the dinner table, broken by a tiny chuckle from Moira. She put up a dainty hand to cover her mouth in what to Annette didn't really convey any regret for her spontaneous outburst of amusement.

'Sorry,' Moira said, 'I shouldn't have laughed, but honestly, Marianne,' she went on, 'are there no limits to your tactlessness? You know what actresses are like.' she added, mimicking Marianne to perfection.

'Moira,' David said, smiling at her. 'I make no apologies for my sister. It seems to have slipped Marianne's memory that you, one of my best friends, were once an actress. Also,' he went on, 'the founder of the New Theatre which is good news for all of us interested in the profession.'

'Talking about the theatre,' Annette said in the hope of diffusing the atmosphere which she was finding embarrassing, 'I had a call from Caroline Johnson earlier this evening.'

'Oh dear,' Moira said, 'she's been away and wouldn't have known about Jenny. Poor girl, it must have come as a dreadful shock to her. They have known each other for a long time as you probably know, Annette.'

'I didn't, actually. I've been trying to remember whether I ever heard Jenny mention her, but I'm not sure.'

'They first met when they were at RADA and started off in repertory together.'

'I remember now, yes. Years ago, but I'm sure I never met her. Jenny has so many friends.'

'I know; that's the lovely thing about her. How did Caroline sound?'

'Quite upset actually, she wants to see me, so I'm going along to the theatre tomorrow morning.'

'Why?' Marianne butted in, presumably unable to remain quiet for much longer.

'Why?'

'Yes, Annette, why does this friend of Jenny's want to see you?'

'I don't know, Marianne,' Annette answered slowly, 'to talk about Jenny, I expect. It would be only natural, wouldn't you say?' There was no way she was going to elaborate, and couldn't help thinking Marianne's interest somewhat excessive given as she had made it abundantly clear she had no time for Jenny.

'Come for lunch tomorrow, Annette.' Moira invited, 'I would love it if you could.'

'Thank you, Moira. David has already told me what good friends you and Jenny are.'

'You really will have to get out of the habit of talking about your sister in the present tense, you know.' Marianne, once again treading a treacherous path, but apparently impervious to the waves of distaste she was creating.

'You believe Jenny is still alive, don't you?' Edward asked her quietly, his intelligent eyes looking at her closely.

'Yes, I do.'

'You must feel very strongly.'

'I do,' Annette said, 'you see, I know my sister probably better than anyone else, except for our parents, of course. We grew up together, we've always been close and it didn't matter that several months would often go by without us seeing each other. That didn't diminish the bond. Jenny may be impulsive at times, I don't think that is a crime, Marianne,' she shifted her gaze for a moment to look at her before turning back to Edward, 'and neither is it one solely attributable to the acting profession, but Jenny is not irresponsible, especially when it comes to the sea. I cannot believe she would have taken David's boat out if the conditions had been bad.'

After she had spoken there was silence in the room, broken only by the soft movement of the muslin curtains fluttering against the open balcony windows and, in the distance, the harsh sound of a dog barking.

'Well,' true to form, Marianne was the first to speak, 'all I can say is, everyone is entitled to their own opinion, whether they are right or wrong.' she added, looking pointedly at Annette.

Conversation from then on went along more predictably, normal after dinner chat: the incessant heat which apparently was unusual even for the month of June; the tourists, and the way they treated the island as their own; the rising prices, in fact relatively safe topics guaranteed to have each guest more or less agreeing.

The party broke up around ten-thirty; Edward offering to drive Annette back to Sliema and Moira, after arranging a time for lunch the following day, to walk the short distance to her villa.

'Thank you, David,' Annette said as they all prepared to leave, 'that was a lovely meal. Does your housekeeper do the cooking?'

'Yes, she does,' he smiled at her and she was glad to see he looked a little more relaxed than he had earlier, 'I'm very lucky to have her and am the envy of all my friends. Maria's late husband was a chef and as you have experienced for yourself this evening, he must have taught her well.'

'Yes,' Marianne put in quickly, 'I have been trying to persuade her to come and work for us; for years, as a matter of fact, but to no avail. I can't understand why, especially as I've offered to pay her more than David does.'

This time, Annette could not hide her amusement. Marianne, if nothing else, was consistent. Anyone unfortunate enough to work for her would have an impossible task in satisfying her every whim and Annette rather thought she had met her match with Jenny. It probably explained the woman's open criticism of her.

Chapter Five

Annette had already planned how she was going to spend the day, but first she needed to have some transport. She didn't like depending on other people and it was far too hot to use the buses, also it would give her more flexibility. The girl at the Hertz desk in the hotel, after taking down her details, promised she would only have to wait ten or fifteen minutes for one to be delivered.

The New Theatre, situated in one of the many side streets half-way up Manwel Dimech Street from the Strand, was an imposing three-storey building, converted and renovated from two old merchant houses. Now, there was only one front door built into the original stonework, and although there was a balcony, it was purely decorative, the iron struts curving outwards; 'pregnant windows', as Annette had heard them described. Dark green wooden shutters, firmly closed, giving it an air of secretiveness and if it had not been for the sign, discreetly positioned above the doorway, with 'New Theatre' written in gold lettering, she would never have guessed what lay beyond the ancient frontage.

As Angela had said, there was a parking area at the front of the building and although there wasn't a great deal of space, Annette managed to find a space between a Renault and an open-topped coupé; an unpleasant reminder of Marianne's husband and with an involuntary shudder, she switched off the engine and stepped out on to the cobbled car park.

The Green Room, she was told by one of the two girls standing on the steps outside, was on the second floor, also that rehearsals would soon be starting. Thanking them, Annette went inside and walked up the two wide flights of stairs noticing with pleasure they had retained the old wrought iron balustrades. She needed no further directions: the sound of voices and laughter floating out from the end of the long, red-carpeted corridor, led her there.

'Hi, there! I'm Linda, can I help you?' an auburn-haired woman in jeans and a white tee-shirt with New Theatre printed across the front, called over to her, waving the clipboard she was carrying in a vain effort to quieten the noise. This would be the assistant David had mentioned Annette thought, going further into the room.

'I'm looking for Caroline Johnson,' she said, 'she asked me to meet her here.'

'Caroline hasn't arrived yet, I'm afraid. She should have done; we're just about to start our first read-through.'

'Do you mind if I wait for her?'

'No problem. Sit wherever you like, take your pick.' she said, pointing towards the empty rows of seats.

'If that's alright? I don't want to get in the way.'

'Don't worry; you won't be,' she laughed, 'once Adam arrives, he's our director by the way, this lot will soon settle down.'

Annette sat on the nearest seat at the end of the back row and watched as Linda with a cheerful smile left her to rejoin the others at the far end of the room, where a semi-circle of chairs had been placed on a raised platform. If her mind had not been so preoccupied with Jenny and the forthcoming meeting with Caroline, she would have enjoyed the experience; being in at the very beginning of a new play, but it wasn't possible; her presence here, at the theatre and in the Green Room where Jenny must have been in dozens of times, only made it worse.

Linda, she noticed, had almost finished re-arranging everyone: three women and two men were now on the platform and the other actors seated along the front row and then, as she had predicted, with the appearance of the tall, broad-shouldered man walking up the length of the room towards the platform, there was a hushed silence. Impressive, she thought. So far, he hadn't said a word but there was still no sign of Caroline. A second man had now joined him; thick-set with spiky-blond hair and like most of them, wearing jeans and the theatre's tee-shirt.

Linda said something to them both; Annette was too far away to hear, but the two men turned round to look at her. Immediately, the taller man broke away and walked up to where she was sitting.

'I think you must be Jenny's sister.'

'I am, yes,' Annette said, 'but how did you know?'

'Simple;' he gave her a slow, lazy smile, 'you look like her.'

'Do I? Nobody has ever said so before.'

'Haven't they?' a look of genuine surprise on his face, 'well, they're probably not as observant as I am.'

'Did you know I was in Malta?' she asked him.

'Yes, Moira Refalo told me.'

'I was with her last night.'

'I was sorry to hear about Jenny. We all were,' he added, his expression now grave as he looked at her more closely, 'tragic, in fact. Absolutely tragic; we're going to miss her dreadfully.'

Annette quietly acknowledged his condolences; she wasn't going to voice her doubts about the boating accident. She had learned a lot in the last thirty-six hours. Something was drastically wrong and whether Jenny's disappearance had anything to do with anyone in the theatre or not, she decided from now on she would be more circumspect in what she said to people.

'Caroline Johnson phoned me last evening,' Annette went on, 'she had only just heard about Jenny and wanted to see me. That's why I'm here.' she added.

'Yes,' he said, 'Linda told me, but it looks as if you're going to be unlucky. Caroline isn't usually late; it isn't like her at all. Slept in, I expect. Incidentally,' he added, 'I'm Adam Bond.' and rather belatedly shaking hands with her, 'Look, you're more than welcome to stay.'

'Well – ' Annette hesitated.

'I tell you what; I'll get someone to show you around. That would be more interesting than having to listen to an endless read-through; can be somewhat monotonous.'

This was what she wanted, not necessarily to see the rest of the theatre, as much as she would have normally enjoyed it, but what she did want, was to speak to someone; ask questions and somehow form a picture of Jenny's life and involvement here and any special friends she had.

Adam Bond led her back downstairs to the foyer and introduced her to a young man who had been leaning against the booking desk talking to the girl behind the counter.

'Ah, Pete,' he said, 'just the chap I'm looking for. This is Annette Graham and I'd like you to give her a guided tour.'

'Jenny's sister?' the young man gave her a keen, sad look and the girl at the desk looked across and smiled.

'I am, yes.' Annette said, trying to put him at his ease. He looked uncomfortable; whether it was because he was in the presence of his director or he didn't know what to say to her, she couldn't make out.

'I'll leave you to it, then.' Adam said, the quick smile returning, but she could tell by his distracted expression he was anxious to get back to work; she had already taken up too much of his time.

'I'll show you the main part of the theatre first,' Pete said to her as soon as Adam had gone, 'it's on the first floor.'

'What kind of plays do you put on?' Annette asked him, once they had reached the auditorium, surprised to see so much activity: electricians, soundmen, set-painters, men and women running across the stage, pulling and dragging pieces of set into position and, below, in the orchestra pit, musicians tuning up and running through their various chords, pausing to make pencilled notes on their scores.

'Contemporary mainly;' Pete said, 'we open with a new one tonight,' he went on, 'hence all this activity.'

'And are you in it?'

'Yes, but only a small part; no more than a walk-on, but it's a start.'

'Exciting.'

'You're right, it is.' he agreed.

'Would Jenny have been in this one?'

'No,' he said slowly, looking at her anxiously, as if not knowing whether she really wanted to talk about Jenny and was merely trying to be politely interested, 'but the play-reading they're having this morning,' he hesitated for a second, 'well, she'd already been given a part; the lead, actually, but –' he stopped altogether, at a complete loss for words.

'It's alright you know, Pete,' Annette said, 'I do understand how you must be feeling. I just want to learn as much as I can about my sister's life here, especially in the theatre, but if you would rather not discuss her.'

'No, it's not that,' he said, 'I suppose the fact is we can't believe she's gone. None of us can.'

'She has a lot of friends here, hasn't she?' she asked him.

'Oh, yes, Jenny knew everyone. Also, although she was far more experienced than most of us, there was no side to her; she always had time to stop and have a chat.'

'Does she have any friends in particular?'

'There was Caroline Johnson and a few others she spent time with outside the theatre.'

'I've already spoken to Caroline,' Annette said, 'who are the others, Pete?'

'Jeannette Summers; she started here at the same time as Jenny and Caroline and then there was Tony Borg and his cousin, Lawrence, and Evelyn Peterson.'

None of the names meant anything to her, but hardly surprising she thought when Jenny had not even mentioned Caroline's name in any of her letters, but then this is the way she is. A people-collector, but it didn't mean she treated any of her friends differently. They were never placed on any particular level of importance, that wasn't Jenny's way. She liked them all equally and could move comfortably from one to the other and easily pick up from where she had left off the last time she was with them.

Annette spent the next half hour accompanying Pete around the building: behind the auditorium, the dressing rooms with the lingering smell of grease paint, reminding her of the times after a show she had gone back-stage to meet up with Jenny; the vast wardrobes, full to capacity; rows of shoes, various sizes and styles; a pile of hat boxes and trays of costume jewellery and accessories; the stock room, shelves stacked with a treasure trove of stage props; the café and bar where Pete bought her a coffee and then he took her up to the roof garden. Carpenters were in the process of constructing a stage, not along traditional lines, but circular. Theatre-in-the-round Annette commented and Pete agreed, saying it was a new venture, adding proudly, an enthusiastic smile on his face, that they were planning a mid-summer production. Finally, going back down to the second floor he showed her the main office; a long room, glass-partitioned work stations each with their own desk top computer; the screens flickering and telephones ringing constantly. By the time they had finished, she was glad to leave, but before she did Annette asked him if he would mind finding out whether Caroline was in the Green Room yet and when he came back to say she still hadn't come in, she felt a twinge of unease. She could not explain to herself why, but it persisted all the same, niggling away in her already troubled mind.

She took the top road to Balluta; a short cut, continuing up Manwel Dimech Street until she reached Depiro Street, past tired-looking houses, but each of them, without exception, and in spite of the prevailing dust from the incessant traffic, with gleaming brass door knobs and freshly scrubbed steps; interspersed by a mini-market; a pharmacy; a hairdressing salon; a bread and pastry shop and a greengrocers displaying locally-grown products: potatoes, beans, cabbages, broccoli, peas and some she didn't recognise; all of them in their pink plastic baskets and taking up most of the narrow pavement, and then she was dropping down to join Tower Road and immediately in front of her, the glittering blue of the bay. She drew up outside the florists close to the Carmelite church: the predominant feature of Balluta Bay, its stone edifice facing out towards the Mediterranean as it had done for more than a hundred years; wide shallow steps embracing the frontage and above, the bell towers; the twin clocks, one faceless and the other, the hands approaching midday.

"The Bells of Saint Mary's", disturbing the pigeons scrabbling for crumbs on the grass beside the café on the green mound, began their melodious chiming as Annette emerged from the shop with a gift-wrapped bouquet of red and yellow roses. The tune; when she had first heard it years ago, had struck her as inappropriate, taking her back to childhood days in the school playground, when they would take it in turns to jump in and out of skipping ropes; the latest craze, and singing the song at the top of their young voices.

Shutters had been flung wide open in David's villa and Maria, wiping along the top of the balcony rail, waved to her as she drove past.

Moira was already there, waiting for her on the balcony, and today was wearing a loose tunic in delicate shades of green and blue, a matching swathe of the same fabric tied bandana-style around her head and, as before, wayward curls fast escaping.

'The door is open, Annette,' she called down, 'do come in.'

While the exterior of her villa was identical to that of David's and the others further up the road, once inside, there the resemblance ended. As Annette pushed open the inner screen door to the lounge she felt she had entered another world; one where vibrant colour intermingled with even more vibrant colour, where conformity of style and fashion had no place. The contrast was to her, as she stood in the open doorway, staggering. Where David went for the minimalistic, his friend and neighbour went for something entirely different. Two enormous cream leather sofas dominated the room; Indian square rugs, richly patterned in an exotic mixture of deep blues, greens and reds, covered the polished parquet floor; a couple of solid hand-carved tables had been placed in front of the sofas, but it was one of the walls in particular which immediately caught her interest; every spare inch was taken up by framed photographs. Of course it was theatrical and Annette wondered for a moment what Quenton's reaction would have been if he had been here with her, but she liked it; it truly reflected the personality of the lady who was now walking towards her. How Jenny must love coming here.

'What a fascinating room, Moira.' Annette said, unable to take her eyes away from everything. There was so much to see and absorb; delightful.

'It's different, I suppose,' she smiled, giving one of her tinkling laughs and kissing Annette on both cheeks, 'not to everyone's taste, but there you are; it's me and a constant reminder of my past, which I might add,' she gave a small rueful smile, 'now seems a very long time ago.'

'And so many photographs.'

'Self-indulgence, I'm afraid,' she admitted, 'but once an actress, always an actress, I guess.'

Moira led the way out on to the terrace at the rear of the villa; a wide terracotta tiled area with a red-painted wrought-iron railing curving along the whole length. Pots of shrubs were scattered haphazardly: flowering begonias; clumps of large white daisies, sturdy geraniums and a couple of healthy-looking ferns. A blue and white awning projected half-way, giving protection from the sun which was now almost overhead. A matching swing-seat with plump scarlet cushions was next to the round rattan table together with half a dozen chairs; all covered with the same fabric.

'I thought we could have lunch out here,' Moira suggested, taking out a bottle of 'Green Label' which had been cooling in the ice bucket, 'but a glass of wine first, wouldn't you agree?'

'This is really lovely,' Annette said, 'and your view, Moira! So pretty.' she added, gesturing towards the un-tamed terrain beyond the railings which had long ago given up on resembling what it must have once been like and further back, higher from where she was sitting, a lovely old villa: orange-roofed, green roller blinds and a two-tiered balcony; a tiny orange grove, still, in spite of the apparent neglect, flourishing; the fallen fruit scattered on the long grass, but more than anything, it was all so peaceful.

'I'm lucky.' Moira said simply, sitting down next to her and following her gaze beyond the terrace.

'You are.'

'Tell me, Annette,' she said, raising her glass, 'how was Caroline when you saw her this morning?'

'I didn't see her, Moira; she wasn't there.'

'Really?'

'No, she didn't turn up at the theatre.'

'How odd. That's not like her.'

'That's what Adam Bond said.'

'You've met him? That's good, but did they try to phone her and find out if she was alright?'

'I don't think so; they were assuming she had overslept.'

'She may have done, I suppose, but I'll give her a ring later,' Moira said, taking a sip of her wine, a puzzled frown on her face.

'Does she live on her own?'

'As far as I know, yes.'

'When I spoke to her last evening she sounded really keen to see me.'

'Yes, that's worrying me slightly, but perhaps she was just late in getting there.'

'It's possible.'

'Tell me,' Moira smiled, 'what did you think of last evening? You had already met David, I know, but it would have been the first time you met any of the others. His sister, for instance?' she added, a teasing smile hovering on her lips.

'Not an easy woman.'

'Diplomatically put, Annette,' she laughed, 'Marianne suffers from rather a bad dose of big-sister syndrome.'

'I rather thought so, but they are in business together, so presumably their relationship must work?'

'Oh, it does; she is an extremely good businesswoman, an excellent foil for David; he deals with their clients and Marianne the financial side of their business.'

'She gave me the impression she doesn't think a great deal of Jenny.'

'No,' Moira agreed slowly, 'but then any girlfriend of David's would find it extremely difficult, if not impossible, to come up to her standards. Mind you,' she laughed again, 'Jenny was a match for her alright. Gave as good as she got, in fact!'

'I'm not surprised,' Annette smiled, 'but, Moira,' she went on, seriously now, 'you have already heard my views about what everyone believes about Jenny, but what do you think?'

She had not meant to come out with it, but there was something about this woman which invited confidences. Annette needed someone she could talk to, express what she felt without coming up against a mental barrier. If she was to find out, or get any closer to what happened, she would have to delve deeper and ask more questions.

'I honestly don't know what to think, Annette,' Moira said at last, placing a hand gently on Annette's arm, 'and I believe David feels the same, but everything points to Jenny having gone out there that morning; the boat being found, even her car which apparently David found parked in its usual place. So far, there has been nothing to suggest any other explanation for her disappearance.'

'I know,' Annette said, but she still held back mentioning Angela; perhaps later she would mention her to Moira, but not yet, 'but I cannot help feeling there is something else; something nobody has thought about.'

'Such as?'

'Well, and please don't misunderstand me, Moira,' Annette said, 'perhaps Jenny wasn't happy. Perhaps she wanted to get away. Oh, I know, if that had been the case it would have been out of character for her to do it in such a way, but she may not have known anything about the boat being taken out and being found on the rocks. She might not realise what people are thinking, even to the police being involved. I'm sorry, I'm rambling, clutching at straws.'

'No, my dear, I don't think you are,' she smiled gently, 'it is only natural for you to be thinking about other possibilities. You had never met David before; you probably don't know the strength or the depth of their relationship.'

'Do you?'

'Ah, there's a question,' she sighed, 'does anyone know that sort of thing? I very much doubt it. I am extremely fond of David; I've known him ever since I came to Malta, even before I married Julian and I have always liked him. Both of us did. During that time he has had a number of girlfriends, but none like your sister. She was like a breath of fresh air to him; he was instantly captivated. Jenny was like a beautiful butterfly, but don't get me wrong, Annette; by that I don't mean to imply she was skittish in any way, because she wasn't, but what I am trying to say is, I didn't really believe she would stay for very long. Oh, they were in love, there was no doubt about that. We were all aware of that, but passion, well –' she paused, holding both hands up; who can put any length of time on passion she was implying, without putting her thoughts into words.

'She seemed to believe David was the man for her.' Annette said, remembering the excited telephone call from Jenny, also her own, albeit sceptical reaction, but then it had not been the first time Jenny had professed to be madly in love.

'I believe she did,' Moira smiled, 'and certainly as time went by, I did begin to think she was settling down, but –'

' – but?'

'Oh, I don't know, Annette. I really don't, but you know what happens to a butterfly when you attempt to pin it down, keep it in one place?'

'I've already asked David,' Annette said, understanding exactly what she meant and hadn't she thought of Jenny like that so many times over the years, 'what she had been like in those days leading up to the accident? He described her as being nervy, a bit jittery, putting it down to the impending production.'

'She was, but then Jenny was always like that. Although, having had some time to think about it and to try and think back to what is really not so long ago, she did seem more so than usual. Edward noticed it also and I did ask her if there was anything wrong, anything worrying her, but she said there wasn't.'

'Perhaps there was.'

'Perhaps, but then I can remember what I used to be like during rehearsals and before a performance. I must have been impossible to live with; in fact, my first husband used to tell me so frequently, but then he never had wanted me to continue with my career after we were married.'

'But you did?'

'Oh, yes, I did, and paid the price; he left me.'

'I'm sorry, Moira.'

'Please do not be, my dear. It was a long time ago and I probably deserved it, but it was a bit of a blow to my ego when he went off with a girl a good ten years younger than me.'

'Oh dear.'

'Yes, anyway, I learned a salutary lesson from that. I realise now, in retrospect, if I had really loved him I would have been prepared to give up my acting career. After all, Annette, a career, however enjoyable and satisfying can never replace a loving marriage, can it?'

'No,' Annette said quietly, 'it doesn't work, does it?' she added, thinking of the bitter end to her affair with Steve and the last words he had said to her when he had walked out of her apartment: "I love you, Annette," he had said, standing in the doorway, his whole expression tight with suppressed emotion, "and I thought we could make a go of things. Get married, even, but in any relationship there has to be give and take and I am tired of coming second-best to your job. You are only able to give what is left in you to give, Annette and it isn't enough for me." The words had hurt for a long time, but he had been right; she hadn't loved him enough.

'What do you plan to do next, Annette?' Moira asked.

'I need to see the Inspector of Police in charge of the case, even although from what I've been told it's now closed, but I want to talk to him, perhaps discover how they reached their conclusions. I can't at the moment think of anything else.'

'It makes sense,' she agreed, leaning over to top up her glass, 'but what about your parents? Jenny told me they were in Australia.'

'I haven't been in touch with them yet, perhaps that's wrong of me, but, Moira, I must find out more and until then I don't think it would be fair to phone them. What do you think?'

'Oh, Annette, it has to be your decision and a few days aren't going to make much difference, are they? Provided that is,' she added, 'they don't hear about it from someone else.'

'I think that's the risk I will have to take.'

'It doesn't seem right that you have to take on all of this on your own. You need some support, some moral support. Is there anyone in England you could ask to come out?'

'No, there isn't,' Annette said, 'it's something I have to do on my own, at least for the time being.' she added, putting Quenton to the back of her mind. It was now Friday and this evening he would be phoning her and she still had to decide what she was going to say to him.

'Inspector Secluna is the man you should be talking to.' Moira said, 'I know him quite well; he's a fair man and approachable, but please, Annette, don't hold out any hope of him performing miracles.'

'I won't.'

'We'll eat soon,' she said, 'but first, have you planned anything for this evening?'

'No.'

'Aren't you seeing David?'

'We didn't make any arrangements and apart from waiting for a telephone call from my boss, I thought I would probably have a meal in the hotel and have an early night.'

'Would you like to come with me to the airport?' Moira asked, again with the little smile on her lips and her lovely blue eyes sparkling, 'I'm meeting Andy; he's coming for a few days as he usually does at this time of year.'

'Andy?'

'My son; from my first marriage,' she explained, 'and I can tell by the way you're looking at me, in that very enigmatic way, so like Jenny, exactly what you're thinking.'

'Which is?' she couldn't help smiling; her vivaciousness was so refreshing, making her realise just how serious she had become over the years, especially those spent working for Quenton. "Lighten up, Annette", Jenny would have said and she could almost hear her chuckle of amusement.

'My lips are sealed,' Moira said, 'but I know you don't believe me; I'm not trying to match-make, but I would appreciate your company. I don't like the drive to the airport, especially at that time of the evening when there is so much traffic. You would be doing me an enormous favour.'

'Put like that,' Annette laughed, 'how could I possibly refuse.'

*

It was almost four by the time Annette reached the police station in Sliema. She could have gone back the same way; it would have taken less time, but instead, she had decided on the coast road. On her immediate left sweeping past the Barracuda Restaurant; the washed-out blue wooden balconies overhanging Balluta Bay, and continuing around the second deep curve to Saint Julian's Tower, followed by the straight stretch of road with the sea on her left, passing the red and white painted Captain Morgan ferries; their top decks packed with tourists as they set off on their trips around the island, before finally turning right; still in Tower Road, until she was once again in Manwel Dimech Street and at the top, before it dipped down where she had driven earlier, the police station.

Inspector Secluna was able to see her immediately. It was almost Annette thought as if he had been expecting her. A short, broad-shouldered man, with black hair greying at the temples, rose up from behind his desk as the sergeant showed her into his office.

'Miss Graham,' he said, leaning over to shake her hand, 'I knew you were in Malta. I have been expecting you to call into the station.' he said, confirming her thoughts. Very little happened on this island she thought cynically which escaped notice. No doubt as soon as she arrived at Luqa Airport the metaphoric bells had started ringing.

'Inspector Secluna.' Annette said, sitting down on one of the chairs in front of his desk.

'First,' he said, 'I would like to extend our condolences on your loss. A tragic accident.'

'Thank you, Inspector,' she replied at the same time taking a deep breath. What she was going to say would, she knew, be hardly acceptable to him, but it had to be said; she wouldn't get another chance, 'please don't think I am criticising your police force in any way, but I have to tell you that I do not believe the verdict.'

'I see.' he replied, leaning back in his chair, his hands folded neatly in front of him. 'Perhaps you would like to tell me why you think this way.'

'Jenny is an experienced sailor, Inspector Secluna. We both are, in fact, and she would never have taken the risk of going out if the conditions had been remotely dangerous.'

'Yes, but there is always an element of spontaneity, Miss Graham.'

'Spontaneity? '

'Let me explain,' he went on, his hands remaining in the same position, 'however expert or responsible a person may be, there are times when these factors quite frankly are disregarded.'

'Of course,' Annette nodded, 'I realise this can happen, but what proof have you that my sister actually took the boat out?'

'The boat was found, Miss Graham, also your sister's car.'

'And do you consider that as sufficient proof?' Annette replied quickly and not missing his flash of irritation.

'As for *sufficient* proof,' he emphasised, 'in an accident of this nature, given there is no body, excuse me, Miss Graham for being so frank, we have to look at what we do have.'

'A boat smashed against the rocks, my sister's car parked on the road above the boat-sheds, a man out walking his dog early that morning reporting the boat-shed door open and the boat missing'

'Miss Graham,' he was trying to placate her now, but this only acted as a stimulus for her to continue, not to let go, 'I do appreciate how difficult this must be for you; to come to terms with your sister's death, but believe me with my experience in the force, I am afraid you have no choice.'

'Don't I?'

'No, frankly, I don't believe you do.'

'Alright, Inspector,' Annette said, stifling a sigh, 'I hear what you say, but I will not let this rest. I would like to ask you if, when you made your enquiries, you asked whether anyone had seen my sister that morning, perhaps seen her driving towards Saint Paul's Bay, parking in her usual place on the road there, walking down to the boat-shed, opening the door and actually taking the boat out on to the water. Even being on the water! That man with the dog, for instance, was he the only person around that Friday morning; it wasn't exactly the middle of the night.'

'I really have nothing more to say to you, Miss Graham,' he said, getting to his feet and coming round to the front of the desk, 'I sympathise with your distress, but the case is closed.'

One of the telephones on his desk rang at that moment and she could tell he was no longer interested in her. She had no alternative but to leave. There was so much more she could have said, but knew she would be wasting her breath; they had reached their decision and that, as far as they were concerned, was that. Where on earth could she go from here she wondered as she re-traced her steps along the corridor to the front desk? There must be something else she could do; someone she could talk to.

'Miss Graham!' the desk sergeant called out to her as she pushed open the double glass doors on to the small courtyard outside the station, 'Would you mind coming back, please. Inspector Secluna would like to talk to you again.'

What now, Annette thought; as she followed him back along to the inspector's office, watching distractedly as he tapped on the door. This time, the inspector didn't get to his feet; instead he remained behind his desk, his hands in front of him, fingers forming a neat pyramid.

'Sit down, Miss Graham, please,' he said; gesturing to the chair she had just vacated, 'I have just heard some distressing news –'

' – Jenny!'

'No, I'm sorry to alarm you, it wasn't my intention, but I have just heard that Caroline Johnson was found in her apartment this afternoon.'

'Found?' Annette gasped, 'You mean she's dead?'

'Yes, it's too early to say how she died, but it may have been a drug overdose.'

'I don't understand! We had an appointment this morning to meet at the theatre. She was a friend of Jenny's and she wanted to see me.'

'We didn't know this, Miss Graham, but we did know she was a friend of your sister, and like her, an actress at the New Theatre, and even at such an early stage, we have to view this – incident,' he hesitated slightly before continuing, 'as suspicious.'

'Do you mean there could be a connection, between Caroline and Jenny?'

'It is too soon to tell, or even to speculate.' he said slowly.

'Poor Moira,' Annette said, 'she's going to be terribly upset.'

'Mrs Refalo already knows, Miss Graham,' he said, 'it was she who contacted us a few minutes ago. You see, the young woman who found the body, well, naturally she panicked and the first person she called, rather than the police, was Mrs Refalo.'

'How absolutely awful; I just cannot believe this. What is going on, Inspector Secluna?'

'That is something we intend to find out, Miss Graham. Now, you say Miss Johnson wanted to see you?'

'Yes, she phoned me last evening; she had only just heard about Jenny and wanted to talk to me, that's all. I had never met her, but apparently, she had been a friend of Jenny's for a long time; from when they both started out on their careers.'

'And you have no idea why she wanted to speak to you?'

'None at all.'

Chapter Six

As it turned out, Annette drove to Luqa Airport on her own. Moira had phoned her as soon as she returned to her hotel saying she had to spend some time at the theatre that evening.

'I realise it is a terrible imposition, Annette,' she had said, her voice trembling as though she was, with considerable effort, holding back tears, 'but do you think you could meet Andy for me?'

'Of course I will, Moira.'

'You see,' she went on, 'they need me at the theatre. Adam is doing his best to keep up their morale, but it's difficult. Inspector Secluna telephoned me after you left his office telling me he had told you about Caroline –' her voice breaking.

'Please,' Annette said gently, 'try not to distress yourself any further.'

'I'll try not to,' she said, her voice a little stronger, 'but Evelyn, she was in a dreadful state –'

'It's understandable,' Annette said, remembering she was one of the names Pete had given her, 'it must have been dreadful for her.'

'It was,' Moira said, 'when she phoned me she was absolutely frantic. I honestly didn't know what to do to try and calm her; she was hysterical, Annette. She had been worried, you see when Caroline hadn't turned up earlier and she went along to her apartment to find out what was wrong. The very last thing she expected was –'

'Moira,' Annette interrupted, 'how did she get into the apartment? Did she have a key?'

'No, she didn't. Apparently, the door wasn't locked. Caroline –' again she stumbled over the name, 'Caroline,' she repeated, 'must have forgotten to do it last night.'

'I see.' but she didn't see at all. Surely Caroline would have been more security conscious? A woman living on her own; alright, in a country with a relatively low crime rate, but that should not have made any difference. It would, Annette reasoned, have been automatic to make certain all the windows and the door to her apartment were closed up for the night. Nobody, unless they were either in the habit of being so remiss or they were too distressed to realise what they were doing, would neglect to do something so important.

'You probably know the play opens tonight?' Moira asked her.

'I do, yes.'

'Evelyn is in it, Annette, and although I have tried to dissuade her not to go on this evening, she is quite adamant, so you can probably appreciate why I should be there.'

'I understand.'

'I knew you would. And so will Andy when I tell him.'

'Moira, how will I recognise him?'

'Don't worry about that, my dear,' Moira said and Annette could hear the smile in her voice, 'I'll send him a text message on his mobile; he'll get it as soon as they land and I'll tell him what you look like, so that won't be a problem.'

The lady who thinks of everything and accustomed to being in control, Annette thought as they brought the call to a close and wondering what *he* would look like! She didn't even know his surname. It could be Refalo, but perhaps not. In fact, she knew absolutely nothing about him.

The Air Malta flight from Heathrow was on time and Annette, standing further back from the barrier and those waiting for the passengers to filter into Arrivals, had a good vantage point; she was able to look up and watch them as they filed past on the other side of the glass from baggage reclaim on the floor above, curiously silent as they glided down the escalator. She tried to look out for men who were travelling on their own. She counted to twenty and then gave up. It was useless; there were far too many people and too close together and even when they started to trickle through from customs she realised she would have no alternative but to wait for him to find her. Three, four minutes, not much longer and she noticed the tall, slim man, about her own age, with the thick unruly hair, blond as his mother's may once have been, walk swiftly and unhesitatingly towards her.

'Annette Graham?' the smile, an uncanny replica of Moira's.

'Yes, that's right.' Annette said as they formerly shook hands. 'Your mother must have given you a good description of me.' she added as they walked along the concourse and out to the car park.

'I would have recognised you anyway.'

'Really?'

'Yes, you look like your sister.'

'Do you know,' Annette smiled up at him, 'only two people have ever mentioned the resemblance between us before and you are the second one and both on the same day!'

Andy placed his bag in the boot and settled into the passenger seat. They said little on the way out of the airport, not until after the fast stretch of dual-carriageway and heading towards the quieter and, to Annette, the more familiar road towards Sliema. He seemed to sense she needed all of her concentration and she was grateful. She would have much preferred for him to have driven, but she hadn't extended the insurance, not thinking for one moment she would want any additional cover.

'Where do you want to go, Andy?' she asked, 'to the villa or the theatre? I think Moira will still be there.'

'Why don't we go for a coffee or something; although I must admit I feel more in the need of a beer after being cramped up on that plane for the last three hours?'

'Why not?' she agreed, wanting a break from the driving. Although the distance to Luqa was short, she had nevertheless found it a strain and would be glad to get out of the car, 'there are plenty of places along here. We could try 'Sandals',' she added, nodding towards the red and white fluorescent sign of a bistro a couple of hundred yards further along.

'Looks alright to me,' Andy said, 'and I can call my mother from there; find out what time she expects to finish.'

There were tables outside under the gazebo-style canopy; all of them set for the evening meal, but inside there were places along the front of the bar. As soon as Andy's beer and her glass of wine had been brought to their table and he had spoken to Moira, only a brief call, he leaned back against the leather seat with a deep sigh.

'Tired?'

'More weary than anything else,' he admitted, 'this will be a good pick-me-up, though.' pointing to his beer.

'How was she?' Annette asked him, at the same time raising her glass to his.

'She sounded okay,' he said, 'but I think it's pretty grim there at the moment.'

'What about the girl? Evelyn?'

'She's fine apparently. Of course it must have been one hell of a shock for her, but like many people in the acting profession she's tough. They have to be.' he added.

'I'm sure you're right.'

'Moira has already told me about Jenny.' he said, picking up his glass again.

'I thought she may have done.'

'She's also told me that you are reluctant to accept the verdict.'

'I am, but so far I am finding it extremely difficult to get anyone to listen to me. I spoke to the Inspector of Police this afternoon; the one who was in charge of the case, but it was like coming up against the proverbial brick wall.'

'I can imagine.' he said, looking at her over the rim of his glass. 'It's difficult to know where you can go from here, isn't it?'

'Yes,' Annette agreed, 'and now the shocking news about Caroline.'

'They were friends, weren't they?' he asked, his voice casual, but she could tell by his expression that what she had said, or perhaps the manner in which she had mentioned Caroline's name, had made an impact on him and at that moment she made a decision. She had to talk to someone. She had to find someone in whom she could confide, someone she could trust and wouldn't fob her off the way most of them had done since she had arrived. Annette rapidly felt she was getting out of her depth and was in danger of doing what everyone else was doing; assuming.

'Yes,' she repeated, 'they had known each other for a long time, but I only learned this last night when Moira and I were talking. When I had the call from Caroline earlier I had no idea who she was.

'Presumably she knew who you were though?'

'Yes, anyway and this is really what is worrying me, Andy, making me sceptical about this drug overdose thing especially, but she had only just heard about Jenny and was anxious to meet me. Really anxious, I mean. Not just her manner but something she said.'

'Which was?' she had all of his attention; his half-drunk beer for the moment forgotten.

'She said, "Something isn't right", also I am sure she was interrupted because her voice changed abruptly towards the end of the call, she was practically whispering. It was as though someone had come into the room; she was phoning from the theatre.' Annette added.

'And didn't want to be overheard?'

'Quite. What do you think?'

'God knows, Annette and perhaps we will never know. Something else we don't know, at least not yet, and that is whether she took drugs.'

'I would be very surprised if she had, you know. Jenny holds strong views on that sort of thing. I don't believe she would have much time for anyone who did take them, far less be friends with them and over a period of time she would certainly have known, wouldn't you say?'

'I would, yes;' Andy replied thoughtfully, 'why had Caroline only just heard about your sister? Had she been away?'

'Yes, she only got back yesterday.'

'I see.'

'There's something else,' Annette said, 'about Jenny. I don't know whether Moira told you, but they had pinned down the time when Jenny was meant to have taken the boat out.'

'Yes, apparently someone walking their dog had noticed the empty boat-shed at eight-thirty that morning.'

'That's right. Well, Jenny was seen arriving at the theatre at more or less the same time.'

'What!' he gasped, 'How did you find out? Have you told anyone?'

'Not yet, no,' she admitted and went on to tell him about everything Angela had said and how she shouldn't have been at the theatre helping her sister and concerned that once it was found out her sister could lose her job, 'I felt really sorry for the woman. I suppose I have had this hope that someone else may have seen Jenny around that time. Oh, I don't know.'

'If she is correct about the time and everything, this could be crucial evidence.'

'I know, what do you suggest I do? Have another word with her?'

'Why not try and speak to the sister. She might have seen Jenny as well; also, she may have recognised the Renault.'

'Appeal to her better nature, you mean?'

'Something like that, yes,' he smiled for the first time since they had come into the Bistro, 'it would be a start wouldn't it?'

'It would and if Angela did agree to make a statement, this would mean the police might re-open the case.'

'I think they would have to. Mind you, they wouldn't like it, but tough.'

'I wonder where Jenny went. Even if she did go by her own free will I am still desperately worried about her. A person just can't disappear from a small island like this! Can they?'

Andy ordered another round of drinks and Annette took Jenny's letter from her bag and handed it to him, saying she had received it nearly two weeks ago. She watched him as he read and re-read the relevant section, a small frown furrowing his forehead.

'Odd.' was his only comment as he handed it back to her.

'Did you ever meet Jenny?'

'Yes, once,' he said, 'at Easter; I'd managed a couple days' break and Moira had invited some of the theatre crowd for drinks.'

'You probably didn't have the opportunity to gauge her personality properly. When I got the letter, I didn't put a great deal of importance on what she'd written. Jenny is like that, over-dramatising, starting off excitedly and very often what she had to tell you would have petered out to insignificance the next time you either saw or heard from her. But,' Annette went on, 'that's no excuse, I should have asked her what she was talking about. Her letter arrived on the same morning I flew out to California and it wasn't until I got back to London last Tuesday I heard she was missing.'

'You shouldn't be so hard on yourself, Annette,' he said, pausing as their drinks were brought over to their table, 'if Jenny had wanted you to know more, she would have told you.'

'I suppose so.'

'Cheers.' he said.

Before Annette had time to respond a car with a screech of brakes pulled up outside and with a flourish of lilac chiffon and lace Moira emerged, running up the couple of steps into the bistro.

'She always drives like that,' Andy said under his breath, 'actually she is, believe it or not, a very good driver.'

'Andy, darling!' Moira enveloped him, throwing her arms around his neck and kissing him exuberantly on both cheeks, 'Forgive me?'

'There is absolutely nothing to forgive,' Andy smiled and looking over the top of her head towards Annette, 'you couldn't have sent a better ambassadress.'

'I simply had no choice, Andy.' Moira went on, slightly out of breath and flouncing down on to one of the empty seats, wafts of Chanel Number Five drifting towards them.

'How did it go this evening?' Annette asked her.

'The play you mean?'

'Yes, but everything else?'

'The play is going well; there's still another half an hour to go and Evelyn, well, she really is a little trooper. I was proud of her. She had an absolutely dreadful experience this afternoon; I don't think I can possibly imagine how bad it must have been for her, but tonight – she was superb; a credit to not only the New Theatre, but to the acting profession.'

'But afterwards,' Andy put in, 'at the end of the performance, what then, Moira? She may just crack up.'

'I don't think she will,' Moira said, 'anyway; she's staying with Jeannette tonight, so,' she added, 'she won't be on her own.'

'Good.' he said, beckoning over to the waiter, 'what would you like? A cognac?'

'How did you guess, darling?' Moira gave him a tired smile, 'It's been a ghastly day, also,' she paused for a second, looking at them both, 'I had a call from Inspector Secluna as I was leaving the theatre –'

' – yes,' Andy prompted, placing a hand protectively on her arm.

'There is no easy way of saying this,' she went on, 'but he had received the autopsy report. Caroline was murdered.'

There was silence. Andy, his arm remaining on her arm, staring at her in what seemed to Annette as she watched him to be total disbelief. While, she? Well, the only way to describe how she felt was a complete numbness. Also, she realised this was what she had been dreading to hear ever since Inspector Secluna had told her about Caroline. There was no rational or logical reason why she should have thought this, except that something was indeed very wrong here. Something sinister and she gave a silent prayer that Jenny was alive and well, wherever that might be.

'Apparently,' Moira spoke at last, 'the first prognosis was correct. She did die from a drug overdose; so far, an unknown substance and it had been administered to her late last night. The pathologist could find no trace in her blood stream of a history of any intake of drugs.'

'Oh, no!' Annette whispered, 'This is terrible!'

'I simply cannot believe it.' Moira said. 'I told you, didn't I, Annette,' she went on, 'about the door to Caroline's apartment and I think the police are considering the possibility that she must have opened it to let someone in and that would have to be someone she knew.'

'From the theatre?' Andy asked.

'It's impossible to tell, darling,' she said turning to face him again, her eyes filling with tears, 'she was such a lovely young woman. I simply cannot imagine why anyone would want to do such a wicked and despicable thing.'

'You're tired, Moira,' Annette said leaning towards her, 'you need to get some rest.'

'You're right, my dear,' she said patting her hand, 'I'll just drink this and then I'll go home.'

They all left the bistro at the same time; Annette, to drive the short distance back to her hotel and Andy and Moira on to Balluta with Andy driving. Before he pulled away from the kerb he leaned out of the window telling her he would call her in the morning. And, heartened, feeling she was no longer on her own and trying to solve an insurmountable problem, followed them until the road branched off to Tower Road and up towards the Holiday Inn, Moira waving from the open window to her as they continued towards Balluta.

Annette was surprised to find it was not yet nine, also that she hadn't eaten since lunchtime. The time since she had left for the airport seemed hours ago; so much had been said, so much ground had been covered and now with the latest about Caroline, she wanted nothing more than a quick shower, a change of clothing and something light to eat.

As soon as she opened the door to her room, the first thing she noticed was the light flashing on the telephone console. This time it had to be Quenton. She called reception and yes, a Mr Barton had phoned earlier in the evening and left a message: No matter how late, he had demanded, he wanted her to call him. I really do not need this she thought, tossing her bag on to the bed, and as so many times before, dialled his mobile number, one she could have done quite easily in her sleep. He answered immediately.

'Annette!' his first words, even before she had time to say anything. 'Where the hell have you been?'

'You could always have phoned me on my mobile, Quenton.' she reminded him.

'I could have, yes,' he replied, sounding to her a little surprised by her reaction, 'but I didn't want to bother you. It may not have been convenient.'

'I wouldn't have minded,' she lied, not fooled for a minute by the change in his tone, 'things,' she added, 'are not easy here.'

'What about your sister?'

'Quenton,' she started, selecting her words carefully, not wanting to aggravate him, but prepared for once in their long business relationship to be resolute, 'it is becoming clear – at least to me – that Jenny didn't have an accident at sea.'

'Oh?'

'She was seen outside the theatre about the same time as the empty boat-shed was discovered.'

'So what happens now?'

'I don't know.'

'What do you mean, Annette, you don't know! What sort of answer is that?'

Annette took a deep breath before attempting the impossible; to try and make him understand what the situation was like; however futile. Quenton Barton's impatience knew no bounds.

'For a number of reasons;' she went on, 'the first being, the police still don't know about anyone seeing Jenny —'

' — why not?' interrupting her and she experienced for the first time during all the years she had worked for him, her temper beginning to rise.

'Perhaps, Quenton,' she said quietly, 'you would give me a chance to explain.'

It must have worked because there was silence at the other end of the line. 'I was told in confidence, that's why,' Annette said, 'but I'm hoping to persuade the woman; Angela she's called, to tell the police herself. She had personal reasons for keeping quiet; she shouldn't have been in the theatre, but she was there that morning helping her sister, who works as a cleaner. Angela had got it into her head her sister may lose her job if it was found out. Anyway, I'm going to try and have a word with her tomorrow.'

'And Jenny? Still no sign of her?'

'No.'

'She must have gone somewhere!'

'I know,' holding back an involuntary sigh, 'it is possible she may have decided to go, leave the island, I mean, although it wouldn't be like her, totally out of character, but —'

' — you mean she may have been forced to?'

'Yes,' Annette said softly, 'and that's what I'm afraid of, Quenton, especially after what has happened now.'

'Which is?' his impatience rapidly returning.

'One of her friends has been murdered.' bluntly said, she knew, but how else could she tell him and didn't have long to wait for his reaction which was instantaneous.

'What's going on out there, Annette?'

'I wish I knew; so you see,' she continued quickly, not giving him the opportunity to interrupt, 'I have to stay on for a bit longer; see if I can discover what has happened to Jenny.'

'What are you now, Annette,' he was practically shouting down the phone, 'some sort of detective! That is why there is a police force, in case you are not aware of it!'

'All I can say,' she answered slowly, forcing herself not to over-react to his sarcasm, distasteful though she was finding it, 'as far as Jenny's disappearance goes, they haven't done a very good job. They have, like most of the other people on this island, assumed!'

'Alright, alright, don't let us get heated, Annette. There is obviously something pretty odd going on, but do you honestly believe you can help unravel things? Now, do you?'

'Perhaps.'

'Listen to me, Annette,' here it comes she thought; the cajoling, let-us-be-reasonable approach, 'there is something I don't believe you have taken into consideration which is, if you are determined to go ahead and try to dig into what has been happening, your own safety could be in jeopardy. Have you thought of that?'

'No. No, I haven't, but I don't think it would be.'

'Come on, Annette, where is your logic? Unless you are just prepared to sit down and wait for clues to land in your lap, you are bound to alert someone and that someone could be the killer whether there is any connection with Jenny or not! Now, do you see what I'm getting at?'

'Yes, but -'

'- I don't think there are any buts here,' he went on, still wearing his persuasive hat, 'you could be putting yourself in a predicament from which you may very well find it impossible to extricate yourself and with tragic results, Annette. You are listening to what I'm saying, I hope?'

'Of course,' she said, 'but, Quenton, I cannot abandon this.'

'Which is?'

'Trying to find Jenny.'

'And how long do you think that is going to take?'

She dearly wanted to say for as long as it takes, but she didn't think her reluctantly given leave of absence would extend that far. She needed time, without the constant pressures from him hampering her; time to work out in her mind whether there really was anything to be gained by staying on in Malta. But to leave now, she felt, would be tantamount to literally throwing up her hands and admitting she had not done all she could.

'Well, Annette,' he persisted, 'how long?'

'I don't know, Quenton. I don't know.'

'Right,' exasperation in his voice, 'this is Friday; shall we give it until the middle of next week? I want you back at work, Annette,' he went on, 'also, I need you out in Oakland again pretty damn quick. In fact, I'm going to book a flight out to San Francisco for you for next Friday. What do you say?'

'What do you expect me to say?'

'You tell me, Annette, you should know better than to answer a question with a question. Look,' he persisted, 'I have a business to run and of course I sympathise with you, but it is vital you get back out there. Your report was succinct, as always to the point and confirming what I had already suspected: the whole set-up in Oakland is like a pack of bloody cards! Mandy has taken leave of absence,' he continued, 'for some unspecified reason.'

Mandy, her counterpart in the States; a woman she had been working alongside for the last three years: tough, staunch Mandy; a New Yorker and one who could be relied upon in any crisis and she had to admit there had been a few, but each time, between them, they had managed to dilute the situation which had, at times, been volatile.

'Alright, Quenton,' Annette sighed, 'I hear what you say. I have a job to do, but I want you to realise I may have to return to Malta.'

'Of course.' And she could so easily read into what he was thinking. Quenton had won this round as he very well knew he would and that was why he was so brilliant at his job. She knew that. Many called him ruthless and they were right, but although she acknowledged this, she did wonder how much longer she would continue to act as his 'yes man'.

'I know I said I would come out to join you, Annette,' he said and she held her breath, dreading what he was going to say next, 'but I have more to do here and I must be back in London by Tuesday at the latest. Now, is there anyone there you can trust, someone you can talk to? It strikes me you are very much on your own on that island.'

'Well, there is Moira Refalo,' Annette said, 'she's Scottish and years ago used to be an actress. She founded the New Theatre in Sliema; the one Jenny is with, also there's her son who arrived this evening. I am sure I could trust both of them.'

'Not *the* Moira Henderson?'

'You know her?'

'If it is the same woman, Annette;' Quenton said, 'she was the darling of the London stage about twenty years ago. She was an exquisite creature; a mass of blonde hair and the ability to captivate her audience. She left at the height of her profession, more is the pity and I had always believed she had married some Italian.'

'It could be Moira,' she said, 'but I only met her for the first time last night.'

'You say she has a son?'

'Yes, Andy, by her first marriage. She did tell me that much.'

'Her first husband was Cameron Henderson,' Quenton put in, 'and he had no time for her acting, at least that was what I read; in fact he left her quite early on in the marriage. He was a Scottish landowner, I believe, loads of money. In fact, that is something she has never lacked and, now it would appear she's living in Malta. What about this Refalo chap?'

'She's a widow, Quenton and when he died she set up the theatre. It does sound as if it is the same person.'

'She would be in her sixties by now.'

'Yes, probably.'

'Okay, Annette,' he said quickly, back to his normal brisk self, no doubt feeling he had given her enough of his time and anxious now to ring off, 'it sounds as if you have found someone you can talk to, but for goodness sake, be careful, won't you?'

'I will.'

'Watch your back and, Annette?'

'Ye?'

'I expect to see you in the office first thing on Friday morning, if not before! And,' he added, 'bring your travel bag with you; you'll be flying out to San Francisco later that night.'

Chapter Seven

Annette telephoned David early the following morning before she went down for breakfast, wanting to catch him before he left for work. She was surprised not to have heard from him since the night before last, especially when he had given her the impression he wanted her to be there, needed to talk to her in fact about Jenny and to go over all the various scenarios of what could have happened to her. But then, she didn't know him; he may be the sort of person who found it difficult to get too close to people, especially those he had only recently met, even although she was Jenny's sister. Also, she reminded herself, he had a business to run and perhaps by this time, in spite of the glimmer of doubt she thought she had detected, had once again become reconciled to the fact that Jenny had drowned. Marianne would certainly be no help in giving him time to breathe and consider other possibilities, Annette thought, as she waited for him to answer.

'Annette,' he said at last, just as she was about to hang up, 'I've been meaning to phone you, but quite frankly,' he faltered for a moment, 'with work and everything I haven't been able to get my head round what's been happening.'

'You mean Caroline?'

'Caroline?' he said her name slowly, hesitatingly, as if he had no idea who she was talking about, 'Oh, yes, of course, Caroline; tragic. '

'How well did you know her, David?'

'Hardly at all.'

'But she was one of Jenny's closest friends,' Annette couldn't prevent a note of criticism creeping into her voice. He was sounding so vague and matter of fact.

'She was, yes,' he admitted and to her, said with some reluctance. What was wrong with him, she wondered; he sounded spaced out, as if he was on another planet; unaware or disinterested in what was going on around him. First, his girlfriend disappears, presumed drowned and now her best friend has been found murdered and all he could muster was this half-hearted response, 'but,' he went on, 'Jenny always kept that side of her life, the theatre I mean, quite separate.'

'Really?' again she couldn't hold back her disapproval, not really believing his indifference. The girl had been killed, for God's sake, Annette thought with exasperation.

'Okay, David,' she said slowly, 'you didn't know Caroline, but you must have been in her company at some time, surely; perhaps at Moira's?'

'Oh, yes, of course, but you should understand, Annette, as much as I like and admire Moira, Jenny was the only woman who interested me and I have to admit I was rather selfish there. I did want her all to myself, a little bit jealous of all the competition, you might say.' he tried to laugh, but she wasn't fooled. There was something wrong with the man and she couldn't make it out. His whole manner was totally different to what it had been the other night, indeed from when they had first met.

'The reason I'm phoning,' she went on, thinking it was time she tried to move the conversation forward, if she could, and get him to focus on what she was saying, 'Jenny's papers and things, David.'

'Yes?'

'I was wondering whether there could be anything, perhaps a clue as to how she had been thinking these last few weeks. Years ago she used to keep a diary; I don't know whether she still does, but she was a great scribbler, jotting down on odd pieces of paper little comments about people she had met, that sort of thing.' she finished lamely.

'You are still insisting it wasn't an accident, then?'

'Of course, David; I thought I had already made that clear to everyone the other evening.'

'I have to say, Annette,' he said, 'I admire your tenacity. You never let go, do you?'

'Not when I think I shouldn't, no.' she replied quickly, objecting to his tone.

'Well,' he said, 'as far as Jenny's things, anything in fact, are concerned, I want you to feel free to go through everything and if there is anything you would like to take back to England with you, I won't mind.'

'It's not that,' Annette insisted, wondering why he was being so obtuse. Alright, it would appear he was giving her full reign to look through Jenny's possessions, but to imply she might want to have any of them struck her as insulting as well as extremely hurtful, but she let it go, 'I don't want to take anything away with me, David. As I've said, I want to get some sort of picture of what her life, her personal life that is, not necessarily in the theatre, has been like for the last six months or so.'

'I see,' he said, 'I'm sorry, Annette, you must forgive me. I'm still distraught and I don't know what to think about Jenny anymore. I don't expect you to understand; I can only hope that you will one day. I loved her, you see.' he finished; the past tense again. 'When were you thinking of coming to the villa?' he asked.

'Well, as soon as possible, really. This morning, if that would be alright.'

'That's no problem. I won't be here though, but Maria knows where everything is. I'll tell her to expect you.'

'Thank you, David. I do realise how painful all of this must be for you.' she added.

'That's alright,' he said, 'anyway, Annette; no doubt I'll see you tomorrow afternoon at Moira's. She's giving a small informal drinks party, all in the effort, I believe of boosting morale.'

*

By the time Annette had finished talking to him she had completely lost any appetite for breakfast and decided to settle instead for coffee and a savoury cheese-cake; unique to the island. She needed to get out, finding the atmosphere in the hotel uncomfortably claustrophobic. She remembered a small café on the Strand; she had been there a number of times before and she was glad to see it was still there and sitting outside on the terrace and wiping crumbs of flaky pastry from her mouth, was where Andy found her.

'Hello,' he smiled, 'I expect you're going to ask how I knew you would be here.'

'How did you?' she returned his smile, looking up at him, shielding her eyes from the sun which was creating a hazy golden halo around his head.

'I didn't,' he said, pulling out the chair opposite, 'do you mind?' he added before sitting down.

'Of course not.'

'Moira dropped me off on her way up to the theatre; too early to call you, so I thought I would have a wander around the town and find somewhere for a coffee. Also,' he added, 'I recognised your car.'

The waitress arrived to take his order. Being with him again made her realise how devoid her life had been of convivial male company. Although her working life was predominantly male it wasn't quite the same; each day revolving around endless meetings either in California or in London; there was little difference and the miles across the Atlantic did not prevent her from being at Quenton's beck and call. Since she had broken up with Steve, Annette couldn't remember when she had last sat down as she was doing now and relaxing over a coffee and when the conversation was so undemanding. If only, she stifled a sigh. If only the situation had been different; if only Jenny could have been here, or at least to know she was safe.

'How is Moira this morning?'

'She appears to be alright, as resilient as ever, but I don't think she slept very well last night; I heard her moving around in the early hours.'

'She's taking the news about Caroline very hard;' Annette said, 'I realise that, and from what I've seen so far, she is very much a mother-figure to them all.'

'You're right, of course. The theatre is Moira's life and always has been.' he added quietly. And she looked across at him wondering about the reflective expression which cast a brief shadow across his eyes, as though he was thinking back; to his childhood perhaps and remembering. Whatever his thoughts were, Annette didn't think they were all that happy.

'I believe she was quite famous,' she said to him, 'in London,' she added, 'before she came to Malta.'

'And married Julian you mean?'

'Yes.'

'He was a good step-father,' Andy said, 'in fact; he was the only father I ever really knew.'

'That's sad.'

'I don't mean it to sound like that,' again the Moira-like smile, 'I had a good childhood. Okay, most of the time was spent away at boarding school, but Moira was always there for me. She far made up for the lack of my real father; mind you, she didn't have much choice considering he left us when I was only four years of age.'

'That's terrible.'

'Don't think that, Annette. Please. Of course I didn't realise it at the time, but much later I knew why their marriage could never have worked; he couldn't tolerate her having another life.'

'You mean the theatre?'

'Yes.'

'Difficult.'

'Yes, but it happens, so when she met Julian I truly believed he was the only person for her. She was in her late forties by then and some may have thought she wanted a way out, but I didn't think so. Quite simply, she fell in love with him and from that moment her career faded into insignificance.'

'I got that impression yesterday when we had lunch; I rather think she was trying to give me advice.'

'Oh,' he laughed, 'she would. My mother never misses an opportunity, but I mean that in the nicest way. I love her to bits, you know.' he added.

'She's a very sensitive woman.'

'In what way?'

'Well, although she hasn't said too much about Jenny, apart from how much she likes her, it's the way she is reacting to Caroline's death.'

'I know what you mean. Anyway,' he continued, 'she asked me to tell you she's having a few people round tomorrow afternoon and would like you to come.'

'I'd already heard about her drinks party.'

'Had you?' a look of surprise on his face. 'How?'

'David Grech told me.'

'Ah.'

'I phoned him earlier, because I wanted to know if he would allow me to look through Jenny's things.'

'I understand,' he was quick to answer, the blue eyes looking at her directly, 'in case you can find out anything about her life here on the island?'

'Exactly.'

'And what did he say?'

'He didn't seem to mind, so I plan to drive along to Balluta this morning, not that I really hold out a great deal of hope, Andy, but you never know. I know I said I would try and speak to Angela's sister today, but I thought going to the villa would be a start, may even give me some sort of lead. There might be something among Jenny's papers, photographs, perhaps; in fact, anything.'

'It's a good idea. Do you want me to come with you?'

As much as she would have liked him to have been there with her, she didn't think it would be wise. She couldn't explain to herself why she should feel this way. Perhaps it was something to do with David; the change in his manner towards her and one she was finding it difficult to fathom out. Even although he wouldn't be at the villa, she was sure he would hear she hadn't been on her own. No, she decided, not a good idea.

'You don't have to say anything, Annette,' he broke into her thoughts, 'Why don't we meet later on today; back here in Sliema. Have dinner together. I don't really know David Grech all that well,' he added, 'and perhaps he wouldn't take too kindly if he learned I had been there with you.'

'Perhaps not,' she agreed, grateful for his understanding. Here was a man, she thought, with perception.

'How much longer do you plan to stay in Malta?' he asked her.

'A good question,' she gave him a quick smile, 'if you had asked me yesterday I would have said indefinitely, but it looks as if I will have to leave at least by Thursday.'

'I take it you've been issued with an ultimatum?' once again surprising her by his intuitiveness.

'You could say that,' she nodded, 'my boss, a difficult man, is rapidly reaching the end of his endurance. He's even booked me on a flight out to San Francisco on Friday night.'

'Wow!'

'Exactly.' Annette laughed, 'But that's what Quenton is like.'

'Quenton Barton?'

'Yes, but how did you guess?'

'It wasn't exactly a guess,' he admitted, 'but Moira had already told me you worked for a publishing house in London and as far as I know there is only one Quenton Barton.'

'I'm sure there is! So,' she added, 'how is it you know him?'

'Because I'm in the same business, that's why.'

'Really?'

'But, I might add, by comparison in a very small way. I only started up a couple of years ago and it's still very much in its infancy, but it was something I always wanted to do.'

'In London?'

'Yes, Notting Hill.'

'Like the film?' she smiled.

'Not quite, so far nobody famous has wanted me to publish their masterpiece.'

'It must be fun, though,' Annette said, envying him the freedom of working for himself, 'not having anyone cracking the whip!'

'I have heard he's a bit of a tyrant.'

'You heard right!'

'But you cope?'

'I do for most of the time, but usually only when I agree with him. For instance, apart from not being at all happy about me taking time off, he even suggested coming out here.'

'Oh dear, but he obviously changed his mind?'

'Only because he had to be in London.'

'He offered me a job once.' Andy said.

'And you turned him down? He wouldn't have been too pleased about that.'

'No,' he gave a rueful smile, 'I don't think I am one of his favourite people. Mind you, there have been a few times when I have thought I may have made the wrong decision.'

'Why?'

'Because I know now I would have learned a lot from him; perhaps it would have made the first few months when I was starting up the business less stressful. I seemed to fall into one pitfall after another.'

'It's strange, isn't it?' she said thoughtfully, 'but we could have been colleagues.'

'Life does move in an odd way, doesn't it?' he agreed, 'And, Annette, have you always been in publishing?'

'Yes, ever since I left college. My first job was with the large publishing firm in Dundee as a secretary, although really no more than a copy-typist, and when my parents left Scotland to move south, I went with them.'

'A good grounding though, but I bet it didn't prepare you for Quenton Barton.'

'How right you are, but then I learned; he made certain of that.'

How good it was to talk to him. He sounded genuinely interested in what she had been doing, not making a polite pretence like so many other people she had met. He was a good listener and that was a gift, once more reminding her of Moira. She also had the same ability; a real interest in people and wanting to learn more about them.

'And what about you, Andy,' she asked him, 'did you take on your step-father's name?'

'No, I was too old when Moira re-married, almost twenty-two and still at university, so there was no point. And,' he hesitated, the quick smile reappearing, 'I remained Andrew C Henderson.'

'What does the C stand for?'

'I was hoping you wouldn't ask me that,' he smiled, 'but it's Cassius.'

'Obviously your mother's choice?'

'Correct!'

'I rather like it,' she said tactfully, looking at him closely, 'but I think Andrew suits you much better.'

'Thank you.'

'Do you go back to Scotland very often?' she asked him.

'Not as often as I should perhaps, but my father and I have never been all that close. Too many years away from home; first boarding school, and followed immediately by university, but what about you,' he asked her, 'have you any family there?'

'Not now,' she said, 'after our grandparents died it didn't seem the same, even although they left Jenny and me their lovely old house with one of the most spectacular views overlooking the north sea.'

'Ah, the east coast; I know it well.'

'Do you?' surprised; the coincidences were building up and she was wondering why their paths had taken so long to cross. 'It's in Saint Angus; a village between Arbroath and Montrose. Just talking about it makes me feel nostalgic; Jenny and I have been promising ourselves to take some time off together and spend a summer there as we used to do when we were girls, but of course it's never been possible.'

'Perhaps one day.'

'Perhaps.' she agreed, silently praying his words would come true.

*

It was nearly eleven when Annette reached David's villa; their early morning coffee extending as they found more to talk about; discovering similarities, not only their Scottish backgrounds, but in the publishing world. She had been fascinated to hear about his business, how he had taken the risk in giving up a steady job and branching out on his own. She knew she could never do that; she lacked the entrepreneur spirit, preferring the relative safety of being employed, even although it meant being subjected to constant pressures, but she loved her work, especially the satisfaction when she submitted her final report on any assignment Quenton delegated to her.

Jenny had used one of the bedrooms as a dressing-room: two racks of her shoes, alongside a double wardrobe filled with her clothes; a multitude of colours: skirts, dresses, trousers, shirts and jackets and all fighting for space. There was a small desk; a pretty piece of furniture in oak, the darkness of the wood relieved by a scroll of delicately etched vine leaves. It had been placed in front of the window and as from the lounge windows, overlooking the bay. She could picture Jenny sitting there, exactly where she was at that moment, reading through a script and memorising her lines, the thought filling her with an overwhelming helplessness. Taking a deep breath, she opened the first drawer on the right-hand side of the desk.

On top was the green leather-bound note-case their father had given Jenny on her sixteenth birthday. She was about to leave home for the first time; she had, after months of nagging, managed to persuade him to allow her to go to drama school. No doubt, Annette thought, the gift was to encourage her to keep in touch. He should have known better, she smiled to herself; it would have taken more than that to make Jenny write home if she didn't feel in the mood. Annette unzipped the case. It had hardly been used; the envelopes on one side looked as if they had always been there; the writing-pad, cream velum paper was as new, except she had started to write to someone called James, but hadn't got very far and had drawn an impatient line diagonally across the page. The date, Annette noticed, was over two weeks ago.

There was a diary in the same drawer, but disappointedly it was for the previous year; some months before she had arrived in Malta and, predictably, only the first few weeks of January had been filled in.

Annette's own letters to her were at the bottom of the drawer, neatly tied together in their arranged date order. She pushed them to one side, not too surprised to find Jenny had kept them. She was a hoarder and would hardly ever throw anything away, even when she had been quite young, protesting vigorously when asked to tidy her room and indignantly insisting that everything was important to her.

There was only one other letter, still in its envelope. Disliking intensely what she was doing, Annette picked it up, holding it unopened for a moment and trying to decipher the partially obliterated post-mark. She couldn't make out the day, but the month and year were clear enough: October, nineteen-ninety-three; ten years ago. Pulling the letter out; a single sheet written in a small back-slanting hand and, with the same reluctance she began to read: "Dear Jenny, I expect you will be surprised to hear from me since we are no longer together," and at this point she glanced down to the bottom of the page. It was signed simply, with no embellishments and no endearments: James. The same James, she wondered and carried on reading: "but Paul phoned me last night to tell me what he had been able to find out about Ben Standish. It would appear he was not as squeaky-clean as he tried to make us believe. He was involved in a massive fraud here, in London, over three years ago apparently and still very much sought after by the authorities, but from what the four of us saw that night it would seem they are going to be out of luck. I thought you should know about this, Jenny, as I know how upset you were after it happened. I always thought you rather fancied him, but then, it's as they say, now water under the bridge. Anyway, we had a good holiday and one I will always remember. James."

Thoughtfully, but not understanding any of it, Annette replaced it in the envelope and, putting it back where she had found it, closed the drawer. These were names she had never heard Jenny mention, nor, she was certain, had ever met; James who had obviously been her boyfriend around this time and their friend, Paul. And then, there was this other person, Ben. A dubious character by all accounts, she concluded with a shrug and opened the second drawer.

As in the other one, everything had been placed in separate neat piles: old Christmas and birthday cards; wedding and christening invitations; postcards going back years, except for four of them: from Australia and replicas of the ones she had received from their parents on each stage of their trip; Sydney with the much-photographed Opera House in the background; Canberra's Houses of Parliament; Melbourne, the high-rise buildings reminding Annette of the Hong Kong sky-line and the fourth card where they both were now; Brisbane, and the long stretch of sandy beaches. All of which served to remind her that soon she would have to get in touch with them.

There wasn't much else in there, except a small photo album. Most of the photographs Annette was looking at were familiar; mainly from when they were children, right through to their teenage years and nearly all of them taken by their grandfather who had been a keen photographer. Unwilling to continue down such a sentimental path, which she knew would only sadden her, she made to close the album when a couple of photographs fell out, landing on the desk.

The first one: a group, taken in front of a villa somewhere; a backdrop of blue and purple wisteria, possibly the south of France. She remembered Jenny spending a holiday there once, but it was years ago. Jenny was there, posing dramatically, both arms wrapped around the young man standing next to her with an embarrassed looking smile on his face. Another girl; blonde curls framing a heart-shaped face and holding hands with the man beside her and further back in the picture, but not directly facing the camera, a third man, older than any of them. Annette turned the photograph over and sure enough in her usual precise way Jenny had written in the details: "Our idyllic holiday in the south of France – me (of course!), James, Caroline, Paul and Ben, August, nineteen-ninety-three". The same year as James' letter, so he must be the same person, Annette decided, picking up the second photograph. Once again, he wasn't looking at the camera; in fact, he didn't appear to know the photograph was being taken. This time, not at the villa, but on a boat, a yacht perhaps, with a vivid blue sea merging with an equally blue sky. Jenny had simply written on the back: "Ben – Cap d'Ail, August, nineteen-ninety-three."

Not having any clear notion of why she did so, Annette took out the letter again from the drawer, tucking the two photographs inside the envelope and putting it into her bag. They could be nothing important and nothing to get excited about, but Jenny had started to write to someone called James; that was enough to be going on with for the moment. There was nothing else for her to see, no more cupboards or drawers, and she drew the line at going through any of her clothes. Besides, she knew all too well that Jenny was too meticulous to keep anything in pockets or in bags she wasn't using; she liked to have everything separated, documented and stored neatly away.

Annette called out to Maria as she left the villa. There was no car in Moira's drive she noticed and, presuming she was still at the theatre, Annette reversed down the drive and headed back towards Sliema, not sure whether she had achieved anything that morning or not. What did she actually have? Not much, except for a reference made to something which happened ten years ago; a letter from around that time from an old boyfriend of Jenny's and the start of one written two weeks ago to the same person. Who was this Ben she wondered. As she drove along the coast road, Annette tried to make sense of everything hurtling through her brain but by the time she got back to Sliema she was no further forward; if possible, more bewildered than ever.

She was driving past 'Tony's' when she saw Angela sitting out on the terrace at the same table as before, but this time she wasn't alone. There was another woman with her; a few years older, but with such a striking resemblance Annette thought she could be her sister and with luck the one who worked at the theatre. This was too good an opportunity to miss she decided and pulled into an empty space across the road.

'Miss Graham,' Angela called out to her as soon as she stepped on to the terrace, 'would you like to join us?'

'Hello, Angela,' Annette smiled at her, noticing the dark circles around her eyes.

'This is my sister, Joanne.' Angela explained.

'I'm glad to meet you, Miss Graham,' Joanne said after they had shaken hands, 'Angela has just been telling me she saw your sister last Friday morning when everyone thought she was out in the boat. Of course she should have told the police, but, well, what can I say,' she gave her thin shoulders a tiny shrug, 'she was only being protective towards me.'

'I understood that.' Annette said quietly.

'I just want you to know, Miss Graham,' she continued, 'in fact, we both want you to know, Angela is going to make a statement to the police and I'll be going along with her this afternoon.'

'You don't know how relieved this makes me feel,' Annette said quickly, 'and should your employer make any difficulties for you, Joanne, I'll speak to him. I've already met Adam Bond and I'm sure he will be sympathetic.'

'Thank you, Miss Graham, but I don't think that will be necessary.'

'Well,' Annette smiled, 'remember my offer still stands.'

'I do hope they find your sister soon,' she said, 'her safety is far more important than my job.'

Chapter Eight

'Ten years.' Andy said, handing the photographs back to her, 'A long time.'

They were in the lounge bar of the Holiday Inn before going into the restaurant and had chosen a table close to one of the open windows looking out to the hotel's swimming pool where there were still a few guests enjoying a final swim before changing for dinner. Annette had shown him the photographs and the letter she had brought from David's villa; she had also told him about talking to Angela and her sister. He had read the letter first, before looking at the two photographs and, as she had done, turned them over to see if anything had been written on the other side.

'I know.' she agreed, trying to remember back to that time. What had she been doing ten years ago? It had been shortly before she started working for Quenton and she had spent a good part of the year juggling her secretarial job with studying for her marketing degree, having come to the conclusion her career had become stymied, uninteresting and taking her nowhere.

She had not seen Jenny for at least three months, but there was nothing unusual in that. Jenny was in rep then and the very nature of her work meant she had little free time; therefore, she had been surprised to receive a postcard from her that summer. She hadn't said she was going on holiday, not that Annette expected to be told in any case. Jenny only communicated when she had something important to say; usually a part of her life, the good part, she wanted to share. Annette looked again at the group, this time more closely, certain she had never met any of her friends. As for the man in the background, he didn't look English; sun-tanned and casually, but expensively, dressed. Also, as she had already noticed, he was considerably older. Had Jenny fallen for him, she wondered. Annette tried to remember how long it had been after the postcard arrived before she had seen her again. Slowly, fragmented pieces of memory were coming back. It must have been towards the end of the summer; a Saturday morning and they had met for coffee. Jenny had looked tired, but Annette had put it down to too many late nights. She didn't have much to say about her holiday in France, had appeared reluctant to talk about it. And that was all.

'This guy, Ben Standish,' Andy said, 'there's something of a mystery here. If James was right and he was involved in a major fraud around then, I could try and find out the details. This would presumably have been during nineteen-ninety sometime; a bit vague, but I should be able to unearth something.'

'He would have changed his name, wouldn't he?'

'I would think so. That would be the first thing he would do if he wanted to create a new identity for himself, but there could be a picture of him in the archives. At least then,' he added, 'we could tie it up with these photographs.'

'It all sounds rather incredible, doesn't it?'

'It does, yes,' he agreed, 'but perhaps this is what we've been looking for, Annette. A lead, maybe a connection to what is happening here. I've been thinking about the letter Jenny sent to you. She saw someone she recognised, or at least she thought she did. It could have been Ben Standish.'

'It was the man's voice she recognised.' Annette reminded him.

'I know,' Andy smiled, 'and you and I have no idea what he sounds like. But, let's try and narrow this down a bit. It's ten years on, Annette, and in this photograph he would have been at least thirty, perhaps even older, so he is bound to look different now.'

'Andy?'

'Yes?'

'Do you think Caroline's murder has anything to do with any of this?'

'I don't know,' he said, putting a hand on her arm, 'but I can't help feeling it could have.'

'I think so, too.' she said quietly; too afraid to put her thoughts into words, that, at the time Jenny had got into the Renault outside the theatre, there was no-one else around and she had apparently remained there, in the passenger seat, and waited for the driver. It must have been someone she knew. From the theatre, but not necessarily; Angela had said the parking area was used by people with nothing to do with the theatre? So, she concluded, when Jenny did leave she must have done so willingly; she hadn't been forced. But, where did she go? There were so many questions and not one of them with any answer.

'Look, Annette,' Andy said, 'I can tell your mind is in a whirl. Why don't we give it a rest for a while? I suppose there is one redeeming fact though.' he added.

'What?'

'Now that the police will have the statement from Angela they will have no option but to re-open the case.'

'That's true.'

'And this means they will start going round, asking questions; trying to find out whether Jenny was seen by anyone else. At least,' he went on, 'the official verdict will now be reversed.'

'She could have left the island.'

'That's always possible and I would imagine they'll check all the flights from the Friday onwards.'

'It still doesn't make any sense.'

'I know; none of it does.'

'Well, I suppose,' Annette said, 'if the police are going to continue trying to find her, there is not much point in me staying on here.'

'Perhaps not.'

'As I've said, I have to be back at work by next Friday, so it looks as if I have no option but to book a flight out the day before; that is, if I can.'

'I have to get back as well,' he said, 'perhaps we can get the same flight.'

'That would be good.' she said, realising she meant what she said; she wanted him to be with her.

'Annette,' he said, 'I know we've only known each other for a very short time and under stressful circumstances, but I would like to hope we can see each other when we're back in London. What do you think?'

'I think,' she smiled at him, 'I would like that very much.'

*

'It's good of you to call into the station, Miss Graham,' Inspector Secluna said the following morning as she was ushered into his office, 'at such short notice and on a Sunday.'

'It's alright, Inspector,' Annette assured him, 'I wasn't too surprised to hear from you.'

'Ah, yes,' he said, 'the young lady who now remembers seeing your sister. Yes, well this does make a difference; that is, if she wasn't mistaken.'

'She sounded quite positive to me.'

'Yes,' he repeated slowly, pressing both palms together, 'but apart from her, Miss Graham, we have since spoken to someone else who saw your sister on the same morning.'

She waited as patiently as she could for him to continue. His whole manner, pedantic and deliberate, was irritating. Why couldn't the man come to the point? It seemed to Annette as she sat there in front of his large paper-free desk, as if he was keeping her in suspense intentionally.

'This second witness,' he said at last, 'lives in the apartment below the one in which Caroline Johnson rented. She recalls seeing Miss Graham's car parked outside on the Thursday night and,' he went on, 'it was still there the following morning.'

'But –'

'I believe I know what you're going to say,' he interrupted, 'how could she have been in two places at once? Although Mr Grech had told us earlier that when he left for work on the Friday morning your sister was still in bed; asleep he'd said, but he now claims this wasn't the case.'

'I don't understand.'

'Believe me, Miss Graham, at the moment neither do we. But, rest assured, we will; given some more time.'

'You say that Caroline's neighbour actually saw Jenny on the Friday morning?'

'Yes,' the inspector said, 'in fact she spoke to her. Only briefly, you understand, merely to say good morning and this was before your sister drove off.'

'And, this was around eight-thirty?'

'Yes, indeed.'

'It wouldn't have taken her long to reach the theatre, would it?'

'No, minutes only.'

'Did she know Jenny then?'

'Not well, no,' he said, 'but your sister had often been to Miss Johnson's apartment.'

'I'm puzzled, Inspector.'

'Yes?'

'Why should Caroline Johnson's neighbour mention now something which occurred over a week ago? Especially when she had only just learned about Caroline; surely that would have been uppermost in her mind?'

'Under normal circumstances, yes, but these are far from normal, Miss Graham. You see, according to her, Caroline Johnson had expected your sister to be waiting at the airport for her when she arrived back on Thursday afternoon and when she wasn't there, she had taken a taxi directly to the theatre only to learn about —' here, he hesitated, but only for a fraction of a second, '- the boating accident.'

'Which we now know didn't happen.'

'Miss Graham,' he held up a hand, 'we still have no proof whether there was an accident or not. However, as I was explaining to you, Caroline Johnson saw her neighbour when she eventually got back to her apartment and told her about your sister.'

'And didn't her neighbour know?'

'Surprising though it may seem, she didn't. But, she told us that she mentioned to Caroline Johnson that she had seen your sister on the Friday, the morning after the storm.'

'I see.' And for the first time Annette did begin to understand a little bit more of what may have happened, although it didn't explain why Caroline had wanted to see her so urgently; she had been at the theatre when she phoned and this was before she spoke to her neighbour. "Something isn't right" she had said. Had her murderer been there as she was making the call? Caroline's door had been open the following day Moira had said. This did indicate that Caroline probably knew who had called at her apartment that night.

'So, Inspector,' Annette said, 'do I take it you are still trying to find my sister?'

'We are, yes,' he said and she recognised his reluctance. How he must have disliked making such an admission, but the thought gave her no satisfaction; nothing altered the fact that Jenny was still missing.

'How much longer do you intend to stay in Malta, Miss Graham? he asked her.

'I'm returning to England next week,' she said, 'Wednesday or Thursday, whenever I can get a flight. There's nothing I can do here.'

'I am sorry, Miss Graham,' and for the first time she heard a faint trace of sympathy in his voice, 'we don't have some good news for you. I do realise how distressing all of this must be for you. Perhaps, on reflection, it would be best if you did return home.'

'You're probably right. Inspector Secluna, you will no doubt think this a stupid question, but –' she hesitated, beginning to wish she had not decided to say anything more.

'Yes, Miss Graham?' he was already getting to his feet. Obviously the interview was at an end.

'The car my sister was seen getting into. I know you weren't given a registration number, but, how many silver grey Renaults are there on the island?'

'Quite a number, I can assure you,' he permitted her one of his rare smiles, 'in fact, Miss Graham, I own one myself.'

*

'Annette! You're here at last!'

'I'm sorry, Moira,' Annette smiled, leaning over to the back seat to pick up the bottle of wine she had brought with her, 'I got a bit delayed.'

'The traffic is awful on Sundays,' Moira sympathised, 'if anything, worse than on any other day in the week, at least along the coast road. But, you're here, safe and sound and that's the main thing. Come on in, my dear,' she added, putting an arm around her shoulders and taking her into the lounge; radiantly bright with the early afternoon sun streaming in from the open balcony windows.

Marianne and Frank were there; Frank, looking quite startling in a red and white striped blazer and a loosely-tied red silk cravat. All he needed Annette thought uncharitably was a straw boater to complete whatever character he was attempting to portray. Edward Coppini gallantly rose to his feet to shake hands with her. There was no sign of David, but for the moment, her meeting with Inspector Secluna still uppermost on her mind, she wasn't sorry. Ever since the inspector had told her that Jenny hadn't spent that last night in the villa, she didn't want to acknowledge the unsavoury fact that David had lied.

'Hi!' Andy said, coming through from the kitchen carrying a couple of bottles of wine, 'Are you alright?'

'I'm fine,' she answered automatically. At that precise moment, fine was definitely something she did not feel. Why was it she wondered the British were never straight-forward when they were asked how they were. All she had to say was: no, I am not fine; far from it, in fact. My sister is missing; the police appear to be going round and round in ever diminishing circles and I have to return to London next week having resolved nothing! Also, my boss, who has as much sympathy as a wet dish cloth, is only going to make me feel a whole heap worse!

'I know you're not really,' Andy whispered to her, 'but we'll go out later, shall we? Have a quiet uninterrupted drink somewhere.'

'So, Annette,' Marianne bore down on her; her navy and white floral dress managing by a fraction of an inch to skim her wide hips and the neckline cut dangerously low revealing a large expanse of bosom, 'you're still here.'

'Yes, Marianne,' Annette answered, accepting a glass of wine from Andy, 'I'm still here.'

'And when do you propose returning to England?' she persisted, not in the slightest put off by her coolness.

'Probably Thursday.'

'I see and what about Jenny's things?'

'What about them, Marianne?'

'Somebody needs to sort them out and honestly you cannot expect David to do it. He has got quite enough to cope with at the moment.'

I bet he has, Annette thought bitterly, longing to be anywhere but in this woman's company. She was not only unbearable, but unbelievably rude. Why had Moira invited them; surely they could have nothing in common?

'It would seem you were right, Annette,' Edward Coppini said, guiding her gently but firmly away and out on to the balcony, 'in disbelieving Jenny had taken the boat out.'

'You've heard then?' she asked. And she wondered if he also knew about the second witness, but she wasn't going to be the one to enlighten him. Presumably, he would hear in time.

'Yes, David phoned me this morning,' he said once they were outside, 'he was in a bit of a state actually.'

'Why?'

'Well,' Edward went on, lowering his voice, although they had the balcony to themselves. Behind them, more guests were arriving and Annette heard Adam Bond's voice; a higher cadence from the others. Looking over Edward's shoulder she couldn't see David and wondered if he had decided not to turn up, 'after we had left that evening, apparently he and Jenny had a terrific argument and Jenny in a fit of temper – his words, you understand, Annette, not mine, walked out.'

'And of course he hadn't told this to the police.'

'No,' he said slowly, 'David is a proud man. I've known him for a long time; since he was a boy in fact, and he has always been a very private person; keeping things to himself. I don't think he wanted to admit to something as personal as an argument which may in the end have proved to be merely a lover's tiff. I don't know. I didn't ask him.'

'But,' Annette said, trying to make some sort of sense out of what he was saying and wanting to believe it had been just that; a lover's tiff. 'all the same,' she went on, 'he should have told the police. Don't you think so, Edward? It might have made their job easier.'

'I don't know about that,' he smiled at her, 'it may have done, but David really believed Jenny had gone to Saint Paul's Bay and taken the boat out. So, he wasn't wrong when he reported her missing.'

'I'm sorry, Edward,' she said, 'but I don't quite see it like that. And,' Annette continued, 'as it has turned out she didn't go anywhere near Saint Paul's Bay, at least around the time they had thought.'

'You're right, of course, and unfortunately he has landed himself into something of a predicament.'

'They don't believe him?'

'Let's say, Annette,' he sighed, 'they are asking him a great number of questions.'

'And, meanwhile,' she pointed out, trying to keep her voice steady, 'nobody knows where Jenny is.'

'All we can do, my dear, is hope.' he said, 'That's all we can do; hope and pray Jenny is alright. I've always thought her to be a very resilient young woman; determined and headstrong, yes, but not without strength. There is something going on here, Annette and I can't help feeling there is some sort of sinister connection. Caroline's death, for instance; it's too much of a coincidence not to believe your sister's disappearance is not somehow connected. But, whatever you may be thinking of David, I don't believe for one minute he is involved in any way.'

'He's just arrived now,' Annette said looking down to see David walking up the steps to the front door. Even from where she was standing she could see the strain in his face; more haggard than ever and he looked unbelievably tired, as if he hadn't slept and in spite of her reservations, she couldn't help feeling sorry for him. He looked like a man who was not only extremely unhappy, but had given up all hope. Wherever you are, Jenny, she thought, and if you have left the island, are you really aware of what you are putting him through.

Jenny could be thoughtless at times; she knew that very well, but never cruel, at least not intentionally. But had she gone? And where was she? Annette watched as Moira went over to greet him, noticing how she enveloped him in her arms and the way, for a moment, he put his head on her shoulder. For that fraction of a second he looked the epitome of misery. Marianne, she saw, made no move towards him, but remained where she was at the far end of the room, apparently engrossed in what the young man, incongruously dressed in a Hawaii-style shirt, was telling her, accompanied by a great deal of arm flapping. Annette remembered seeing him in the Green Room; he had been one of the actors on the platform.

'That's Tony Borg,' Edward smiled, following her gaze, 'he's one of the theatre's more flamboyant characters, but he's a good actor.'

'And the girl next to him; the one with the mass of auburn hair?'

'Jeannette Summers; she's in our current production,' he told her, 'the play which opened on Friday night.'

Jeannette was one of Jenny's friends, also Tony Borg. She remembered Pete mentioning his cousin; Lawrence he'd said his name was and wondered if he would also be here this afternoon. It felt strange putting faces to the names she had been given and picturing Jenny with them.

'Edward,' she said, 'the girl who found Caroline, is she here?'

'Evelyn? Not yet, but I'm sure she will be. She was also one of Jenny's friends, you know.'

'I knew that. Jenny makes friends so easily; I've always envied her for that.'

'We're all different, Annette,' Edward smiled, 'would you like me to replenish your glass or do you want to come back into the lounge and – mingle?' he finished, his eyes twinkling. How well suited he is to Moira she thought, giving him her glass; simpatico, with a charming, although old-fashioned manner, and extremely easy to talk to. She liked that and watched him walk back into the lounge, touching Moira gently on the arm as he passed her.

'Hello, Annette.'

'David. How are you?' she felt forced to ask him, taken aback by his dreadful pallor.

'Not too great. I had quite a harrowing interview with Inspector Secluna last evening and it has rather taken it out of me. Why is it, I wonder,' he went on, 'the police have this nasty habit of making one feel guilty?'

'Was it as bad as that?'

'I lied you see, Annette, but at the time I felt justified. It was stupid, of course. I realise that now; someone was bound to have seen Jenny. I just didn't think.'

'Did you believe she would come back?'

'I did, yes, but when I noticed the boat wasn't in the shed I started to think the worse; I didn't want to, Annette, believe me, but then when they spoke to that man who'd been walking along there earlier, well-'

'But you reported her missing before you heard about that, didn't you?'

'I did, because I had absolutely no idea of where she could have gone. I didn't know then she had a key to Caroline's apartment; she never told me. It hadn't been the first time she'd walked out you know,' he went on, 'and each time she always did the same. She drove to Saint Paul's Bay and went out on the water. She explained it was her way of unwinding.'

'I can understand that,' Annette said slowly, 'but not if the conditions had been bad.'

'I realise that now, Annette.'

'I saw Inspector Secluna this morning,' she told him, 'but I got the impression they are still no further forward. He isn't even ruling out that Jenny may have had a boating accident.'

'He implied a little bit more than that to me,' David's voice was bitter as he turned abruptly away from her to stare out across the bay, 'he practically accused me of being involved, not only in Jenny's disappearance, but for Caroline Johnson's murder.'

'I don't believe it!'

'Don't you?' surprise in her reaction made him turn round to face her again.

'No, I do not. I don't think they know very much at all at this stage. He's clutching at straws, David. Don't you think it is his way? Police have to suspect everyone they question. At least that is how it is in detective novels, so why should real life be all that different?'

'Easy to say, Annette,' he said, a cynical smile momentarily appearing, 'but not so when one is at the brunt end of their suspicions, whether pure fabrications or not, which they are, of course. I have got to the stage that I honestly do not know what to think. The last thing I want to do,' he went on, 'is to criticise Jenny in any way. I loved her.'

'Loved, David?'

'Sorry?'

'You used the past tense,' she reminded him, 'you either believe she is dead or you don't love her anymore.'

'Please, Annette,' he protested sharply, 'don't try to be clever.'

'I'm not.'

'I'm sorry,' he sighed, 'that was rude of me. Perhaps I shouldn't have come here this afternoon. It wasn't a good idea, but I wanted to see you; to try and explain, convince you if possible, that in spite of what you are no doubt thinking about me, I am utterly devastated.'

'Okay,' Annette said quickly, placing a hand on his arm, 'I don't mean to be smart, but I am worried about her as well. You should realise that, David.'

'I do. Of course I do. You see,' he went on quietly, 'I had hoped that Jenny and I would have had a future together, but –' leaving his sentence unfinished, no doubt waiting for her to prompt him.

But she didn't. She had no wish to hear any of this. His whole manner was beginning to embarrass her; he was so intense. The Mediterranean way, she concluded. So different from the type of man she was used to. She wondered whether in the end Jenny had felt the same. Annette had only been in his company for a matter of minutes, but already she felt hemmed in, stifled by the intensity of his emotions. All she wanted was to move away; she didn't want any further involvement in what he had to say, but, she didn't have a great deal of choice, other than to resort to a bluntness which wasn't in her nature.

Edward, she saw with relief, was on his way back to her, one glass of wine in each hand, but then, half-way across the room, he was stopped by Adam Bond.

'You haven't asked what our argument was about, Annette.' David said, a hint of impatience in his voice.

'It's none of my business, David. That was between you and Jenny.'

'I know it was, but it was one we'd had a number of times and one neither of us could resolve, at least not in the foreseeable future.'

'I don't understand.'

'She wanted me to marry her. She wanted children.'

'And you didn't?' suddenly she did want to know more. Had Jenny been so serious about this man? Did she feel, as she was approaching thirty, it was time she settled down and had a family?

'I'm married already, Annette.'

'And Jenny knows this?'

'Oh, yes, she knew alright, but she couldn't get it into her head that in Malta divorce is not easy, in fact well nigh impossible in many cases. Annulment can be obtained, but it can take years and as I already have a child, well –' he finished with a shrug, '- what more can I say?'

Not a lot Annette thought. Poor Jenny; it would seem for once in her life she had come up against a problem which couldn't be overcome. How frustrated she must have felt. Jenny was used to getting what she wanted and always had been. It wasn't her fault; it was how she was, and the way since a very young child she had been allowed to wind everyone around her little finger. No wonder she had lost her temper and walked out on him, walked away from what must have been to her an impossible situation.

'I didn't know, David.' was all she could say to him. What else could she say? At last Edward was coming back. And, wondering how she was going to excuse herself politely, without offending either of them, she took her glass from him.

'Evelyn isn't here yet, Annette.' Edward said.

'It doesn't matter. Perhaps I'll go along to the theatre tomorrow and try to see her there. Now might not be the best time.'

'True,' Edward said, 'by the way, I believe Andy wants a word with you.'

Was he being diplomatic she wondered as she took a sip of her wine, but his expression, bland and inscrutable, told her nothing. It was time she returned to the lounge in any case; she had spent long enough away from the rest of the party. Also, she did want to speak to Andy. Someone normal she thought; someone more like herself with roots firmly established in England and not confined to, what she considered to be an insular way of life, living on such a small island where everyone appeared to know everyone else. Apart from wanting to spend some time periodically with his mother, she doubted whether Andy had any real interest in being here for long periods.

'Before you go, Annette,' David said, taking out an envelope from his shirt pocket, 'this arrived for Jenny yesterday. I didn't know what to do with it.' he added quickly. 'I felt it wasn't right for me to open her mail.'

He handed her the envelope with the blue airmail sticker in the top left-hand corner. What was she meant to do with this? To open any mail not addressed to her, even if Jenny was her sister and for the moment not here, she still felt repugnance in doing so. Without saying a word, she accepted it from him and slipped it into her bag. There was nothing she could say. She may or she may not open it. She would decide later; when she'd had time to think through the other things she had learned that afternoon. Not only what the inspector had told her, but what David had admitted about his relationship with Jenny. Emotional stuff; made even more difficult because she knew Jenny would never have told her about any of it. Being sisters, no matter how close, didn't give either of them *carte blanche* to encroach into each other's affairs. One's private life, which included everything from confidences from personal friends to the exchange of letters, was sacrosanct to her and Jenny was the same. It was the way they had both been brought up. But perhaps, Annette realised now, she would have no choice. It had been distasteful enough going through Jenny's papers without opening her mail.

Annette mingled as Edward had so succinctly put it, adroitly managing to avoid having to talk to Marianne again, although she wasn't so lucky with her husband. Frank; the dark, almost black eyes, undressing her with every suggestive word he uttered. He really believed he was some sort of latter day screen idol. In his dreams she thought with distaste as for the second time that afternoon she pulled away from an uncomfortable situation, thanks this time to the appearance of Andy.

'Shall we go then?' he asked her.

Music to her ears she thought, finishing off her wine. She had caught Andy's eye a few times when she had been talking to David Grech and had read the sympathy in his expression.

'Moira won't mind, will she?'

'Not at all; she understands.'

'What?' Frank leaned forward, completely ignoring Andy; so close she couldn't help but inhale his overpowering after-shave mixed with a strong whiff of brandy, 'You're not leaving already? The party has hardly begun!'

'I'm not really in a party mood, Frank,' she said, letting him off lightly and curbing her annoyance at his total lack of tact, wanting to wipe the ingratiating smile from his face and tell him what she thought of him. But instead, knowing he would be insensitive to any reminder of the reason why she was in Malta, she attempted a smile, 'you probably consider me to be unsociable, Frank, but quite honestly, it can't be helped. Say goodbye to Marianne for me, won't you?'

She had the satisfaction of seeing his expression change and she was sure his jaw dropped slightly, but it may have been the result of too many brandies, rather than that her words had managed to penetrate through to his brain.

'Well done, Annette,' Andy said, taking her arm and leading her away. 'he had that coming to him. I couldn't have put it better myself.'

'I was rather rude though.'

'Forget it,' he chuckled, 'the man is a creep and you won't be too surprised to hear he has a reputation around the island. Marianne, I am sure, doesn't know half of it!'

'I would like to say, poor Marianne, but I can't bring myself to feel sorry for her. In her way, she isn't much better.'

'They certainly haven't a great deal of charm between the pair of them.'

'How well do you really know David Grech, Andy?' she asked him when they were in the car and heading back towards Sliema?

'Not all that well,' he said, 'I've never really had much of a conversation with him. Moira has known him for years and is very fond of him. He's okay, I suppose, but not too easy to get to know.'

'He can be charming, at least that was my first impression when I met him,' Annette said, 'and I can understand why Jenny was attracted to him, but —'

'– but?'

'Well,' she gave him a quick smile, taking her eyes off the road for a second, 'I'm probably being unkind; doing him an injustice, but I find him lacking in substance.'

'In what way?'

'It's his manner, or rather the noticeable change in it. He seems to have gone completely to pieces since Thursday evening. He's convincing himself now that the police suspect him of having something to do with Caroline Johnson's death, not to mention Jenny's disappearance, especially as he lied to them about Jenny walking out on him. Did you know about that, Andy?'

'Yes, Moira told me.'

'Where shall we go?' she asked as they approached the centre of the town. 'You suggested somewhere quiet; not easy on a Sunday afternoon. It seems to be the one day in the week when everyone is out and about!'

'Why not the same place we went to the other evening? ' Sandals', we may be able to get a table outside and make the most of this marvellous weather.'

The bistro was busy but there were some empty tables at the edge of the terrace and Andy ordered their drinks from one of the waiters standing in the open doorway.

'Do you think I should open this letter?' she asked him when their wine had been brought to them. She had already told him about David giving the letter to her and mentioned her reluctance in opening it.

'Not an easy decision; I can understand how you feel, Annette. I would be exactly the same, but,' he added, raising his glass to her, 'apart from your own feelings how do you think Jenny would re-act when she learns you've opened her mail?'

'I don't think she would be all that pleased, but perhaps I should. It may help us in some way. Jenny isn't a regular correspondent, much preferring to pick up the phone and I rather think most of her friends are the same. But,' she went on slowly, thoughtfully, 'I didn't mention it to you before, Andy, but when I was looking through her desk yesterday, I came across a letter she had started and then, as if changing her mind, she had scribbled across it.'

'Had she put a date on it?'

'Yes, the sixth of June; a few days after she wrote to me. Also, and this could be the relevant bit, it was to James.'

'The same James you think?'

'It could be, couldn't it? I've been thinking; perhaps she did write to him and this letter is his reply.'

'In that case,' Andy said, 'perhaps you should read it.'

Slowly, trying to dispel the insistent pin pricks of guilt, Annette opened the envelope and pulled out the sheet of airmail paper and taking a deep breath started to read: "Dear Jenny," it began, in a strong flowing hand, "no doubt you will be surprised to hear from me, but James gave me your letter." She stopped there, scanning down to the bottom to read the signature.

'It's from Paul,' Annette said glancing up at him, 'not James.'

'Jenny's other friend; the one in the photograph?'

'Yes, that's right,' she nodded, continuing to read: "James is married now with a family and for, I suppose, natural-enough reasons didn't want to get involved. Sorry, I guess that sounds pretty thoughtless, but I hope you will understand, especially if you are right, and it was Ben you saw. Anyway, I have mentioned this to my editor who has always believed Ben could still be alive. I don't know whether James ever told you, but we, my paper that is, sent a reporter to the south of France to find out what they could about Ben Standish, but came up against a brick wall. Someone else was already living in his villa in Cap d'Ail by then and no-one in the area seemed to know anything about him; all very frustrating. It would have been quite a scoop if we had been able to find him, but perhaps we will have more luck this time. I'll keep in touch, but meanwhile be careful and remember he mixed with a pretty rum crowd. Best wishes, Paul."

Silently, she passed the letter over to Andy and waited while he read it. His expression was serious as he came to the end, folding the letter and putting it back into the envelope.

'I don't like the sound of this.'

'I'm afraid to think what it could mean, Andy. If Jenny had recognised Ben Standish, she could be in danger. What do you think we should do?'

'I honestly don't know. We could tell the police, but what would that achieve? There is one thing, though.'

'Yes?'

'It looks very much as if Paul's paper will send out another reporter and that may stir things up a bit. Whether that would be good or not, again I don't know.

'I can't get rid of the feeling that Jenny has left Malta.' Annette said, 'She'd walked out on David; perhaps she had had enough and her disappearance has nothing to do with Ben Standish. Oh, I don't know, Andy. I'm only guessing.'

'The police will now have checked the flights going out over those couple of days and presumably she wasn't on any of them or we would have heard.'

'But how thorough would they have been?' she insisted, 'Would they have checked every flight, not only those to London? It seems to me they have been doing so much assuming, perhaps they have assumed that if she did leave the island she would make her way back there.'

'You could be right.'

'Andy, I've just had a thought. Jenny said in her letter to me that she was going back to the casino which she probably did. Perhaps Ben Standish was there again and that prompted her to write to James, after she had decided to scrap her first attempt.'

'You mean she was certain it was him?'

'Yes, and that means the man is on the island. Why don't we go along to the casino? I realise even if we thought we recognised Ben from the photograph, there wouldn't be much we could do, but it would be something.'

'You're right,' he agreed, 'we could find out who he is; presumably the name he's using now and where he lives; that sort of thing. It would be better than just sitting here speculating.'

'So, when shall we go?'

'No time like the present,' Andy smiled at her, 'we'll go this evening.'

Chapter Nine

It was after nine when they arrived at Malta's oldest casino; a beautifully proportioned classical villa on the promontory which is Dragonara Point. Andy had insisted they take a taxi, telling her he felt guilty about all the driving she had been doing while he had enjoyed the luxury of not having to drive on roads which at times were frenetic with impatient locals overtaking with practised and breath-taking alacrity.

'A pity about the neon signs,' Annette remarked as they walked across the forecourt to the main door, 'and this statue! It's bizarre.' she added, stopping to read the plaque below the bottle-green effigy.

'I know,' he agreed, taking her arm, 'I don't think the old Marquis would have liked it very much, but no doubt he would have approved of his home being used as a casino.'

'The Marquis Emanuele Scicluna.' Annette read out, 'Was he very famous then?'

'I don't know about that,' he said, 'although it's likely. He was made a Marquis in the late nineteenth century on the strength of a loan to Pope Pius IX and the villa was built as his summer residence, named at that time, the Dragonara Palace.'

'You're very knowledgeable, Andy; I am really impressed.'

'Well, my stepfather told me a great deal about the Maltese history. He had a wonderful gift for making the past come alive.'

'Our grandfather was like that,' Annette said, remembering, 'he was a fantastic story-teller. There was nothing he didn't know about Scotland and its folklore. Jenny and I used to sit and listen to him for hours on those long summer evenings when it seemed to take for- ever to get dark.'

The gaming rooms were in the colonnaded centre of the rectangular building in what Andy told her had once been the courtyard. They paused for a moment at the entrance before going into the rooms. It was too early for any serious gamblers, but already there were a few at the

Baccarat and Black Jack tables. There was more than one man there who could have been Ben Standish: early middle-age; hair greying slightly at the temples; suavely attired in a dark jacket and white shirt: the unwritten dress code for the casino.

'We'll just stroll around, Annette,' Andy said, guiding her towards the first table, 'I know it's a long shot, pretty hopeless I guess, but you never know.'

'These men all look the same,' she complained, 'like penguins!'

'I suppose they do,' he smiled, 'come on; let's go over to the Black Jack players. The man we're looking for is a gambler, remember.'

'Do we really know that?'

'If what we've learned about him so far is true, he certainly manages to gamble successfully with his life, so what's so different from playing the tables. It's in their blood, Annette.'

'Do you gamble?' she asked him.

'No, I was far too rigidly brought up. My Scottish background I expect. I have played a couple of times here; years ago, with friends who had no such hang-ups.'

'And did you ever win?'

'Never. Even at a young age I realised it was a mug's game.'

'I suppose,' she said thoughtfully, 'you're either born with a gambling instinct or not.'

'I've always thought so.'

They spent ten or fifteen minutes, standing at each of the tables in turn, affecting an interest in what was going on. More people had come in, but most of them had positioned themselves in front of the fruit machines at the end of the room; the clatter of chips sounding harsh against the hushed and subdued tones around the tables, interspersed with the croupiers calling for bets to be placed.

There was a totally different atmosphere in the bar: a piano being played softly in the far corner; the lilting chords of 'Chariots of Fire' as background to the chink of glasses; the popping of a champagne cork; a sudden burst of laughter from a party seated in the centre of the room and the rise and fall of voices. They chose one of the window tables from where they would be able to see everyone without making their scrutiny too obvious.

The group in the centre appeared to be celebrating; one of them, quite elderly, had stood up and was raising his glass in the direction of the couple facing him. Another burst of laughter as more champagne was poured out for them all. There were ten of them; Annette counted, watching with interest. They looked Italian and three of the men, once again in identical dark lounge suits, would be around Ben Standish's age. Would he look like them now she wondered. She tried to add the ten years on to the photographs she had. Ben Standish had given every appearance of being Italian and as she did so, the thought occurred to her; of course, why hadn't she realised before, it was something to do with his voice; Jenny had remarked it had been that which she had recognised.

'Andy?'

'Yes.'

'Ben Standish would have an English accent, wouldn't he?'

'You're right! With a name like that he would be English; you're absolutely right,' he repeated, 'and all this time I've been thinking Jenny had meant there was something distinctive about his voice.'

'I have as well. It could narrow things down a bit though, couldn't it?'

'Yes,' he agreed slowly, thoughtfully, 'but we can't walk around listening to every man who superficially fits him.'

'No,' Annette said, 'but we could try. What I mean is, try to tune in. For instance,' she nodded slightly towards the party, 'over there. Jenny and I used to have a game we played when we were young. She was pretty good at it, but then she has always had a good ear for voices; picking up the odd word and phrase. Cheeky, I know, but it was fun.'

'So,' Andy smiled at her; no doubt thinking she had some odd ideas, 'how do you do this tuning-in?'

'You're laughing at me.'

'No, I'm not, Annette,' he insisted, 'I'm intrigued, honestly.'

'Well,' she went on, 'the knack is to blot out all the other sounds around you and concentrate on those you want to hear. Eventually, their voices will become clearer, more distinct, and nearly always there is one which predominates, higher pitched perhaps or a deeper intonation. Do you know what I mean?'

'I do, yes, but that lot just sound a babble to me. They're all talking at once.'

'I know.' she agreed, 'Alright, Andy, would you say that so far this evening there appears to be an equal mix of Maltese and Italians?'

'Yes.'

'Speaking in Italian or, if in English, with an Italian accent and easy to distinguish.'

'And the Maltese?'

'You know them far better than I do, Andy. Unless they were born and brought up in England it is more than likely they would have similar accents to us, but if not they would have formed their own accent.'

'Yes, that's true,' he said, 'as you know, English is their second language. In fact, I've found if they are not speaking in English, invariably it would be in Italian.'

'So,' Annette put in, for the first time a tiny flicker of hope raised her spirits, 'if and I know it is a big if, but *if* Ben Standish is here tonight and given we have quite a good idea of how he may look, we could spot him.'

'Let's not get too carried away,' he warned, 'so far it is mostly supposition, isn't it? We don't know whether he is on the island. Also, we don't know whether it was Ben Standish Jenny had arranged to meet on the Friday morning or not.'

'I know, but you've said yourself there is something going on here.

Too much is happening, Andy and so much we don't understand.'

'Have you considered what we would do if we should find him?'

'Not really, no.'

'I think you ought to, Annette. Remember Paul's warning to Jenny.'

'I haven't forgotten.'

'To get back to what we were saying,' he said, giving her hand a slight squeeze of encouragement, 'those characters over there?'

'Oh, they're Italian.'

'You're very confident.'

'Although three of them could resemble Ben Standish, they are definitely not English.'

'Now I am impressed.'

'I've had plenty of practice.' she laughed, amused by his expression. She had noticed before that when he was puzzled a tiny frown would appear which gave him a quizzical and at the same time a bemused look. Again, she was being reminded of how much she enjoyed being with him. It had been a long time since she had felt so much at ease with anyone, especially after such a short acquaintance; a rarity in fact. She tried to think back to the Steve days, but it was difficult. The memory of him was fast diminishing; had grown less and less as the months had gone by. Steve wasn't the sort of man to read into her thoughts the way Andy was doing. With Steve, everything had to be cut and dried, placed out neatly in an invisible and non-deviating straight line. He had his work and she had hers and although in the beginning of their relationship she had genuinely attempted to take an interest in what he was doing, he had always pulled down the shutters. He had been prickly, over-sensitive and she had been uncomfortably aware of the competition he managed to imply and it had become worse when she started to spend as much time in the States as in England; he couldn't handle the situation. In retrospect, Annette now realised, he'd had a point, but they hadn't been on the same wave-length, not even from the beginning. Steve and she never had a future; it would not have worked and, in hindsight, she knew that.

'We may as well make a night of it, Annette.' Andy said, pulling her back to the present. 'Don't think I am making light of everything,' he went on, his expression serious for a moment, 'I realise how terribly worried you are about Jenny.'

Again, he placed his hand on hers, the warmth not only comforting, but she felt a frisson of excitement, of anticipation. Oh, God, Jenny where are you she thought, trying to curb the uncharitable thoughts which were running through her brain. Here I am in Malta for the sole purpose of trying to find out what has happened to you, if indeed anything has, and for the first time in my life I meet someone I can relate to, but you keep on intruding. She wasn't being fair, but that was how she was feeling, wanting more than anything for the situation to be different, to feel free to enjoy the moment. She was instantly ashamed of these thoughts, but unwanted, they persisted.

'Annette,' he said softly, suddenly leaning over and kissing her on the cheek, 'come back.'

'I'm sorry. I keep thinking about her.'

'I know. Shall we have another drink and then continue with our tuning-in. No,' he raised both hands in mock surrender, 'I'm not being facetious.'

'Okay.' amused, but then how could she not be but at the same time reading the sympathy in his expression, 'Where shall start?'

'Well,' he said, beckoning over towards one of the waiters, 'we have dismissed the riotous party which has so far predominated; shall we concentrate on some of the other customers? This couple at the table next to us, for example,' he continued, lowering his voice, 'another Ben Standish look-alike, wouldn't you say?'

'He is, yes,' she admitted slowly, turning a little in her seat: the right age and the right build; hair greyer than she would have expected, but then ten years can take its toll. He looked wealthily confident, but so far she had been unable to pick up on his voice. The woman; young, still in her twenties, was striking in an obvious sort of way. Raven-black hair, piled high; an off-the-shoulder lace dress, short and displaying long, slim tanned legs. She could be either Maltese or Italian, impossible to tell. She was, Annette noticed, wearing an enormous single diamond ring on her wedding finger. There was a haughty spoilt look about her, probably used to getting her own way. He had his arm around her shoulders, his fingers lightly stroking the back of her neck.

'She's Maltese and I would say from Sliema.' Andy said quickly.

'How do you know?'

'Because their accent is quite different from anywhere else on the island; it's their diction. I wouldn't describe it as refined exactly, but they emphasise each syllable meticulously as if they'd had elocution lessons. I don't suppose you have had time to notice it yet.' he added.

'No, I haven't.'

Their drinks arrived at that moment distracting them. Could this man actually be Ben Standish Annette thought, looking at him again. Surely they couldn't be so lucky and so soon? If she was being honest, he really didn't look much different from at least half a dozen other men she had seen this evening. And, just because she hadn't heard his voice, there was no reason why she should be experiencing this quickening flow of adrenalin. Was this the man Jenny had fallen for ten years ago? Annette had already come to the conclusion there had been something going on between them. She made an attempt to peel those years from him; replace the way he looked now with how he could have been back then, also to put a nineteen year-old Jenny beside him; in place of the woman who was sitting there at that moment, but it was impossible, also foolish conjecture. She wasn't normally so fanciful, but this business was making her like that; inexorably changing her normal steady viewpoint and logical thought process. Suddenly, Quenton's voice came to her, as always unheralded, but she had no option but to listen: "For goodness sake, Annette," he would have said in the gruff, no-nonsense way of his, "you're not cracking up on me, are you! I hope not. Why don't you face facts? That sister of yours has gone walk-about!" Shut up, Quenton, but wondering if what she heard him telling her could be part of her own conscience; what she really believed herself. Quite simply, Jenny had fallen out with David and had left.

'Cheers.' Andy said, raising his glass to her, 'They're going.' he added and they watched as the couple stood up; the woman collecting her small diamond-studded bag from the seat beside her and linking her arm with his.

They sat for a while, continuing to watch as customers came and went, but apart from a couple of Englishmen who didn't remotely resemble Ben Standish, everyone else was from other parts of Europe. Andy suggested they have another walk around the gaming rooms before leaving, although by now Annette realised they weren't going to achieve anything. It had been a wild goose chase. And, there was something else worrying her. Soon, when she was back in London and if there still had been no news of Jenny, she would have to get in touch with her parents. Already, too much time had passed. It was now over a week since the night of the storm; too long for them not to be told. And there was always the chance, heaven forbid, they may read about it in the press, especially now, if Paul's paper was sending someone out. There was no saying what they would uncover. Their mother and father had been accustomed over the years to Jenny not keeping in touch, but this was different; entirely different. Annette didn't look forward to that moment and knew, as she walked across the lobby to the 'Ladies', she would probably put it off for as long as she could.

She was sitting in front of one of the vanity units in the ladies cloakroom when the woman who had been sitting at the table next to them came in. Normally, Annette would have paid no attention, but the decisive way she snapped shut the door behind her, leaning against it as though she wanted to prevent anyone coming in, made her swivel round to face her, the lipstick half-way to her lips.

'I don't know who you are,' the woman began, her voice a hiss, her eyes narrowing as she glared at Annette, 'but I want you to go.'

'I'm sorry?'

'If you don't,' she continued, her voice rising an octave, 'you will be sorry, lady. Very sorry.'

'I have no idea what you're talking about,' Annette said, 'but that sounds very much like a threat to me.'

'I do not care what it sounds like! You have been staring at my fiancé for the last twenty minutes; doing your best in fact to attract his attention.'

'You are being ridiculous.'

'I am not being ridiculous! Oh, I know your sort: not married; English; coming out here and trying to find a man, some wealthy husband. You don't fool me!'

'I don't intend to fool you.' Annette replied, appalled at the ludicrous situation she was in. Why on earth didn't someone come in? Slowly, deliberately, she put the lipstick back in her bag, closed it and stood up; moving over towards the door, but she remained where she was, her back firmly pressed against it.

'Excuse me,' Annette said quietly, 'I would like to leave, if you don't mind.'

'I do mind, as a matter of fact; I haven't finished talking to you yet!' spitting out each word.

'Would you please move aside?'

Fortuitously, the door handle turned and she had no option but to step away. The two women who came in threw them both a puzzled look, glancing at each of them in turn, but Annette didn't hesitate. She moved quickly, slipping out before the door had closed and once more in the lobby, walked over to where Andy was waiting for her.

'Annette,' he said, moving towards her and taking both her hands in his, 'are you alright? You're shaking.'

'I think so,' she tried to give him a reassuring smile and failing, 'but I've just had a rather unpleasant experience and I still can't believe it happened.'

'We'll go back into the bar,' he said gently, 'and then you can tell me about it. I was worried about you; you were such a long time.'

They managed to get the same table and once Andy had ordered a couple of drinks, she told him. By the time she had finished his expression had changed from concern for her to one of outrage. She had never seen him angry before, also she sensed it was rare for him. Andy, she was discovering, was a calm man; while not exactly laid back, he did give the impression it would take a lot to rile him and this, it would appear, was one of those occasions.

'You say she threatened you?' he asked at last.

'Yes, it was tantamount to that. She told me,' Annette went on, recalling every word the woman had said, 'that if I didn't go, I would be sorry; very sorry, in fact.'

'Strong words.'

'Exactly. What do you think, Andy? Is she just a neurotic and hysterical female who doesn't know how to behave?'

'She could be, I suppose,' he said, 'but extreme behaviour all the same. Mind you,' he continued, 'some of these girls are inclined to be over-possessive. I've heard some tales over the years. Any sign, imagined or otherwise, of another woman trying to poach can result in a pretty nasty situation. The hot Mediterranean temperament, I guess. Not that that's much comfort to you.'

'Also, it was totally unprovoked.'

'I know,' he agreed, 'best to forget it, Annette.'

'She's just come back in again.' Annette said, watching as the woman walked over to join two men at the bar, one of them being the same person she had been with earlier.

'I've a damn good mind to go over there.'

'No, Andy! Don't please. It wouldn't achieve anything.'

'I suppose you're right, but it makes my blood boil! Who the hell does she think she is?'

'More importantly,' Annette said, calmer now, 'what about the man she's with; she said he was her fiancé? Do you think, by some chance, he could be Ben Standish?'

'Anything is possible,' he said wryly and she could tell he was still angry, 'and before we leave tonight I'm going to find out who he is. It shouldn't be too difficult. This island is a village, Annette, especially in places like this. If they are regular customers, the barman will know him.'

'I've suddenly recognised the man who's with them.'

'Yes,' Andy said, 'so do I. I've seen him a couple of times at Moira's soirees, but I can't for the life of me remember his name.'

'He works for the theatre, doesn't he?' Annette put in, 'I saw him on Friday when I was there. He came into the rehearsal room at the same time as Adam Bond.' she added, remembering in particular the contrast in his appearance to the impeccably groomed director, although this evening he had smoothed his hair down and made some effort to appear more presentable.

'Yes, you would have done,' Andy said, still with his eyes on the three of them, 'he's their stage manager. He's been on the island some time; eight or nine years I think.'

'English?'

'Yes, he is as a matter of fact. I'm remembering now, Annette; snippets of conversation I've heard. Nobody appears to know much about him; keeps himself very much to himself. Apparently, Adam thinks a great deal of his abilities and to please him is not one of the easiest things in the world to do.'

'He'll know who I am though, Andy. He's seen us, but he's not making any attempt to come over.'

'Good,' Andy said, getting to his feet, 'this might be the opportunity we want, Annette. I won't be long, but I'll go and shake hands with him and that way try and find out where his friend comes from.'

'You won't say anything to her, will you?'

'No, I won't, so don't worry. A couple of minutes; that's all it will take.'

Annette watched as he strode across the room and at the same time noticed the way the two men glanced at each other as he approached them. The look lasted seconds only, but she wasn't mistaken. These two knew each other well. But, it was so fleeting and now, as the blond-haired man moved slightly forward to greet Andy, a smile on his broad face, she began to wonder if she had been mistaken. The woman's body language on the other hand was palpable. From where she was sitting, Annette could see her visibly cringe; the way she stepped back, leaning against the man she was with and taking hold of his hand. She really thought Andy was going over intentionally to have it out with her. And, even when Andy, making a point of openly ignoring her presence, she still didn't relax. Instead, with her free hand, lifted up the glass on the bar in front of her and took a long sip of her drink, taking even longer to put it back. There were no introductions and very few words were exchanged and for once Andy's expression as he returned to her, although grim, was unreadable. Annette, taking a sip of her own drink, waited with a patience she was far from feeling and dragging her eyes away from the three at the bar, looked across at him as he sat down.

'He's English, Annette.'

Chapter Ten

It was not conclusive. How could it be? An Englishman who gave every appearance of being Italian? It wasn't much to go on. They had both been quick to agree on that, but the following morning, waking early, Annette could not ignore the possibility, slight though it may be. Okay, she thought, pushing back the sheet, the chances of the man being Ben Standish were improbable, but it might be him. For instance, she reasoned, going through the automatic actions of walking over to the windows, pulling back the curtains and sliding open the glass doors to the balcony, she could dismiss the distasteful confrontation with the girlfriend, but perhaps more significantly was the relationship between her fiancé, as she had so emphatically described him, and spiky hair; the name with which Annette had now labelled him. He was odd-looking; reminding her of those identikit pictures, a put-together face and one which somehow did not seem altogether real; a face which didn't conform. And, another Englishman, which shouldn't be all that surprising; from what she had gathered, the theatre seemed to employ a large proportion of English men and women. There was one thing she thought, going into the bathroom, there was no way spiky hair could be Ben Standish, which brought her back full-circle to the other man. She turned on the shower, but her mind continued working overtime, refusing to let up. Where could they go from here? Perhaps Andy had some ideas. She hoped so, because she was at a complete loss what they could do next. Should they hand over all their information to Inspector Secluna? And what would he do with it? She knew in advance what his reaction would be, so there really was no point and she was sure Andy would feel the same, but it still didn't take them any further forward. In fact, she realised with resignation minutes later as she stepped out of the shower, wrapping one of the hotel's towels around her, who could they talk to? The situation was the same; nothing had changed.

Before breakfast, Annette phoned Moira's number. She wanted to thank her for yesterday and to apologise for leaving the party so early, but it was Andy who answered, the warmth of his voice, familiar to her now and sounding as though he was in the room beside her.

'Annette, good morning, how are you?'

'I suppose the only answer to that,' she laughed ruefully, 'is for the want of a better word, confused.'

'I know what you mean,' he said, 'the deeper we delve and all that?'

'Quite.'

'I'm glad you've phoned,' he went on, 'in fact; I was just about to give you a ring. I've managed to get us two seats on an early morning flight tomorrow. That is,' he hesitated, 'if you still want to get back and it isn't too soon.'

'No, that's fine. I don't think I can do any more here, Andy, not that I've managed to do much anyway. In spite of last night, there really isn't much to go on.' she said. 'It's time I left. I think if I stayed here any longer it would quite literally do my head in!'

'I think you're right, also I don't like the idea of you being here on your own and I really do need to get back to the office.'

'I understand.' And she did; it would have been selfish of her to think otherwise.

'Annette,' he said, 'the inquest on Caroline is this morning and Moira has asked me to go with her. She's worried about Evelyn as naturally she will have to be there to give evidence; it could well prove quite distressing for her.'

'I'm sure it will be.'

'Can we meet for lunch?'

'Of course,' Annette agreed, 'where would you like to go?'

'Can you face another Italian?'

'After last night,' she said, 'why not? They keep cropping up, don't they?'

'They do,' he agreed, 'how about Luigi's, the Sicilian restaurant? I don't know whether you know the place. It's in Valletta, half-way down Saint Ursula Street with a fantastic view across to the Grand Harbour. I hope you don't mind, but I'm not sure how long the inquest will last?'

'It doesn't matter; perhaps I'll take the bus in, it's practically impossible to park in the city and I know where Luigi's is, Andy; I've been there before.'

'Great,' he said, 'and I will have something to tell you.'

'Yes?'

'You remember I said I would try and get some more background on Ben Standish?'

'Yes.'

'Well, a friend of mine e-mailed some stuff to me this morning and it's extremely interesting, but I'll give you the details when I see you later.'

And on that tantalising note he rang off. She only had one more phone call to make before going to the theatre, even although she now knew Evelyn wouldn't be there; perhaps Jenny's other friend, Jeannette, would be though.

David answered immediately. She had half-expected to hear Maria's voice, realising as she finished dialling he could have left for work, but it was just as well he was still there. She wanted to get the call, necessary although it was, over and done with. There was not much she had to say, only to tell him she would be leaving. The thought of having to speak to him at all, far less having to see him again, filled her with distaste. She could not forget the lies he had told to the police. In Annette's opinion, he had been wrong; unless, and this thought she tried to push to the back of her mind, there was another reason. She hadn't even worked out what that could be, but the unpalatable fact remained; she didn't trust him

'Listen,' he said, immediately pre-empting what she was about to say, 'you probably think I'm a bastard, Annette, and I wouldn't blame you if you did, but I could tell by your expression yesterday exactly what you thought of me.'

'David, please,' she interrupted the flow. He sounded no better than he had at Moira's; if anything, worse. Had he been waiting for her to call with his script at the ready? 'there is absolutely nothing to be gained by this conversation,' she said, doing her best to explain and get through to him, 'and I certainly don't view you in that light. Let's leave it at that, shall we?'

'I apologise, Annette,' immediately contrite, 'I always seem to be wrong-footing with you; I don't know why.'

'Does it really matter?'

She was tired, drained by this pointless and going-nowhere conversation. He was incredibly heavy-going. How could Jenny have put up with so much intensity? Jenny, who always had the ability, consciously or not, to evade and side-step people whom she described as mentally suffocating.

'As a matter of fact,' he was going on, relentlessly, 'it *does* matter. To me.' he added, his voice dropping.

'The reason I'm phoning, David,' Annette put in quickly before he had the opportunity to say more, 'is to let you know I'm flying back to London tomorrow.'

'Tomorrow! So soon? What about Jenny?' petulance creeping into his voice now.

'David,' she said as patiently as she could when she wanted to yell at him, try to make him understand, but there was no point; David Grech was enmeshed too deeply in what was worrying him and she sensed it wasn't entirely all to do with Jenny. Perhaps it was no more than his pride which had been hurt. It could be his ego: his girlfriend had left him; something which may never have happened to him before to upset the equilibrium of a previously well-organised life, but there was nothing she could do about that, even if she had wanted to. 'I came out to Malta because I didn't believe, even from the beginning when you told me

Jenny had died in a boating accident and since then I've learned she actually walked out on you the night before and, well,' she hesitated; not really knowing what more she could say. 'well,' Annette repeated, 'she's gone somewhere and it's up to the Maltese police to do all they can to find her. My presence here is superfluous. I'm wasting my time, David and incidentally, no use whatsoever to Jenny.'

'I see,' he said quietly, 'you're deserting us.'

'If you wish to see it like that; it's up to you.'

'You are not at all like her you know, Annette.'

'Probably not,' she answered, realising only too well what he meant. He thought her hard, but if that was the way he viewed her she didn't care. She only wanted this futile conversation to come to an end.

'By the way,' he said, 'someone broke into my villa yesterday when I was at Moira's.'

'No!' wondering why he had taken so long to tell her, 'Was there much damage? Did they take anything?'

'As far as I can make out, everything is still here, although they made quite an upheaval in the room Jenny used. Her clothes, papers from her desk, everything in fact, were all strewn across the floor.'

'Have you reported it to the police?'

'You should know better than to ask me that, Annette,' he said, 'there was no damage done and, quite frankly, the way I'm feeling now I have had more than I can take from them; they probably wouldn't believe me.'

'It's your decision, of course,' she said, 'but it could be important, you know.'

'How?'

'To their investigation, David. Haven't you wondered why your intruder appeared to be only interested in Jenny's things? I would imagine the police *would*,' she emphasised, 'and don't forget Caroline's death is now part of the same enquiry.'

'I'm hardly likely to forget.'

'It's the inquest this morning.'

'Is it?'

She could tell he was lying. How could he have not known? And why should he tell such a stupid lie? Another one, she thought cynically. Moira would have told him. As Annette finally replaced the receiver the main impression from their conversation was once again his manner; the rapid change this time from belligerence to self-pity, which could mean that David Grech was afraid. Of what? She didn't have an answer to that either.

*

Rehearsals were in full swing when Annette reached the theatre. There was a different girl on reception and, as before, Pete was there, leaning against the counter and gave her a welcoming smile, immediately offering to take her up to the Green Room, but she said it was alright; she knew the way.

Adam Bond was at the end of the room, pacing up and down. Every line of his body exuded the strength of his personality; the way he controlled and manipulated everyone there; his impatience, his exasperation even and his pent-up energy. It was all there and obvious to Annette as she sat down on one of the seats at the back and watched, fascinated, as he proceeded to do what he undoubtedly excelled in; directing. It wasn't as if he said much, but as the actors moved and re-positioned themselves throughout the scene, by a lift of an eyebrow, critical and verging on intolerance, it was sufficient. Each of his actions, whether by expression or the raising of a hand, was those of a master puppeteer. He had absolute control. Not only was he a perfectionist, but he was relentless, persistent in achieving exactly what he wanted as he walked, his feet making no sound, between the actors. She noticed when each one of them spoke; words which to her uneducated ear, sounded perfect, he would close his eyes, listening and slowly, trance-like, nod his head, which could convey he was satisfied, but more often, again without uttering a word, he would wave dismissively at whoever was at fault and the whole speech would be repeated. Meanwhile, Linda, sitting on one of the chairs facing the platform continued to make notes. From time to time, Adam would look across at her and the nod would be repeated; a secret code perhaps. And this is Jenny's world. How different from her own, but, then was it? Was there so much difference between Adam Bond and Quenton Barton; probably not that much!

Annette recognised the girl she had seen at Moira's; Jeanette Summers. When she wasn't up on the platform, she would be sitting beside Linda, waiting for her cue, but there was no way Annette could interrupt. She waited in the hope they might have a break soon. She didn't know what she was going to say to her, except to find out who had gone with Jenny to the casino. She couldn't see Jenny going there on her own and somehow she didn't think David Grech was a gambler. Pete had told her she spent time with her friends outside the theatre. It was possible Jeannette had been with her. Annette wasn't over-hopeful of finding out much, but she had to try. There were also Jenny's other two friends; Lawrence and Tony Borg. Tony, the flashily dressed one, but he wasn't here this morning, and she had no idea what his cousin looked like.

'Hello, you're Jenny's sister.' A statement; and she watched as spiky hair sat down next to her.

'Yes, that's right. I don't know your name, but I've heard you're the stage manager.'

'You seem to be well informed.'

'Not really,' she answered, 'but I saw you last night at the casino and the friend I was with told me.' She, too, could play games. Not that it mattered that he had, for some inexplicable reason, omitted to give her his name, but that would be simple enough to find out.

'Ah, the casino.'

'Yes, I'm afraid I may have upset your friend's girlfriend. Perhaps he mentioned the slight misunderstanding we had?'

'Lawrence? No, he didn't say anything. Couldn't have been all that important.'

'She seemed to think so.' Annette went on innocently, watching his expression closely. He did have a strange face. She hadn't been far wrong in her first impression of him. It occurred to her he may have been involved in an accident at sometime; a car crash perhaps. The skin was stretched tightly above the cheekbones, also he had the coldest eyes she had ever seen: a washed out grey colour, below eyebrows which were practically hairless, in sharp contrast to the blond hair which today was back to how it had been before.

'How long are you staying in Malta?' a quick change of subject.

'I'm leaving tomorrow.'

'It was bad news about your sister.'

'Yes, it was.'

Either he hadn't heard the latest about Jenny, which she found difficult to believe, or he was being deliberately obtuse; why, she had no idea. It was not often Annette took an instant dislike to anyone, but this nameless person fell into that category; a dislike even more than her reaction towards Marianne's husband.

'You said your friend is called Lawrence.' Annette said, making an attempt she hoped to sound only mildly interested, 'Is he Lawrence Borg, Tony's cousin?'

'Good heavens, no. He's Lawrence Stanton. I don't think he would be too flattered to hear you say that.' he said quickly, falling into her trap. Stanton; not all that much different from Standish and he *is* English. Annette could feel her heartbeat quicken. Now what? Should she let it drop or try to find out more?

'Stanton,' she began, deciding to forge ahead. It was obvious that spiky hair wasn't going to be more forthcoming with anything else unless asked a direct question, 'that's an English name.'

'Yes.' back to playing games again.

'Which part of England does he come from?'

'Why so interested, Miss Graham?' alarm bells were ringing; it was time she stopped.

'Just wondering, that's all,' she answered, trying hard to read the expression in those colourless eyes. They reminded her of the marbles Jenny and she used to have; shreds of blurred colour; opaque. They were dead eyes; you could see them, but they appeared not to see you. But she had learned enough; at least for the moment. She had needled him. He was giving nothing away; also he knew there was more to her so-called innocent questions. There was a strong message here she thought. Annette knew when she was being warned to back off.

'Well, Miss Graham,' he said, standing up, 'I've enjoyed talking to you, but I have work to do.' he added over his shoulder as he left, walking up to join Adam Bond.

There was no point staying any longer. It didn't look as though there was going to be a break in the rehearsal. Also, it was almost time to meet Andy. She would take the car after all, she decided, remembering she could park in the Floriana car park. It wouldn't take her long to walk down the hill to Ursula Street from there. She wanted to get away, leave the theatre, and also leave behind her an atmosphere which she didn't like. The few words she had exchanged with spiky hair had unsettled her. It was more than her dislike for the man, but what exactly; she couldn't make up her mind. She needed to talk to Andy and share this new concern with him.

Pete wasn't around when she went downstairs, nor was there anyone behind the desk. Her heels echoed as she walked across the tiled floor. Eerie; the thought coming into her mind; as if she was the only person in this old building, also she couldn't get rid of the feeling of being watched. You are being ridiculous Annette Graham. Jenny is the dramatic and imaginative one in the family, not you! Impatiently shrugging off such notions which were entirely alien to her character she pushed open the front door; the feeling of unease immediately lifting once she was outside.

About to pull out of the car park Annette saw Jeannette in her rear view mirror waving to her from the top of the steps and then running down them until she reached the car.

'Annette?' she said, out of breath, 'I'm sorry, but I saw you in the Green Room and –'

'– I was hoping to have a chance to talk to you actually,' Annette said, helping her out, 'Pete told me you are one of Jenny's friends.'

'I know; he told me he'd spoken to you.' she said, breathing more evenly now.

'Jeannette,' Annette said, 'I haven't much time, but there is something I would like to ask you.'

'Yes?'

'You see,' Annette went on, deciding on the direct approach, 'Jenny wrote to me a couple of weeks ago, telling me about her life out here and, in particular, how she enjoyed going to the casino; she told me she went with one of her girlfriends, but she didn't say which one.'

'Oh, it was me. We went there quite recently, in fact. Only days –' she faltered, '-before she disappeared.'

'What was Jenny like? What I mean is, was she the same as she always was; not worried or anything?'

'No more than usual.' was the quick response.

'Was this something to do with David, or perhaps someone else?'

'Oh, there was no other man in Jenny's life, Annette. Okay, she did mention she thought she recognised someone there she used to know years ago, but I don't think it unduly bothered her.'

'What about her and David?' Annette knew she was being forthright, but felt it was really the only way to be, 'Was she happy?'

'You mean with David?'

'Yes.'

'I don't think she *was* happy.' she emphasised, 'At the beginning, when they got together, she was crazy about him, but these last couple of months I think she had become disenchanted.'

'Disenchanted?'

'A quaint word to use, I suppose,' she smiled, 'especially in relation to Jenny, but that was the way I saw it. I actually tackled her about it, you know, but she told me everything was fine.'

'But everything wasn't fine, was it?'

'No, it wasn't.'

'So, Jeannette,' she pressed her, 'what do you think happened?'

'Well,' she said slowly, for the first time showing some reluctance; perhaps regretting saying as much as she had, 'she walked out on him.'

'I know that. At least I know it now, but how did you hear?'

'Because Jenny telephoned me; she was really upset.'

'When was this?'

'Very early on the Friday morning.'

'Did she tell you where she was phoning from?'

'No, and I didn't think to ask. I assumed she must have booked into a hotel. And, then later, when we heard she had taken David's boat out, well, I believed everything they were all saying.'

'But she didn't.'

'No, I'm sorry, Annette,' she said, 'I am so sorry I couldn't be more helpful and I hope with all my heart Jenny turns up.'

'I hope so too, Jeannette. I hope so.' Annette said softly.

*

It had been a harrowing couple of hours and it was good to see Andy waiting for her when she finally arrived at Luigi's. He had chosen a table on the far side of the terrace and saw her as soon as she reached the bottom of the steps. Standing up, he waved; the gesture immediately making her feel better.

'Hi,' he said, kissing her lightly on the cheek, 'I won't ask how your morning has gone. I can tell by your expression, it hasn't been good.'

'Mind reader!' she accused, smiling up at him. 'But, first, tell me about your morning. The inquest; was it grim?'

'I suppose so,' he answered, 'but as I had never been to one before, I couldn't say whether it was more so than any other. But,' he went on, 'enough of that, shall we order?'

Once the waitress had taken their order and brought their drinks, Annette told him about David's break-in and how depressed he'd sounded, also about talking to spiky hair and the way he had unnerved her and then what Jeannette had been able to tell her, although not a great deal, it had told her something; that all had not been well between Jenny and David.

'Well.' Andy said when she finished, 'It's all very interesting, isn't it? By the way, Annette, your spiky hair is called Gerald Smith.'

'Smith,' she repeated, 'an ordinary name. I didn't like him at all, Andy. Also,' she added, 'I don't believe he thought much of me either.'

'Don't worry about it; you don't have to see him again. Perhaps best if you keep away from the theatre.'

'You're right. And now I've spoken to Jeannette there's no need to go back.'

'From what you've said,' Andy went on, 'this Gerald Smith seemed to go to some lengths not to answer you directly. Naturally secretive, dislikes personal questions perhaps or is there something else behind his behaviour. He also appears to be quite protective towards his friend. Lawrence Stanton, you said he called him?'

'Yes, that's right. Andy, what have we really achieved in all of this? As far as I can make out a load of loose ends leading us nowhere and Jenny, according to Jeannette, sounding so upset earlier that morning. But why had Jenny waited so long? Why didn't she phone Jeannette as soon as she got to Caroline's apartment the night before?'

'I know,' he agreed, 'and why *was* she so upset? Have you thought about that? Could it have been because of the row she'd had with David or was there another reason?'

'Jeannette already knew she wasn't happy with him, so I think there could have been.'

'And then there's this poor girl, Caroline Johnson,' Andy said, 'from what I was able to make out at the inquest, I got the impression the police are totally at a loss; I think mainly because they can't find a motive.'

'But, Andy, we think there *is* a motive. Oh, I know, in every murder there has to be one, but if we are right in the way we're thinking we could be ahead of them.'

'You're thinking about when Caroline phoned you earlier on Thursday evening?'

'And being sure she was interrupted? Yes, but it's more than that. Remember Caroline was with Jenny and the others in France all those years ago, when they first met Ben Standish.'

'True.'

'I think Jenny would have told Caroline she'd seen him at the casino.'

'And, of course, it had been Jeannette who'd been with Jenny, not Caroline.'

'Exactly.' she said, 'Caroline may have known too much, Andy. You know what I'm getting at, don't you?'

'Jenny.' he said quietly, putting an arm around her shoulder, holding it there for a moment before releasing her. His closeness, his warmth, comforted her, reminding her she was not on her own.

'I'm so terribly afraid for her, Andy.'

'I know. I know.'

'Do you think we should tell Inspector Secluna?'

'A good question and one I've been trying to sort out. But, apart from a couple of letters and photographs of Ben Standish who does, it is true, bear a marked resemblance to Lawrence Stanton, it wouldn't be much for them to go on, would it?'

'No.'

'If Lawrence Stanton is the man we're looking for and if the police thought it worthwhile to check him out, question him even, it might have an adverse affect on everything.'

'In what way?' she asked him.

'What I'm trying to say is, it could alert him and if that should happen I don't think it would be a good thing. This Stanton guy; he looked pretty affluent to me. He's English and, apart from those two facts, that is about all we do know. It's not enough, Annette.'

'Is there any way we could find out something more about him. Not just his name, but where he lives for example and what sort of business he's in. Also, there's his girlfriend. She said she was his fiancée; perhaps they're living together.'

'As to that,' Andy smiled, 'I don't think so; at least not openly. She's Maltese and they have very strict rules about the behaviour of their unmarried daughters. It would never be permitted. But I suppose we could find out who she is, which should inevitably lead us to him.'

'And then, what if we did find out, where would it take us? To Jenny? I don't think so. It's such a muddle.' Annette sighed, leaning back in the chair, exhausted by it all: the speculations; the suspicions; the worry; the constant worry about Jenny. It was as if there was an impenetrable silence surrounding her.

'We don't appear to be getting much closer, do we?' he agreed, 'Alright, we keep coming across these pointers, because that's all they are: a man who looks like Ben Standish; the odd behaviour of his girlfriend, which may mean absolutely nothing; the enigmatic Smith guy; the break-in at David's place and, of course, Caroline Johnson's death. There has to be a connection.'

'With Jenny, you mean?'

'Yes, with Jenny.'

'I'd almost forgotten, Andy, what was it you were going to tell me?'

'Ah,' he smiled, 'I was wondering when you were going to mention that.'

'Please,' she said, answering his smile, 'don't keep me in suspense.'

'I'm not,' he said, 'but the data which I got this morning, although not all that enlightening, apart from the vast amount of money Ben Standish, not his real name naturally, managed to get away with, did come out with something unexpected.'

'Which was?'

'It appears,' Andy continued, 'there were two of them: Ben Standish and another guy called Ted Bryant. They were colleagues apparently and they both left England at the same time, literally hours before it all came to light. They must have decided to go their own separate ways because the police managed to trace Ted Bryant to Spain, across to Italy and even as far as Sicily, but from there they lost trace of him. And, according to the report, as soon as Ben Standish left London on a flight booked for the States, although they received confirmation he had arrived in New York, after that there was nothing. In fact,' he went on, 'the pair of them must have planned their escape down to the last minute detail. More than ten years now, Annette, and the case still remains open.'

'So, if Jenny and her friends were right and it was Ben they met in France, he must have made his way back to Europe, having already created a new identity for himself by then.'

'And now, perhaps he's here.'

'What about the other man? Annette asked, 'I wonder what he looks like.'

'Nothing like Standish.'

'How do you know; have you a photograph?'

'It's not too great,' Andy said, taking out a folded piece of paper from his pocket and handing it to her, 'a bit blurred, I'm afraid.'

Eagerly she took it from him, trying to distinguish the features of the man who looked disinterestedly in the direction of the camera: taken on a busy pavement somewhere, waiting to cross the road at a set of traffic lights; a short, stocky frame, straight light brown hair; in fact, he was quite indistinguishable from any other guy you might see in the street and pass him by without a second glance.

'You said their last sighting of him was in Sicily, Andy?'

'Yes, that's right.'

'That is only a hop, skip and a jump from Malta.'

'True.'

'I wonder.'

'What do you wonder?' Andy asked, the now familiar smile hovering on his lips.

'Oh, I don't know,' she hesitated, 'you'll think I'm being absurd.'

'No, I won't. Why should I?'

'Well,' she took a deep breath, 'Ben Standish; what was his real name by the way? Not that it matters all that much, it certainly wouldn't have been Lawrence Stanton.'

'He was called Phillip Jackson.'

'Right. It would seem those two were in this together right up to their necks. They would have a tremendous lot to lose if either of them was discovered. In fact, find one and I believe you would find the other. There is no honour among thieves, is there?'

'No.' unsmiling now, his eyes never leaving her face.

'So, let's say, only an idea mind you, Andy, nothing else. Let's say,' she repeated, slowly warming to her theory, 'they are both in Malta and by some fluke, some coincidence, Jenny recognised – '

'– them both.' he finished for her.

'I wasn't going to say that,' it was her turn to smile at him now, 'and I don't know whether she did, but what I do think is that she recognised the man she once knew as Ben Standish.'

'Go on.' Andy urged.

'What if,' she paused, not for effect, but to prepare herself for his reaction, 'and I realise this may sound a bit farfetched, what if Ted Bryant is spiky hair?' There, she had said it. And now she waited. It was Andy's turn to tell her she was talking nonsense.

'What makes you think that?'

'Because,' Annette went on, 'when I saw him today, close up, I mean, I came to the conclusion he had perhaps been involved in an accident at some time. Remember I said to you how he reminded me of one of those identikit pictures; a put-together sort of face.'

'Yes, you did.'

'He's had plastic surgery, Andy. I am sure of it. Also, from what you've told me, Jenny would never have seen him before because he wouldn't have been in the south of France, so how could she have connected the pair of them.'

'You could be right, you know, Annette,' he said thoughtfully, 'and to think, if you are, Jenny had seen him every day in the theatre and she would have had no idea!'

Chapter Eleven

Rabat; situated outside the walls of the citadel of Mdina, which had, more than four hundred years ago, been the capital of Malta, resembles a sprawling suburb and like no other part of the island. There had been two addresses for Lawrence Stanton in the telephone directory; one in Saint John's Street in Valletta and the other one on the outskirts of Rabat.

The converted farmhouse had not been easy to find; it had taken them longer than they expected to get on to the right road; no more than a track, until, without passing any sign of habitation, they reached a dead-end and came face to face with it: a child's drawing; a tall flat-faced building with steps leading up to the front door and placed neatly and symmetrically on either side and on the floor above, square windows, all with the traditionally green-painted shutters; the whole edifice demanding privacy.

'It doesn't look occupied.' Annette commented, pulling up outside.

'No,' Andy said, unfastening his seat belt, 'but there might be someone in there. Surely he won't keep it empty?'

'I don't know,' she said, switching off the engine, 'but now we are here, what explanation can we give?'

'Oh,' he grinned at her, 'simple. We're lost. Tourists frequently do get lost, you know!'

But, she needn't have concerned herself; the place was deserted. Against her better judgement she followed him up to the front door, watching nervously as he rang the bell; the sound resounding hollowly inside the house.

'No one at home.' he said, 'Come on, Annette, let's walk round to the back; see what we can discover.'

'Andy Henderson,' she said quietly, not really knowing why she should be lowering her voice, 'I do believe you are enjoying yourself!'

'Not really, my love,' he gave her his gentle and understanding smile,

'I'm only trying to make it easier for you.'

'Andy!' she gasped, stopping in her tracks.

'What's wrong?'

'You don't think she's here? Please tell me I'm wrong. Please.'

'Annette. Annette.' the smile immediately wiped from his face, he put both his arms around her and held her close, 'Don't jump to conclusions.'

Together, her hand in his, they walked round the side of the farmhouse. Nothing stirred; no birds were singing. It was the middle of the afternoon; hot and silent. She tried to stop trembling, willing herself not to panic; to ignore the tightening in her chest as they approached the back door and, as before, no-one answered when Andy rang the bell. Here, there were no shutters, only blinds; modern vertical ones, set to the mid-position, making it practically impossible to see inside, except for the kitchen; chromium fitments along the length of one wall, gleaming white, even in the limited light filtering in from another part of the house and worktops with a range of copper pans suspended from an ironwork bracket.

'Expensive, but quite ordinary,' Andy remarked, 'what do you think?'

'You're right,' she answered, 'it doesn't look lived in though, does it?'

'No, it doesn't. I wonder if there is another entrance, a way of gaining access.'

'You're not suggesting we should –' she faltered, ' - break in?'

'Not to put too fine a point on it, yes.'

'But, Andy, what if we are totally wrong and this Lawrence Stanton isn't Ben Standish?'

'Annette,' he turned round to look at her, 'we have to do something. I'm prepared to take the risk and if someone should turn up, we'll think of something.'

'I suppose so.' still doubtful, but he was right. Soon, they would be back in England and she knew she would find it difficult to live with herself if, at this stage, she got cold feet. As Andy had said, they would think of something: they had found a door open, or a window; they were lost; their car had broken down; they needed to find a telephone. The excuses could be endless. Whether they would fool anyone was another matter, but they couldn't turn back now. They were here; it was too late.

There were a number of outhouses and all securely padlocked. An annexe had been built at the far end of the building; a low modern structure, flat-roofed with sliding glass doors but again locked. And then they noticed a window had been left open on the first floor above the annexe, close to what must be the boundary wall, but only slightly; they could easily have missed it.

'We need something to stand on,' Andy said looking round as if she thought he expected a pair of stepladders to suddenly materialise.

'Andy, I don't think we should be doing this.'

'Don't worry, Annette. I know it's wrong, illegal in fact, but have we really got any choice?'

'No.' she admitted.

'So, help me find something to stand on. A box, anything; it doesn't have to be all that high.'

'There's one of those, I suppose,' she suggested, pointing to a stack of garden chairs at the edge of the terrace, what do you think?'

'Just the thing,' he said taking the top one down, 'I'll easily be able to reach the roof of the annexe and all I have to do then is walk over to the window.'

'I don't know, Andy; you're heavier than me, it's only a plastic one. Perhaps I should try.'

'No, it's okay,' he said, one foot already on the chair, 'just hold it steady for me.'

After he had hoisted himself on to the roof, pushed the window up half-way and climbed over the sill and she could no longer see him, she felt the thick stillness even more. She stood there, rigidly, her hands continuing to grip the back of the chair; her palms sticking to the hot plastic and expecting to hear at any moment a car approaching the farmhouse, imagining the slamming of a door and footsteps striding along the path towards her. But there was nothing. The track to the farmhouse was deserted and she couldn't hear anything from the main road; this fact making her feeling of isolation total. This was a desolate place and she wondered if Jenny had been here. Had she met Ben Standish, or Lawrence Stanton if he was the same person, on the Friday morning and had he brought her here? Her brain and her imaginings refused to take her any further. She couldn't afford to fall apart now; to break down; she would be no help like that. So far, ever since she had heard about Jenny, she had managed to keep control and to make an attempt to think positively.

At last, he was coming back and, as before, she steadied the chair for him. He didn't keep her waiting; no doubt sensing what she had been going through. He placed both hands on her shoulders and kissed her lightly on the forehead.

'I've been right through the house, Annette,' he said, 'it's quite empty. In fact, it doesn't look as if anyone is living here. There's some food in the fridge; a few clothes in one of the bedroom wardrobes, but no sign that it's actually being occupied. A sterile sort of atmosphere.' he added with a grimace.

'I think we should go, Andy,' the mixture of relief and nervousness making her feel lightheaded, 'I don't like it here.'

Taking her hand as he had done before, they walked back to the car, closing the gate behind them. Quickly now, wanting to get as far away from there as possible, Annette slid the key into the ignition, reversed to face the way they had come, taking the most direct route towards Birkirkara. Seconds only after they had joined the main road, a car coming in the opposite direction passed them, reducing speed to turn into the track they had been on. There was a brief eye-contact as both vehicles drew level and there was no mistaking the look of surprise on

Gerald Smith's face, also, the open hostility in those strange eyes. And then he had gone and once again, their vehicle was the only one on the road.

'You saw him, didn't you?' she asked him.

'Yes,' Andy said, 'I saw him alright; spiky hair and making his way to the farmhouse. Indeed, where else; it's the only building along there.'

'Thank God we managed to leave in time;' Annette said, expelling a deep breath of tension which had been building up ever since they had started out on this journey. 'he would have seen us getting back on to this road.'

'I'm afraid so,' Andy said, 'but he won't know we were able to get into the farmhouse.'

'It won't stop him being suspicious though, will it? He's going to wonder why we are so interested in his friend's property.'

'That's all he can do, my love; wonder. It won't get him very far.'

'I wish we hadn't seen him though; he scares me, Andy.'

'Don't let him. What can he do?'

She didn't like to remind him, not that there was any need to, they could be up against something really evil here. Also, she couldn't bring herself to mention what had happened to Caroline; to do that, would merely put into words her increasing fears for Jenny.

'Annette,' he asked, 'did you notice what he was driving?'

'Not really.' she admitted, trying to remember, but she had been so completely thrown by seeing him, she hadn't given a thought to anything else. 'Why?'

'It was a Renault; a silver grey one.'

'Oh, my god! How stupid of me.'

'Not stupid,' the smile in his voice, 'you probably got enough of a shock just seeing him.'

'I did, that's true, but I should have done, Andy. Some things are beginning to slot into place though, aren't they? Slowly, I know, but we still don't have much to go on.'

'Jenny would have known him of course.' he said thoughtfully, 'If he was at the theatre on the Friday morning and they had actually arranged to meet, she would have had no hesitation in getting into his car.'

'Which she may very well have done; perhaps she wasn't meeting Ben Standish, or whatever his name is, after all. She could have arranged to meet spiky hair.'

'Can you truly see your sister having anything to do with a character like that?'

'No, I can't, but there could have been a reason.'

'He may have been taking her to meet the guy. They are friends after all; partners in crime!'

'I don't like the sound of this, Andy. What should we do now?'

'There's not a lot we can do,' he said, 'but it's possible our presence on the island is making the pair of them jittery and they may start making mistakes. Jenny could be perfectly alright, you know. From how you've described her, she sounds very resourceful; used to looking after herself. I think we'll just have to leave it to Inspector Secluna and as you said the other day,' he added, 'she may have already left Malta'

'I know.' Annette agreed hopefully, 'I suppose we could tell the inspector about Gerald Smith having a car the same make as the one Angela saw. Gerald Smith does work for the theatre after all and that was where Jenny was last seen.'

'We could,' he said slowly, thoughtfully, 'but would it really help them in finding Jenny?'

'Oh, I don't know; it's a bit thin, isn't it,' she admitted, but wanting to get something moving, 'and perhaps it wouldn't be so clever. Inspector Secluna may not be as keen to accept the silver grey Renault bit as we are. I got the impression last time I spoke to him they were putting more emphasis on Caroline's murder, which in a way is understandable, rather than focusing on Jenny.'

'You could be right. I wonder what conclusions they've reached on how David's boat managed to end up on the rocks.'

'Do you know, Andy,' she said, wondering why the thought hadn't occurred to her before, 'I suppose I've just been thinking all along that Jenny hadn't taken it out, but of course someone did; the question is, who?'

'Also,' he put in, 'when was this? Okay, the man with the dog noticed the boat-shed door open at eight-thirty, but what about the day before or come to that, the night before? And, does anyone know exactly when the boat was taken out? Again, that is a job for the police, Annette.'

'And,' wishing she could turn to look at him, but it was impossible. They were driving past the outskirts of Birkirkara and now, late afternoon and packed with home-going traffic she needed all her concentration, 'what about Jenny's car? Someone drove it from the theatre to Saint Paul's Bay. If spiky hair did pick her up, he couldn't have taken the car there. It would have needed someone else.'

'I see what you're getting at,' Andy said and she could hear the increased interest in his voice, 'that would mean there are two people involved. If we are right in suspecting those two worked together on this fraud thing, it looks as if they could still be together now in whatever it is they are up to. Leopards don't change their spots.' he finished.

'I couldn't have put it better myself.' she smiled for the first time that afternoon.

*

'Andy! And, Annette, my dear! How lovely. I'm so glad you're both here.' Moira called out to them.

She must have heard them coming as she was already on her balcony before Annette had pulled up outside the villa; sweet strains of Mantovani drifting out from the open windows.

'My mother,' Andy said to her, 'as I'm sure you have already realised is a complete romantic.'

Annette smiled up at him, 'And why shouldn't she be?'

'No reason,' he grinned, 'she's my mother and she is forgiven!'

'Admit it, Andy Henderson; you love this kind of music as much as she does. And,' she added, giving him a nudge as they reached the top of the steps, 'I do as well.'

Edward was there and immediately got to his feet when they went into the lounge. At the same time, Moira emerged from the kitchen with a bottle of wine and as though she had been expecting them four glasses had been placed on the coffee table.

'It's alright,' Moira smiled, putting the bottle down and kissing her as she had done before, 'I'm not clairvoyant but I hoped Andy would bring you back here. You look tired, Annette.' she added, concern in her expression as she looked at her.

'I'm fine.' Annette reassured her, and wishing it was true.

'This must all be so difficult for you, Annette,' Edward said quietly, 'both Moira and I realise that.'

'Thank you.'

'We have to keep hoping she's alright.' Moira said, passing the bottle to Andy to open, 'At the moment all of us are going through a very distressing period. Poor Caroline and not knowing where Jenny is, also, David, who quite honestly is in a dreadful state.'

'It's not good, is it?'

'You're right, Andy,' Edward said, smiling sadly and accepting a glass of wine from him, 'it's very much like living in a dense fog.'

'So, Annette,' Moira said sitting down next to her, 'you're going back home tomorrow.'

Was this a criticism or was she being over-sensitive, remembering what David had said earlier? She didn't think so, but then how could she be sure? Perhaps Moira believed she should stay on until there was some news of Jenny. Annette hoped she was wrong, but again, how could she know? She had only been in Malta for less than a week; she hardly knew these people. How could she tell what they were thinking or what they thought of her? David had made it abundantly clear; he had more or less accused her of abandoning him. Abandoning him to wallow in his self-inflicted martyrdom?

'I feel I have to get back, Moira.'

'Of course,' she said, tapping her gently on the arm, 'indeed,' she went on, 'what else can you do? What else can you be expected to do?'

'Thank you, I hoped you would understand.'

'I do, my dear; absolutely. We'll still be here, you know, Edward and I and we will keep in touch with you. I believe its best you go home.'

'Moira is right,' Edward said quietly, 'it's a sad business. In fact, all of it is.'

'Have you and Annette made any plans for this evening?' Moira asked, turning to look at Andy.

'I thought we could have a quiet dinner somewhere, perhaps the restaurant in Annette's hotel.'

'That's a lovely idea.' Moira said. 'Do try to relax, Annette, my dear.' she added, putting an arm around her shoulders. 'You've had a lot to contend with since you arrived here; I don't like to think what you must be going through; the worry and everything. Trite words, I know,' she gave a shrug, 'but what more can I say? It isn't really advice, but it's the best I can do.'

'You haven't told them about the wedding invitation.' Edward said and Annette was sure he was not only trying to change the subject, but wanted to lighten the atmosphere.

'I haven't, no!' Moira said, jumping quickly to her feet and going over to the mantelpiece and picking up a large cream-embossed card; at the same time putting on a small pair of spectacles which Annette had already noticed she kept suspended around her neck on a thin silver chain, but had never seen her use before. 'The Giannini family; their youngest daughter, the last one to leave the nest,' Moira said, looking at them over the top of her glasses, 'Sylvanna; a pretty creature, terribly spoilt of course, but they all treated her as the baby of the family and now it seems she has decided to settle down. It should be quite a splendid occasion. Don't you think so, Edward?'

'Undoubtedly,' he smiled up at her, his eyes twinkling; obviously, Annette thought, enjoying every moment of Moira's dramatic explanation, 'Sylvanna has always been quite a handful.' he went on, 'I've known her since she was a child and even then she was able to make herself heard.'

'Giannini?' Andy said, 'I don't think I've heard you mention them before, Moira?'

'Probably not, darling. Edward knows them far better than I do. All I do know is, they are one of Malta's oldest families and very much respected on the island.'

'And who is this lady planning to marry? Someone up to coping with her, I hope.' Andy asked, taking the invitation from her.

Annette was only half-listening to them, her mind refusing to move away from what had been happening; from the unpleasant conversation with spiky hair earlier in the day; the nail-biting moments outside the farmhouse waiting for Andy to return and then, to seeing spiky hair again and driving what could have been the same car Jenny had been in, gradually became aware of Andy looking across at her, the invitation held in front of him. It was as if he was trying to say something to her; an imperceptible shake of his head as he handed it to her.

She took the invitation from him, moving her eyes from his face to read the elaborate script: "Marco and Rosalind Giannini request the pleasure of your company to attend the marriage of their youngest daughter, Sylvanna Antonia, to Lawrence Stanton on Saturday, the eleventh of July ...."

She didn't read any further; there was no need. Lawrence Stanton; the man from the casino, the one they thought could be Ben Standish and the girl; her rudeness instantly returning to her. Annette's first thought was it must surely be a coincidence and with an island as small as Malta, she supposed it could very well be. She looked up from the invitation and met Andy's eyes, sensing he didn't want her to say anything in front of the others.

'I would imagine,' she said to Moira, 'a Maltese wedding must be quite different from an English one.'

'Oh, yes, my dear,' she laughed, putting the invitation back on the mantelpiece, 'you can't imagine! Terribly formal in many ways, but then after the ceremony a real celebration! They have this charming and riotous custom when all the guests pin lira bank notes on to the bride's dress! And, the outfits! I will have to find something quite outstanding, Edward.'

'Whatever you choose, my darling,' the brown eyes tender as he looked at her, 'you will look stunning.'

'Flatterer.'

'With a name like Stanton,' Andy said, 'he must be English.'

'He is,' Edward said, 'I've only met him a couple of times. He's in banking, I believe; an attractive fellow and quite a number of years older than Sylvanna. Lived on the island for some time; I can't remember exactly how long, but it must be at least nine or ten years. Actually,' he went on meditatively, 'I've always thought he must have some Italian blood in him. He's not your typical Englishman.'

'Why do you think that; does he look Italian?'

'He does, yes; very much so in fact, but I've been told he's English alright. It's his general appearance, I suppose; very Latin, if you know what I mean.'

Annette thought she did know. She also realised that they were not likely to find out very much more about the man; if he is Ben Standish, he would have made sure of that. A master of disguise no doubt and she felt a shiver of apprehension.

*

'He wouldn't want anything to rock the boat, would he?' Andy said to her later when they were back at her hotel, having a drink before their meal.

'You mean Lawrence Stanton?'

'Who else?' he smiled at her.

'If he is Ben Standish and on the verge of marrying into the prestigious Giannini family, I think he might be more than a little concerned about the possibility of his past catching up with him.'

'Which it might.'

'Do you really think so?'

'I do, yes. Too much is happening here,' he said, 'and all too quickly, perhaps too quickly for him, also, there's the other guy.'

'Spiky hair?'

'Yes, spiky hair or Gerald Smith or whatever else he's called.'

'He might do another disappearing act, or should I say, they both might.'

'That's what I'm worried about,' Andy said, 'and then once again, for years maybe, the trail will go cold. There doesn't seem to be any shortage of money, does there?'

'No,' Annette agreed, 'you're right. The farmhouse; the property in Valletta, presumably he owns both of them. Also, the way he looks. Wealthy.'

'And about to marry into one of Malta's oldest family; perhaps it's the prestige he's after now, good for his ego.'

'If the family do find out about him, they aren't going to be too pleased.'

'An understatement, my love and I would say they would not only be outraged, but utterly humiliated. The Maltese are an extremely proud race of people and they don't like being made a fool of.'

'We could be quite wrong.'

'We could, yes, but I don't think so. Do you?'

'No, not really.'

And it was true. Instinct or not, she felt sure they had found the man. There were too many indications for them to be mistaken, but thinking about them all made her head spin.

It was still too soon to go into the restaurant and Andy was about to order another round of drinks when they both noticed the woman standing in the open doorway and looking over towards them. Catching Annette's eye and without any hesitation, she walked over to their table. A tall, youngish woman: dark brown hair cut short; a lemon two-piece; linen and not a visible crease in sight and a voluminous cream leather bag slung over her shoulder.

'I'm sorry to disturb you,' she was standing in front of them now; her body leaning slightly forward, pink glossy lips arranged in a cool professional smile, 'and I do hope you won't mind, but you are Miss Graham, aren't you? Annette Graham; Jenny's sister?'

'And who are you?' Andy asked her.

'I'm Julia Warburton from London.' she answered, taking out a wallet from her bag, extracting a card and handing it to him.

'Julia Warburton.' Andy read aloud, the frown remaining, 'Journalist.'

'Investigative journalist,' she corrected him, 'freelance, but I've been sent out here by my paper to report on the murder of Caroline Johnson.'

'You mentioned my sister's name.' Annette said quietly, 'Why?'

'Because,' the woman turned to her, 'of the mystery surrounding her disappearance. She was, I understand, a close friend of Caroline Johnson.'

'That's true, but you're quite wrong about any mystery surrounding my sister.' She had said it but hoping this Julia Warburton hadn't already spoken to the police and, if she had, Annette had no way of knowing how much information they would have given her. She didn't believe it would be much, but she had to bank on that.

'Really?' smoothly, 'But I understand there is some talk about a boating accident.'

'There may be talk, Miss Warburton, but that is all it is. Talk and speculation; there was no boating accident. My sister had a row with her boyfriend and left.'

'Oh,' clearly taken aback; Annette felt the intelligent grey eyes with surprisingly long lashes appraising her, 'but you don't know where she is?'

'That's right.' a game of chess and Annette hoped it was a clever game. She rather thought this woman would be familiar with all the moves while she was feeling her way by instinct.

'Miss Warburton,' Andy said, 'we don't think we can help you in your enquiries, so if you don't mind, we would like to continue with our evening.'

Nicely put Annette thought. Why couldn't she be as cool and dismissive?

'I have tried to speak to Mr Grech, your sister's boyfriend, Miss Graham.' she wasn't going to let go so easily, Annette thought with a sigh. She was a journalist and by the very nature of her job she had to be this way.

'Yes?' she, too, was giving nothing away. She hadn't worked for Quenton Barton all these years and not learned how to parry. This part should not be too difficult.

'He refused to talk about Jenny.'

'I don't find that so surprising.'

'Don't you?' a faint raising of an eyebrow to show her reply had not been what she had expected.

'No, I don't,' Annette went on and as Andy had done, keeping her voice low, 'David is extremely upset about their relationship breaking up. I can quite appreciate why he doesn't want to talk about it; especially to the press.' She couldn't resist that one.

'Perhaps you're right, but it isn't all that straightforward, is it?'

'Miss Warburton,' Andy repeated and Annette could hear the exasperation in his voice; he'd had enough, 'if you have anything further to say, please say it.'

'Does the name Ben Standish mean anything to you? Either of you?' she added.

'No,' Annette said, looking at her directly, 'should it?'

'And you, sir?' turning to Andy.

'I've never heard of him.'

'Perhaps you've never heard his name mentioned,' she said, 'but,' opening her bag again and taking out a beige folder, she spread it out on the table in front of them. Pulling out a black and white photograph, she passed it to them.

Annette's breath caught painfully at the back of her throat, making it impossible for her to stretch out and take the photograph from her, but Andy did.

'You've seen him before, haven't you?' she asked, the intelligent eyes focused on Annette.

Why was she re-acting in this way Annette thought. All she wanted was to find Jenny; to learn that she was alright. She had no wish to discuss with this woman or with anyone in fact, the man calling himself Ben Standish. At that moment she didn't care one iota about trying to bring him to justice. What did it really matter? Not that much she thought. So what, he was an out and out crook; an embezzler, a fraudster of some magnitude, or whatever. The way things were developing, including this intrusion, was beginning to nauseate her. She was literally sick of the undercurrents: David's peculiar behaviour; Gerald Smith's unpleasantness; the casino experience and this Lawrence Stanton who may or may not be Ben Standish. It was all too much and she was tired of it all and longed to leave the island and go home.

'Actually, he does look a little like a man we saw last night at the casino,' Andy was saying, 'but I can't be sure. He looks Italian, doesn't he, and there are many Italians in Malta?'

'Ben Standish did look Italian.' was all she contributed. She was giving nothing away, Annette thought bitterly, wondering how much Julia Warburton actually knew about the whole business.

'Ben Standish is not his real name' she said at last, 'but your sister, Miss Graham, knew him by that name when she was holidaying in the south of France ten years ago. Caroline Johnson was with her at the time.'

'I didn't know this. Oh, I knew Jenny did have a holiday there, but I had no idea who was with her.'

'This man,' Julia Warburton continued, ignoring her response, 'has been on the run for almost fifteen years now, Miss Graham and we have in our possession a letter written by your sister, which was passed to me by a colleague, saying she had seen Ben Standish in Malta.'

'Why don't you get to the point?' Andy said.

'I intend to.' she smiled at him, 'He was involved in a major fraud involving millions of pounds and from what we have learned he is not only adept at evading the law, but mixes with a ruthless and unscrupulous set of people. In her letter Jenny mentioned that she had told Caroline Johnson about seeing Ben Standish, although Caroline, to quote your sister, Miss Graham, didn't want to know and that is why she wrote it. She wanted support.'

'There is absolutely nothing either of us can say to help you in any of this,' Andy said, 'it's obvious you and your paper are making a connection between Caroline's death and the hunt for this man —'

'Don't forget,' she interrupted, standing upright and moving away from their table, 'Miss Graham must have felt strongly enough to have written that letter.'

*

Luqa Airport; eight-thirty, Tuesday morning, and the queue at the check-out extended in a straggling line outwards across the concourse. Moira had wanted to bring them, but knowing she disliked the drive to the airport, Andy persuaded her against it. They'd had breakfast with her; a subdued affair, before they left in the taxi. Moira had told them Caroline Johnson's parents would be arriving later in the day and typically, she had invited them to stay with her. The mother hen syndrome, Andy had whispered to Annette after she had told them, but Annette couldn't help worrying about her. Although Moira was putting on a brave face it was apparent, no matter how much she tried to hide it from them, that she was distressed by Caroline's death and having to go over it all again with Caroline's parents, was not going to be easy. Thank God, Annette thought, for the support she would get from Edward; she was going to need it.

At last, after what seemed an interminable length of time, but was in fact no more than fifteen minutes, they had checked in, reached the top of the escalator and finally, relatively unscathed, emerged from immigration when Annette's mobile rang. Groaning, scrabbling to the bottom of her bag and wondering for about the hundredth time why it was that mobiles, like keys, were so frustratingly elusive, she found it and pressed the button.

'Annette! Where the hell are you?'

Quenton. Indeed, who else? Trust him to choose this moment to call. The man didn't let up at all and, taking a deep breath and raising her eyes at Andy, she answered.

'I'm at Luqa Airport, Quenton; in Departures.'

'Ah, that's good,' his voice sounding far too loud to her, 'at least you're on your way back. Now, Annette, can you hear me alright?'

'I can hear you, Quenton.'

'I've had a message from that sister of yours.'

'You what! Jenny?' noticing immediately the change in Andy's expression; from one of tolerant amusement to one of astonishment.

'You've only got one sister, haven't you?' facetious now; clever, infuriating Quenton, switching into yet another of his personae, 'At least that's what you told me.'

'Quenton,' there was no point trying to rush him, but every fibre in her being wanted to shout out, force him to stop playing games, because that was what he was doing, 'you've heard from Jenny?'

'Not personally, but she telephoned the office and spoke to Penelope; apparently she had been trying to get hold of you, left a message on your answering machine, but why the hell she didn't phone you on your mobile, I do not know.'

'She doesn't have the number, Quenton. If you remember, I had to change it a couple of months ago and I never told her. Remiss of me, I know, but she's alright then?'

'Sounded okay,' another irritating answer, 'Penelope thought she sounded a bit stressed out, but she could be exaggerating. I wouldn't know.'

'Quenton,' Annette said slowly, trying to bring him back on track. She knew only too well how he was perfectly capable of going off at a tangent, 'where is she? Did she say?'

'In Scotland.' Two little words; two comforting little words and for the first time in a week she felt the huge cloud begin to lift, 'A place called Saint Angus; said you had the number.'

Chapter Twelve

Thursday, 9th June

The day of the storm began like any other day in June; the sky, bright blue, matching to perfection the wide sweeping curve of the bay as it spread outwards to meet the Mediterranean. The panoramic view from David's balcony never failed to delight her: the water, a vast inviting expanse of blue, luring her, enticing her, and making her long to be out there and part of it all; to be surrounded and in a way protected by non-human sounds; to be able to think, which lately she was finding crushingly impossible. There were too many distractions, too many people demanding her attention, infiltrating, and making it difficult to distance herself, mentally or physically. And now, she sighed, leaning against the balcony, with this latest problem, more than ever she needed some space. She needed to have a plan; some sort of direction and that was something she was at this particular moment incapable of finding.

The telephone rang in the room behind her; another intrusion. It was relentless she thought, going back inside and picking up the receiver. Caroline; sounding as she always did, ever since she had first known her, way back in the RADA days, slightly out of breath as though she couldn't wait to tell you something of momentous importance. And then, characteristically, she would slow down, immediately giving the impression she had suddenly lost interest in what she had wanted to say in the first place.

'Jenny, it's me! I know I'm being a nuisance and I do realise how busy you are. I could get a taxi; but you see it's like this .....' she continued and Jenny let her run on until she either came to the point or ran out of steam. It never mattered to her which came first. She was used to her. '.... so you see,' Caroline repeated, 'could you possibly give me a lift to the airport this afternoon?'

Of course she agreed. It didn't concern her why Caroline couldn't merely pick up the phone and call for a taxi. Luqa Airport was only a twenty-minute drive away and it wasn't the money. Although neither of them earned high salaries, neither did they consider the cost of anything. Easy come; easy go. That's the way it was with them. So, what was different now she thought, replacing the receiver. They had both come out to Malta together; a spur of the moment decision, having found themselves at a bit of a dead end in London. 'Resting' they had called it and had laughed at the appropriate description which really meant they couldn't get work. It had, at the time, seemed the obvious thing to do; have a holiday, and they had chosen Malta, not too far away and less expensive than other holiday resorts. Their timing had been good; the New Theatre was in its infancy and they were looking for actors. Both of them had, without spending too much time discussing the wisdom of severing their ties, even temporarily, from London, accepted the offers made to them, mostly thanks to meeting Moira Refalo who instantly became a close friend to them.

It had been a good year and after she had met David and moved in with him she truly thought she had made the right decision. She often remembered what she had said on that holiday years ago in the south of France how she had wanted above anything else was to live somewhere in the sun; somewhere warm. Back then, she did not have any particular place in mind, had never even been to Malta, but it matched her dreams well enough. But, like most dreams and, if she was honest, that was all it had been; this one could never come true. She had been caught up in one of them; meeting a man who instantly, although only fleetingly, had reminded her of Ben. In essence, David had mesmerised her, making her believe they could have a future together, but she now realised this couldn't happen. David would never marry her. Even if he had been in the position of making that commitment, Jenny had learned it wasn't what he really wanted and now, especially with what had happened, she wasn't sure about anything anymore. She didn't even know whether she still loved him. Not in the way she had at the beginning; passionately, wanting to be with him, and only him and wanting him to feel the same way. He did love her; she knew that, but he made her feel more like one of his precious porcelain pieces; to be looked at, to be admired and to be put back while he got on with his life; his everyday life in which there was no place for her. Also, she had, over the months, begun to realise he didn't want to share her, wasn't interested in what she was doing in the theatre and did not mix naturally with any of her friends. He was jealous, making it plain he wanted her to himself and she was finding it suffocating. Recently, he had begun checking up on her; phoning the theatre to find out if she was there. This, she was finding intolerable. Jenny was accustomed to being free, moving away when relationships got too heavy. At nearly thirty she knew she should be settling down, seriously committing herself to someone and to leading a more responsible life, but she didn't believe now that David was that person.

She wondered whether seeing Ben again had something to do with the way she was feeling: disorientated and discontented, perhaps yearning back to those halcyon days when she had first met him and thought he was the most exciting man she had ever known. The others hadn't suspected how she had felt, except for James perhaps, but he was only guessing, sensing perhaps that she was attracted to Ben because he had been so different. But it had been far more than that; those stolen afternoons when she had made the excuse of preferring a siesta instead of going with them to the beach had added an intoxicating additive to her emotions. She had only been nineteen and although not inexperienced, she had never been made love to in that way before, or since. Ben had made her feel desirable, beautiful and that there was no-one else in his world. Of course she had not been stupid enough to believe it could ever be anything more than a brief holiday romance; secretive, because that was the way she wanted it, but not a serious relationship. She hadn't wanted to hurt James, also, it would have ruined the holiday for the rest of them and that would have been difficult to live with, so instead, they met as they had and it had been sensational.

And now? The man she had seen at the casino looked different from the Ben she had known; older, thinner, but there was no doubt, it was him alright, but the old magnetism had gone. Since then she had been told too much about him. Ben Standish, not even his real name; a fugitive and goodness knows what else. If she had known back then would she have given herself so freely and with such absolute abandon she wondered. How could she tell now, ten years on? In retrospect, she really hoped her upbringing would have intervened, made her see sense to realise that what she was doing was wrong. Well, she thought resignedly, she had done all she could think of doing, but the fact remained: he was in Malta and so was she and it was such a small island. She didn't think he had recognised her, but if there was a next time and the chances were there would be, what then?

*

'Coffee, Jenny? I don't need to go up to Departures for another thirty minutes.'

'Okay.'

She watched Caroline walk up to the counter, wishing she was going back to London with her. There was nothing stopping her; she knew that. She could leave Malta at any time. It wouldn't be too difficult; book the flight back and pick up all the old threads. But, she couldn't; not yet. There was too much going on in her head and there was no way she would let the theatre down. Not for the first time she regretted having had such a strict upbringing; being taught from an early age the difference between right and wrong and to treat people the way she would want to be treated herself.

'Penny for them?' Caroline smiled, coming back with two mugs of coffee.

'Oh, nothing special,' she smiled back at her although she knew it was a poor effort. She didn't feel like smiling and was sure it showed, 'I was just thinking, that's all.'

'Come on, Jenny,' she said, sliding into the seat opposite, 'there's something on your mind, isn't there? Is it David?'

'Partly.'

'You're not still thinking about Ben, are you?'

'Well, I am, yes. Caroline, I honestly do not know what to do. We are probably the only two people who know he's here.'

'For goodness sake,' Caroline sighed, taking a spoonful of sugar and stirring her coffee for what Jenny thought was for an unnecessarily length of time, 'don't be so intense about it all.'

'I'm not.'

'You seem like it to me. What does it really matter if you think you've found him?'

'I don't think. I'm positive.'

'Okay. Okay. So it's Ben Standish. So what?'

'There are times when I don't understand you, Caroline. The man's wanted by the police and has been for years. Don't you feel a little bit responsible?'

'No, I don't.'

'So, you're not going to back me up?'

'Listen to me, Jenny, please, that's not the point and as you know I wasn't with you when you saw him. I only have your word for it; besides I have to be honest, it would seem I am not as public spirited as you.'

'I wish you felt differently, I really do.'

'And I wish I wasn't going to be away for the next week. I don't want you doing something silly.'

'Such as?'

'Oh, I don't know,' Caroline looked across at her; deep blue eyes wide with concern, 'get out of your depth in all of this, I suppose. That shooting on Ben's yacht, remember? That was really weird. Paul always thought it was a put up job, you know.'

'Did he? What; especially for our benefit, you mean?'

'Yes, and he could have been right, but honestly, Jenny, it's not up to people like you and me to get involved. You know what they say: Let sleeping dogs lie.'

'Perhaps,' Jenny said slowly, 'anyway, I've written to James.'

'You have?'

'Yes,' Jenny nodded, 'I thought he might know what should be done. Who to speak to, I mean.'

'It's possible, I suppose,' Caroline agreed, glancing at her watch, 'look, Jenny, I'll have to go now. Don't do anything rash will you and I'll see you when I get back next Thursday.'

'I'll try not to,' she smiled at her, 'and I'll come and meet you if you like.'

'I like.' she grinned, looking so much like the young Caroline she knew all those years ago. 'And don't let the dragon wear you down!' she added as they walked arm in arm towards the bottom of the escalator.

'What?'

'It's Thursday, isn't it?' Caroline was laughing now, 'your weekly dinner party when you will have to be polite and smile sweetly to the overbearing Marianne!'

'Please do not remind me!'

*

By the time Jenny returned to Sliema, the air was heavy and sluggish and the taken-for-granted unblemished sky now overcast. The first drops of rain hit the windscreen as she drew up outside the villa.

'We're in for a storm, Miss Graham,' Maria greeted her at the front door; 'I've just heard the forecast and it is not good.'

'Perhaps it will pass, Maria.'

'I don't think so,' she said, shaking her head knowingly and going back into the kitchen from where the succulent aroma of roasting lamb was wafting through.

Maria was right Jenny thought, kicking off her sandals and standing at the balcony window. The wind was getting up, rapidly churning the water along the edges of the bay, sprays of foam rising high and splashing down on to the esplanade. She would have time for a shower before they arrived; not all that surprised to find David hadn't come home yet. The depression of earlier in the day was still with her; she would have to make an extreme effort this evening. Being in Marianne's company at the best of times was never easy and she knew she was going to find it even more difficult than usual to be civil to her. Jenny had known from the first moment David had introduced them that his sister didn't like her, but as she had philosophically reminded herself many times, the feeling was after all reciprocal. They were quite literally poles apart and nothing in the world was going to change that. The annoying thing was David did not seem to sense anything antagonistic between them, making it impossible for her to complain about the critical vibes she had to put up with. At least Moira would be here. Her company always made these Thursday evenings bearable and of course, Edward. Who could dislike him; charming Edward, the epitome of diplomacy? She refused to even think about Marianne's husband; the loathsome Frank; Frank the lech, Jenny thought, as she pulled off her clothes and stepped into the shower, surrendering to the luxury as the water cascaded over her shoulders. It was time she snapped out of this hopeless attitude. Tomorrow she decided turning off the spray and reaching for a towel, she would make up her mind what she was going to do. David first. An ultimatum? She didn't know. And Ben? In spite of Caroline's advice and she knew it was good advice, she didn't know the answer to that either. Perhaps she would wait for James' reply; that is, if he did get back to her. But, again, she would think about it all tomorrow, ignoring the little words which came into her brain. Something her grandfather would often say: "Jenny, remember, tomorrow never comes."

David arrived as she was finishing dressing, quickly putting his head round the bedroom door and blowing her an apologetic kiss.

'Sorry, Jenny, I got held up at the last minute. I didn't expect you to be here; you're early, aren't you?'

'I didn't need to go to the theatre this afternoon,' she explained, surprised he should have noticed. It was true she often didn't get home until nearer seven, but there were many times when she was still back before him, 'I drove Caroline to the airport; she's off to England for a week.'

'I see,' he said; by this time in the bathroom, and she could hear the shower, 'good, we'll have time for a drink before the others get here. That will make a change, won't it?'

There was a time Jenny thought when she would have loved to hear those words; to know that he really wanted to spend some time with her; just the two of them, but now this was something she would rather avoid.

As it happened, they were half-way through their aperitifs when Marianne and Frank arrived, followed shortly after by Edward and a wind-swept Moira; her curls even more wayward than ever, but looking extraordinarily pretty and reminding Jenny what a lovely woman she was; so utterly refreshing and wonderful company; funny and entertaining and full of fascinating snippets of theatre gossip. It was a pity Marianne was always invited to these dinners; no-one else really had the chance to say very much and Moira, on these occasions had little to say and who could blame her Jenny thought, stifling a sigh as she made a supreme effort to welcome David's sister and her husband.

'You look divine, Jenny.' Frank said, keeping hold of her hand longer than he needed and, as always, his face far too close to her own.

'Thank you, Frank,' politely; swallowing the words she would really like to say, 'you look pretty dapper yourself.' she said instead, which wasn't exactly true, but it pleased him as she very well knew it would, as she looked at what he was dressed up in this evening: a tailored navy blazer with brass buttons; a cream shirt open at the neck and another cravat from his collection; this one, the same colour as the shirt, with large navy dots, the whole thing resembling an elongated domino tied around his scrawny neck!

More drinks were served. As always, as if they hadn't spent enough time together during the day, Marianne and David were at the far end of the room, no doubt going over various aspects and deals of the business. She should be used to this by now Jenny thought bitterly, but the truth was, she wasn't. These Thursday evenings were meant to be relaxing, a wind-down towards the end of a busy week, but they weren't like that. David brought his work home with him and there was no room for anything else.

'So, Jenny, you saw Caroline off this afternoon?' Moira said to her when they were at last in the dining room; each of them seated as they usually were: David at the head of the table, while she sat opposite to him; Edward on her right, with Moira next to him and Frank on her left and Marianne, as always, between him and David. A Thursday night ritual Jenny thought and how I am beginning to hate every minute of it.

'I did, yes,' Jenny said, 'I'll miss her.'

'Of course you will,' Moira smiled her sweet smile at her, 'but she'll only be away for a week.'

'I know.'

'Perhaps it is time you also had a break, my dear;' Edward said quietly, 'if you don't mind me saying so, you seem tired.'

'Oh, Edward,' she touched him lightly on the hand, 'I'm okay. Honestly,' she said, 'don't worry about me.'

'But I do,' he said, 'we both do. You know if there is anything worrying you, you only have to say.'

How could she possibly tell either of them? She had wanted so much to confide in Moira the other afternoon when they'd had lunch together. Not just her reservations about David but about Ben, but she couldn't bring herself to say anything. Moira loved David almost as if he was her son and while Jenny would never have criticised him in any way, she realised if she had it would have been not only pointless, but damaging to the friendship she had built up with her since she had first arrived in Malta. They all knew David was married and had a child. She, also, had known; known the rules, but Ben Standish was an entirely different matter and what she had learned about him could never be shared with these people.

Jenny sat through most of the evening an outsider, contributing little and only half-listening to what was being said. Frank was nagging away, without making any headway, at Marianne; something about wanting a holiday. Marianne quite rudely had turned her back on him and was talking to David about work. It was always work; some property deal they were currently involved in; meetings which would have to be arranged for the following week; all top priority stuff. Frank, she noticed had finally given up on Marianne and had turned his attentions to Edward, 'You've recently come back from the Seychelles, haven't you, Edward?' he was saying.

'Yes, that's right. A splendid holiday; in fact, I'm trying to persuade Moira to come with me next time.' he said, putting an arm around her, 'that is if I can drag her away from the theatre.'

'I won't need much dragging Edward, darling,' Moira smiled up at him, 'I think it is high time I had a holiday. One can get a trifle insular don't you think, Marianne?' trying to draw her into their conversation.

Was she being intentionally provocative Jenny thought, amused and waiting for Marianne's reaction, but at that moment the telephone rang in the lounge, followed shortly by Maria in the open doorway. It was for her. Thank goodness for that, Jenny thought; an interruption from all of this and excusing herself, although she didn't think anyone had really noticed, left the room.

'Jenny?'

'Ben!' recognising his voice instantly, 'It *is* you, isn't it? After all this time! So you *did* see me the other night?'

'We need to meet.'

'Do we?' deflated by his tone, at the same time remembering what Caroline had said. Did she want to meet him? Was that wise? There was only one answer. She did want to see him; for the very last time.

'Tomorrow morning, Jenny,' he said, 'I'll be at the theatre. Eight-thirty.' and that was all; nothing else. She heard the final click as he replaced the receiver.

She didn't know how she got through the remainder of the evening. The wind had risen, making it difficult to hear what they were talking about which was just as well. She didn't think anyone had noticed her agitation; certainly not David. He was still engrossed in what sounded like the same conversation with Marianne. Frank was too intent on refilling his glass; his face becoming more flushed by the second. She couldn't be sure about Moira, although she recognised the same unfathomable little smile hovering on her lips, but she was saying nothing. Edward did glance at her several times and she hoped he didn't have the ability to sense her nervousness. This was something she had to think about; to keep to herself. No-one, absolutely no-one, must know that the following day she would be going to meet Ben. She could not trust one single person; she was on her own. A tiny shred of common sense told her she didn't have to go to the theatre; nobody was forcing her, but she knew she would.

'It's a wild night,' Edward remarked, 'I pity anyone who is out there.'

'You mean on the water?' Marianne's strident voice reached out across the table.

'Well, yes, I suppose I do.'

'Only a fool would be out there! Would you not agree, Jenny?'

'Of course,' Jenny answered, although not with her full attention, 'but then like many storms, it will probably be quite calm tomorrow.'

'Don't you believe it! These are treacherous waters. Always have been, haven't they, Frank?'

'Indubitably, my dear; can't trust them.'

'It's true, Jenny,' David said, 'I hope you're listening to what Marianne is saying.'

'I'm listening, David.' For God's sake; she was only making a comment. As much as she loved the sea, loved being out on it, she also had the utmost of respect for it. It would appear that in spite of what she had told David about her sailing experiences, probably in far more dangerous waters than these, he hadn't really believed her. All she wanted now was for the evening to end and for everyone to leave. More than anything she wanted to get to bed and to sleep. Try and put to the back of her mind, if that was at all possible, which she doubted, what was threatening to literally drive her crazy.

'Nightcap, darling?' David asked her when they were on their own.

'No thank you; I'm tired. Do you mind very much if I go to bed, David?'

'What's wrong, Jenny?'

'Nothing's wrong;' she sighed, 'I'm just tired, that's all.'

'I think it's more than that,' he persisted, 'you've been quiet tonight; nervy as well. What's the matter?'

'Do you really, truly want to know, David?' she asked him, deciding it was best to come out with it all now; far better than bottling it up for another day; one more day of wallowing in this debilitating depression and uncertainty, and reaching no conclusions. It wasn't only her future, but she had to consider David. He, also, had a future and it looked very much as if it would be one which wouldn't include her. She had now at last come to terms with this, but the hard part was still to come.

'Well, I do yes?' he answered quietly, 'I hope it isn't the same old problem.'

'It's rather more than that, David.'

'Yes?' surprise furrowing his brow.

'Yes; your possessiveness. I feel I am constantly under a microscope. Everything I do, everywhere I go, is being monitored by you and it's getting worse. You phoned the theatre at least four times this week; asking if I was there and although I was, not once did you ask to speak to me.'

'I just wanted to make sure you were alright.'

'That's feeble and you know it. You were checking up on me, David. Admit it!'

'There's nothing to admit, Jenny. I worry about you when you're not here; in the villa.'

'And why? What do you think is going to happen to me?'

'An accident.'

'If that happened, you would be the first to know. This is another example of you exercising control over me which, quite frankly, is becoming paranoid. Your behaviour is just not normal.'

'Jenny, come on, relax. You're overwrought, tired; let's drop it, shall we? You'll feel better tomorrow.'

'That's where you are quite wrong. I will not feel better tomorrow, or the day after that. Now you're telling me how I feel. What else, I wonder. What time I should go to bed? What time I should get up? What time I can go out? Would you like me to clock in and out, David? Is that what you want?'

'I give you a lot of freedom, you know. You can come and go as you please –'

'– there you go again!' she interrupted, her voice rising, her exasperation made worse by his calmness, calculated she was sure; the way he just stood there, as though he had no intention of taking her seriously, only the hardening expression in his eyes, which had never left her face since she first began her tirade, giving her any hint that perhaps he was beginning to get more than mildly annoyed. 'I don't need to be given permission, David.' she continued, on a roll now, uncaring whether he, too, might lose his temper, 'I don't have to be *allowed* anything. I'm a big girl now. I've had to work hard for my independence and I treasure it; in other words, David, my freedom.'

'But you're not, Jenny, as you describe it, free,' he said, 'you're with me.'

'Am I?' sarcastically now, wanting to hit out at him, to make a final attempt to get through to him, force him to understand.

'Of course; you're living with me now.'

'I'm living with you? Well, I suppose that's technically correct but I would prefer to think we were living together.'

'It's the same thing, surely.'

'It is not! I've become your prisoner, David! If I was your wife, would you treat me the same way, or perhaps even more so? But then you would have *bought* me, wouldn't you?'

'Jenny.' making a half-hearted attempt to pacify her, but she had gone too far. There was no going back; the situation would be the same in six, twelve months' time.

'Right.' the die was cast and her voice breaking as she pulled herself upright, moving away from him, 'I don't intend to spend one more night with you. I'm going!'

'You can't!'

'Watch me, David; just watch me! I've had enough!' she finished, running from the room and banging the door behind her. He didn't follow her. Not that she expected him to. He never had before when she had walked out on him, but this time it was different. There would be no change of mind, no tearful making-up and promising to make the best of the situation. She knew at last the plain and unadorned fact; he just didn't love her. It should not have taken her so long to realise this, but it had.

She pulled down one of her travel bags from the top of the wardrobe, throwing in the first things which came to hand; shoes, a couple of skirts, some tee-shirts, her make-up and that was about all. She would come back later and sort out everything else. For now, all she wanted to do was leave before she weakened and she didn't want that to happen.

She didn't see him before she left; at least she was spared that. The rain had stopped, but the wind was as strong as it had been earlier in the evening. She flung her bag on to the back seat of the car, switched on the ignition and pulled away from the villa. There was no David standing forlornly at the open door, begging her to stay; in fact there were no lights on at all. That said everything. Perhaps he realised that this time she meant it. Also, that was what he wanted. Whatever, it didn't matter a damn; she didn't need him. She was fine on her own; absolutely fine.

Chapter Thirteen

It took her a long time to get to sleep and it wasn't only because of the wind rattling the window frames and whistling angrily around Caroline's apartment block. The scene with David had unsettled her, but even as she tossed and turned, trying to find a cool part in the bed, she could not forget his expression; how he had looked when she had run from the room, out of her mind. Those eyes of his had seared into her and there was no love or even affection in them and she wondered, reliving those last few moments, what she had ever seen in him in the first place. She had been a fool. Old enough to have known better, but mesmerised by his charm and of that he had in abundance and, especially in the early days before she had moved in with him, lavished unsparingly on her, wrapping her up as it were, binding her to him. Yes, that was it, were her last troubled thoughts before finally drifting off to sleep; she had been right to describe him as possessive because that was what he had been trying to do; possess her and he had very nearly succeeded .....

..... morning came too soon. The telephone ringing in the other room finally brought her reluctantly to the surface of wherever she had been. She wouldn't answer it; there was no need. It would be for Caroline; no-one knew she was here. Jenny hadn't told anyone Caroline had given her a key to the apartment. "If you don't mind, Jenny," Caroline had said to her, "if you could call in now and again and make sure everything is okay." She hadn't even told David. No specific reason, except she didn't think he would have been interested. So, she thought, kicking off the sheet, for the moment she was incommunicado. There was much she had to do, but first things first and before she left to meet Ben, she should let them know at the theatre where she was, but perhaps later. She was certain Caroline wouldn't object to her staying on in her apartment, at least until she found somewhere else. It was too early to telephone Moira; instead, she dialled Jeannette's number and waited for what seemed an age for her to answer.

'Hi, Jeannette, it's me. Did I wake you?'

'You did, actually, but it doesn't matter. What's wrong?'

'Everything and nothing,' Jenny said, feeling for the first time since she had confronted David, waves of emotion threatening to swamp her. She so much wanted to talk to someone; she had already spent too long on her own, thinking and getting absolutely nowhere. She felt so terribly isolated. 'It's David.'

'You've left him?'

'How did you guess?'

'Come on, Jenny, it's been obvious to us all for weeks now that you haven't been happy with him; it was a matter of time. You are alright, aren't you?' she added and Jenny could hear the concern in her voice which only made her more emotional and tearful. She would really have to take a grip on herself; she had too much to do. She mustn't crack up; she mustn't!

'I will be,' she said slowly, taking a deep breath, 'I couldn't take anymore, Jeannette. I just couldn't.'

'I know. I know.'

'I've left him. And this time,' she added, 'it's for good.'

'Are you sure?'

'Positive.'

'Look, love,' Jeannette said, her warmth comforting her, 'it couldn't have been easy for you, I realise that, and I know Caroline would agree with me. She got off okay yesterday?'

'Oh, yes, no problem. Is there any chance of meeting later on today, for a coffee or something?'

They rang off, the apartment feeling strangely silent without hearing Jeannette's voice. I am not suited to living on my own Jenny thought, going into the kitchen, opening the fridge and taking out a carton of orange juice and making a mental note to replenish it later she poured some into a glass. She had over an hour before she needed to leave for the theatre. Already, the sun was streaming through the window with no apology for the storm the night before. It promised to be another hot day; far too hot for rushing around like a fool and that meant going back to David's place and clearing out all her things; that could wait, there was plenty of time. The orange juice was refreshing, also the shower. Repetitive lines from a musical kept running through her brain as she stood under the spray: "I'm gonna wash that man right out of my hair – I'm gonna wash that man right out of my hair -" and that is what it felt like when she finally stepped out from the shower; a return to independence. She was her own woman again. She *had* loved David, or at least she had believed so; any further speculation she refused to pursue. To do so would be pointless and she was determined that from now on her life was going to have more purpose and, more importantly, she would be more circumspect in her choice of men. Brave words she thought, rubbing her hair dry, but not a bad way to start the day.

Caroline's neighbour; she didn't know her name, but Jenny had seen her a number of times, was returning to the apartment block with a carrier bag and smiled at her as she reached her car.

'A lovely morning,' she called out, 'especially after the storm.'

'It is, yes,' Jenny agreed, opening the door and sliding into the seat which felt uncomfortably hot against her legs.'

'Caroline is away, isn't she?'

'Yes, only for a week.'

'To England, I expect?'

'That's right,' Jenny answered trying, without being rude, to cut the conversation short. She was beginning to feel edgy about the forthcoming meeting; the last thing she needed at the moment was this. The woman probably knew already where Caroline had gone. Nosey parker! With a final wave, she pulled away from the kerb and saw in her rear view mirror that she remained standing there, feet apart, clutching the carrier bag and a curious expression on her face. No doubt longing to ask what she's doing here, Jenny thought as she accelerated up the road, turning left at the top and climbing again until she reached the theatre.

There was only one car in the car park; a silver grey Renault. Was this Ben's she wondered, pulling up alongside and switching off the engine. It could be. He had said to meet him here; a strange choice, although last night she hadn't placed all that much importance to it. Too surprised, she supposed, to have received a call from him in the first place. There was no-one in the car and the whole area was deserted which was what she would have expected at that time of the morning. No doubt the cleaning woman was inside somewhere, but none of the office staff would have arrived yet. It was only eight-thirty and rehearsals didn't start for at least another hour and a half. Normally, like her fellow actors, Jenny would still have been in bed, but circumstances that morning were far from normal she thought wryly, walking up the steps to the main door and going inside.

There was no-one around; the slatted shutters were still down at the front desk, but, from upstairs she could hear the muffled drone of a vacuum cleaner. Perhaps she was too early for him she thought going up to the second floor; not really expecting to find Ben inside the theatre, but curious about the Renault. It might not belong to him. The door to Adam and Gerald's office was open and as she reached the top of the stairs, Gerald appeared.

'Ah, Jenny, you're here.'

'Good morning, Gerald, I didn't expect to see you so early. I've arranged to meet someone,' she began, hesitating for a moment, taken aback by his manner. It was as if he had been waiting for her, 'the car outside,' she went on slowly, 'I thought it might belong to Ben.' realising immediately the un-wisdom of mentioning Ben's name, but seeing Gerald there had caught her off-guard.

'No, it's mine.' he smiled that strange smile of his, as though it was an effort for him. She had known Gerald Smith ever since she joined the theatre and had always considered him to be somewhat of an oddity. She knew she wasn't alone thinking like this; they all thought the same: Caroline, Evelyn, Jeannette; in fact all of them. He was anti-social, very single-minded and like Adam, a perfectionist. No-one knew anything about his background, only that he had arrived in Malta about ten years ago; something like that; she wasn't sure, and apart from the rare occasion she had seen him socially, he had given every appearance of only being interested in his work.

'There's been a slight change of plan, Jenny,' he said, coming out on to the landing, half-closing the door behind him, 'Ben has been held up and wants you to meet him at the farmhouse; you don't mind, do you?'

'No -,' she paused, 'I suppose not, but –'

'Don't look so worried,' the smile made another brief appearance, 'I'll drive you there. Twenty minutes, that's all; we can come back later and you can pick up your car if you like. No point taking two vehicles, is there?'

'I suppose not.' she repeated.

'That's fine then,' he said, 'I just have to make one quick phone call and then we can go. Why not wait for me in the car?' he suggested, handing her his car keys and, giving her no time to say anything, went back into the office, this time closing the door behind him.

She could still hear the vacuum cleaner in the distance and apart from a door closing somewhere in another part of the building, she didn't meet anyone on the stairs on the way down to the front door. There were many questions she wanted to ask him. It was obvious Gerald Smith knew Ben. For how long she wondered, unlocking the car door and getting into the passenger seat. Presumably she would find out eventually. As she sat there waiting for him, she was more interested in meeting Ben again and discovering why he wanted to see her. Those long ago memories were still with her, especially the last time they had been together; just the two of them. She'd had no idea then it was going to be the last time. She had been naive and young enough to believe that after the holiday they might see each other again. Back then, she had allowed herself to dream, but the night of the accident on the yacht had shattered that dream for her and his re-appearance here, in Malta, and wanting to see her, could only mean one thing; he wanted to pick up the threads from where they had left off. She had always been reluctant to believe the story James had told her. How could he have been so certain anyway; it wasn't as if he had any real proof? James, she remembered, had always been reluctant to be friendly with Ben; right from the very first evening in the restaurant, how, when they had been invited to join Ben's table, he'd made that pathetic excuse about it getting late. James, she had discovered, had been a real stick-in-the-mud and that was the reason why she had finished with him only a matter of weeks after their return to London.

'How long have you known Ben?' Jenny asked as soon as they had driven out of the car park, turning right at the bottom of Dimech Street along the Strand towards Gzira and Msida.

'Some time now, Jenny.'

She might have known better than to expect much more of an answer from him. Gerald Smith was always frugal with his responses, rationing each word. She supposed, in retrospect, what he had told her was quite a lot for him.

'Where is the farmhouse?' she asked, deciding on a different tack.

'On the outskirts of Rabat.'

'Oh,' she said slowly, not wanting to press him; realising how fruitless that would be, 'and does the property belong to Ben?'

'Yes.'

'It's rather a long way to go, isn't it; just for a chat?'

'Nowhere is very far on this island,' he reminded her, at the same time negotiating the Msida roundabout, 'it's quieter there than in town.'

'Gerald,' she asked, 'why all this secrecy?'

'I think you know the answer to that, Jenny.'

An enigmatic reply and it looked as if that was all she was going to get from him, so shrugging, she gave up. The drive to Rabat was not unpleasant; the Renault was air-conditioned and the suspension rode the potholes, once they had left the main road, with ease. She guessed the turn-off to the farmhouse; no more than a dust track, could only be a couple of kilometres from Rabat. She had already seen the high walls of Mdina; Malta's ancient capital. David had taken her there not long after they had met and she loved the compactness of it all; the cleanliness, the cool narrow alleys and the street signs scripted on china plaques. She had found it quite charming and had always meant to come back again and spend more time exploring and absorbing its history. But one day she would, she promised herself as they finally drew up outside the farmhouse which was a bit of a misnomer. Once, yes, there was no doubt that was what it had been, but since then the building had been completely renovated and although the actual shape of the stone building had been retained, the whole place had a modern look about it.

'Here we are,' Gerald said and he led the way up the path to the front door. 'after you, Jenny.' he added, opening the door and pointing inside. It was at that moment she felt the first twinge of unease. It wasn't anything he said, or the way he glanced at her, but something else. Unexplainable; it was only an impression, but she sensed it all the same.

He followed her into the hall and she walked a few yards to the first open door she came to. The kitchen: gleaming chrome fitments, marble worktops, copper pans on a wrought-iron rack above a cherry red Aga and high stools around a central breakfast bar. Luxurious but didn't look lived in she decided, turning round to speak to Gerald but he wasn't there.

'Gerald,' she called out, going back into the hall, 'where are you?' in time to see the front door closing; the sound of the double lock being turned jolting her into action, but she was too late. He had gone and within seconds she heard the slam of a car door followed by the screech of tyres. What an absolute idiot she had been, allowing herself to be brought here, believing in her stupid and trusting way she was going to meet Ben. What a naive fool!

There was no way she would be able to open the door, so that way out was hopeless. A quick tour round the ground floor, doing her best not to panic, showed her that it would be impossible to open any of the windows; they were all securely fastened with safety locks. Upstairs, although there were no locks on the windows, the drop to the ground below was too much and she had no intention of flinging herself out; she wasn't that desperate. There must be a way; there had to be! She stared down to the track at the front; the place was isolated. The main road was at least half a mile away and even if she saw anyone out there, they would never be able to hear her no matter how loudly she shouted. From the back windows the view was even more desolate; if that was possible, but from a small room at the end of the passageway she noticed that the roof of an annexe to the property was practically level with the window ledge. She just may be able to do it.

Getting out of the window and on to the roof would be the easy part, but how she wondered, would she manage to reach the ground. Adjacent to the annexe was an old stone wall which looked as though it separated the property; a boundary wall perhaps. On the other side, grass; long, tufted and much-neglected, stretched out, although further along, over the years it had grown and crept up against the wall, creating a bank. It looked reasonably solid. It would have to do she decided and without hesitating and slinging her bag across her shoulders, she lifted the window up higher and stepped over the sill and on to the roof of the annexe. So far, so good. The trickiest part was scrambling on to the top of the wall. The stone was crumbling in places and as she did so, pieces came away in her hands, falling in a shower to the field below, but the self-made bank was solid enough which was more than her legs felt when she finally reached the bottom. Also, her throat felt dry and she wished she had taken the time to see if there had been any water in the fridge, but too late now.

Walking as best she could through the parched grass and around scraggy clumps of scrub, she kept close to the wall until she reached the end of the field and found herself on the track a few yards further up from the farmhouse but, although she knew there was no-one around, she couldn't help feeling exposed. So far, she had not given any thought why she had been brought here and more importantly, and this was the frightening bit, why he'd locked her in.

Jenny walked quickly now, anxious to reach the road and take the direction towards Rabat; well away from where they had come. Once there, she would feel safe. There, she had used the word. She *was* in danger! These were not games they were playing; this was serious stuff.

Why had she not listened to Caroline and to James when he had told her about Ben. Ben Standish; how many other names has he got she wondered. And what did they plan to do with her? A good question. She was now on the main road and ahead she could make out the first signs of habitation; a few houses only.

The sound of a vehicle behind her made her jump over to the side, praying it wasn't Gerald, but too afraid to look round.

'Can I give you a lift into Rabat, lady?'

No silver grey Renault and no Gerald Smith leaning over to open the passenger door and dragging her inside. The relief was enormous. She hadn't realised how tense she had been, realising now what was meant by the expression holding your breath. She had been doing that from the moment she'd heard the lock being turned in the front door of the farmhouse. Instead, the ruddy-faced man, a checked cloth cap perched on the side of his head – a damn good replacement to Gerald Smith – who was now smiling at her. Just an ordinary Maltese guy, nothing else on his mind that morning but to drive his truck laden with freshly picked vegetables into Rabat; a market man. Jenny couldn't believe her luck. Was she really going to get away?

'Thank you,' she smiled weakly at him, 'that's kind of you.'

'Hop in, then,' he said, 'it will only take us five minutes or so, but better than having to walk, eh?'

'Yes,' she agreed, 'and in this heat,' she added. She was babbling, but she couldn't help it. Only now, as the distance increased between her and the farmhouse, was she becoming to realise how dire it could have been. What would have happened if she hadn't been able to get out? Would he have come back? The thought didn't bear thinking about. One step at a time she told herself, grateful he didn't ask for any explanation why she should have been on that stretch of road.

'Here we are,' he said, pulling up in the centre of the town, 'you'll be alright from here, won't you?'

'I will, yes, and thank you,' she said, climbing down from the truck, 'I really am very grateful.'

'Don't mention it, lady. You'll be able to get a cool drink in there,' he added, pointing over to a café on the corner of the square, 'you look as if you might be in need of one.'

On the bus to Sliema, Jenny tried to get her thoughts together, but it wasn't easy. Prioritise she told herself; what comes first? What should she do and what should she not do? Looking out of the window, but not actually focusing on anything they passed, she forced herself to think. She had left David and there was no going back. That was the first positive and she knew her decision had been the right one. Next; it was obvious Ben Standish was not happy about finding she was in Malta and had recognised him. Also Gerald Smith who, up to now, had always appeared to be the theatre's stage manager and nothing else, but again how wrong can one be? Somehow the pair of them were working together; a chilling thought. Even if she went to the police, what could she tell them? They would never believe her. In fact, she concluded, there was only one thing she could do and that was to leave the island and the sooner the better. Thank goodness for Caroline's apartment. She was afraid to go back to the theatre, also she couldn't contact anyone remotely connected. She was on her own in this. It would be too simple to go straight to Moira, tell her everything, but it wouldn't be right to involve her. However friendly they had become over the months, the theatre was Moira's life; she adored David, also she respected both Adam and Gerald. Jenny could imagine only too well what her reaction would be if she were to turn up at her villa, not forgetting it was next door to David's, and try to get her on her side. Stupid thoughts and best forgotten. No, as she had already decided, this was something only she could resolve. Once she was back in England she would sort things out. She would write to Moira and to Adam giving him her resignation, cringing in advance, imagining what his response would be. She would also write to David; she owed him that much. And, then, perhaps she could put the whole wretched business out of her mind and get on with her life. There was also Caroline, but she would phone her next week. Another apology, but did she have much choice? At that moment, as her bus pulled into the Strand, she didn't think she had any. She simply had to get away.

It was the middle of the afternoon when Jenny finally let herself into Caroline's apartment. Everything was exactly as she had left it. Was it only that morning? It seemed days, weeks, since she had driven to the theatre with one thought uppermost in her mind and that was to see Ben again. But that was finished; over and done with. There was absolutely no point in going on and on about it all. Ben Standish was well and truly in the past. She had lost interest in trying to expose him. What was it Caroline had said, something about being public spirited? Well, it was true; she had been, but not anymore. Enough was enough. The experience that morning had scared her and she still couldn't believe she had managed to get away. A nightmare in fact. The only occasion in her life when she had witnessed anything remotely violent had been on Ben's yacht; the night of the shooting and he had been pushed overboard; all of which now seemed to her remarkably like a bad stage setting. Once again, she remembered something else Caroline had said; that Paul had always believed it had been a put-up job especially for their benefit. But, she concluded, dialling Air Malta, it doesn't matter anymore; it was history.

She was in luck; they had one seat available on an evening flight to Glasgow. That suited her fine. She had thought of going direct to London and perhaps staying with Annette for a couple of weeks; it wouldn't take her all that long to get organised, find work and get back into the swing of things again, but for now, Saint Angus seemed to her to be the ideal place in which to relax, disappear for a while. Her grandfather would have said, with that twinkle in his eye: "to lick your wounds". A truism, she thought. Such a wise man and how she wished he was still there. She so much wanted someone she could lean on, but there was no-one; absolutely no-one. You are one sad cow, Jenny Graham, she said to herself. One sad cow.

Chapter Fourteen

'There's a call for you, Gerald.'

'Who is it?'

'He didn't give his name,' the receptionist said, 'shall I tell him you're not available?'

'No. No, it's okay; put him through, Amanda.'

'Gerry, it's me.'

'Lawrence! What's wrong?' his free hand pushing the office door shut.

'Plenty. She's gone.'

'That just isn't possible! That place of yours is like Fort Knox!'

'I thought so, but it seems not!'

'Are you there now?'

'No, I'm in the apartment.'

'So, how did you find out?'

'Because I sent someone out there this afternoon; let's say with the sole intention of finishing off the job for us.'

'I see.' but he didn't. He had thoroughly checked the doors and windows and as for jumping from any of them, well it would have been a sheer drop.

'We have to meet, Gerry. This is bloody serious.'

'I can't until later this evening. We open in less than an hour and I need to be here; you know that.'

'Blast!'

'Look, Lawrence, let's try and stay calm, shall we?'

'I am trying, believe me, but where the hell is she?'

'I've no idea, but there is one thing for sure, she hasn't come back here. I don't expect you know this, but David has reported her as missing. According to Moira, he's worried sick, especially as they found the boat smashed up on the rocks.'

'What about the car?'

'Oh, they found that as well, so everybody is jumping to the accident theory.'

'Well,' a dry humourless laugh at the other end of the line, 'at least that part of our plan worked.'

'What now?'

'You may well ask, Gerry and that's why we need to meet. She's a bloody loose cannon. You and I have far too much to lose.'

'You mean you have,' Gerald said, 'I can just pack my bags and move on. It won't be the first time, but then you have quite a different agenda.'

'You're referring to the wedding, I suppose.'

'That yes; I don't think your future in-laws would take kindly to having all the dirty linen washed in public.'

'You have a delightful way of expressing yourself, Gerry,' he said, 'most eloquent.'

'It's true, though, isn't it?'

'Yep, it's true, so when will you be free? Tonight; after the production? It doesn't matter how late.'

They arranged a time and Gerald rang off, for a moment remaining at the side of his desk. He now had a great deal to think about. It was still inconceivable to him that she had managed to escape from the farmhouse. Where could she have gone; she had no transport? Perhaps she had telephoned someone, but he had been at the theatre all afternoon and he was certain by the concern the cast were showing over her disappearance she hadn't contacted any of them. And, it would appear she hadn't told David Grech she was planning to meet Lawrence, or as she called him, Ben. Well, she wouldn't would she? She must be somewhere on the island, no doubt scared witless, wondering what was going to happen to her next. As well she might, Gerald concluded. The man Jenny Graham had known as Ben would not let it rest. He wouldn't mentally shrug his shoulders and hope he had heard the last of her; he wasn't like that. Gerald had known him for too long. As for himself, it was true what he had said to him; he could quite easily move away, but he didn't believe his position was in any immediate danger. He hadn't been in the south of France back then; time enough to worry about his own skin when that moment arrived. Meanwhile, they were together in this business and had been since day one when they had pulled off one of the largest financial swindles of the time and had managed to get away with it; so far, that is.

Also, although he had never questioned him, he was almost one hundred per cent sure Lawrence was continuing with his 'siphoning' as they jokingly used to describe it. His financial consultancy firm had prospered on the island over the years and he did not believe for one moment Lawrence would not be averse to speculating with someone else's money. But, although a gambler, he was shrewd. Gerald had never known him to make one impetuous move; not once, and he didn't think he was going to start now. At that precise moment, he had no idea which direction they should take. Perhaps Lawrence would come up with some ideas. For both their sakes he hoped so.

*

'Any news, David?'

'Moira,' David said, opening the door for her, 'I'm so glad to see you. No, there's nothing.'

'My dear,' she said, putting her arms around him, 'what can I say?'

'What can anyone say? She's gone. I've lost her, Moira.'

'We can hope.'

'That's not what the police are doing. To them,' he added bitterly, 'Jenny is already dead. Everything points to it, Moira.' he went on, leading her into the lounge and going over to the drinks cabinet to pour them both, without asking her whether she wanted one or not, a couple of whiskies. 'The boat smashed up against the rocks, the guy with the dog reporting the boat-shed empty and there's her car. What else can anyone think?'

'I simply cannot believe it,' Moira said, taking her glass from him and sitting down on the edge of the sofa, 'Jenny knew what the conditions would have been like out there.'

'I know.'

'Have the police given up looking for her?'

'I think so. At least that's the impression I got when I spoke to the inspector earlier.'

'Who's handling the case?'

'Inspector Secluna.' he told her, 'Do you know him?'

'Yes, I do; he's a sound man, David. Perhaps you're wrong; perhaps they *are* continuing with their search.'

'She wouldn't still be alive, would she, Moira?' stark words, but deep down she believed he was right. Her heart went out to him, also to Jenny. She had grown very fond of her, had loved her vivacity, her love of life. She would miss her dreadfully. Sighing, she took a sip of the amber liquid. As comforting as it was to feel the warmth, she hoped David wouldn't go down that particular road. He worried her. He had closed up; a taut spring and she realised as she watched him drinking deeply from his glass, realising how much he was suffering. He had really loved the girl. She had never doubted this, although lately she had wondered what Jenny's feelings were. She was, already she was thinking of her in the past tense, very much a will-o'-the-wisp character, sprite-like, beautiful, yes, that as well, but had from the first moment she had met her, the day Jenny and Caroline had arrived at the theatre, recognised her. It was like looking in the mirror; as she had been herself at that age; young, embracing life, expecting everything from it, always on the move, reluctant to settle for long in one place and, she had to admit, reaching out for the moon. Jenny was enchanting and she rather thought David had caught and been captivated by this special essence she exuded. It was now Sunday; more than two days since Jenny had gone and she had no idea how she could help him.

'I don't expect you've eaten today,' she asked practically;' the only approach she could think of, 'why not have dinner with us, David. It will do you good to talk to Edward. He's as upset as we all are, you know.'

'That's kind of you,' he said, putting his empty glass down on the table, 'I'd like that.'

The telephone rang at that moment and walking over to the desk in the corner of the room he picked up the receiver.

'Yes, Marianne,' were his first words, making her move away, not wanting to eavesdrop, on to the balcony, but the conversation was brief and he was soon back to stand beside her. For some seconds he said nothing and knowing Marianne well, she didn't think the call would have helped him much.

'You know, Moira, there are times when I dearly wish my sister was a hundred miles away. It seems as though when there is any moment of crisis, which this is of course, she comes to the fore, always there with her tactless advice and platitudes. She drives me mad!'

'I can well imagine,' Moira chuckled softly, linking her arm with his, 'but that's Marianne, isn't it? She's her own worst enemy. At least I have always thought so.'

'Wise, Moira,' he smiled at her wanly, kissing her lightly on the cheek, 'and Edward is a very, very lucky man. And,' he added, 'thank you for inviting me for a meal. At least I didn't have to invent an excuse. Marianne's dinners are apt to be one long tirade and Frank is no help whatsoever.'

'Come on,' she said, 'let's go. I expect you've had enough of these four walls for one day.'

'How right you are. I'll just lock up and I'll be with you.'

'By the way,' Moira smiled, 'you're in for a treat this evening. Edward is cooking the meal. How does chicken *chasseur* sound?'

'It sounds delicious.'

*

'I've found her.'

'It's about time.'

'I didn't have a great deal to go on, Lawrence.'

'Perhaps not, but it shouldn't have taken you three days, Alan. I'd already told you the area: the east coast of Scotland, south of Aberdeen, also her name.'

'Do you know how many Grahams there are in the telephone directory? Dozens.'

'Enough of all this,' Lawrence interrupted impatiently, 'where are you?'

'In a village, if you can call it that, called Saint Angus. After a few enquiries, discreet ones, I may add, at the one and only hotel here, it would appear she owns a property along the cliff.'

'That's fine, go on –' Lawrence prompted him. They had already wasted too many days since Friday. Alan was right though; he hadn't given him much information to help him. It had been a long shot; a very long one. His friend, Ricardo Mion, Head of Reservations at the airport, had been quick to confirm she had taken the Glasgow flight. And from there, it had triggered off what she had told him on one of those almost forgotten long afternoons how much she loved that part of the country, going there as often as she could. She had also mentioned grandparents, although she hadn't said exactly where the house was and he had never thought to ask; those hours spent with her had made talking superfluous.

'– well,' Alan went on, 'she appears to be on her own in the house apart from her housekeeper, also there's a gardener. In fact, since she arrived she's hardly budged, except to go to the local village shop for bread and that sort of stuff.'

'No visitors?'

'Not so far. Do you want me to go in there, Lawrence?'

'No, not yet; it's too soon. Just continue to keep an eye on her. She can't stay there indefinitely. She'll emerge sometime and then I want you to follow her.'

'Okay.'

'Have you seen any car outside?'

'Yes, it's a hired one; she probably picked it up at Glasgow airport.'

'No doubt.'

'She's got a small boat, though; spends quite a bit of time out in it.'

'That's interesting.' he couldn't keep the sarcasm from his voice. He wasn't in the least interested whether she had a boat or not; she wasn't likely to sail off in it! He merely wanted him to watch her and, when he issued the final instructions, for him to get on with what he was paying him for. But, first, he had to make sure whether Jenny Graham was the only one he need be concerned about. One of her crowd, Paul Watson, concerned him. When he had left Cap d'Ail and had learned a reporter from Paul Watson's newspaper had been snooping around the Côte d'Azur and asking questions about him he realised he had been recognised. Not by Jenny, but Lawrence was fairly certain he would have told her; it would have been natural. The four of them would have spent some time mulling over that business on the yacht, also his housekeeper had told him they had called at the villa asking for him. He could not afford to take the risk. Jenny Graham was smart; he had never had any doubts about that, remembering how attracted he had been to her; foolhardy although that had been, but he mentally shrugged his shoulders, how the hell did he ever think she would turn up in Malta ten years later? It was a chance in a million; damned unlucky, not for him, but for her.

'Alright,' Alan said, 'I get the message, Lawrence. I continue with the surveillance and report anything untoward. Okay?'

'Okay, Alan. You've got it.'

*

'Are you alright, Moira?'

'I'm fine, Adam. Sad, but,' she shrugged, 'but then it's a sad business, isn't it? I still can't believe I'll never see her again.'

'I know,' Adam Bond smiled down at her, resting a hand gently on her arm, 'but you know better than any of us —'

' — the show must go on,' she finished for him, 'a cliché, but a truism for all that, especially in our profession. David managed to speak to Jenny's sister last night, by the way.'

'Good.'

'She'll be arriving later this evening.'

'She's coming out? Why?'

'Well,' Moira hesitated, 'according to David she refuses to believe the verdict and I suppose she wants to see for herself —'

'- but there's nothing to see.'

'I know. I know. But she's her sister, Adam and they were very close. Jenny often talked about her.'

'What about the parents? Do they know yet?'

'As far as I know, they don't, but then I rather think that will be up to Annette.'

'That's the sister?'

'Yes. It will be her decision, poor girl. Apparently, her parents are in Australia; a trip they had been planning for years. And, thank goodness, there's been nothing in the press about the accident.'

'Are you sure?'

' I can't be of course, but what I do know is if it had been mentioned, they wouldn't have given Jenny's name.'

'Because of the next- of- kin thing?'

'Yes.'

'Moira,' he smiled, 'you do take everything to heart so. No —' he held up a hand to stop her interrupting, 'listen to me and don't get me wrong. This whole business is tragic and Jenny, her personality and talent, will be greatly missed. And I do realise how you are feeling, but try to become a little, dare I say, more detached.'

'Good advice, Adam, but it isn't easy.'

*

'Really, David,' Marianne slammed shut the file she had been working on, 'you should have dissuaded her from coming out here. Why didn't you?'

'She's Jenny's sister, Marianne and I would think it was perfectly natural she would want to see where Jenny lived and worked, also to talk to her friends.'

'Natural! That's rubbish! She sounds to me like a hysterical female.'

'She didn't strike me that way. Of course she was shocked, but quite calm and her first response had been to say she would be here as soon as she could get a flight.'

'Which is today! Quick work!'

'A little bit of compassion wouldn't go amiss, you know, Marianne.'

'Quite frankly, David, that is something I do not have any time for. We have a business to run and I have a heavy workload today.'

'So do I, Marianne.' David answered quietly, turning abruptly on his heels and walking out of her office.

The telephone was ringing as he reached his own office and as he leaned over the desk to pick up the receiver Marianne's callous remarks were running through his brain. It wasn't as if he wasn't used to her but he had managed over the years, especially since they started the business, to build up a defensive mental barrier against her sharp tongue. He had realised from the beginning that she had never liked Jenny, but even so, her total indifference to her accident was, even for her, quite staggering.

Marianne had never made any attempt to disguise her animosity towards her. It was far more than jealousy; that he could have understood, at least partly, it was something else. He had noticed the way Marianne had looked at her when he'd introduced them. It had been one of sheer malice. There was no other way of describing it; remembering how her eyes had narrowed as she had scrutinised the younger woman. He'd seen it before, but it had been some years ago. He had been given a particularly fine piece of porcelain and she had reacted in exactly the same way. It wasn't because she wanted it; she had no interest in acquiring such items. It was almost as if she objected to him having it; objected to him owning something as beautiful and objected to him being happy. Perhaps it was as simple as that David concluded bitterly.

Somehow, he managed to bring his mind back to business, switched to professional,talked earnestly and persuasively to the caller; another potential buyer for one of the apartments on the new marina development and jotted down in his diary the time for the appointment later that afternoon, squeezing it in between two others, as he rang off. Business was incredible and had been for the last year or two. At least he had that and with the thought he guiltily remembered how Jenny used to complain that she hardly ever saw him. "It's all you ever think about, David. Work! Work! Work!" And of course she had been right, but then she hadn't objected to the comfortable lifestyle he had provided for her. Leave me alone, Jenny, he muttered under his breath. Just leave me alone!

Chapter Fifteen
SCOTLAND

He was there again; on the beach directly below the house. He'd been there the day before. She had seen him from the boat: a short figure, thin, quite nondescript, wearing fawn coloured trousers and a multi-checked shirt, but when she had reached the shore he had gone. She hadn't given any further thought to him, except to wonder who he could be. He didn't look like the ordinary tourist who came to Saint Angus and she didn't think he was local. Looking at him now, dressed as he had been yesterday, she wondered what he was doing down there. He wasn't sunbathing, although it was warm enough. He wasn't even walking along the sand at the edge of the water as most people did and he had no yapping dog at his heels. He was merely standing there, leaning against a pile of ancient driftwood. Aimless, as though he was waiting for someone. For two days?

Moving away from the window, Jenny put him out of her mind. She had been on her own for too long and apart from the Robertsons, who looked after the house and the garden and the woman in the village shop, she had not spoken to anyone else since she had arrived. Five days. It was too long; time to think about leaving. She couldn't spend the rest of her life like this; hiding herself away. She had had sufficient time to think through what had happened, to rationalise and re-arrange everything; put it all into perspective. The fear was still there, but not occupying her every waking moment. She was learning slowly to push it back, reduce its importance. She *would* write those letters and later in the week make her way back to London; find work. It had been a rash decision to leave Malta the way she had, but she still thought she'd had no alternative. Anyway, she concluded philosophically, her characteristic optimism returning, it wasn't so bad. She could start afresh. After all, what had she lost? A year in her life, that was all. David had been a mistake. She should learn from that. She had let the theatre down, especially Moira and she regretted that. But, it was time to move on. How did it go again? "Shake yourself down and start all over again"; that was it. And that was what she would do and it wouldn't be the first time.

The house, giving the impression of perching on the cliff edge, overlooking the North Sea and several hundred yards from its neighbour, although appearing to be isolated was only a short five-minute walk away from the village. No need even to take the car. The village shop, Annette and her had always referred to it as that; they had never learned the name of the people who owned it and although they must have changed over the years, the woman behind the counter always seemed to Jenny a replica of her predecessor: plump, rosy-cheeked, the grey hair tightly permed.

'It's another grand day, Miss Graham,' her usual greeting, in the soft lilting accent of the east coast and always reminding Jenny of her grandmother. She could remember coming in here when a child; she couldn't have been more than five or six, and having to go on tip-toe to reach the counter; how long ago that seemed and such sweet sun-filled memories. 'what is it you'll be wanting today, then? I've got some very nice ham, only arrived in this morning.'

Jenny bought some slices of the ham, also a lettuce, tomatoes and radishes; all of which she knew were grown in the nursery further along the road. She also bought a small wholemeal loaf and some farm butter. This would be her lunch. Later, to break what was becoming too much of a monotonous routine, she would go to the hotel for a meal. Perhaps even have a carafe of wine to celebrate; to celebrate what? Her new freedom she decided positively, paying for her shopping and walking slowly back up to the house. Mr Robertson was working on the rockery at the far end of the front garden and as she opened the gate, he pushed back his cloth cap and gave her a wave. He and his wife had worked for her grandparents as far back as she could remember. She had no idea how old they must be, but they had to be well on in their seventies; the strange thing was Jenny thought as she walked up the path to the front door, neither of them looked any different. To her, perhaps also to Annette, they had always looked the same; Mrs Robertson, not unlike the woman in the village shop; placid, hardworking and continuing to treat her like a girl, which, if she was honest, she rather liked. Such vanity, she thought smiling to herself and opening the door. After her grandparents had died, they had been more than willing to keep an eye on the property as they had inadequately put it, but Annette and she knew very well they did far more than that. It could be months before either of them were there, but always the house smelled sweet; every room well-aired, even flowers in their grandmother's tall crystal vase placed in the centre of the table in the hall.

Jenny took her lunch out on to the paved terrace, rearranging the table and chairs to face the sun. Sounds of laughter drifted up from the beach; children's laughter. A family; a boy and a girl, running round and round their parents, hindering their attempt to spread out a tartan travelling rug on the sand; a small baby, plump arms and legs kicking strenuously in its stroller and joining in their shrieks of joy. How lovely, she thought; a family picnic, reminding her suddenly and painfully of what she had hoped from David; marriage, children. But it wasn't to be, she sighed, bringing out her own picnic, also a copy of the 'Glasgow Herald' she had bought in the shop. She had become these last few days completely ignorant of what was going on in the rest of the world; she should make an effort to catch up.

The ham was good and the salad; the lettuce crispy, in fact perfect, also the sun was warm on her face and shoulders as she laid her head back on the lounger and closed her eyes. Tomorrow she would make a start. Definitely. She must have drifted off for longer than she thought, because when she woke up the sun had gone in. Scudding grey clouds were drifting in from the sea and puffs of wind were rustling the leaves of the plants on the terrace and blowing the bread crumbs from the table on to the paving stones. The family on the beach were rapidly packing up now, hampered by the children who had lost none of their boisterousness and the baby was beginning to cry plaintively. The downside to family life Jenny thought cynically. Soon they'd be gone, leaving only in their wake a patch of churned up sand. There was no sign of the stranger; probably given up waiting for whoever it had been she decided, going inside and closing the terrace doors.

The hotel was in the main street of the village. The Saint Angus Arms had been a coaching house at one time and still retained its old world appearance; both inside and out. Stone-built, like so many buildings in that part of the country, a low lintel over the heavy oak door and wood-beamed ceilings. There was no separate bar; it was part of the restaurant, a comfortable and cosy atmosphere. She was glad she had decided to break the pattern of eating on her own. Gregarious by nature, Jenny knew she had had enough of her enforced isolation and with her newly formed resolve was looking forward to getting away now and back into what she was beginning to think of as civilisation; her world. Back to London; she had been away for far too long.

Seven-thirty and the restaurant was beginning to fill up, but she was able to find a table next to one of the windows. The storm, only a brief one, had passed swiftly and the air now felt pleasantly cool. A typical summer's evening in the north of Scotland Jenny thought with pleasure, when it would remain light up until midnight. She wished Annette could have been here and together they could have wallowed in a little nostalgia. She must make an attempt to keep in touch with her more she decided. Another resolution! Don't overdo it, Jenny, she told herself, but she was well aware she had always been a hopeless correspondent; absolutely hopeless and however busy Annette was, she always managed to find time to call or write to her. A couple of lines from an early school report came into her head as she sat there: "Jenny, although a bright child, lacks concentration and really should try harder." So, stifling a grin, that is what I am going to do in future; try harder.

She noticed him straight away, even although she had only seen him from a distance. He peered short-sightedly into the restaurant before coming in and walking up to the bar. Jenny heard him ordering a drink: campari and soda. Somehow, she thought, looking at him over the top of her menu, he did not strike her as a campari and soda person. Prejudiced and snobbish she knew, but just look at him! Dead scruffy! Whether in deference to a smart restaurant or because of the drop in temperature, he was now wearing a jacket. Nothing special; muddy brown linen and much crumpled, but the idea occurring to her the effect could be a contrived one. Designer scruffy. That was it. All is not as it first seems and this guy sitting at the end of the bar, half-turned to face the restaurant, could be just that. A real swarthy-looking character; his face, more gaunt than thin; the only prominent feature, a narrow pencil-drawn moustache above bloodless lips.

'What would you like, Miss Graham?' the waiter was at her elbow, 'We would recommend the sole; freshly caught today,' he added, 'and new potatoes.'

Jenny took his advice and waited for her food to arrive, realising she was hungry. It seemed a long time since she'd had a meal prepared for her, missing Maria's cooking. That was not all she would miss from Malta she thought, pouring wine into her glass.

He was still there; not looking at anyone in particular. At least that was what it seemed like to her, but she couldn't be sure. He had that kind of face; shifty, and those eyes. Not actually focusing, but she had the impression he missed nothing. What on earth was he doing here? In Saint Angus; a small village on the coast road between Montrose and Aberdeen, not the sort of place for a person like him. He wasn't Scottish; she would have picked up on the accent as soon as he had spoken, but he wasn't English either. In fact, she decided, he could be from anywhere in Europe, taking a sip of her wine and moving her head to avoid looking at him.

'You're Jenny, aren't you? Jenny Graham?'

She had never seen the woman in her life before and hadn't even noticed her coming over to her table. Jenny watched appalled as she pulled out a chair and flopped her large frame down; layers of white cotton organdie flouncing out around her wide hips.

'That's right,' Jenny answered slowly affecting a politeness she didn't feel and taking another sip of her wine, 'and you are?'

'Oh,' she said waving an arm dismissively; the dozen or so bead bangles on her wrist jangling, 'that doesn't matter. I've been one of your most ardent admirers for simply ages.' she enthused without taking a breath. Oh, come on, Jenny thought, I haven't been in the acting profession all that long! Who is this woman; is she real? But, rather than be rude and cause a scene in the restaurant which was the last thing she wanted to do, also at the same time aware of how the man at the bar had moved his stool over slightly, obviously interested. What the hell, Jenny thought; this is becoming bizarre, but, for the moment, decided to go along with it. Tomorrow, or the next day, she would have left Saint Angus, so it didn't really matter.

'That's kind of you.' Jenny said, forcing politeness.

'I saw you in "Blythe Spirit"; also in "Separate Tables",' she went on, 'I went down to London to see them especially.'

'It's a long way to go.' Jenny said, not having a clue what else she could say to this theatre-obsessed woman and realising she should feel flattered.

'It was, yes,' she continued, 'but I knew your family, you see. In fact, you could say I have been following your career ever since you left the repertory company in Dundee. Anyway, Jenny,' she said leaning over towards her, 'I don't mean to intrude, but it's for my grand-daughter, you see, but do you think I could have your autograph? It would mean such a lot to her. She wants to be an actress, just like you.' she added on a triumphant note, handing her a small leather-bound autograph book.

The woman was irritating; she could have done without her and noticing how he had now turned round completely on his bar stool and making a blatant attempt to hear what they were saying. Jenny signed her name with her usual flourish; a scrawl which didn't resemble Jenny Graham in the slightest, but she seemed quite happy.

'Thank you very much, Jenny,' she said, closing the book quickly, 'I am sorry to have disturbed you. I know how much you actresses like to preserve your privacy.'

'That's right, but it's been a pleasure talking to you.'

'And how long are you planning to stay in Saint Angus?' she asked, snapping her handbag shut and slinging it over her shoulder.

'I'll be leaving soon.' Jenny answered, again only too conscious of the man's interest. It wasn't as though he made any movement this time, but she could tell by the way, without actually looking in their direction, his head on one side he was doing his best to hear.

'Mrs Robertson thought you would be;' she garrulously went on, 'by the end of the week perhaps?'

'Perhaps.' Jenny said dismissively, raising her glass to her lips, 'well, Mrs —'

'— Doreen. Everybody knows me in the village.'

I'm sure they do Jenny thought and now could you please leave. As if in answer to her silent prayer, Doreen, patting her bulging handbag and making sure it still remained securely suspended from her shoulder, left the restaurant as quickly as her varicose veins would allow.

He had gone and without finishing his drink. Jenny couldn't remember at what point she had last seen him at the bar, but it could only have been minutes before Doreen left. Anyway, he wasn't there now. Thank goodness for that she thought; he was beginning to get on her nerves. Normally she would have dismissed his continual presence, but perhaps she had spent too much time on her own and had started imagining things. Malta and everything which had happened had perhaps not entirely reduced in importance after all, she concluded, asking for the bill.

The terrace was still bathed in sunshine although less intense than it had been earlier in the day. Jenny opened the French windows, pulling one of the chairs over to the rail to catch the last warmth. Soon, she thought, she would be back down south and by this time in the evening, dusk would be falling; she wanted to make the most of it. Tomorrow would be the day of action she had decided, but first she must try and phone Annette again, but as before there was no reply and she was loath to leave a message on her answering machine, disliking intensely speaking into a machine and receiving no feedback. She would make some coffee, but it would have to be instant; she was too tired to fill the cafétière and then perhaps she would have an early night.

Taking her mug out to the terrace with her, she sat down, reluctant for the moment to go back inside . Jenny felt, not only lonely, but very much on her own, as she looked out towards the horizon; a perfectly drawn navy blue line. This was an entirely new experience for her and these last few days had proved she did not like the situation one little bit. She had to leave. By Friday at the latest, she promised herself. If Annette wasn't in London, she would find somewhere else. It didn't matter; she just had to get away.

Later, much darker now, and restless Jenny threw back the duvet and slipping on a cotton bathrobe; one Annette and she shared, around her shoulders, walked over to the window, pulling back the curtains, instantly flooding the bedroom with pale moonlight. He was there again. He was standing quite still, once more against the driftwood, waiting. But he wasn't! He wasn't waiting at all, he was watching! Watching her! She should have realised this from the first or at least the second time she had seen him out there. They had sent him! *They*? Who were they; instant panic making her catch her breath? Hands moist, she clutched at the curtains and moved further back from the window. Her immediate instinct at that moment was to run; get in the car and drive, anywhere! But what would that achieve; perhaps that was what he wanted her to do. How on earth was she going to get through the remainder of this night? There was no-one she could call and there was no point in phoning the local police station. What would she have to say to them? There's a man loitering on the beach in front of my house, officer. I think he's .... What? She could all too well imagine what their reaction would be: "Now, now, Miss Graham, I don't think you have anything to worry about. It isn't as if he has broken into your property. He's on the beach you say; no harm in that, Miss Graham." And technically they would be right. She couldn't tell them about Ben Standish; the threats to her life and how she'd had to leave Malta in such a hurry. Even to her, as she stood shivering in spite of the warmth, it sounded too far-fetched. Somehow, she must try to get some sleep and tomorrow she would make plans. There was one thing for certain; she had no intention of spending another night alone in the house. Tomorrow she would be somewhere else, but not here.

She slept badly. Half-way through the night; it must have been around two or three, she ventured over to the window and looked out. He could be out there but it was impossible to tell; there were too many dark shadows. The dense outline of the driftwood predominated and whether the wider fingers of shadow were him or not she had no way of telling. After that, she slept very little until finally waking well before seven, with the sun already beginning to filter through the half-open curtains. The beach was deserted. The fears of the early hours seemed foolish now, making her think she had allowed her imagination to run away with her; it wouldn't have been the first time, but however everything appeared in the clear light of day, she couldn't dismiss the figure on the beach or in the restaurant. Unless he was merely one of life's loners, his behaviour was just not normal.

Opening the back door and breathing in the familiar smells of the sea, she tried to think back to when she had been with Ben. Had she ever mentioned Saint Angus? She didn't think so, but she had told him about the holidays she had spent in Scotland as a girl. Had she said where? Then, with total recall she could hear her voice describing those times: the east coast; the unspoilt white sandy beaches; the indulgent grandparents and how it had always been a sanctuary to her. Was it possible she thought, he had remembered. The man on the beach; of course it wasn't Ben, but neither had the person who had taken her out to the farmhouse been Ben. The fear was returning. Would Ben go to such lengths, but she already knew the answer.

An hour later, having made some fresh coffee, she stepped out on to the terrace and forced herself to look down on to the sands below. He was back; in exactly the same place. Moving out of his line of vision, she sat down and lifted the mug to her lips. Keep calm. Just keep calm. Pretend you haven't noticed him. Come on, Jenny, she told herself, you're an actress; you should be good at this sort of thing. But I'm not she thought, holding the mug tightly in both hands. She could not ignore the situation she was in. In spite of her earlier firm resolutions of turning a blind eye and believing she would be allowed to get on with her life, they had gone. Completely. She had no choice; she must get help. She could not just pack, get into the car and drive back to Glasgow and make her way down to London and to normality. They would only follow her. She had made the fatal mistake of recognising Ben and that had been enough. Jenny was no longer kidding herself. Locking her in the farmhouse had been done for a specific purpose and she still hadn't worked out what they would have done next but she didn't really want to know or even guess. She was too much of an ostrich, although not too much of one not to realise her life had been in danger and it would appear still was.

Sounds from the kitchen broke into her troubled thoughts; the familiar soft tread of Mrs Robertson as she walked across the stone flagged floor, opening the door to the utility room and dragging out the vacuum cleaner. Now that was normality she thought with a sigh, calling out to her.

'Hello, dear,' Mrs Robertson said, a floral apron tied around her waist, putting her head around the lounge door, 'you're up early this morning.'

'I know,' Jenny smiled at her, 'I couldn't sleep.'

'I dare say you've had enough of the quiet life. Must be a wee bit dull for you.' she added as though she could read her mind Jenny thought, as no doubt she could; she had known her long enough.

'I think it's time I went back down south,' Jenny said, 'I've been idle for too long.'

'At least you've got more colour in your cheeks, Jenny. You were looking a wee bit peaky when you arrived. Mr Robertson and I were quite worried about you.'

'I'm alright.' Jenny assured her. A lie. She was far from that, but this was something she couldn't share with her.

'I don't suppose you'll have heard the news this morning, Jenny?'

'What news?'

'Well,' she went on, wiping her hands on her apron, 'fortunately she wasn't hurt, but it was a terrible thing to happen; a good woman like that. She never did anyone any harm in her entire life.'

'What happened?'

Mrs Robertson had always been like this, taking such a long time to come to the point. It was best not to prompt her; she would reach what she had to say eventually.

'Well,' she repeated, 'last night. She was on her way home; it wasn't late and as you know it would still have been light and —' she paused for a moment. Not for effect. Jenny knew that, but she could tell by the indignant set of her mouth she was struggling to put her distress into words, '- and someone came up behind her, Jenny, and snatched her bag from her!'

'My goodness, in Saint Angus! Surely that's unheard of?'

'It is, dear and that is why I'm so upset. We all are in fact. That sort of thing goes on in the cities; everyone knows that, but not here. Poor Doreen, it will take her a while to recover.'

'Doreen?'

'Yes, Doreen Cameron, I don't expect you will know her.'

'It may not be the same person,' Jenny began but knowing in her own mind; a dreadful sinking feeling in the pit of her stomach, that it was, 'but when I was in the hotel restaurant last night a lady who told me her name was Doreen came over to my table.'

'Och, that would have been Doreen alright. She knew you were back. She's one of your greatest fans, Jenny and has followed your career ever since you started acting.'

'But this is terrible. Why would anyone do such a thing?' but as she spoke she didn't really need, far less expect, an answer. She recalled the brief conversation they'd had, only a few words, and the way Doreen had leaned over to ask her to sign in her autograph book and how she had quickly put it back into her bag, but most of all, Jenny remembered how interested the man on the beach had been. He may not have heard what they were saying, but he would certainly have seen her writing something down. For the first time since the moment she had seen Ben in the casino, right through to managing to get out of the farmhouse, she felt the stirrings of anger; anger against Ben Standish; anger against his sidekick, Gerald Smith and anger against this weirdo who was obviously following her, but more importantly, anger that the life of an innocent woman had been affected like this. She knew now what she was going to do and wondered why she hadn't thought of it sooner. She had already wasted five days hanging around, hiding away and hoping everything would improve, that they would dismiss her, forget about her. Again, how wrong she had been.

Jenny had James' telephone number; the one of his firm in London and with hands which were not quite steady, she dialled. It was a strange feeling, waiting to speak to a man she had once known, had loved being with although not actually being in love with, but she had been happy then. How much had he changed she wondered as she waited to be put through. The answer to that was instantaneous; the coolness in his voice told her everything. Was this the same person she thought she had known so well, the man who had made love to her, had told her she was the most wonderful girl he had ever met? People, as well as time, she thought sadly, move on and changes do happen. It was not often Jenny was lost for words, finding it difficult to express herself, say what she wanted to, but that was how she felt. James may not want to talk to her, but she had to try. He had been there, in France, and he had been the first one to raise any doubts about Ben. Also, she remembered, he had right from the beginning, not trusted him.

'Jenny, this is a surprise. A pleasant one, of course.' this new James said, 'How can I help you?'

How can he help me! Honestly, what sort of person am I trying to talk to here? She attempted but failing badly, to imagine him as he had looked the last time she saw him. Young. Naturally, they had all been, but it was only ten years on for goodness sake! The man who had that night on Ben's yacht stood beside her, his arm around her shoulders, as the four of them stood at the rail, the way he had tried to protect her from what they had all seen; Ben Standish being pushed overboard and then followed by the shot being fired. This James was a totally different person.

'I had to call you, James,' she said at last, 'I'm sorry if it isn't convenient, but –'

' – well, actually,' this stranger interrupted, 'as it happens, I am rather tied up at the moment.'

'This won't take long,' Jenny said, by now regretting the impulse to phone him, his coldness reaching her and making her feel even more isolated than she was already, 'but did you receive my letter? About Ben.' she added.

'Ah, your letter, Jenny; it arrived some days ago and I must admit I was rather surprised to hear from you.'

'And the contents? What do you think we should do, James? It's Ben alright; I have absolutely no doubt about that.'

'Jenny, just a moment, don't think you're getting somewhat carried away here. I, personally, don't intend to do anything.'

'Oh.'

'I did pass your letter on to Paul, though,' he said, 'he told me he would be getting in touch with you. I take it you haven't heard from him?'

'No – no, not yet,' she answered, 'but I'm not in Malta now. I – I had to leave rather suddenly.'

'Sorry to hear that, Jenny,' he said smoothly, quickly and insincerely, 'afraid I will have to ring off now; I'm about to go into a meeting. Nice to hear from you and I hope you get things sorted.'

And that was it. She was left, the receiver in her hand and with the dialling tone. He had quite simply, rung off. What an absolute bastard! At least that was one right decision she had made; finishing with him. He always had been a cold fish, she concluded, banging the receiver down in disgust.

James had not even bothered to give her Paul's telephone number, but she remembered the newspaper he used to work for. Perhaps he was still with them. Another five minutes getting the number from directory of enquiries and she was once again dialling London. Better luck this time she thought as she waited to be connected. She was passed from one office to another before at last Paul came on the line and he sounded exactly the same. At least, he hadn't turned himself into a stuffed dummy of a city man!

'Jenny! Where are you? I've been waiting to hear from you. Are you still in Malta?'

Then it all tumbled out. Or at least as much as she was capable of, but she managed to tell him the gist of what had happened and he listened, without interrupting, until she came to the end, slightly out of breath, unbelievably relieved to have been able to unburden herself. He was silent for a moment and she wondered if they had been cut off. More than anything she needed some sort of contact, to know there was someone out there to whom she could relate. After Paul, she realised there was no-one else.

'Jenny,' Paul said quietly, the calmness in his voice immediately steadying her, 'you are on your own up there in Scotland?'

'Yes.'

'Right. You shouldn't be and have you any transport?'

'Yes, but –' she hesitated, 'I'm afraid to leave. I really believe he would follow me. He's out there now; on the beach. He never moves anywhere else, but stays in the same place all the time. Even last night, he was out there.' and she told him about seeing him in the hotel restaurant and again later, in the early hours on the beach.

'Alright,' Paul said, 'from what you've told me, it looks as though he must have some connection with Ben Standish. And you're probably right, Jenny; he would follow you. It looks as if he's been sent there to keep an eye on you. This bag-snatching thing last night; perhaps he thought you were trying to give something to the woman. Somewhat extreme, I must admit, but he could be desperate. There is no doubt a great deal at stake. Ben Standish has managed to evade the authorities for the last fourteen years or so, he's not going to give up now without a fight. Unfortunately, and this is what is worrying me, you seem to be very much in his line of fire.'

'I know. What do you think I should do?'

'Stay where you are. Don't do anything out of the ordinary and don't let him see you've noticed him. I think that's the main thing.'

'I feel – so trapped.'

'Of course you do,' he said, 'you've done pretty well so far, Jenny, and if it's any consolation, on the strength of your letter; the one you sent to James, my editor didn't take a great deal of persuasion to believe our Ben Standish is the same guy you saw in Malta.'

'Thank goodness for that.'

'We're sending out one of our journalists. She'll be arriving there sometime this week-end.'

'She?'

'Yes,' he chuckled, no doubt amused by her reaction, 'Ben Standish is an extremely vain man, Jenny, as I am sure you will remember. Thinks he is God's gift to women and I don't suppose he will have changed very much over the years.'

'You're probably right.'

'Jenny?'

'Yes.'

'I'll have to pass it by my editor, of course, but I don't think he'll have any objections to me taking some time off. I can get to you sometime tomorrow afternoon. Do you think you can hang on in there until then?'

'You mean you are actually prepared to come all this way?'

'Of course I am. Look,' he went on, 'we're in this together. You can forget James by the way; he's a respectably married man now and to be blunt, he just does not want to get involved.'

'I see,' she said, 'I got that impression when I phoned him earlier. Understandable, I suppose.'

'If you're James, yes,' he laughed again, 'sorry,' he added, 'don't mean to be such a cynic.'

'Paul.'

'Yes?'

'Thank you.'

'You don't have to thank me,' he said, 'and I'll give you my mobile number; just in case.'

'You don't think I'm over-reacting do you?'

'You know better than to ask me that, Jenny. I've believed for a long time, ever since we came back from France, actually, that Ben Standish was the man the police had been looking for. And,' he went on, 'I trust your judgement and from what you've told me, what further proof do I need. I think it's him alright.'

Chapter Sixteen
MALTA

When Caroline Johnson arrived back at Luqa on Thursday afternoon fully expecting to see Jenny waiting for her, Jenny had been missing for seven days. At first, as Caroline emerged from customs, the sea of faces a blur as she pushed what must be one of the most wayward of the airport's trolleys; each set of wheels going which-way, intent on taking her with it into the roped-off barrier. The usual scene confronted her: the anxious faces of those waiting to meet their loved ones, craning their necks above the heads of others; tour operators holding up high cardboard placards with the names of passengers they were to meet; taxi drivers, as always in their friendly tittle-tattle huddle, but no Jenny.

She wasn't there. Surely, she hadn't forgotten, Caroline thought, giving her trolley another angry jerk; this time narrowly missing a woman with three screeching toddlers around her ankles and a baby in a stroller perched on the top of her luggage. It was not like Jenny. Tiny pricks of unease followed Caroline as she penetrated with difficulty through the crowded concourse to make her way over to the exit. Queuing to pay for the ticket for her taxi into Sliema, she remembered how Jenny was the last time she was with her. She hadn't liked to leave her like that. Jenny had been absolutely convinced the man she had seen in the casino was Ben Standish and this worried her; too much in fact. Jenny was impetuous. The man to her mind was bad news and she had a premonition Jenny would not let the matter drop. Dragging her mobile out from the bottom of her bag she quickly stabbed in Jenny's number. No answer. It sounded as if it had been switched off, but knowing how Jenny had this inbuilt dislike for being easily contactable, was not all that surprised. On the other hand, she could have forgotten to re-charge the thing. There was no reply from David's villa either. She must be at the theatre Caroline concluded, telling the driver to take her there instead of to her apartment and, leaning back in the seat, tried to stop worrying.

It had been ten years since they had all been in France and those holiday memories were still vivid in her mind. How very young they had been she thought; at that moment feeling much older than her twenty-nine years. Where did all those years go she wondered; each one blending far too quickly into the next until suddenly you were ten years older! She should not be feeling like this. Stupid, but Jenny concerned her. Caroline had not been fooled back in Villefranche. Not for one minute had she believed those excuses Jenny had made of wanting to spend the afternoons at the villa. She hadn't said anything to Paul and certainly not to James, but she had known Jenny too well not to have read the signs; not to put too fine a point on it, Jenny had had the hots for Ben Standish. As simple as that. Even later, when she had finished with James, Caroline had never said anything to her. What would have been the point? None whatsoever, and besides, it was really none of her business. Ben Standish, she had to admit, had been an attractive guy, not her type, but she could see how quickly Jenny had been instantly mesmerised by him. He'd had bags of confidence. Yes, he had fancied Jenny. Fancied her like mad, but he was a playboy. It had always surprised her Jenny hadn't cottoned on to that straight away, but she hadn't, but then that was Jenny, Caroline thought resignedly; she was always reaching for the unattainable. For the dream. Utopia. Whatever.

The taxi dropped her outside the theatre; there were only two cars in the car park, but no sign of Jenny's. It was still too early for the frenzy of activity before the evening's performance; another couple of hours at least, but there was always the chance Jenny may be in there. There was a play-reading scheduled for the following morning and she already knew Jenny would be taking the lead, perhaps she was talking it over with Adam. By this time Caroline was unable to still the growing concern which had increased with each kilometre from the airport; there had to be a logical and quite simple explanation for her not coming to meet her.

There was no-one in reception and Caroline, leaving her travel bag behind the desk ran upstairs to the second floor. The door to Adam's office was open and tapping lightly, she went in.

'Caroline,' Adam Bond got up from behind his desk, 'you're back safely. I'm glad. Did you have a good holiday?'

'It was great, especially to see my parents and everyone, but,' she said, 'I'm worried about Jenny, Adam. She said she would be at Luqa to meet me –'

' – sit down, Caroline,' he interrupted, coming round and guiding her towards one of the chairs in the centre of the office and sitting down beside her, 'it's difficult for me to know how to break this to you, but,' he paused and she felt the colour draining from her face, her hands gripping too tightly the soft fabric of the arms of the chair, 'there's been an accident.'

'Accident? To Jenny?' she hardly recognised her own voice. Desperately wanting him to tell her what had happened, but equally afraid to hear the truth. This is my friend we are talking about she thought aghast, dreading what he was going to say.

'A boating accident,' he began quietly, 'it happened last Friday, early in the morning, she had taken David's boat out and, well,' spreading out his hands in an endeavour to explain more graphically, 'they found the boat; smashed up against the rocks in the north of the island, but no sign of Jenny.'

'Jenny was an experienced sailor, Adam. She knew what she was doing out there.'

'I know that, Caroline, but the police have now called off their search. The case is now closed; their verdict being death by misadventure.'

'But –'she was stumbling, groping to make sense of it all. It was just not possible! ' – they haven't found – they haven't found her?'

'No, they haven't. I know what a dreadful shock this must be for you, and I also know how close you two were –'

' – Adam,' it was her turn to interrupt, 'you believe she is dead? Really believe it?'

'What else, Caroline. She must be. We had one of the worse storms the night before.'

'I just cannot take it in,' she said quietly, 'are they absolutely sure she went out there?'

'Oh, yes, there's no doubt apparently. She'd left her car parked on the top road above the boat-sheds and someone walking along the beach about eight-thirty that morning noticed the door to David's boat-shed swinging open and no sign of his boat. I'm sorry, Caroline,' he said, getting to his feet. 'we all are.' he added.

'I don't understand.' Caroline whispered the words, her brain refusing to believe what he'd told her, 'What about David? He must be terribly upset?'

'Of course, also Moira. She was telling me yesterday that Jenny's sister was flying out; she should have arrived last night.'

'Annette?'

'Yes, that's right. Do you know her, then?'

'I've never met her, but Jenny talks – I mean, talked about her a lot. It isn't going to be easy for her being here, seeing where Jenny used to spend most of her time and everything. Where is she staying, Adam? At David's?'

'No,' he answered, 'he did invite her Moira said, but she was booking into the Crowne Plaza. Look, Caroline, I'm afraid I have to leave you now, but stay here for a while, give yourself time to recover. Shall I get someone to bring you some tea? It would help, you know.'

'No, no thanks, Adam, I'll be okay.' she smiled up at him, appreciating his sympathy, watching him leave the room.

She had to see Jenny's sister. She needed to speak to someone and there was no-one else she could think of. Directory of enquiries gave her the number of the hotel and with trembling fingers she dialled the number. Perhaps she should have had that tea after all she thought as she waited to be put through to Annette Graham's room.

It was really weird hearing her voice; so like Jenny's with the faint trace in the Scottish vowels; the way she pronounced each syllable was uncannily identical. Caroline knew she was prattling, aware she should slow down and then becoming even more annoyed with herself forgetting even to say who she was.

Annette was asking if she was a friend of Jenny's when she heard a shuffling outside the door. Lowering her voice, expecting someone to come in at any moment and not wanting to be overhead, she quickly explained how she had been away and had only just heard about Jenny. She had hesitated then, puzzled, because whoever it was, was still out there.

Annette's prompting brought her attention back. Caroline now wanted the conversation to come to an end as speedily as possible, but first she had to stress the importance of seeing her and tried to hide her disappointment when Annette said she would not be able to make it until tomorrow. Somehow, she had to get through the hours ahead, to ward off the disturbing thoughts which were surging through her brain.

There was no-one in the corridor; in fact, the floor she was on, the one above the auditorium was deserted. She could have gone backstage or to the coffee shop, but she didn't feel like speaking to anyone, not even Jeannette. The news was too raw, too shocking and she couldn't trust herself not to mention her suspicions. Nobody would believe her anyway she decided resignedly, picking up her bag from the deserted foyer and going back outside.

Caroline could have taken a taxi to her apartment, but she didn't even feel up to that. Besides, the walk would do her good; help her to sort things through in her mind. It was a warm evening and the back streets behind the theatre were quiet, with many of the older residents sitting in their front doorways chatting easily and familiarly with their neighbours as they had no doubt been doing for years she thought as she walked past them. Her neighbour, Joyce, was outside the apartment block and gave her a cheerful wave as she approached.

'Welcome back, Caroline,' she greeted her; the smile instantly fading, 'what's wrong, dear?'

'I've just heard some terribly sad news, Joyce,' she answered, 'about my friend, Jenny.'

'What's happened to her?'

'You haven't heard then?'

'Has there been an accident?'

'Yes, apparently she took her boyfriend's boat out last Friday morning and –'

' – that would have been the morning after the storm, Caroline. It was awful, one of the worst we have ever had on the island. We're all still talking about it; such a lot of damage, but you say your friend went out. The sea would have been very, very rough.'

'I realise that, Joyce, but I've been told the boat was found later – on the rocks.'

'Oh, no! And, Jenny?'

'They still haven't found her.'

'How very, very sad. She was such a lovely girl. I'm not surprised you're so upset.'

'I just can't believe it.'

'That's quite natural to feel like that, dear,' she sympathised, 'and I saw her that morning, you know. It was quite early.'

'You did?'

'Yes, she had spent the night in your apartment. She arrived quite late the night before; the rain had stopped, but the wind hadn't. I couldn't sleep and I saw her drive up and park outside.'

So, Jenny didn't spend the night at the villa, how odd. But then, she thought, perhaps not. Caroline had been expecting David and her to split up for weeks; perhaps they'd had a row and she had finally left him. It wouldn't have been the first time.

'What time did you see Jenny on the Friday morning, Joyce?'

'It would have been around eight-thirty.'

'Jenny never gets up early.' Caroline said; her mind instantly going into overdrive. There was something wrong here; it was to do with the time; Adam had told her that the guy with the dog had noticed David's boat wasn't in the boat-shed then. It didn't make sense.

'Are you sure about the time Joyce?' she asked her.

'Oh, yes, I always go for my bread around then every single morning.'

'She couldn't have taken David's boat out.' Caroline murmured.

'What did you say, dear?' Joyce leaned closer, putting an arm around her shoulders, 'You're shivering; why don't you come in and I'll make you a hot drink. You shouldn't be on your own at a time like this.'

'It's kind of you,' Caroline said abstractedly, 'but I'll be alright. Honestly. I'm tired, Joyce, I think I'll have an early night.'

'If you're sure, dear?'

'I'm sure.' Caroline attempted a smile, but it was a weak attempt. She didn't feel like smiling and wondered as she let herself into her apartment when she ever would again. Her worse fears for Jenny had come true. She had told her to forget about seeing Ben Standish again, but had known Jenny wouldn't have paid any heed. And now; what had really happened to her?

The possibilities which were coursing through her mind were too terrifying to envisage, to put into words even, but she had to. She had to inform someone, but she would speak to Moira first; she would know the right person to talk to.

She knew Moira's number off by heart and pulling the telephone towards her dialled, letting it ring for several minutes before finally giving up and replacing the receiver. She had no alternative now but to wait until the following morning and somehow get through the hours until then.

Caroline had not meant it when she had told Joyce she was going to have an early night. It had been true to say she was tired, but she knew it would be impossible to sleep and the last thing she wanted to do was spend hours tossing and turning. Instead, in an attempt to distract herself, she took out the script for their new play from her travel bag. It might work she thought, curling up on the sofa, with a large mug of tea on the table in front of her.

She had finished highlighting the lines she would be reading when the door bell rang. It would be Jeannette. Bound to be, Caroline thought, tossing the script on to the table and getting up. Eleven-thirty, she noted as she passed the wall clock in the tiny hall; the performance would have finished thirty minutes ago and it was not unusual for them to spend a couple of hours drinking coffee before going to bed. She unlocked the door, fully expecting to see her standing on the step.

'Oh, it's you?'

'Yes, Caroline, it's me.' he said.

'So Jenny was right.'

'Aren't you going to invite me in,' he asked her, 'I've brought a bottle of wine, for old times' sake.' he added.

Chapter Seventeen
SCOTLAND

Mrs Robertson had shown no surprise on the Friday morning when Jenny told her there would be a friend arriving for the weekend, not even a quizzical raising of one silver-grey eyebrow. In fact, the only surprise she did show was when Jenny said he would be sleeping in Annette's room. Mrs Robertson, Church of Scotland, stalwart supporter of the proper way to live had, it would appear, moved into the twenty-first century, Jenny thought, stifling a smile.

'It will be good for you, Jenny,' she had said, her plump arms folded in front of her, 'you've been too much on your own these last few days. Not like you at all.' she added, nodding her head.

How right you are Jenny thought wryly. She had never felt less like her old self. It would, she decided, be a long time before she would recover from what had been happening and it would appear, she frowned, looking out of the window down on to the beach, was still continuing. He was making no attempt to be inconspicuous and was still wearing the same clothes, but perhaps he had more than one pair of trousers and a shirt; all of them in the same drab colours.

'What about food, Jenny,' Mrs Robertson broke into her thoughts, 'do you want me to cook you both a meal this evening? It would be no trouble, you know.'

'No, please,' Jenny smiled, not wishing to offend, but at the same time hoping Paul and she could have the house to themselves. What they had to discuss, she didn't want Mrs Robertson to hear. That would not be fair. This was her problem and she was tremendously grateful Paul had been so quick to come to her rescue. Speaking to James had been a total waste of time. As she had thought, time could change people and he had always been a bit stuffy. So, now he was married, no surprises there. He had, even in his early twenties, an inbuilt desire for settling down; owning his own property and everything which went with it: a hefty mortgage; the latest model, a BMW no less, parked in the drive; a couple of kids, with places already reserved for them at one of the best schools in the south of England. She knew she was being cynical, but she couldn't help it. The conversation with him had rankled, but the irony of it all had not escaped her. Here she was, ten years later and she longed for stability; perhaps not the hefty mortgage, but somewhere she could call her own; a place where she could plan to spend the rest of her life with someone she loved and who loved her and, children. The desire for children was strong, but she shrugged sadly, she had picked the wrong man in David. 'It's alright, Mrs Robertson,' she said, 'I think we may well have a meal down at the hotel this evening. Tomorrow though, if you're sure you don't mind?'

'What do you think, dear?' she beamed and Jenny knew she had said the right thing. The Mrs Robertsons of this world were put on this earth to help others. She could remember those late afternoons when she and Annette, hot and hungry from hours spent on the beach, would gravitate to the kitchen and always there would either be a fresh batch of scones, not just plain ones, but full of fat sultanas, or Mrs Robertson's speciality: fairy cakes; small sponges with the tops sliced off and cut in half to look like fairy wings and pressed into the soft cream-filled centre; another world! She really must stop this; it wasn't doing her any good. It was time also she tried to give Annette another ring.

As before, she got Annette's answering machine and curbing her reluctance she left a message for her, and as usual felt the words she did manage to leave were inadequate and pathetic. Some actress, she couldn't help thinking as she rang off, reminding herself as she did so she ought to re-charge her mobile. It had been several days since she had used it and for all she knew Annette may have been trying to call her.

It was after five when Paul arrived, pulling in behind her car at the side of the house.

He looked exactly as she remembered him: tall, slim, and the dark brown hair which still had the tendency to flop over his forehead. She had hardly seen him after the holiday in France. Paul and James had been friends since their university days; Paul had been Caroline's boyfriend and after she had split up with James, it had seemed awkward somehow and shortly after that, Paul and Caroline had also ended their relationship. But, seeing him now, striding towards her, she had an overwhelming feeling of relief. Here was a person she felt she could rely on. Hadn't he come all this way; six hundred miles or so to be with her, to help her through this mess? That says something, she decided, running the short distance to meet him.

'Jenny!' he said, putting his arms around her, 'you haven't changed a bit!'

'Neither have you,' she grinned up at him, 'Oh, Paul, I can't tell you how glad I am that you're here!'

'I couldn't stay away,' he smiled, kissing her on both cheeks, 'I don't know whether I'm going to be much help, but I couldn't let you face all of this on your own.'

'Come on,' she said, pulling at his arm, 'let's go inside. First, I'll introduce you to Mrs Robertson and then we can have some tea or something. You must be parched!'

'Mrs Robertson?' he asked, allowing himself to be led up the steps to the open front door.

'She's our housekeeper and has been with the family for more years than I can remember. Annette and I were left the house when our grandparents died and she and her husband look after everything for us. She's marvellous; you'll love her!'

Introductions over, Mrs Robertson followed them both out on to the terrace, her cheeks rosy-red from the kitchen where Jenny knew she had spent most of the afternoon baking.

There was no stopping her and she only hoped Paul still had a good appetite.

'Jenny,' he said once they were on their own, 'I've something to tell you.'

'What is it?' she asked quickly, her heart beat quickening. She could tell by his expression whatever it was would not be good.

'It's distressing news, I'm afraid,' he said, sitting down beside her in one of the wicker chairs and taking both her hands in his, 'I phoned my office at the last service station and –'

' – not, Annette!'

'No, nothing to do with her.'

'Thank God.' she breathed.

'It's Caroline.'

'Caroline?' she frowned, the last name she expected to hear.

'Yes, information had just come in from Reuters. She was found earlier today, Jenny; in her apartment and they're suggesting a drug overdose.'

'Caroline is dead?' a cold sweat breaking out on her forehead. Suddenly, it was overbearingly stuffy and she felt her body begin to sway.

'Yes,' he said quietly, keeping a firm grip of her hands, 'I'm sorry, Jenny, I should have waited, told you in a different, more sensitive way. I'm sorry.' he repeated, releasing one of her hands to gently smooth back strands of damp hair from her cheeks. 'Are you okay?' he asked, his eyes filled with concern, 'Can I get you something?'

'No,' she gulped, taking a deep breath, filling her lungs with air until the dizziness passed, 'I'll be fine; just give me a couple of minutes and, Paul?'

'Yes?'

'Mrs Robertson mustn't see me like this. She knows nothing about any of this awful business.' Jenny added, getting to her feet and walking over to the edge of the terrace, standing with her back to him and looking far beyond the wide expanse of white virgin sand and trying to absorb what he'd told her. He was respecting her need to be on her own and she was thankful. She could hear Mrs Robertson behind her; the scrape of Paul's chair as he stood up to help her with the tray of drinks. Mrs Robertson had guessed it would be beer for him and a jug of her home-made lemonade for her. Reluctantly, dragging her eyes back to the beach immediately below the terrace to where the man she had mentally labelled as the stalker usually positioned himself, noticing there was no sign of him. Not knowing whether to be relieved or not, she took another deep breath and turned round to face them both.

'You're wonderful, Mrs Robertson,' she said, 'just what is needed in this heat.'

'It will do you good, dear,' she smiled, 'and I've made some sausage rolls; not too many because I don't want to spoil your appetite for the evening meal.' she added, putting a far from small plate of sausage rolls in the centre of the table and deftly, as though she had been doing it for years, opened a beer for Paul, pouring it out for him without spilling a drop.

'There you are,' she said, handing him the brimming glass, 'you will probably be in need of that after the long drive. Now, unless you want me to do anything else, Jenny, I'll be off.'

'You've already done more than enough,' Jenny said, 'and thank you, Mrs Robertson.'

'Och, lassie, it's nothing. It's a real pleasure; so I'll see you both in the morning. And,' she added as she made to walk back inside, an unreadable expression on her face, 'I hope, Mr Watson, you won't find your room too much like taking a step back into the eighties.'

'Do call me, Paul,' he said and Jenny could tell he was trying to keep his face straight, 'but aren't you going to explain?'

'Och, Paul,' she said, 'you'll find out soon enough.'

'Quite a character,' Paul said when she had gone, 'you're lucky, Jenny, having someone like her to look after you when you're up here.'

'I know,' she said, sitting down beside him again and taking a long sip of her lemonade; cool and not too sweet, 'Paul,' she went on, putting her glass back on the table, 'Caroline. You said something about a drug overdose?'

'Yes, that's right. The message was brief, but there will be more later. They said they'd let me know as soon as anything further comes through.'

'I see,' she said, 'but Caroline didn't take drugs, Paul. I could swear to that. She never would. Never!'

'I didn't think so either,' he agreed quietly, 'so; I expect you're beginning to come to the same conclusions as I am.'

'Something to do with Ben Standish.'

'I would say that was fairly certain, but we should learn more once the post mortem results come through.'

'It's all my fault.' Jenny said, stifling a shudder at the thought of what his words meant. Like most people, having watched numerous police thrillers, she only had a modicum idea of the basic rudimentary technicalities of a post mortem. Pretty Caroline. No longer here; in this world. The girl she had known since the very first day they had both joined RADA, shared many a bottle of cheap plonk, talking about boyfriends, catty fellow actors, short-tempered producers, sleazy hand-groping agents promising them lead parts in the next box office success and never once during those years had they ever fallen out, had an argument even. Caroline had been the down to earth one and she had relied on that, but now, there was nothing.

'Jenny. Jenny, listen, don't torture yourself like this. Please. Caroline's death is not your fault.'

'But, Paul, I think it is,' she insisted, 'if I hadn't opened my big mouth, if I hadn't said I had seen Ben, she – she would still be alive.'

'You don't know that.'

'I *feel* it, Paul. And that is enough. I don't *need* proof. She warned me, you know. Do you know what she said to me, only minutes before she went through to Departures?'

'What did she say, then?'

'She told me to let sleeping dogs lie. And I didn't bloody listen, did I? As soon as I got that call from Ben, I agreed without the slightest hesitation to meet him.'

'This still doesn't mean you should hold yourself responsible. I don't see it like that at all. Okay,' he continued, 'she probably gave you sound advice. Perhaps she was thinking it would be wiser if you ignored the fact you had seen him, but by telling her didn't automatically mean that once she had that knowledge she would be in any danger herself.'

'You believe she was murdered, don't you, Paul?'

'I do, yes. Don't you?'

'Yes,' quietly, feeling prickles of what she could describe as sheer terror flowing through the whole length of her body. Her best friend was dead. She would never see her again. That knowledge alone was devastating and with the thought, the first tears began to fall, unchecked and unheeded down her cheeks.

'Darling, Jenny,' he was on his feet immediately, his arms around her and holding her tight, 'don't. Don't. Look,' he went on softly, his face close to hers, 'this is dreadful, but we are in it together. I know Caroline will never be there, but we have to be strong. We have to be.'

'What do you think we should do,' she asked, pulling herself away and impatiently wiping her face with the back of her hand, 'do we go to the police? Tell them what we know? Would it help? It won't help Caroline though, will it?' she sighed.

'No, it won't help Caroline. Nothing will; we both know that, but if we are right and I believe we are, this is all to do with Ben Standish and his need to stay clear of the authorities and somehow – God knows how – he has to be stopped.'

'I know.'

'I think we should wait until we have more information.'

'You mean about –' she hesitated, not wanting to say the words, 'about how Caroline died?'

'Yes,' he said, 'and then we should go back down south. I'll speak to my editor; hear what he has to say. Given what's happened, it is unlikely we will be able to go to the press with this, he'll have no option but to check it out with the police. I would imagine they will be quick to put a block on any exposure.'

'What about this creep who's been watching everything I've been doing for most of this week?'

'He's a problem. I don't underestimate his presence here for one minute, so we must be careful, Jenny. Not to do anything untoward and give him the least idea we have even noticed him, in fact. It seems to me he's been told to keep a close watch on you, see where you go, who you talk to, that sort of thing.'

'I wonder if he saw you arrive.'

'I'm sure he did,' he said, his expression hardening, 'that is, if he's doing his job properly, which I'm sure he is. When did you last see him, Jenny?'

'Earlier this afternoon, but he's not there now.'

'He'll be somewhere nearby.'

'I find him scary. It's not knowing what he might do next, I suppose. Surely he can't keep this up indefinitely.'

'No,' he agreed, 'and this is why we must move as swiftly as we can. I suggest we drive down on Monday; early in the morning. He might not be expecting that.'

'My car is a bit of a problem. I hired it at Glasgow airport; I suppose it should really go back there.'

'No, best not, Jenny. Who did you hire it from?'

'Avis.'

'Right; Montrose is the nearest town, isn't it?'

'Yes.'

'Well, they'll have a branch there. Why not give them a ring and ask them to pick it up here. I don't think that should pose any problem for them.'

'That's a good idea,' Jenny said, 'now, I'll show you your room, Paul, and then you can see what Mrs Robertson was going on about. I thought we could eat in the hotel this evening, if that's alright with you.'

'Suits me.'

Annette's bedroom, like her own, had changed little since they were young girls, barely into their teens: the single bed with the pink quilted headboard and matching coloured duvet; the faded posters covering most of the walls: a larger-than-life posturing Mick Jagger above the frilled kidney-shaped dressing table; a long-legged Tina Turner; Gemini, Phil Collins in the forefront; Eric Clapton, sad and lugubrious; a cheeky and extremely young Rod Stewart; Freddie Mercury in full exaggerated gear and, obviously pride of place, above the bed, a signed poster of the Beach Boys in concert at Knebworth Park in England.

'Wow!' Paul stood in the open doorway, a look of delight on his face, 'Hall of fame, eh? Fantastic!'

'You mean that?' she asked; not quite believing him. She'd lived with this particular decor for so long, or at least Annette had, but then they had spent quite a number of hours in here and being only about nine years of age compared to what she had considered Annette's grown-up fourteen, having to listen to endless records of all her favourites.

'Of course I do. It's great, Jenny. Quite a collection in fact.'

'My room is totally different,' she laughed, 'I was never into rock; my whole young life was centred on ballet and the theatre. Mostly of Margot Fontaine, whom I considered to be the most fabulous person in the whole of the universe, my extremely tiny universe of course, but I absolutely idolised her. And then, I think I was eleven, my mother took me to see Lawrence Olivier performing in London and from that moment I was hooked. Ballet for me paled into insignificance.'

'So,' he was smiling, 'instead of becoming a ballerina you became an actress.'

'I suppose so,' she shrugged, 'but I have rather made a bit of a muck-up of that, at least for the moment. You see, Paul, I love being on stage, pulling the audience towards the character I'm portraying. A bit of a show-off really, I suppose.' she smiled, but sadly, immediately and inevitably being reminded of Caroline.

'Okay,' he put an arm around her, giving her a quick hug, 'I think I know what you're thinking. I'll grab a quick shower, if that's alright and then we can walk down to the hotel.'

'No problem,' she said, making an effort to lighten her mood, at the same time trying to come to terms with losing Caroline. Not easy, but she knew she would manage it. She had to.

*

The restaurant in the Saint Angus Arms was busy, but as soon as Jenny and Paul arrived, the same waiter who had served her the other night, hurried forward.

'Good evening, Miss Graham,' he smiled. Does everyone here know who I am, she wondered; it was a bit like living in a goldfish bowl. Don't become paranoid, Jenny, she quickly chided herself, 'would you like the same table?' he asked.

'Please, that would be fine.' she answered and turning to Paul suggested they have a drink at the bar before ordering their meal.

They ordered two champagne kirs; Paul's idea and one she wasn't going to argue with. While they waited Jenny looked around the restaurant, almost as full so early in the early evening as it had been before and, fortunately, no sign of either the theatre fanatic or the stalker. Good she thought, but she had no intention of holding her breath. There was time yet for them to appear.

'Do you think he's staying here?' Paul asked, as though reading her mind.

'There would be nowhere else in the village,' Jenny said, 'and considering what he's up to, he would have to be on the spot.'

'Right,' he said, 'give me a minute, Jenny;' taking a short sip of his drink, 'I won't be long.'

And before she had time to say anything he had gone. Through the glass doors she saw him at the reception desk. As far as she could make out there was no-one else out there. What was he doing? Ah, the idea suddenly occurring to her; of course, the hotel register. Trying not to make it obvious and raising her glass to her lips, she watched him. Although slim, his shoulders were wide and it was impossible to see what he was doing. This is all becoming like an Agatha Christie! When on earth was all this nightmare going to end and more importantly, how was it going to end?

'Okay?' Paul asked, coming back.

'I think so.'

'You guessed what I was up to, didn't you?'

'Checking to see if the stalker had booked in here?'

'Oh,' he smiled, 'is that what you're calling him. I could think of other names!'

'What did you find out then?'

'There haven't been many new arrivals this week,' Paul said, frowning as he tried to remember exactly what he had read, 'one woman booked in on Monday, two couples the following day and one man, again on the Tuesday.'

It could be him, but he wouldn't have used his real name, would he?'

'Probably not.'

'What is it?' she couldn't help smiling at his expression. Paul had, she was finding, one of those faces it was easy to read what he was thinking.

'You'll never believe this.'

'I might.'

'David Jones.'

'Typical, I suppose. How many David Jones do you think there are in Britain, Paul?'

'A lot,' he said wryly, 'but one thing; I made a note of his car registration number; it could come in useful.'

They had been shown to their table and the menus had been handed to them with a friendly and professional flourish when the stalker came into the restaurant, and, as he had done two evenings ago, chose the same bar stool.

'That's him, isn't it?' Paul asked softly.

'Yes.'

'A shabby individual, isn't he?'

'He doesn't make much of an effort.'

'I saw him earlier, you know, Jenny.'

'Did you?' surprised; he had only been in Saint Angus for a few hours and already he was making headway, or at least some sort of headway; more than she had done anyway in the last six days.

'Yes,' he explained, 'when I drove past the hotel he had just come out and I saw him in my rear view mirror as I climbed the hill towards your house. He was behind me, walking in the same direction. Can you get down to the beach that way?'

'Yes,' Jenny said, 'it's rather a steep path. Not many people use it, preferring to take the longer and easier route further along, through the village. But that's funny, Paul, he wasn't on the beach after you arrived; at least not in his usual place.'

'He was probably hanging around though,' Paul suggested, 'perhaps he's found a new vantage point.'

Realising he was out there, lurking, unnerved her. And now, here he was back in the hotel. He knew she was here. It was almost as though he wanted her to notice him. But why? The man was an out and out repulsive creep.

They had almost finished their meal when she saw Doreen. Is everyone around here Jenny thought irritably creatures of bloody habit? But, apart from the village pub at the end of the road, there really was nowhere else for people to go in the evenings. Could it be as simple as that? And she braced herself for the moment when the woman spotted her. She didn't have long to wait and neither did she have any time to warn Paul what he was in for.

'Hello, Jenny, you're still here, then?' she called out to her. What was the matter with her? Stifling her annoyance Jenny smiled which was a mistake; she was on her way over.

'Yes,' Jenny said, 'I'm still here, Mrs —'

'— call me Doreen; everyone else does.' she interrupted, managing at the same time to throw an inquisitive look in Paul's direction.

'Doreen,' Jenny said, wondering how she was going to get rid of her, noticing Paul's bewildered expression; she really should spare him this, 'how are you after your dreadful experience the other night?'

'Och, not too bad,' she shrugged, her eyes continuing to focus on Paul, 'Mrs Robertson told me you would be having a visitor to stay this weekend.'

The woman was a pain in the neck. Village life! She should have grown used to it, but she hadn't. It was only natural that Mrs Robertson, who presumably had been doing her shopping at the same time as Doreen, would have mentioned someone new arriving in the village. After all, Jenny thought, what else did they have to talk about in a small place like this when not much happened from one week to the next? She couldn't blame Mrs Robertson and never would.

'This is Paul,' Jenny said at last, turning towards him and smiling apologetically at him, 'he's from London.' she added; not to enlighten the silly woman, but for something to say.

'Hello, Paul,' Doreen stretched out a large hand, a look of undisguised delight on her face, 'and are you an actor, like Jenny?'

'No,' he said, shaking her hand, 'nothing as glamorous as that, I'm afraid.'

'Och, that's a pity. I would have loved to tell people that I knew *two* famous actors!'

'I'm sorry to disappoint you, Doreen,' Paul smiled, 'but what was this unfortunate experience Jenny mentioned?'

'It was terrible, Paul,' she said quickly, for once ignoring Jenny and no doubt about to repeat her tale for the hundredth time, 'I'm surprised Jenny didn't tell you about it.'

'Paul has only just arrived, Doreen.'

'Och, I know, dear, I'm not blaming you. But, Paul,' she continued relentlessly, confident she had in him the new audience she wanted; 'I was mugged.'

'Mugged?' Paul said and Jenny was sure she could see a slight quivering at the side of his mouth. Please, Paul, she thought, do not smile and do not laugh. Farcical although Doreen's behaviour was, this was the last thing she wanted, also once again very much aware of the stalker at the bar doing his utmost to follow their conversation.

'Yes I was walking home; I live at the end of the village,' she explained for Paul's enlightenment, 'and I had almost reached my front gate when somebody crept up behind me and pushed me right down on to the pavement. It was terrible, really terrible. In fact,' she stressed,' I have never been so frightened in all my life.'

'Were you hurt?' he asked her.

'No, not really, Paul,' she answered, using his name in such a familiar way even Jenny was beginning to see the amusing side, 'a bit bruised, that's all. It was the shock, you know, and when I managed to get to my feet, whoever he was had gone; also my handbag.' she added 'And it was one I'd had for years; ever since I was first married and I can tell you that was a very long time ago. I won't tell you how long, Paul.' she finished with a coquettish smile.

'And you didn't see who it was?'

'No, I didn't; it all happened far too quickly.'

'As long as you're alright, Doreen,' Jenny said, deciding it was time she made an attempt to stop the tirade, 'that's the main thing.' A platitude she knew, but what else could she say to her.

'He was listening to every word of that.' Jenny said once Doreen, with obvious reluctance had moved over to the bar.

'Damn!'

'What? Does it matter all that much?'

'I think it might very well,' he answered, keeping his voice low, 'if he's been assigned to keep an eye on you by Standish, hearing my name mentioned is bound to be passed on to him.'

'I'm sorry,' Jenny said puzzled, 'I'm probably being stupid, but I still don't see the importance; you'll have to explain.'

'Well,' he said, taking one of her hands in his, 'think about it, Jenny. Go back in your mind to our holiday: the four of us; you, me, Caroline and James.'

'No!' she gasped and feeling his grip tightening, warning her to take it easy, to remain calm and for the second time that day she felt waves of fear coursing through her, 'Caroline, of course, she's – she's gone. Ben knows where I am and now – Oh, God, Paul! – he'll soon know you're here as well. It's like being caught in some ghastly trap!'

'We'll get through this,' he soothed, keeping her hand in his, 'we've just got to be a lot smarter, that's all. I could be mistaken, but that guy over there with the over-developed antenna doesn't strike me as all that bright.'

'I hope you're right, I really do.'

'Shall we have some more coffee, Jenny?'

'No thanks, let's go back. I find his continual presence disturbing. Believe me, Paul, I am trying very hard not to get paranoid about him, but he frightens me.'

The walk back to the house did not take long. She and Annette had done it many times: turn right outside the hotel, a few hundred yards along the narrow pavement, past the high beech hedge bordering the manse, across the road and up the pebbly incline to the top and they were there.

It was only ten; there would still be more than an hour of daylight and the evening was warm, the sweet smell of honeysuckle reaching out to them as they opened the gate.

'Your garden is lovely, Jenny.' Paul said, looking around with obvious pleasure. And he was right. The perfectly manicured lawn stretching down towards the front hedge, the borders; a mass of early summer colour: geraniums, their tight clusters of tiny red, pink and white flowers; marigolds, thick clumps of yellow and orange; pansies, velvety purple and their cross little yellow faces, interspersed with the bluish-purple of a scattering of violets.

'It is, isn't it,' she agreed, taking the key from her bag, 'I do believe he takes as much pride out here as he does in his own garden.'

'I take it you're talking about Mr Robertson?'

'Who else? As you said earlier, I'm lucky, or I should say both Annette and I are. Without the Robertsons' tender loving care of the place I don't know what it would look like. It is just a shame we can't spend more time up here.'

As soon as they were inside, Paul helped her to open some windows, also the glass doors on to the terrace. The tide was out, probably as far as it would go; the sand in its wake perfectly smooth. As she had been in the habit of doing lately, Jenny walked to the edge of the terrace, although she realised he wouldn't be down there; he was still in the restaurant and with this knowledge, a feeling of relief. She felt they had the whole beach to themselves. How lovely it would be to take the boat out tonight. She was imagining what it would be like: the slight ripple on the water as they gently left the shore, the cool night air caressingly soothing and then returning with the moon behind them lighting up the watery path back to the beach. Perhaps another evening she thought. They'd had a few glasses of wine, so not wise, she decided.

'Jenny,' Paul called to her from the lounge, 'can you come here for a minute.'

'Sure.' still with her thoughts elsewhere, she turned away and walked back inside to where he was standing in the centre of the lounge. The expression on his face brought her immediately back to the present.

'What's wrong?'

'Just come in here,' he said quietly, taking her hand and leading her into Annette's bedroom, 'somebody's been in here, Jenny.'

'What!' following him into the bedroom. The window was still closed; there was no sign as far as she could see of any break-in, so what did he mean? How did he know?

'My bag,' he explained, pointing over to the chair next to the dressing-table, 'look at it, Jenny. I didn't leave it like that.'

All the contents had been pulled out, most of them tossed on to the floor in a heap.

'My God,' she said, sitting down on the edge of the bed, 'what is going on, Paul?'

'Something not very pleasant, darling.' he answered, his mouth set in a tight grim line, 'but whatever he hoped to find he must have been disappointed. As you can see, these are only clothes. As I've already thought, the man is an inept fool.'

'So he might be, Paul,' she said, 'but he did manage to get into the house.'

'For people like that,' Paul went on, his expression not relaxing, 'that would not be difficult.'

'What do you think he was looking for?'

'My passport maybe; papers to explain what I did for a living. Oh, I don't know. I suppose anything which they might find and consider relevant. Let's face it, Jenny, Standish already knew I was a journalist and that knowledge alone must be bothering him.'

'And,' she began slowly, trying to make sense of it all, 'and,' she repeated, 'did you have anything this creep could pass on to him?'

'Not a thing. I've been around long enough,' Paul said, 'to learn to keep anything like that firmly on my person. Not that I have very much in any case, but if, for example, he was to attack me the way he did poor Doreen, he would at least have discovered which newspaper I work for and my address.'

'Do you still want a coffee?' Jenny asked practically, getting up from the bed, 'or would you prefer a brandy?'

'A brandy would be the answer, I think. It would help take away the very unpleasant taste of this invasion of privacy.'

Chapter Eighteen

"I wonder who he is. Someone pretty important I would say." Caroline's voice, coming from a long way away and echoing down the years. They were on the yacht. Ben Standish's yacht: the four of them, leaning against the rail. The moon, an enormous white globe, balancing on the horizon, the string of coloured lights along the deck reflecting on to the water: blue, red, yellow, purple, gold and silver. A shadow, dark and shapeless, passed across the face of the moon, a sudden cold breath of air drifted along the deck ruffling their hair, tugging at their clothes. A splash, louder even than the music from inside, disturbed the stillness. "It's only a flesh wound!" a disembodied voice called out.

"I have to go now." Again, Caroline's voice and they watched helplessly as she pulled herself up on to the top of the rail and her body, a perfect arc, dived into the sea. Her limbs although Jenny knew they were deeply suntanned showed up white against the darkness of the water below them. "No, Jenny," Caroline called up, her voice now rapidly receding, "don't come in! You'll only get out of your depth ..... you'll only get out of your depth ...."

They stood there. No-one moved and not one of them made any attempt to follow her. Caroline wasn't in any danger. Of course she wasn't. It was not possible. She was swimming further away from the boat, distancing herself from them and then she was returning, closer now; her blonde curls encircling her face and then silently she had gone. Sinking, only the once; a stream of technicolour bubbles rising slowly to the surface before finally dissipating into the night. Jenny felt an arm around her shoulders and looked up expecting to see James, but it wasn't him. The cold, dispassionate eyes of Gerald Smith stared into her own. At this point she woke up, her body bathed in sweat. She must have shouted out, she couldn't be sure, but she must have done.

'Jenny, Jenny, you're okay,' Paul whispered, bringing her back, 'you've had a nightmare.'

'Oh, Paul,' she said, leaning her head against him, 'Caroline was there. I saw her. She spoke to me.'

'Sssh, come on,' he said, 'let's go into the other room. I'll make us a hot drink.'

'It was awful, Paul. Awful.'

'I know, come on,' he repeated, 'you can tell me all about it.'

'I don't know whether I want to.' she was sobbing uncontrollably, allowing him to help her.

She did tell him; as much as she could remember. He sat beside her on the sofa, his arm still around her, until she came to the end. The tea helped, but she didn't think she would sleep again that night. She was afraid to even try; afraid the nightmare would return, but, it didn't. Although it must have been almost dawn before she finally dropped off into a thankful oblivion and this time she slept soundly, awaking to the soft voices of Paul and Mrs Robertson coming from the kitchen. He had left her bedroom door open, just in case he had explained the demons returned. Jenny Graham she thought, swinging her legs out of bed, you are becoming a wimp! Where has all that Scottish backbone gone? The shower helped and pulling on the cotton robe and wrapping a towel around her damp hair, she padded barefoot into the kitchen, drawn by the comforting smells of freshly made coffee.

'There you are, dear,' Mrs Robertson greeted her, 'it's a lovely morning and Paul tells me he's going to take you for a drive. Blow the cobwebs away he said.' smiling and filling her coffee mug up to the brim.

'Sounds good to me,' Jenny smiled across the room at him, noticing how very much at home he appeared, perched on the ledge by the open window and devouring a large slice of toast generously spread with Mrs Robertson's home-made strawberry jam, 'but first, I must try to call Annette.'

'Why don't you both take your coffee out on to the terrace?' Mrs

Robertson suggested which really meant she wanted to get on with her chores, but Jenny didn't mind. She needed to be outside, to fill her lungs with sea air; always to her more potent in the mornings than at any other time of the day.

As before, there was no reply from Annette's number. She didn't leave any message this time, but decided instead to try her office and wondering as she dialled the unfamiliar number why she hadn't thought of doing this before. They should know where she was, she decided, listening impatiently to the dialling tone.

'Barton Publishing. Good morning, how may I help you?'

'I'd like to speak to Miss Graham, please.'

'Sorry,' came the quick, pert reply, 'but Annette's on leave. Is there anyone else who could help you?'

'Er –' the last thing she expected to hear. She couldn't think why; it wasn't as if Annette would have told her she was going away. Stifling a sigh of disappointment she hesitated. She could, she supposed, try and speak to the great man; Quenton Barton himself, at least he would know when Annette would be back in the office. 'well,' Jenny continued, 'could I possibly have a word with Mr Barton? It is important.' she added, not expecting that to carry much weight. It was like talking to a robot. Why, she wondered, did so many London receptionists possess this air of disdainful disinterest.

'I'm sorry, but Mr Barton is away on business.'

'Oh.'

'I can put you through to his secretary, though.' the suggestion surprising her. She may be more forthcoming Jenny thought waiting to be put through.

'I'm terribly sorry,' a voice drawled, as different to the receptionist as it could possibly be, 'but Quenton isn't expected back in the office until Tuesday morning.'

'Oh,' Jenny repeated. This was becoming impossible; how on earth could she find out where Annette was? She could be anywhere! Raising her eyes to Paul in exasperation, she tried again, 'Look,' she went on, trying to curb her impatience, 'I'm Annette's sister and I have been trying to get in touch with her for the last few days.'

'Oh, you're Jenny, aren't you?' so, somebody else who seems to know who I am she thought cynically.

'Yes, that's right. Do you know when she'll be back in London?'

'Not really,' she replied unhelpfully, 'all I can tell you is that she's booked to fly out to the States next Friday. In the evening.' she added.

'I see,' Jenny sighed, 'well, I wonder if you would be kind enough to ask Mr Barton when you see him if he could –' she hesitated, at a loss for words. What could she say? Keep it brief, Jenny, she told herself, '- let Annette know I'm no longer in Malta.'

'Malta?'

'Yes, Malta,' Jenny explained, 'I've been working there for the past year –'

'- acting?'

'Yes, that's right,' she said, curbing her exasperation with difficulty; surely secretaries are not supposed to be like this! 'it's important I speak to Annette as soon as possible.'

'And where are you now, Miss Graham?'

'I'm in Scotland.'

'Scotland?' as if it was at the other end of the world.

'Annette knows the number.'

'Don't worry, Miss Graham, I'll make sure Quenton gets your message.'

Paul's mobile was ringing as she replaced the receiver. Mentally exhausted by the ridiculous exchange, Jenny leaned her head back against the cushion and closed her eyes.

There was nothing for it, but she would have to curb her impatience until she heard from Annette. Meanwhile, she was faced with the problem of trying to find somewhere to live. This wasn't insurmountable, but she would have much preferred the familiar comfort of Annette's flat, at least until she got herself sorted out. Paul had his back to her, facing out towards the sea. She wondered if the stalker was out there; more than likely she thought, but lacking the energy to get to her feet and find out. Soon, she consoled herself, another couple of days and they would be away.

'That was my editor,' Paul explained, coming over to join her and picking up his coffee which must by now be cold, 'they've had the autopsy report, Jenny. It came in first thing this morning.'

'Yes.' bracing herself.

'It's as we thought. A drug overdose was administered to her on Thursday night around eleven-thirty.'

'Administered? How, Paul?' she asked softly.

'In red wine. The actual substance has still to be analysed, but they could find no trace of Caroline having any history of taking drugs.'

'I never thought she had.'

'I know. Also,' Paul went on, taking a deep breath, 'there is something else.'

'Oh, no! What now?'

'It's about –'

' – go on, Paul,' she interrupted him, 'whatever it is, I think I can take it.'

'I hope so.' he said and once again she read the concern in his voice. 'Word has apparently leaked out to the press that the police, the Maltese police, I mean - I really don't know how to say this, but they had recently reached another verdict.'

'It's about me, isn't it?'

'Yes, darling,' he tried to smile, 'apparently David Grech reported you missing and for reasons best known to themselves they –'

' – they what?'

'They believed you died in a boating accident.' he finished lamely, holding up both hands and quickly putting them down again.

'But, why, Paul? Why should they think that? Do you mean to say everyone in Malta thinks I'm – I'm dead?'

'That's what it seems like, yes.'

'This is absolutely incredible! How on earth could they possibly substantiate this – this – I'm at a complete loss for words!'

'Robert, that's my editor,' Paul started, 'says, mind you this is only his opinion, but he reckons the police assumed rather too much on what is really no more than flimsy evidence.'

'Such as?'

'Well, David Grech's boat, for instance; it was found smashed up against the rocks on that Friday, also your car which was parked on the road outside his boat-shed.'

'I just do not believe this! I don't, Paul. It is totally bizarre! Only a fool would have taken a boat out that morning. I've already told you about the storm and, anyone who knew me, David for instance, would have realised that?'

'You would have thought so, yes.'

'This is crazy! Surely someone would have seen me in Sliema, or in Saint Paul's Bay for that matter and my car, Paul; I left it in the parking area in front of the theatre. Do they *really* think I took the boat out? The conditions out there that morning would have been far too treacherous. They seem to have been very quick to reach their conclusions.' she added bitterly.

'I agree with you absolutely; you should realise that, Jenny. Also now, with Caroline's death, they are, according to Robert, connecting the two incidents.'

'Incidents.' Jenny repeated, 'is that how they are describing them? A murder and a missing person presumed drowned, and both of them friends,' she added softly, memory of how Caroline had been as she had last seen her at the airport; excited about her holiday and apart from her rabbiting on about seeing Ben Standish, not one single worry.

'Paul,' she continued, 'are they still sticking with their accident theory?'

'I can't say for sure,' he answered, 'but I would imagine they are now looking somewhat more closely into the evidence they've already got.'

'You mean David's smashed up boat and my car being found where it was?'

'Yes.'

'Ben certainly went to a great deal of trouble to make my death appear an accident, didn't he?'

'True. You got too close for comfort, my love, but fortunately it misfired. So much for their careful planning.'

'Only because I managed to get out of that farmhouse,' she said, giving an involuntary shudder, not wanting to think back to that morning, 'if I hadn't, well who knows?'

'You did, Jenny and that's the main thing.'

'What about your editor? Is he going to tell the police I'm okay?'

'For the moment, no,' Paul said, 'he believes that the best thing is for us both to get away from here and once we're in London, we can make our report to the police and get the protection we need.'

'What about this – this person who's been hanging about?'

'Well,' Paul said, 'I've told Robert, also given him the registration number of the car. He said he would try and find out something about him; not that there will be much to find out; the man will have covered his tracks pretty well, I would imagine. By the way,' he added, 'I haven't seen him out there this morning. Have you?'

'I haven't looked.'

'It doesn't necessarily mean that he isn't around.'

'I know that. Meanwhile,' Jenny said, the full impact of what he had told her finally registering, 'in Malta they all believe I'm dead. I don't like that, Paul. It isn't right.'

'I know how you feel, but I'm afraid you haven't got a great deal of choice, at least for the next couple of days.'

'What do you mean?'

'Look at it this way,' he smiled, touching her lightly on her arm, 'you're in considerable danger, Jenny –'

'– so are you.' she interrupted.

'Okay. We both are. Ben Standish is ruthless; I think we realise that. He will stop at nothing to save his own skin and anyone who comes remotely close to shattering that will, I'm certain, force him to take action.'

'Like Caroline, you mean?'

'Yes, darling, like Caroline. We don't know what she did to arouse his suspicions and chances are we may never know. She may have mentioned Standish's name to someone when she went back to Malta, especially when you weren't there.'

'It's possible. Oh, Paul, it's all so awful. If only I hadn't left the way I did. If only I hadn't mentioned Ben's name to Caroline! If only –'

'– it's pointless to go down that road, Jenny.'

'You're right, of course. Anyway, Paul,' she went on, 'Ben knows where I am, would it matter so much if I came out of hiding now?'

'It's only until Monday, my love. By then, we'll be back in London. There is something else which may not have occurred to you.'

'What?'

'Caroline's murder has, it would appear, reached the headlines here and if the media get the slightest inkling there is a connection with the old story of Ben Standish, they'll be down on you like a pack of wolves. Believe me, Jenny; I know what I'm talking about.'

'I understand,' she said quietly, 'I hadn't realised. But,' the thought suddenly coming to her, 'my disappearance, my accident or whatever they're calling it, why hasn't it been in the newspapers?'

'For the simple reason,' he answered grimly, 'because, before they could do that, mention your name I mean, your next of kin would have to be informed.'

'No! Mum and dad must never hear anything about this, Paul! They mustn't! At least they are far enough away in Australia and will be for a couple of months yet.'

'They won't.'

'And Annette? What if she hears?'

'Let's hope she doesn't.'

And with that she had to be satisfied, but she still found it disturbing. It was as though she no longer existed; had lost her identity. And then she remembered someone else; the journalist Paul had mentioned. She would have been told there had been no boating accident; wouldn't she?

'Paul?'

'Yes.'

'You said your paper would be sending someone out to Malta.'

'Julia. Yes, that's right. Robert said she was booked on a flight on Sunday evening. Why do you ask?'

'Doesn't she know you came up here because of me?'

'Ah,' he said quickly, 'I see what you're thinking. No, she has no idea. Once again my intrepid and single-minded editor has decided to keep that under wraps. Julia's brief will be to find out as much as she can about Caroline's death, undercover of trying to suss out anything she can on Ben Standish. She's got all the background to that business, photographs; the lot.'

'You say photographs. Was there more than Ben involved?'

'Yes, there was,' Paul said, 'when we all came back from France I read up on the story and you're right there was another man involved, but none of Ben's friends we met there resembled him. Most of them, if you remember, were Italian.'

'He would have been English; this other man, I mean?'

'Oh, yes, like Standish, a Londoner.'

'What did he look like?'

'In a word, Jenny: nondescript, nothing like Standish. He was much shorter, quite stocky, in fact; light brown hair, pale blue eyes, hardly memorable. You're looking very thoughtful.' he added, looking at her, his head on one side, a quizzical smile on his lips.

'I could be totally wrong, of course, but it would seem Ben has someone in Malta he trusts and he could be English, although I wouldn't exactly describe the person I'm thinking of as nondescript.

'You mean this Gerald Smith?'

'Yes.' she nodded, trying to work out whether it could be possible. She had always thought Gerald was strange; Caroline had thought the same. They had come to the conclusion he must have had cosmetic surgery at one time. Perhaps they had been right. There had to be a ruthless streak in him and now every time she thought about Ben, that word would keep cropping up; ruthless.

'How long have you known him, Gerald Smith, I mean?'

'Almost a year; that was when Caroline and I first joined the theatre; he was already working there, but I have no idea how long he's been in Malta. A number of years I think.'

'Well, if he is the same person, Julia will be bound to see him when she goes to the theatre, as of course she will. That, I imagine, will be her starting point. Even if he does look different now, there could be other pointers. Like all good investigative journalists, Jenny,' he added, 'she is tenacious.'

'Like a terrier?' she smiled for the first time that morning.

'Like a terrier.' he returned her smile.

*

Jenny changed into white cotton trousers and a yellow and white striped tee-shirt and brushing her hair back from her forehead, she was ready. For the next few hours at least she decided she would put the horrors of what she had learned to the back of her mind, otherwise she would go mad! She simply had to get out; away from the village, which was beginning to feel claustrophobic and she couldn't wait until Monday, but wishing now they had decided to leave before then.

She left the keys to the hire car with Mrs Robertson telling her someone would be along during the morning to collect it and having asked her whether there was anything she wanted them to get for the evening meal, they left to drive along the coast road in the direction of Montrose and as Paul had promised, to stop at the first most likely restaurant they saw.

He reversed the car round to the front of the house and pulled out and on to the incline down towards the village. A lovely June morning, again the smell of honeysuckle hung in the air and Jenny wished things could have been different. If this could have been an ordinary summer's day with no lurking sinister shadows and not knowing what was going to happen next. Lighten up, Jenny, she thought to herself; enjoy the moment. How many times had she said this to Annette; her all-too-serious sister? Now, she sighed, the boot is very firmly on the other foot.

'Oh, no!'

'What's the matter?'

'The Brakes, Jenny! They've gone!'

'No!'

'I can't stop, my darling. Just pray there is nothing coming. I'll have to keep going,' he went on, pumping ineffectually on the brake pedal, 'cover your face! Now! I'm going to steer the best I can towards the hedge. Hold on, Jenny! Hold on!'

Chapter Nineteen
MALTA

'Well, Gerald, from what you've been saying it would seem we have a fall guy and that certainly wasn't in our plans.'

'Grech?'

'Who else? The man's a fool; lying to the police. Tut, tut, tut, he should have known better. Calls himself a businessman!'

'You're a cynical bastard, Lawrence.'

'It's called survival,' he reminded him, 'and I am, you must admit, a past master at that. Avoid, if you can, the truth, admit nothing, but whatever you do, don't put your head in the proverbial noose.'

'You're right, of course. I couldn't have put it more succinctly myself.'

'Of course I'm right.'

'I reckon it's kept us both out of trouble so far.'

'True, but we shouldn't get complacent, Gerald. Time enough for that when we finally get rid of – of these insurgents.'

'One way of describing them.'

They were in the lounge bar in the casino: Sunday night, one of the busiest times of the week. Sylvanna had insisted on coming with him and he'd had to go along with her, but it didn't give him much of an opportunity to have this talk with Gerald. At the best of times, his fiancée was demanding, excessively possessive, wanting his whole attention and was even, ridiculous although it was to him, jealous of his friendship with someone he had known for years. Not that she was aware of that, naturally. She knew next to nothing about his past, merely what he had selected and chosen to tell her. Sylvanna only saw what was on the surface: the way he dressed, designer labels; his confidence and the apparent ease, at least to her, he spent his money. She knew he owned a financial consultancy business on the island and that appeared to be enough for her. She had never once asked what he had done before he came to Malta or even where he had lived. She was, in fact, totally incurious for which he was profoundly grateful. It meant he needed only to keep his fabrications to the bare minimum. Marrying Sylvanna, he had decided, practically from the first moment he had been introduced to her, would be the icing on his cake! Not only was she beautiful, giving him a fillip to be seen out in public with her, but once they were married it would give him automatic acceptance and inclusion into one of the island's most prestigious families. There was nothing, absolutely nothing going to stop him now. And Gerald must realise this; he had to. Lately, he had begun to worry him. He was losing his edge; that all-consuming desire to get out as much as he could from life, regardless of the risks.

'I thought Sylvanna would be with you tonight?' Gerald asked him.

'She is; she's in the rest room, freshening up,' he said, 'so, we haven't got a great deal of time and there are a number of crucial things we have to discuss. Events, Gerald, are moving just a trifle too quickly for my liking.'

'Well, I don't think we need concern ourselves too much about Caroline Johnson's demise, do we?'

'I hope not, but more to the point, there's still Jenny Graham.'

'Ah, Jenny. Yes, she does seem to have an extraordinary knack of being able to extricate herself from dangerous situations.'

'Quite.' Lawrence said, 'And now, another botch-up. Alan could have done a more thorough job. He obviously loosened those nuts and bolts to the brake cables far too much. Saved by a hedge! I ask you! We could have got rid of the pair of them, Gerald. Just like that!' he added, snapping his fingers.

'So, where is Alan now?'

'Oh, he's still over there; at least for the time being, hanging around aimlessly in that back of beyond place, but,' he went on, 'I think it might be best if he didn't stay there for much longer. It's a small village, Gerald, and people may just decide to get curious. There was also that somewhat impulsive action of his the other evening.'

'What was that?'

'I didn't tell you?'

'I don't think so.'

'He was completely out of order and acting without any instructions from me. There was this woman in the hotel restaurant. She was talking to Jenny Graham and he saw Jenny write something on a piece of paper and hand it to her. And then the stupid fool followed her when she left the hotel and would you believe knocked her down and snatched her bag! Hardly the sort of paranoid behaviour I would have expected from him.'

'And what was written on it, then?'

'Jenny Graham's signature, that was all. We seem to have forgotten she's an actress and returning to her old haunts up in Scotland there are apparently a number of people who know her and what, I suppose, would be more natural than to ask for her autograph.'

'I see.'

'Do you, Gerald? I'm glad about that!'

'What about the fourth guy?'

'What fourth guy?'

'James. You told me he was on holiday with them in France.'

'Oh, him. Yes.'

'Well,' Gerald persisted, 'not without small risk to myself I managed to go through Jenny's things and I told you about the letter she had started to write to him.'

'I hadn't forgotten.'

'Do you think we need to concern ourselves about him?'

'Probably not. We've no proof she actually did write to her old boyfriend. She may have done, I suppose.'

'Well,' Gerald asked, 'aren't you going to find out?'

'I honestly don't think we have to worry about him,' Lawrence said, 'I've already made enquiries and from what I've been able to find out I am fairly certain he doesn't pose any threat to us. I know you weren't in France back then, Gerald, but after the four of them left and returned to London, it was Paul Watson who was interested in what had happened to me, not James. Paul was the one who got his paper to send one of their journalists out to the Côte d'Azur and, as you well know, came up with zilch. No,' he added, 'we don't need to concern ourselves with James. He is, I understand, firmly established in his family's accountancy business in the city, also he's married with a couple of kids and they spend their summers at the same villa in Villefranche. I would imagine the last thing he would want was to resurrect something which would bring him no kudos or, if it comes to that, any notoriety, quite the reverse I would say.'

'And you think Paul Watson does?'

'Oh, yes, there's no doubt about that. The man works for one of London's largest newspaper chains; he's a journalist, Gerald, and you know what they're like. Once they get the faintest whiff of, not just a story, but a sensational scoop, they never let go. They are like bloodhounds and in our particular case, let us hope he never gets to smell blood!'

'If you want my opinion,' Gerald said slowly, deliberately emphasising each word, 'things are getting a little too hot!'

'What precisely do you mean by that? You're not thinking of quitting, are you?'

'I might, Lawrence. As you know, I haven't got a great deal to lose by making a speedy exit.'

'While I, as you damned well know, have. There is no way, Gerald, no way, I repeat, that I am going to cut and run. I'm here until the bitter end. I have far too bloody much to lose.'

'There's nothing stopping me, though.'

'Isn't there? That is where you are wrong. Quite wrong, Gerald. We are both in this together and have been since day one and that is something you should not forget!'

Perhaps fortuitously at that moment Sylvanna came back, curtailing anything further which might have been said. Curbing his impatience and wanting Gerald to see reason, he smiled at her, reaching out and putting an around her shoulders.

'Hello, beautiful,' he said, kissing her, 'would you like another drink before I take you home?'

'If you like.' Sylvanna answered.

'What about you, Gerald,' he asked him, 'are you going to join us?'

*

At precisely the same moment that Lawrence Stanton ordered another round of drinks, Julia Warburton's plane from Heathrow touched down at Luqa. Robert had already booked her into the Preluna Hotel, explaining it was best situated; being halfway between the centre of Sliema and Balluta Bay.

Her travel bag was the first piece of luggage to appear on the carousel; going through customs was trouble-free, not that she had anything to declare and within minutes she was in her taxi and on the way to the hotel.

Too late for a meal, besides she had already snacked on the flight over, but not too late for a drink and after booking in she walked through to the bar. Quaintly, or so she thought, a guitarist was playing a selection of sixties music, but it didn't matter; the subdued atmosphere suited her mood. She ordered a whisky and took it over to a free table. It was time to touch base with Robert. He had promised to have some further data for her by the time she arrived and knowing she wouldn't be disappointed, she switched on her laptop and plugged in her mobile phone. Taking a long and appreciative sip of her drink, she watched the screen come to life.

The text came first; no more than half a dozen lines, followed by a photograph of Ben Standish: an artist's impression, using the original photograph of him and superimposed by an image of how he could look now. The dark hair with streaks of grey; the eyes more deep-set; the cheeks gaunt with faint lines running towards the mouth, somewhat thinner than it had been fourteen, fifteen years earlier. It was good she thought and should help. Perhaps the only drawback was that he had never looked English and especially if he was now living here, in the Mediterranean, there would, she was sure, be many look-alikes, but it was better than nothing. She would print it out later. "Well, here you are, Julia," Robert had written, "I think it could prove to be a pretty good likeness. I suggest you start with contacting Jenny Graham, using your cover of writing up on Caroline's death and then take it from there. Good luck and keep in touch. Robert."

After hiring a car from the Hertz desk the following morning, Julia followed the coast road towards Balluta Bay, manipulating between one of the island's buses and an impatiently driven truck, the latter heading rapidly in the same direction. She already had Jenny Graham's address from the letter she had sent to her old boyfriend, perhaps this assignment might prove easier to crack than she had first reckoned. It would be great if she, Julia Warburton, could nail down the elusive Ben Standish where other journalists over the years had failed. These were the thoughts which were coursing through her brain as she drew closer to Balluta, taking the sweep round the bay towards the villa. Owner of the property as she had memorised from her notes: David Grech, forty-one years of age; in partnership with his sister, Marianne, of a fast-growing property investment company; born and brought up in Malta; both parents deceased. The background was faultless, their research department was thorough she acknowledged, finally pulling up in front of David Grech's villa.

The short grey-haired woman wearing an old-fashioned wrap-around apron who answered the door would either be the maid or the housekeeper Julia decided, and after making the briefest of introductions asked if she could see Jenny. Nothing like coming straight to the point; this had always been her way. A man's voice in the room behind them called out, loud, imperious and Julia waited, guessing David Grech was about to make his appearance and she was right. Rudely, he pushed the woman to one side, until he was standing directly in front of her.

'I'm afraid you've had a wasted journey,' he said sharply, the dark-brown eyes looking at her closely, 'Jenny doesn't live here anymore.'

'Oh, really,' it wasn't often Julia was stuck for words, but his manner, if not actually forbidding, was unnerving, 'can you tell me where I can find her. I'm from London.' she added, not thinking for one minute that would make a great deal of difference to him.

'I have no idea where Jenny is,' he replied, 'and if you'll excuse me I'm already late for an important meeting.'

And, without giving her the chance to say anything further, he had stepped out on to the drive and with an impatient tug opened the door of his car; the latest Porsche model, she noticed, and without a backward glance, had driven off down the drive, accelerating as soon as he reached the road. Julia stood where she was for a moment not only bemused by his behaviour, but her journalistic senses well to the fore, she suspected there was more to his hostility. Shrugging, she turned away and walked slowly back to her car when the woman came running down the steps towards her, her cheeks flushed with the effort.

'You have to excuse Mr Grech,' were her first words as she caught up with Julia, 'he's not himself these days. He probably didn't like to tell you about Jenny.'

'He certainly wasn't very forthcoming.'

'No and I don't blame him. He has had a lot to put up with since she disappeared.'

'Disappeared?'

'Yes, well it does seem like that,' she said, 'at first everyone thought she had drowned in a boating accident on the morning after the dreadful storm we had, but now she was actually seen at the theatre around the time the police believed she had taken Mr Grech's boat out.'

'And hadn't she?' Julia asked, trying to fathom out what she was hearing. It was like listening to a story from the end, hoping the woman would get to the beginning eventually and then she may get the whole picture. She was in no hurry and the woman appeared more than willing to talk about Jenny and what may or may not have happened to her.

'No, you see,' she continued, her cheeks becoming more pink by the second in her eagerness to impart what knowledge she had, 'a man on the beach in Saint Paul's Bay – that's where Mr Grech keeps his boat – noticed that the boat-shed door was open and the boat wasn't inside. And this was around eight-thirty and –' pausing to catch her breath and Julia waited patiently for her to continue, 'and, Jenny arrived at the theatre at that time, so, you see, she couldn't have been out in the boat.'

'So,' Julia said slowly, 'the police have had to re-think?'

'Oh, yes, they had already reached their verdict. Death by misadventure.' she finished, obviously repeating what she had heard.

'When was this storm?'

'A week ago last Thursday,' the woman told her quickly, 'Mr Grech held his usual weekly dinner party that evening. His sister and her husband were here, also Mrs Refalo; she lives in the villa next door,' she paused once more. The woman was unstoppable, Julia couldn't believe her luck, never expecting to hear as much as this, 'and her friend Mr Edward Coppini; he was Mr Grech's tutor at university.' she added.

'None of Jenny's friends from the theatre then?' Julia asked her.

'Well, Mrs Refalo is the New Theatre's patron; she and Jenny were very friendly, but you mentioning Jenny's friends has reminded me. She did receive a telephone call that evening; they had just finished their meal, in fact. I answered it and I think it was someone from the theatre; they often did phone her and it didn't matter how late.'

'And,' Julia managed to put in, feeling a frisson of anticipation, of sensing that she was about to learn something important, 'did the caller say who she was?'

'No,' she was quick to answer, 'and it was a man, not one of her girl friends.'

'And he didn't give you his name?'

'No,' she gave a short spontaneous laugh, 'They never do! They just assume I will know who they are, but' she added slowly, 'I did hear, mind you I wasn't listening, I would never do that, but I heard her call him Ben.'

'Ben.' Julia repeated, the tingle now more pronounced, 'and is he one of the actors?'

'I don't know,' she answered, 'he could be. There are quite a few of them and of course, apart from some of Jenny's closest friends, like Caroline and Evelyn for instance, I don't know the names of any of the others.'

'Caroline?' Julia asked, 'Do you mean Caroline Johnson?'

'Yes,' immediately the dark eyes filled with tears, 'poor young woman. So very tragic.'

'I know,' Julia agreed, 'her death was in the papers in the UK, it must have been a dreadful shock to you all.'

'We couldn't believe it, still can't. That sort of thing should never happen on this island. That is what is so shocking and on top of Jenny's disappearance as well. Terrible.'

Julia drove back to Sliema with what she had heard ringing in her ears. Could Jenny Graham be dead? Caroline Johnson was; there was no disputing that. My God, she thought, what a quagmire and there must be a connection with this Standish character. She found the theatre after a couple of wrong turnings and then, by accident, she was suddenly facing the building as she turned at last into Manwel Street.

The foyer was deserted and she made her way up the stairs; her footsteps making no noise on the thick carpeting. There has certainly been no cost spared she thought as she reached the first floor, having still not met anyone and passing double doors which she assumed would lead to the auditorium. She continued up the stairs and hearing voices at the end of the corridor, walked towards them. Here, she discovered was the rehearsal room, or more accurately as the notice outside the half-open door explained, the Green Room.

This was Julia's first experience of seeing a play in the making and her immediate impression was how very disjointed everything appeared. No sooner had one of the actors begun to say their lines, the man striding up and down; a tall imposing figure in jeans and a dark blue polo sweater, would without appearing, at least from where she was standing inside the doorway, to utter a word, they would come to an abrupt halt. A girl, sitting at the front; a clipboard balancing on her knees, had noticed her, but was too pre-occupied to break off from writing her notes to come over and ask if she needed any assistance. This suited her well enough; the fewer fabrications she had to invent the better, but looking at the people watching and listening to everything going on, this was obviously not the right moment. What she needed was a one-to-one approach and she wasn't going to find it here; there was far too much activity. Julia noticed a young woman sitting a couple of rows back from the others and the man on the seat next to her; stocky, square-faced with a shock of spiky hair resembling a rather ugly blond porcupine. Also, he kept looking over in her direction, the expressionless eyes giving her the distinct impression of peering straight through her, although she had the unpleasant feeling he had noted and catalogued everything about her. It was time to leave she decided; she didn't like the look of him and it was obvious she was wasting her time here; at least on this visit.

Going back downstairs she saw the double doors were now open and pushing aside the heavy velvet curtains she went into the auditorium.

Curtains had been drawn across the stage, presumably in readiness for the evening's performance. She walked down the length of one of the aisles until she came to a narrow door at the side of the stage which was slightly ajar and pushed it open; backstage, where everything was happening. Two girls were arranging in neat, chronological order an assortment of props on a long trestle table: a bright red telephone; a goldfish bowl complete with what looked like real live goldfish swimming aimlessly round and round in the bowl; a chess board, the black and white pieces waiting to be placed in their correct positions; a silver cake stand; a matching set of china cups and saucers and incongruously, a wooden monkey on a stick; something she hadn't seen since she was a child. A woman was ironing with smooth and practiced movements along the length of a pleated silk skirt and glanced up briefly.

'Are you looking for someone in particular?' she asked, before returning to her task.

'Well, yes,' Julia said slowly, 'I was actually, a friend of mine; he's an actor and told me he was coming to Malta and I just wondered if he was working here.'

'Yes, dear,' the woman prompted, without taking her eyes away from her ironing, skilfully moving the skirt around on the board, 'and what is his name?'

'Ben.'

'Ben?' she frowned, this time looking up at her, 'Oh, no, we don't have anyone of that name here? And,' she added, 'I would know. I know them all, you see.'

So that was that, Julia thought, and exactly what she expected to hear. Excusing herself, she left and went back into the auditorium. What now, she wondered. There was probably no point in continuing to hang around, but on the other hand, the inquisitive side of her nature and the one which had gained her the reputation of being tenacious, wanted to stay. Thoughtfully, she retraced her steps down to the ground floor.

Outside, on the top step, a young man was leaning against the brickwork, having just lit a cigarette. He would do, she decided.

'Excuse me,' she said, 'but do you work here?'

'Yes,' he nodded, flicking ash down on to the car park.

'I'm a writer,' Julia explained, 'and I'm doing an article on new theatres in Europe; how they evolved, together with the history of the buildings, like this one,' she added.

'Well,' he gave her an engaging smile, 'there's certainly a load of history attached to this old place, but I'm really not the best person to give you much information. You should talk to Moira. She would be able to tell you all you want to know.'

'Moira?'

'Sorry,' he said quickly, 'Moira Refalo. She's our patron.' he added, pride in his voice, 'she was once a very famous actress, you know; in London's West End.'

'Was she? I don't believe I remember the name.'

'Well you wouldn't; she was Moira Henderson then and it was quite a while ago. It must have been at least twenty years since she made her home here, in Malta.'

'She sounds the right person for me to approach.'

'Oh, she is.'

'Is she likely to come to the theatre today, do you think?'

'Well, not this morning,' he began, his expression becoming serious, 'she's attending Caroline's inquest.'

'Do you mean Caroline Johnson?'

'You've heard then?'

'Yes, the news has been in all the papers in England; a terrible business.'

'I know,' he agreed, 'it's almost as if there is a jinx surrounding the theatre. Quite dreadful in fact —'

'Peter!' a voice behind them made him jump and immediately he stubbed out his cigarette, 'You're wanted!'

It was the same man Julia had seen in the Green Room. He was striding towards them, but this time Peter, after a hurried goodbye, adding that he hoped he had been some help to her research, had gone back inside.

'And what sort of research are you involved in?' No introduction, no pleasantries either, but then she rather thought he would be like this and it did not faze her one bit. Julia was well accustomed to antagonism; it was part and parcel of her profession. Nobody really, if they were honest, unless they were one themselves, liked a journalist. The very name had been antipathy to more people than she cared to remember, so she was used to it.

'I'm writing an article about theatres in Europe.'

'Malta is in the Mediterranean.'

'I know, but surely as you are now in the EEC you can describe yourselves, technically at least, as being Europeans.' she parried. He didn't like that.

'Our wardrobe mistress told me you were looking for a friend of yours.'

'Yes, I was,' be careful she told herself, now, Julia, you are entering what could be muddied waters, 'but she told me he wasn't working here. Perhaps he hasn't reached Malta yet.'

'Perhaps not,' and she didn't like the way those cold, colourless eyes stared at her, this time looking at her directly, 'You told her he's called Ben.'

'That's right.'

'Ben, what?' and here was where she had to think rapidly; should she say Standish or not?

'Ben Morrison,' she answered, saying the first name which came into her head, 'we were at university together, but we never kept in touch all that much.' she elaborated.

Whether he believed her or not, she didn't wait to find out. She had said enough and now it really was time to leave. There was something unpleasant about him which, apart from his unattractiveness, made her uneasy. There was also something else she thought as she drove away from the theatre and down to the bottom of Manwel Street, which didn't quite ring true. Difficult to pin-point; it was if he was playing a part. And she didn't mean as an actor; having learned his lines appearing on stage long enough to deliver them before the curtain fell and he could return to his normal self. It was much more; he just was not real.

It was after two when Julia once again drove back to Balluta Bay, past David Grech's villa and stopping outside the one next door. The woman standing on the balcony must be Moira Henderson; Moira Henderson, the actress and now Moira Refalo, the New Theatre's patron. Getting out of the car and looking up at her, Julia was struck by a remarkable resemblance to old photographs she had seen of Isadora Duncan, except perhaps for her hair which may at one time have been a similar shade of auburn, but was now grey, tied loosely back from her face and although no longer young, still retained a youthful eagerness, especially in the eyes; a cornflower blue.

'Hello,' Julia called out, 'I hope I haven't arrived at a bad time, but I've come from the New Theatre and I really would like to talk to you.'

'Hello, there, not at all; do come in; the door is open.'

Julia climbed up the steps to the front door and as she did so tried to make up her mind what her best approach should be. She had already used the one of trying to see Jenny Graham and didn't want to elaborate on that unless she could help it, and of writing an article on new theatres; better not invent a third she decided. In the short time she had been on the island she had quickly come to the conclusion that it was probably very much a village and felt certain that around Sliema and Balluta, most people would know each other and any stranger arriving in their midst would become an instant talking point.

'My name is Julia Warburton,' Julia introduced herself as she entered one of the most stunning and interesting rooms she ever remembered being in before: a rich kaleidoscope of colour which magically blended together in complete harmony and at the same time created a dreamlike impression of another world. The paintings immediately caught and held her attention. There were three of them and all oils. In two, the blue, mauve, yellow and green of the Caribbean had been captured: one at sunset; the sky, multi-coloured streaks radiating from the golden semicircle of the sun as it descended into the abyss of the horizon and in the foreground, the darkening palm trees casting long irregular shadows along the water's edge and in the other, this time the sun directly overhead; the sea, a glittering, shimmering expanse of variegating shades of blue; azure, turquoise, aquamarine and navy, and in the distance the ring-shaped oval of an atoll. Neither of them needed people; they were complete in themselves. The third painting was quite different in both subject and country; a young African boy, his bare legs stained dark red by the laterite dust, seated cross-legged and alone at the side of the road; the verdant greens of the bush behind him dark and impenetrable.

'How lovely they are,' Julia exclaimed, reluctantly dragging her eyes away from the paintings, 'and your ornaments also, Mrs Refalo, from all over the world; you must have done a great deal of travelling?'

'Well, yes,' she smiled, the blue eyes sparkling, 'all of this,' she went on with an elegant wave of her arm, 'was after I stopped acting and came out to Malta. My late husband loved to travel and when he retired, we spent more time away than at home.'

'It's truly impressive.' Julia said, wishing she could have the opportunity to look at everything more closely, but it wasn't possible; she was here for a purpose and that had to come first.

'I've just made some fresh coffee,' Moira said, 'would you like some? And, do make yourself comfortable.'

'Thank you,' Julia accepted, sitting down on one of the leather sofas and placing her bag on the floor beside her.

'You said you had been to the theatre?' Moira Refalo remarked, coming back into the lounge carrying a tray with a silver coffee jug and china cups finely engraved with an eastern scroll.

'Yes, that's right.' watching as she poured out the coffee, waiting until she had filled both cups; all to give her time before replying and then explaining about the article she was writing. Moira Refalo seemed to accept her appearance without question but then why shouldn't she? She probably hadn't had a chance to find out about her visit to David Grech's villa. 'I spoke to a young man there; Peter he's called and he told me you would be the best person to talk to.'

'Peter;' she said, 'he's one of our theatre's budding actors. Modest, too; an admirable quality.'

'He did mention you would be at the inquest this morning,' Julia began tentatively, 'so I hope you don't mind this intrusion, but I did want to speak to you.'

'I don't mind at all, Miss Warburton –'

' – Julia, please.'

'Julia,' the smile reappearing, 'it was stressful, I can't deny it, but I really had no alternative; I had to attend.'

'I understand.'

'Do you?'

For the first time she read something else in her expression, the slight change in her tone of voice. Could she know her real reason for being in Malta, Julia wondered.

'Well, yes,' Julia went on, 'I'd heard about Caroline Johnson's death before I left England and –'

'- you're a journalist, Julia, aren't you?' she interrupted.

The direct question stopped her; immediately. How stupid of her to underestimate this woman. Moira Refalo, those amazing eyes looking at her questioningly as she waited.

'I am, yes,' Julia said at last with a sigh. 'Is it so obvious?'

'I wouldn't say obvious,' she answered, taking a sip of her coffee, 'but you see David was also at the inquest and he told me a young woman had called at his villa earlier today asking for Jenny.'

'I see.'

'And naturally,' she continued, 'I'm putting two and two together.'

'I had no idea Jenny was missing until I spoke to Mr Grech's housekeeper.'

'Didn't you?'

'No, I didn't. Alright, I wasn't being truthful about the article I told them at the theatre I was planning to write, but I am here on the island primarily to find out as much as I can about Caroline's death, get some background to her life here.'

'You say primarily,' she emphasised slowly, 'does this mean you are in Malta for another reason?'

'I'm sorry –'

'Julia,' she interrupted her for the second time, 'I think you know what I mean, what I would like to know is whether you're going to enlighten me.'

'I'm sorry, Moira,' Julia said, 'I really am not at liberty to say anything about that, at least at the present time.'

'I believe it has something to do with Jenny. Alright, Julia, goodness knows, I should understand. During my career, I met a number of people in the same profession as yours and I do realise there are times when you have to be – discreet.'

'Thank you.'

'Don't mention it,' she said, taking the empty cup from her, 'more coffee?'

What a remarkable woman she is Julia thought. There was an aura about her, as though very little would disturb her, or shock her either if it came to that. Moira Refalo possessed an enviable serenity and Julia felt quite humbled by it. She belonged to a totally different world, one for her in which time was at a premium, deadlines had to be met and it didn't matter how many people were upset on the way to reach your particular goal.

'The inquest, Moira,' Julia said, once both their cups had been replenished, 'that is, if you don't mind talking about it, but what was the final verdict?'

'They didn't take long to reach the verdict,' Moira answered quietly, closing her eyes for a moment, as though back in the coroner's court and going over everything again in her mind, 'murder by person or persons unknown, the drug which had been given to her had been in, of all things, a glass of red wine. Would you believe it?'

As Julia could very easily believe it, she chose to remain silent. Also, this way, she had learned often produced more and with the woman sitting opposite, her cup half-raised to her lips, she didn't think she would be any different.

'What was rather telling though, as well as being rather odd, was that there was no sign in the apartment of any bottles of wine, empty or otherwise.'

'And had she drunk the wine while she was in there?'

'Oh, yes, they could tell almost the exact time and Caroline's neighbour spoke to her when she returned to the apartment that evening and she says she didn't hear her go out again. Caroline had told her apparently that she was going to have an early night.'

'Quite conclusive, then?'

'Yes, also her front door hadn't been locked; the key was still on the inside of the door when she was found the following day.'

'What about Caroline's parents?'

'I've spoken to them both and naturally they were utterly distraught. Caroline had in fact only the day before returned from England and had spent time with them.'

'Didn't she have a boyfriend?'

'No-one regular. Caroline was a very independent young woman, you understand. Oh, there had been boyfriends; of course, but nobody serious. I think she was waiting for Mr Right to come along.' she finished, looking across at Julia, the beautiful eyes filling with tears.

'I'm sorry; I'm causing you further distress.' Julia said, putting a hand on her slim wrist, 'I didn't mean to do that. Believe me.'

'I know that, dear. It has all been so dreadful and,' she added sighing heavily, 'continues to be.'

'What do you think yourself, Moira,' Julia asked her, 'Do you think there is a connection between what has happened to Caroline and to Jenny disappearing? What are people saying?'

'Of course rumours are plentiful, as no doubt you can imagine, on such a small island. As for myself, well, I honestly don't know what to think, but then, I am rather an ostrich, Julia. I don't want to think the worse.'

'That's only natural; I can understand. I learned this morning,' Julia went on, moving on from Caroline's murder, 'it's been proved Jenny didn't take the boat out on the water that morning.'

'It would seem not, but the original verdict of a boating accident has not been absolutely ruled out, at least not by the police. It's the old problem, I'm afraid; lack of evidence. Not good either way; Jenny seems to have disappeared into thin air. Her sister never did believe that verdict, you know?'

'I think I would have felt the same.' Julia sympathised.

'She came out to the island; in fact, she's still here. Poor Annette, I know she'll never give up trying to find Jenny.'

'I don't suppose there is a great deal she will be able to do;' Julia said, 'she'll have to leave it to the authorities.'

'You're right, of course. Anyway,' Moira said making a conscious effort to look more cheerful, 'we're all trying to look on the positive side.'

'It can't be easy for her being here and trying to piece things together. Is she staying next door?'

'Oh, no, David did invite her, but she's at the Crowne Plaza in Sliema. She was probably right, she's more independent there and besides, until she arrived on the island she had never met David before.'

'Probably a wise decision,' Julia said and meaning it, 'by the way, I did meet a man at the theatre who struck me as somewhat unwelcoming. Most authoritative; I felt quite sorry for Peter, the way he spoke to him, I mean.'

'Oh,' she laughed, her eyes sparkling again, 'I know who you mean. Did he have short blond hair, and looked as if he'd been a bit heavy-handed with the gel?'

'Yes,' Julia smiled, 'there can't be two of them like him!'

'No,' she continued to chuckle, making her seem considerably younger, 'that would have been Gerald Smith. Mind you, most of the younger actors are in great awe of him and always jump to his commands, but I'm assured by Adam; he's the theatre's director, that Gerald is an excellent stage manager.'

It had taken one hour and two cups of coffee, but Julia had got what she wanted, even more than she had expected. Jenny Graham's sister was actually in Malta and she knew where she should be able to find her. It was always possible Jenny may have confided in her and that could have contributed to her refusal to believe her sister had drowned. Without appearing to make it obvious she wanted to get away, Julia, after remarking and commenting on the collection of framed photographs on the wall above the brick fireplace, many of them autographed, she took her leave. Finally, driving away from the villa she looked back. Moira, a slight slim figure in pale lilac was on the balcony, tendrils of curls escaping from their clasp and a sad little smile on her face as she waved to her.

So, Julia, what have you got so far?' Robert's gravelly voice crackled loudly in her ears later that evening, shortly after she'd spoken to Annette Graham and Andy Henderson.

'I haven't had time to compile my report in any detail yet,' Julia answered, casting her eyes quickly down the list she had been drawing up throughout the day, 'but I'll give you what I've got.'

'Fire ahead then!'

'The inquest for Caroline Johnson was this morning and, as expected, the verdict was murder. I know, Robert, before you say anything, it was already reported in the press, but it's now official.'

'Yes, go on.'

'Her close friend, Jenny Graham is missing – this happened a couple of weeks ago, a week past Friday in fact. At first the police were coming up with a verdict of accidental death, a boating accident, but now they have evidence she didn't take the boat out that morning.'

'Yes?'

'You don't sound surprised.'

'I'm not.'

'What is this, Robert,' she asked, 'have you known about this all the time? Have I been sent out here blind?'

'Hold your horses, Julia,' making as much of an attempt as he could to speak soothingly, 'it was best you didn't know. This way, you would have been more objective, possibly find out more.'

'Okay, if you say so.'

'What about Standish? Any luck there?'

'A little,' she said, 'David Grech, Jenny's boyfriend, but I expect you know about him already,' she added, unable to keep the cynicism from her voice, 'well, when I called at his place this morning all he told me was that Jenny didn't live there anymore. His manner was, to say the least, non-committal, if not downright rude. There's something up with him, Robert, I'm fairly sure of it.'

'Could be.'

'Anyway,' Julia went on, 'his housekeeper was much more forthcoming and she told me Jenny took a call from a man on the Thursday evening and that she called him Ben.'

'Ah.'

'Exactly. It sounds promising, doesn't it?'

'Anything else?'

'Not a great deal, but there is this weird looking guy working at the theatre. I didn't like the look of him; also I don't think he believed my cover story. I'm writing an article on theatres in Europe, by the way,' she went on, 'but before I spoke to him, I'd asked their wardrobe mistress whether they had an actor there called Ben. Not unsurprisingly, she said they didn't, but she did take it upon herself to inform this guy. Or, more to the point,' Julia stressed, 'having already spotted me he'd no doubt seen me going backstage and decided to have a wander round and ask a few questions. The bottom line is, Robert,' Julia continued, 'he appeared more than a little interested, concerned I should say, about my fictitious friend. Since then, I've had time to think and –'

'– What?'

'Well, he could be the other guy; you know, the one Ben Standish had been working with on this fraud thing.'

'What's his name?'

'Gerald Smith.'

'An ordinary name.'

'One could say that.'

'We'll try and get him sussed out, Julia. Now,' he went on briskly, 'unless you have anything of *real* monumental importance, I think that will do for tonight.'

'Okay, Robert.' she agreed. There was little point in telling him at this stage of Jenny's sister and meeting her and Andy earlier. Although Annette Graham's reaction to Ben Standish's photograph had been quite noticeable, it could hardly be taken as proof and she was sure would have meant little to Robert, so she decided not to mention it. She would be including it in her report in any case. 'I'll stay on for a couple more days, shall I? See if I can find out anything else.'

'That's fine,' he agreed, 'keep in touch and Julia?'

'Yes.'

'I know I don't need to tell you this, but watch your back. You know the sort of people we could be dealing with.'

Chapter Twenty

'Do you know, David,' Marianne complained, squarely positioning her large frame in front of his desk, a sheaf of papers in her hand, 'I don't believe you have heard one single word I have said.'

'Sorry, Marianne, I'm finding things rather difficult at the moment.'

'Aren't we all!'

'Please, I don't need this. I really do not. You have no idea what I'm going through.'

'All I do know, David, and I shouldn't have to remind you, we have a business to run and for the last couple of weeks, quite frankly, you have not been pulling your weight. It has meant considerably more work landing on my desk and it is time you pulled yourself together.'

'Easier said than done.'

'Nonsense. She's not worth it, you know,' Marianne said, this time moderating her voice and making, he was sure, some attempt, feeble although it was, but the best she was capable of, to show a modicum of sympathy, 'Jenny has gone. Face facts, David. Isn't it time you got on with the rest of your life? Nothing will come from all this moping.'

'Is that what you call it, Marianne; moping?'

'Well, what would you call it then? Frank said -'

'- I don't wish to hear what Frank said. You do not seem to realise that I have had the police, for some reason best known to themselves, constantly on my back and quite frankly it is beginning to get me down.'

'I can't think why? Do you want me to have a word with Inspector Secluna? I've known him for years. He's always struck me as extremely approachable. Perhaps he has no idea of the pressure he's putting on you.'

Heaven forbid she would do such a thing! Marianne may mean well, there was no doubt in his mind that she did and always had, but on this occasion he wished she would just step back and let him try and cope the best way he could which he admitted wasn't all that satisfactory. He knew he was in danger of losing his grip, not only with the business, but with the way he was feeling. He was finding it increasingly difficult to sleep and when he did it was only for short periods, awaking each time to find the room still in darkness and dawn stretching out interminably. He knew he could not go on like this, but as he sat there in the familiar and once work-inducing surroundings of his office overlooking the water towards the bastion walls of Valletta, he was powerless as Marianne had told him, to pull himself together. Besides, he didn't have the energy; he was so overwhelmingly weary.

'I'm worried about you, David,' she continued, her voice jarring, 'you're not sleeping, are you?'

'No.'

'I thought as much; why don't you make an appointment to see the doctor? Perhaps all you need is a tonic.'

The only tonic I need at the moment he thought was to be left alone. In the vain hope she might take the hint, he pulled his desk diary towards him. Three appointments for the afternoon: one with the bank, another with some more potential clients and the third to finalise on the purchase of the much sought after penthouse suite on the new water-front development. This, he supposed, was what he needed – distraction.

'David,' Marianne shifted the papers to her other hand, 'come for dinner tonight. Nothing too elaborate; pizza and red wine. How does that sound?' She was making an effort and in spite of his irritation with her, was touched. However, he was spared an immediate response by the internal telephone ringing.

'Yes, Angelica?' at the same time nodding an acceptance and hoping Marianne would take the hint. He was finding her continual presence, looming over him as she had the habit of doing, especially lately, more than a little off-putting and making it difficult for him to concentrate. 'Put him through.' David said, stifling a sigh. Here we go again he thought.

'Inspector Secluna here.'

'Yes, Inspector.'

'I wonder if you could call in at the station; this morning, if possible.'

'Again, Inspector?'

'There are a number of points I need to have clarified. It shouldn't take up too much of your time, Mr Grech. Shall we say in half an hour?'

It was an order. Not a request. There was a time when they were on first name terms, but now it would seem all that had come to an abrupt end. He, David Grech, was the suspect, Inspector Secluna the interrogator; the accuser, he thought, replacing the receiver and closing the diary. What was the bloody point? It was completely impossible to get on with anymore work that morning. Pouring himself a large tumbler of spring water from the cooler, he picked up his jacket from where he had flung it earlier on the back of one of the visitor's chairs and left the office, hoping he wouldn't see Marianne on his way out of the building.

The desk sergeant escorted him along the corridor; white tiled and clinical, to the inspector's office. Inspector Secluna was waiting for him; one slim paper folder in front of him on his otherwise clear desk. He waited until the door had closed behind the sergeant before rising from his seat, gesturing David to sit down.

'Coffee?'

'No thank you.'

'Right, well then, we'll get down to business. As I said on the phone it shouldn't take too long, but there are certain –' he hesitated for a fraction of a second, which only served to make David feel more apprehensive than he was already. No doubt a professional tactic he decided, '- certain anomalies' he continued, sitting down once more, 'and they require to be clarified.'

'I really don't know what else I can say to help you; nothing that I haven't already told you.'

'That may be, but,' pausing again, looking directly across at him, 'I don't believe that is so.'

'I don't understand.' David replied wearily and wondering which way the conversation, or as he would more correctly describe an inquisition, was heading.

'Allow me to recap, Mr Grech,' he said, leaning back in his chair, the relaxed gesture not fooling David for a moment, unable to rid himself of the notion that the man was playing with him. He was, David was certain, getting some sort of satisfaction out of it all, but immediately dismissed such thoughts as ridiculous. He was a policeman for goodness sake, an Inspector of Police no less, they didn't play games. Did they?

'Let us return to the morning when you reported Miss Graham as missing. Alright?'

'Alright.'

'You have since told us that she did in fact leave your villa the previous night.'

'Yes.'

'Later that morning,' he went on, 'you telephoned the station to tell us you had located Miss Graham's car parked on the street above the boat-sheds in Saint Paul's Bay. This,' opening the file and pointing to a line of print half-way down the sheet of paper, 'was at eleven.'

'I'm not sure of the exact time, but it was probably around then, yes.'

'You now know that she was seen driving into the theatre's car park and going inside at approximately eight-thirty.'

'Yes.' Where the hell was he coming from? This was old ground; probably everyone on the island knew this by now. Jenny had obviously made arrangements to meet someone at the theatre; she had been seen getting into another car, leaving her own there, and afterwards, nothing.

'You told us,' he said, again consulting his notes, 'you had an early meeting. For seven-thirty, I believe.'

'That's right.'

'Ah,' the sound barely audible as he swivelled his chair round, 'this is where we become somewhat confused, Mr Grech. You see,' he abruptly stopped the chair's movement, 'I would suggest you didn't have any meeting that morning; at least not so early.'

'Why do you think that?'

'It is merely a suggestion. Did you have a meeting?'

Of course he bloody didn't! But how the hell did he know this? He had caught him and he knew it!

'Where did you go, Mr Grech, on that Friday morning when you left the villa?'

'I drove around.'

'You drove around? Could you be more specific?'

'I was distraught,' David attempted to explain, realising whatever he said would not have a great deal of impact or credence with the inspector who had, by this time, become a stranger to him, 'Jenny, leaving the way she had, upset me. We'd been together for almost a year and I truly believed we had something going; I guess I just wanted to get out for a while and, as I said, have a drive around the island.'

'And this was before you telephoned the station the first time?'

'Of course.'

'And where did you go? Around the island, you say.'

'Yes, not really all round the island, that wasn't exactly right, but I took the main road out to the coast, to Marsascala, in fact. It was peaceful there and I sat in the car for quite a while and, well, I just thought about Jenny.'

'I see. And did you wonder, worry even, where she may have gone?'

'Yes, naturally. I've already told you I knew nothing about her having a key to Caroline Johnson's apartment, so I phoned the station.'

'You've already told us that, yes. And then what did you do?'

'I went to Saint Paul's Bay.'

'Why?'

'Because,' David hesitated, reluctant to tell him any more than he felt he should know about Jenny and what had, in recent months, become a turbulent relationship, 'Jenny had walked out on me before when we'd had an argument and each time she had gone there and taken the boat out. She told me she found it helped her to unwind. She was a very keen sailor.'

'So I am led to believe. And then you happened to see her car.'

'I don't know whether I happened to see it,' David emphasised, for the first time feeling a wave of anger at the man's tone; cynical and disbelieving, 'but she always parked there so I wasn't all that surprised to see it.'

'And this would have been at what time?'

'I'm not sure, around ten-thirty I suppose. I waited until I got home before phoning the station.'

'And your boat-shed?'

'Once again, I've already told you the boat wasn't in there. Do I have to repeat myself?'

'Now, let us get this straight, Mr Grech,' the inspector continued, ignoring the question which David already realised he was unlikely to answer anyway, 'you drove to Marsascala, sat for a while in your vehicle, decided to report Miss Graham as missing and then went on to Saint Paul's Bay where you discovered her car, also that your boat wasn't in the shed, then you waited until you came back to Balluta before telephoning us. And by that time it was eleven.'

'That sounds about right, yes.'

'Do you have a mobile, Mr Grech?'

'Yes, hasn't everyone?'

'So, why didn't you use it then? I think I would be correct in saying when you made your first call to the station you were on your mobile.'

'That's right.'

'But when you made your second call to us you decided to drive back home to telephone from there.'

'Because,' David sighed, 'I had this faint hope she may have come back.'

'Leaving her car in Saint Paul's Bay?'

'I suppose I wasn't thinking straight.'

'It so happens, Mr Grech,' the inspector said and David did not like the expression on his face; the way his eyes had narrowed, although his body had remained in more or less the same position, 'someone; a resident of Saint Paul's Bay, saw Miss Graham's car arrive that morning.'

Don't tell me another witness? How many more old busybodies would be climbing out of the woodwork he wondered.

'Really?'

'Yes, she was apparently about a hundred yards away from the car, but she was quite positive about the time.'

'Which was?'

'Nine o'clock.'

'And was Jenny driving?' for the first time for days, ever since that awful night, he had a glimmering of hope.

'Oh no, it wasn't Miss Graham,' hope instantly shattered, 'but the description she gave of the driver could conceivably fit you, Mr Grech.'

'What! This is ridiculous!'

'Is it?'

'Of course it is! How could it have been? I was nowhere near there at the time.'

'But can you substantiate where you were?'

'You know damn well I can't. Anyway, Inspector, how can this person,' he emphasised, 'be so certain it was Jenny's car?'

'The lady lives in one of the apartments opposite and was used to seeing Miss Graham leaving her car there.'

'And did this good citizen see where the man, who apparently bears a remarkable likeness to me, went? Presumably he got out of the car once he'd parked it.'

'A good question, Mr Grech,' grudgingly given David thought, but this gave him small comfort, 'but no, as a matter of fact she didn't.'

'Well, it wasn't me.'

'Perhaps not, but that has still to be either proved or disproved. However,' he paused, shifting in his seat, leaning forward and placing both hands palm down on the desk in front of him, 'you may wish at this stage to have your lawyer present.'

'Why should I? I have nothing to hide.'

'We all have something to conceal, Mr Grech. That is human nature after all. But, if during this interview you should change your mind; it is your prerogative to do so.'

'I see no point.'

'Very well,' he said, 'let's move on, shall we?'

Move on? Where was he going to come from next, but instinctively and with a tightness in his chest, David knew. He had for the moment finished talking about Jenny; this was going to be about Caroline Johnson.

'The night Caroline Johnson was murdered,' predictably and on cue the inspector continued, his eyes never leaving David's face, 'you held a dinner party?'

'Yes, that's right.'

'Five guests you told me when we last spoke,' he said slowly, counting off each one of them on his fingers, 'your sister and her husband, Mrs Refalo, Mr Coppini and Miss Annette Graham, Jenny's sister.'

'Correct.'

'They all left your villa; again this is what you've said, at around ten-thirty?'

'I can't be sure of the exact time, but it wasn't all that late.'

'Time enough for you to drive the relatively short distance into Sliema and call at Miss Johnson's apartment.'

'This is outrageous!' now on his feet and impatiently pushing back the hindrance of the chair.

'Sit down, Mr Grech. Please.' It was an order, although he didn't raise his voice, 'Are you still insisting on not calling your lawyer.'

'I am not insisting, Inspector Secluna. I repeat; I see no point. What you are saying, suggesting in fact, is simply not true. After everyone left that night, I poured myself a final drink and then went to bed.'

'You said last Saturday when you called into the station, that you didn't know Caroline Johnson.'

'I didn't. Oh, I knew she was Jenny's friend; I'd seen her once or twice, but that was all.'

'And yet,' the inspector paused for a second, 'can you explain why Caroline Johnson should have telephoned you that night. Before you say anything,' he went on, holding up a hand, 'we have proof that a call was made from her apartment at eleven-forty-five precisely and it was your number.'

Oh God, was there no escaping the pit he had fallen into? The man had him in a corner and there was nothing, absolutely nothing, he could do to get out of it. The knot in his chest tightened and he swallowed twice, trying to control his nerves. This was all so bloody unfair. His mouth felt dry and he wondered if he would ever regain the full power of speech again. A wave of dizziness threatened, making him feel lightheaded, but all he had to do was tell the truth. That was all and then maybe the nightmare, or at least part of the nightmare, would begin to recede.

'She did phone you, didn't she?'

'Yes.' scarcely recognising his own voice, but he had to go on, had to try and explain, prove he was entirely innocent in whatever was going on. 'I thought she was drunk.'

'What made you think that?'

'Because she was slurring her words, that's why. At first I couldn't make out what she was saying.'

'Which was?'

'That — that she thought she had been poisoned, that she — that she was dying.'

'And you did nothing?'

'No.'

'Why not, Mr Grech?'

'I told you, I thought she was drunk! She wasn't making sense.'

'She wouldn't have been, would she? And she *was* dying, wasn't she?'

'I realise that now, but I didn't then.'

'Why didn't you tell us last Saturday about this call? You had ample opportunity. You were aware we were conducting a murder enquiry.'

'I didn't want to get involved.' he said quietly, hardly trusting his voice and at that moment hating himself.

'But you are involved, Mr Grech,' Inspector Secluna said, his lips set in a thin tight line, 'very much so, in fact.'

'I didn't kill her.'

'No, perhaps you didn't, but it would seem we have a long way to go yet to reach the truth.'

'I hardly knew the woman,' David sighed, 'what possible motive could I have had?'

'Ah, motive,' the inspector permitted a grim smile to crease his face, 'they come in many different guises. Now,' he continued, 'this telephone call. What else did she say to you, apart from asking for help, that is?'

'Not much else.' David said slowly, cringing at the open hostility in his expression.

'I'm waiting. You won't be leaving this room until I am reasonably satisfied you have told me everything you know, even if it means taking you into custody.'

'Custody!'

'I did suggest you should perhaps have your lawyer here.'

'I don't need a lawyer.'

'Be that as it may, but did Caroline Johnson say anything else to you? However garbled it may have sounded to you; it could be important and you never know, Mr Grech, it may work in your favour. I'm sure you don't want to spend much longer here this morning.'

'It didn't make sense.'

'Allow me to be the judge of that.'

'She said – I'm trying to remember her exact words, Inspector – but it sounded like: you must tell them Ben Standish is on the island and he was here tonight and -.'

'And –' the inspector prompted.

'I'm trying to remember,' he said irritated by his impatience, 'I think she was finding it difficult to get her words out, but then she said: Jenny was right, David. I was wrong in telling her to let sleeping dogs lie. You must do something. And that was all, Inspector.'

'Ben Standish?'

'Yes, that was what she said.'

'And do you know anyone of that name?'

'No, I don't.'

'You never heard Miss Graham mention a Ben Standish?'

'No. Never.'

'I see,' the inspector said, getting to his feet, 'it is a great pity you didn't tell us all of this before, Mr Grech.'

'Do I take it I am free to leave?'

'Yes,' dismissively now, as though he had lost interest in him being there, 'but we will, I am sure, need to speak to you again.'

Chapter Twenty-one
ENGLAND

As David Grech was leaving Sliema police station, Annette, with Andy standing beside her, was dialling the Saint Angus number. It rang for several minutes and she was about to hang up when she heard the familiar voice of Mrs Robertson.

'It's Annette here, Mrs Robertson.'

'Och, Annette,' the soft lilting accent reaching out and acting as a soothing balm as it always did, especially when she hadn't heard it for a while, 'it's grand to hear from you.'

'How are you, Mrs Robertson?'

'I'm fine, getting old of course.'

'Not you,' Annette smiled to herself. Mrs Robertson had always been old to her, but the strange paradox being she never seemed to get any older, 'Is Jenny there, Mrs Robertson?'

'Och, Annette, she'll be that sorry to have missed you,' she answered, 'she and Paul only left this morning.'

'Paul?'

'Yes, he's from London. He arrived at the weekend. A nice young man; he really enjoyed my home-cooking,' she added, 'probably doesn't get much of that sort of food in England.'

'I've been away,' Annette started to explain, trying to hide her disappointment; Jenny really was becoming more and more elusive, 'Jenny did leave a message on my answering machine,' she went on, 'but she didn't say very much, not even where she was!'

'Well,' Mrs Robertson paused and Annette could picture her; standing by the telephone on its table in the lounge, the windows wide open to the sea and the soft early summer breeze making the curtains billow gently into the room, 'I'm not sure when that would have been. She arrived here a week past Friday and she did try to phone you, but she doesn't like leaving messages on an answering machine, but you know Jenny?'

Yes, I know Jenny, Annette thought. And how! At least she was safe and the relief she felt knowing this was indescribable. Whatever she had been through and whatever had been happening to her in Malta, somehow she had managed to find a refuge. She looked across at Andy, raising her eyes, hoping he could read her expression, her frustration at once again coming up against a brick wall. Goodness knows what he must be thinking.

'I don't suppose Jenny told you where she would be staying in London, Mrs Robertson?'

'No. No, she didn't, but she was a wee bit shaken after the accident and I think she may very well be going to Paul's; he was very protective towards her –'

'– accident?'

'I'm sorry, Annette,' she said quickly, 'I didn't mean to startle you. And really I should not have even mentioned it, but it happened on Saturday morning. They were going for a drive; Paul was going to take her out for lunch and the brakes on his car failed.'

'Oh, no!'

'It's alright, dear. They were lucky,' she continued, 'very lucky, in fact.'

'What happened exactly?'

'Well,' she said, 'Paul realised as soon as they started going down the lane towards the road, it must have been a frightening experience; for both of them, but they made light of it. They hit that high hedge in front of the manse which was really the only thing he could have done and it was indeed a blessing there was no traffic on the road at the time.'

'That's terrible.'

'But, Annette,' she insisted, 'they were both alright. As I've said, Jenny was a bit shaken and the car survived although it did mean they had to delay going back down south until this morning, but all's well that ends well, dear, so you mustn't worry about her. Jenny is fine.'

'Thank goodness for that! Mrs Robertson?'

'Yes dear?'

'Do you happen to know Paul's surname?'

'Of course I do; it's Watson. I'm sure Jenny will phone you at home, Annette. You mustn't worry about her so much.'

If only you knew Annette thought as she finally rang off and promising to keep in touch, even adding that she hoped to manage a few days up there later in the summer. Once all this business is sorted out she promised herself. If it ever was!

'I take it she's flown?' Andy smiled ruefully at her as she replaced the receiver.

'You guessed right.' and told him about the accident.

'Ominous.' was all he said.

'That's what I thought,' Annette agreed, 'Oh, Andy, what is happening? It's obvious she is still in danger, isn't it?'

'I think so. In fact, I'm pretty sure she is.'

'What do you think we should do? Wait until she phones or what?'

'Well,' Andy said slowly, 'we know the paper Paul works for, don't we?'

'Do we?'

'It was on the letter-heading, remember?'

'Of course. Do you know, Andy, I had completely forgotten that. We can give them a ring and try to get his home number. Presumably, Jenny will be with him.'

Finally, and not without considerable persuasion, they agreed to give Annette Paul Watson's telephone number and for the second time that day and with shaking fingers, not knowing what to expect, she dialled. No answer. As before, she let it ring.

'They may not be back yet,' Andy said, gently taking the receiver from her and replacing it. 'We'll try later. Let's go and get something to eat, Annette. It will do you good. Me as well,' he added with a grin, 'I am starving!'

*

'London!' Jenny said as they left the A1 and joined Camden Road, straight down Albany Street, skirting Regent's Park on their left before turning into a side street, 'It seems so strange to be back, Paul. I feel I've been away for years! In fact,' she went on, looking over towards the park, 'I don't know why I stayed away for so long. Come to that, I don't even know why I left in the first place! Itchy feet, I guess.'

'And do you still have them,' he smiled at her, 'itchy feet, I mean?'

'What do you think?'

'I'm asking you, my sweet.'

'I do believe I'm cured, but don't get me wrong, I'm still ambitious, as far as my acting career is concerned. Okay, it would have been great; perfect in fact, to have lived and worked in the sun, but in retrospect, perhaps not. You know what I mean, don't you?'

'I know what you mean.' he said softly, pulling up in front of a red-brick building; two-storey, window boxes below each of the windows and a small neat garden behind the security gates. 'Well,' he said, switching off the engine and taking the key from the ignition, 'here we are.'

'It's nice.' Jenny said immediately, 'I'm sorry, Paul, that is a paltry way to describe it, but I like it and right in the heart of London too. Unique.'

'I suppose it is,' he replied, 'I was lucky to have found it, especially before property prices in this street soared. Come on, Jenny,' he added, 'shall we go in?'

Paul's apartment, on the second floor, was open-plan and ultra-modern with lots of pale pine woodwork and dark green leather upholstery; a bachelor pad, but she decided instantly, welcoming. She did like it; very much, and slipping off her shoes stretched out full-length on one of the sofas. This was sheer bliss; she could stay here forever, cocooned from the rest of the world, with only the distant hum of traffic from the main road. Here, she felt safe. Malta; David; the theatre; Moira, her dear friend, seemed a million miles away. Of course it couldn't last. She was not foolish enough to believe that, but just for the moment while Paul busied himself in the kitchen, the sounds of windows being opened, and crockery, this was all she wanted to hear and she closed her eyes. She must have fallen asleep, although not for long; the aroma of freshly brewed coffee reaching her as she opened her eyes.

'Better?'

'I'm sorry; I didn't mean to do that.'

'You were tired, Jenny. You've been through a lot recently.'

'When I think of what might have happened, Paul,' she said, sitting up and swinging her feet on to the parquet flooring, 'I can't bear it. There could have been a car, a coach, anything, coming along the road at that precise moment and –'

'– Sshh,' he whispered, placing a finger on her lips, 'don't dwell on it, we survived and that's all that mattered.'

'You're right, but how I wish I could be so –'

'– prosaic?'

'No. No, I don't mean that at all,' she insisted, 'you have loads of imagination, I'm sure, what I meant was that you have the ability to rationalise, make sense of things and I don't.'

'Don't do yourself down, Jenny. Now, coffee, that's the first thing and then we'll go out later; there's a good little Greek restaurant along the road, that is, if that appeals.'

'It appeals,' she smiled up at him and taking the cup from him, 'and what about your office, Paul? When are you going to ring them?'

'I should really do it now; let them know we're here. I have to, Jenny, don't you think?'

'Oh, yes, of course.' she agreed, appreciating the wisdom although at the same time loath to relinquish these moments. Time, when absolutely no-one knew where either of them were, but commonsense told her there really was no choice.

She watched, sipping her coffee, while Paul, taking off his jacket and draping it over the back of a chair, picked up the receiver. She didn't want to listen; he would tell her the outcome of the call and instead, putting her cup down, she wandered into the kitchen, eventually finding the bathroom. She splashed cold water on to her face, revelling in the coolness. Months in the sun meant she didn't need any make-up, although she decided, looking critically at her reflection in the mirror, her hair could do with some urgent attention. Running damp fingers through it, trying to arrange it into some semblance of order, or at least to how her hairdresser in Malta had intended her hair to look, she came to the conclusion it would have to do and went back into the lounge. Paul had finished his call and was sitting on one of the matching leather chairs, waiting for her.

'You look beautiful.' he said.

'Oh, Paul,' she protested, 'please, I don't feel it, but if you think so,' she smiled, 'that's oaky by me. You've spoken to Robert?'

'Yes, I've given him an up-date. You do realise it will mean you will have to meet with the Chief Inspector of Police; in fact, we both will.'

'Oh!'

'You knew that though, didn't you, Jenny?'

'I did, yes,' she admitted slowly, 'it's just so inevitable, that's all. What shall I say to them, Paul?'

'Just the truth, my sweet; exactly as you told me and then, remember I'll be with you.'

'It won't be so bad, then.'

'Not so bad,' he grinned at her, 'more coffee?'

'Please.'

'So,' Paul went on, re-filling her cup, 'we can expect a call either from Robert or the Chief Inspector later on today, or failing that, tomorrow morning.'

'That's okay, I suppose.'

'Don't worry, Jenny. Everything will turn out alright in the end.'

'Will it?'

'Of course it will.'

'It's all been so awful; not just what has been happening to us, but to–' she faltered, once again visions of Caroline running like a never-ending coloured slide across her brain, 'but to Caroline.'

'I know. I know.' he said, putting an arm around her. And, holding her close, kissed her gently on the cheek, 'We'll see it through, my love.'

The telephone rang as they were about to leave the apartment. It was six-thirty, the sun was shining through the ceiling-high plate glass windows and across the road Jenny could see the outer edges of the park, the blueness of the lake in the distance and for the first time for ages she felt relaxed and above all, hopeful. Perhaps there was a good future after all.

'It's for you, Jenny,' Paul said, covering the mouthpiece with his hand, 'Annette.'

'Annette!'

She took the receiver from him, experiencing at the same time a feeling of disorientation. She, Jenny Graham, was in London; nobody knew she was here, except Paul's editor but somehow, by some extraordinary feat of detection, Annette had found her.

'Annette?'

'Jenny, at last!'

'Annette,' she repeated, 'how did you know where I was?'

'More to the point, Jenny,' and she recognised the exasperation in her sister's voice. Annette had always been the calm one; Annette was the one who never, or at least hardly ever, lost her temper. She was cool, level-headed and never, absolutely never, sounded as if she was on the verge of tears, 'and more to the point,' Annette repeated, her voice shaking 'why didn't you let me know you were in Saint Angus? Why didn't you leave a message or something?'

'Hold on a minute, Annette. Hold on! I've been trying to call you, for days in fact. I suppose you were in the States?'

'Today, Jenny Graham' and she heard the anger in her voice, 'I have just returned from Malta!'

'What?'

'David had been trying to contact me and didn't catch up with me until last Tuesday night. I had just returned from California, but the reason he'd called was to tell me you were missing and that the Maltese police had already reached their verdict that you had drowned in a boating accident!'

'I do not believe this!' Jenny gasped, slumping down on the settee, 'I simply had no idea, Annette. Honestly, you have to believe me!'

'Oh, Jenny, love,' sobbing now. Her sister sobbing! Crying like this! Had she been responsible for her terrible distress? 'I can't tell you how desperately worried I have been.'

"I'm sorry, Annette, I truly am, but I didn't know you had gone out there. I didn't think for one minute David would get in touch with you.'

'It's alright, Jenny, you're okay and that's all that matters.'

'But, I have to explain, I have to tell you why I left the island the way I did.'

'Look, love, that isn't important at the moment. I spoke to Mrs Robertson earlier and she told me you were alright and that was all I wanted to hear but we'll talk tomorrow.'

'Okay.'

'Do you want to come here or shall we meet somewhere else?'

'Oh, we'll come to your place; about eleven, if that's alright?'

'We?'

'Yes, Paul will be with me.'

'Oh. That's fine and Jenny?'

'Yes?'

'God Bless.'

*

Andy's mobile rang minutes before Jenny and Paul were due to arrive. Annette watched his expression change, even after so short a time she had learned to read it. This, she felt, was not good news. It was Moira and from where she was standing, at the other side of the lounge, she could hear her voice. Something else has happened. What now, she thought and waited until he had finished talking before going over to him, resting a hand on his arm.

'What's wrong, Andy?'

'It's about David,' he said, switching off and putting the mobile back into his pocket, 'he's not actually been taken into custody, but the police have been giving him a hard time.'

'By the police you mean Inspector Secluna?'

'Yes, apparently David is their number one suspect.'

'Because of Jenny?'

'Not entirely,' he said, 'but for Caroline's murder.'

'This is hard to believe, Andy! How can they not see? What motive could David possibly have?'

'I don't know, my darling,' Andy said, leading her over towards the window, 'at this stage I don't believe motive is very high on the inspector's agenda. You see, David lied and not only that, according to what Moira has just told me, he withheld information from them and that is not exactly in his favour.'

'In what way?'

'Well,' Andy said, pulling her down beside him on to the sofa, pushing the cushions to one side, 'and this could be exactly what the police at this end will want to hear; which is, that Caroline telephoned him that night –'

' – the night she died?'

297

'Yes. David thought she was drunk and didn't take what she was saying seriously.'

'Poor, poor Caroline.'

'Quite. Anyway, she told him that Ben Standish had been to see her.'

'The same night?'

'Yes.'

'And he didn't mention this to the inspector? Why, Andy? Why on earth didn't he?'

'Something about not wanting to get involved.'

'So that is what has been wrong; it explains the dramatic change in him. I *knew* there was something, Andy. I just *knew!*'

'You were right, my love.'

'But,' Annette frowned, 'let's get this straight; the Maltese police know nothing about Ben Standish, do they?'

'I don't think they do; at least not yet, but I'm sure they soon will.'

'What do you mean?'

'We have no option, you know, Annette, now that we know Jenny is safe –'

'– but is she?' she interrupted quickly, 'Sorry, Andy, you were saying?'

'She'll get protection, you can be sure about that, but has it occurred to you we are learning more and more about what could have happened in Malta?'

'You're right, but shall we wait and hear what Jenny has to say? Paul Watson as well, of course.'

'I know.'

'How was Moira by the way?'

'She sounded okay; it's going to take her a long time to come to terms with everything, but she's an old trooper, Annette; resilient to the core and she won't let any of this get her down. Besides,' he added, 'she has Edward.'

'I noticed you didn't mention to her that Jenny had turned up.'

'No, I didn't,' he said slowly, 'until we've spoken to the authorities here I thought it best not to. Ben Standish is still on the island.'

'Don't I know it, also spiky hair!'

'Exactly.'

*

Chief Inspector Westbourne showed no surprise when the four of them were shown into his office on the second floor of New Scotland Yard. They had spent most of the morning, continuing through lunch, comparing notes; one of them filling in when there was a gap in what had happened. An appointment had already been arranged for Jenny and Paul for the afternoon and Annette had unhesitatingly agreed to go with them, followed quickly by Andy. It was obvious to Jenny when she saw her sister and Andy together they were more than just good friends; the way he would look at her as if he could hardly take his eyes away and as for Annette; Jenny had never seen her look so happy. It's strange; she couldn't help thinking that something good may have come out of this whole ghastly affair.

Chief Inspector Westbourne wasn't the only person in the office and after Paul had made the introductions, he beckoned to the tall thin man who had been standing with his back to the window.

'I would like you to meet Mr George Sanderson,' he began formerly; 'he is with the International Police.'

'Interpol!' Jenny said, shaking hands with him, immediately and incongruously being reminded of Adam Bond. A similar bearing; the controlled and concise way he had walked towards them.

'Yes, that's right,' George Sanderson smiled at her, 'you sound surprised, Miss Graham.'

'I shouldn't be, I guess,' she admitted, but ever since she had returned to Britain she'd had this feeling of not being in the real world or was it *she* who was no longer real? 'but, and this is difficult to explain, while I have never doubted the seriousness of what has been going on, it is only now I am beginning to feel the real impact.'

'Mr Sanderson and I worked closely together from the very beginning of the fraud case, fourteen years ago,' the chief inspector said, sitting down again; the only item on the highly polished desk a bulky manila folder, 'a long time and much to our regret with no success and now it looks as though we might be getting close to bringing these two men to justice.'

'Yes,' Mr Sanderson put in quietly, 'Phillip Jackson and Edward Bryant as the pair of them were called back then. We'll probably never learn how many times they have changed their identities since. Apparently,' he said looking closely at Jenny and Paul, 'you believe you knew Phillip Jackson as Ben Standish?'

'That's correct,' Paul agreed, 'and as you've no doubt been told by now, he's known in Malta as Lawrence Stanton.'

'Yes, and Edward Bryant, if he is the same man and the chances are he is, is using the rather ordinary name of Gerald Smith.'

'We have compiled what we hope is a fairly good likeness of what he may look like now,' the chief inspector put in, opening the folder and taking out two photographs; the original taken more than fourteen years ago and the other one, with signs of aging super-imposed, even to the addition of Gerald Smith's bizarre hairstyle. 'What do you think?'

'It's a remarkable likeness.' Annette said, leaning over to get a closer look, 'What do you think, Jenny?'

'It is, isn't it?' she faltered, memory flooding back. She was staring at not only the man who had taken her out to the farmhouse, but at the person who could have had something to do with Caroline's death.

'Are you alright?' Paul asked her softly, but she could only nod, not trusting herself to speak. It still hurt, also, this dreadful burden of guilt which, in spite of Paul's reassurances, was still there, embedded in her mind and refusing to let go.

'You mustn't blame yourself, you know.' Mr Sanderson said to her perceptively. He really did know how she felt.

'But I do; I can't help it.'

'Feeling as you do, Miss Graham,' he said, 'is understandable, but it really won't achieve anything. We have to move forward.'

'I know.'

'We have here,' the chief inspector said, clearing his throat, 'the police reports from Malta.'

'Do you have the one which would have been made yesterday, Chief Inspector?' Andy asked.

'You mean the interview with David Grech?'

'Yes.'

'It was faxed through this morning,' he said, 'but you knew about this meeting?'

'Yes,' Andy explained, 'David Grech is a good friend of my mother and she told me about the interview.'

'I see.'

What else does he see, Jenny wondered. Hearing David's name mentioned in the official environs of this office had shocked her. It should not have done; after all the four of them had already discussed what David had told Moira.

'The net appears to be tightening around these two,' Mr Sanderson was saying, 'but we will require your help, Miss Graham.'

'My help?'

'Yes, that is if you are agreeable –'

' – do I have a choice?' Jenny interrupted.

'Of course you have. Chief Inspector Westbourne and myself have discussed at great length as to how we could, only *could* you understand, proceed.'

'I don't know what you're going to ask my sister,' Annette said, 'but don't you think Jenny has been through enough already?'

'We do appreciate your concern, Miss Graham,' Mr Sanderson said, 'but perhaps if you could both listen to what we have to say, then your sister can decide for herself.'

'Alright.' Annette sighed, leaning back in her chair.

'Miss Graham,' he turned again to look at Jenny, 'what we have in mind will require you returning to Malta.'

'No!' Jenny stood up, pushing her chair back, wincing as it scraped along the wood floor and walked over to the window.

'Hear me out. Please.' he said softly, 'It won't take long.'

'I'm listening,' Jenny said, but with her back turned away from the room, not wanting any of them to see how much this suggestion had distressed her. She had to go back there; to the country which she had at one time loved and where she'd believed she could make her home? Back to where she and Caroline, no more than a year ago, had gone with such eagerness, both of them being taken on at the theatre, even those almost now forgotten days when she had first met David and, once again, been filled with hope; hope for a future which was not meant to be. No, they couldn't ask her to do this! More than anything, she wanted to wipe out the nightmare, but of course she couldn't do that. Also, that would mean dismissing Caroline and their friendship; a very special one. No, Mr Sanderson was wrong saying she had a choice. Whatever they were about to come up with she didn't have one and, deep down, she knew however difficult it would be she would do it; she had to. She owed it to Caroline.

She could feel the silence in the room behind her. Traffic, on the road below; one long moving stream was also silent and then still soundlessly they stopped at the traffic lights; red, amber, green, before continuing. That is what I have to do she thought with a sigh. Go on. And she turned round into the room again and went back to sit down on the chair next to Paul.

'Okay?' he whispered, taking her hand in his.

'Okay.'

'Thank you, Miss Graham,' the chief inspector said, 'we do realise how you must feel, but you will be in no danger.'

'I wasn't thinking about that actually.'

'No, I don't suppose you were,' he smiled, 'you're made of stronger stuff I think.'

'I hope so.'

'Now, here is the plan,' he said, 'Edward Bryant will be the easy part, or as you know him, Gerald Smith. All you have to do there is to make a signed statement to the effect that he took you to the farmhouse and locked you in there. We will then arrest and charge him with abduction.'

'But,' Andy put in, 'how can you follow that up with the fraud business?'

'A good point, Mr Henderson, but by the time we pull him in, hopefully we will have arrested the brains behind this business. I'm going to use a much hackneyed phrase that there is no honour among thieves, but believe me, in my experience and much jaundiced view, it has become a truism.'

'You obviously mean Ben Standish?' Annette asked.

'Yes, I do.'

'But how?' Andy again; a puzzled frown creasing his forehead, 'I don't understand.'

'You will,' the chief inspector promised, 'we are as convinced as you are that Standish is our man. He's not going to escape again. Also, given what David Grech has told Inspector Secluna; namely that Caroline told him that Ben Standish had visited her that night, could result in a possible murder charge.'

'Oh!' Jenny stifled a gasp, putting a hand up to her mouth.

'I'm sorry, Miss Graham,' the chief inspector said to her, 'but it had to be said.'

'I understand. But, how do you think I can help?'

'Well,' he went on slowly, squaring the folder in front of him and appearing satisfied he had it in perfect alignment went on, his eyes never leaving her face, 'we know about his farmhouse and we also know he has another property in Malta.'

'The apartment in Valletta.' Annette said softly.

'Yes, that's right. What we would like you to do Miss Graham,' he went on turning to Jenny once more and holding her breath, she waited, 'is to telephone him there. Have a brief conversation with him, just long enough to draw him out and make him admit he knew you when you were in France.'

'It might not work.' Paul said, 'He's not stupid, Chief Inspector, he might smell a rat. He's had a number of years to perfect more than one new identity.'

'No, Paul, wait a minute, it could work.' Jenny said, 'I have an idea,' she added, her memory effortlessly going back to their holiday and to that first evening when they had met Ben. It had been in the restaurant and she recalled how insistent he had been for them to join his table, also, how reluctant James had been.

'Yes, Miss Graham?' the man from Interpol now. She had all of their attention and for what seemed ages she felt a faint flicker of finding a way; a way of avenging Caroline's murder.

'Do you remember, Paul,' she said, turning in her seat to face him, 'on that first evening Ben introduced us to the couple who owned the villa next door to James' place?'

'Yes,' hesitatingly, 'but only vaguely.'

'You must remember them, Paul,' impatiently tugging at his sleeves, willing him to cast his mind back.

'Wasn't she called Diana; a blonde-haired woman, a bit horsey looking, but I can't remember his name though. Stephan something.'

'That's right,' she nodded, 'he was French, but Diana wasn't.'

'Wasn't she?'

'Of course not. She was one hundred per cent English and she spoke with a Sloane drawl,' Jenny mimicked, 'a bit like the other Diana, in fact.'

'Okay, okay,' Paul gave her a brief involuntary smile, 'but I honestly don't know where you're coming from.'

'Don't you?'

'No, I don't. Do you Chief Inspector? Mr Sanderson?' he asked them both, raising his hands in mock despair.

'I do believe I might.' Mr Sanderson said.

'Chief Inspector, Mr Sanderson,' Jenny went on, unable to keep the excitement from her voice, 'if, as you've suggested, I was able to speak to Ben I don't think he would be the least bit forthcoming, but if —'

'— if you were to pretend you were this Diana person.' Paul provided.

'That's right. I doubt if he's kept in touch with any of his old friends in France, well, he wouldn't have, would he? After all,' she went on, 'I *am* an actress; I should be able to manage to convince him.'

'Remarkable.' Mr Sanderson said, shaking his head.

'But,' Jenny said, soberly now, 'what happens then?'

'Don't worry, Miss Graham,' he said, 'you won't be on your own; the conversation will be taped and we can then go in and arrest him. If you are successful, he will have condemned himself.'

'And then you'll pull in the other guy.' Paul said.

'When do you want me to go out there?' Jenny asked impatiently, before Mr Sanderson could reply to Paul.

'As soon as possible,' the chief inspector said, 'tomorrow in fact.'

'I don't like this.' Annette said quietly, 'you say my sister won't be in any danger, but how can you be sure?'

'Because Miss Graham,' Mr Sanderson said, 'I'll be there with her.'

'But,' Annette persisted, 'why does Jenny have to go to Malta; why can't she just telephone from here?'

'For two reasons, Miss Graham,' he said patiently, 'for identification purposes and as the abduction charge is being made by the Maltese authorities. I appreciate your concern,' he continued, 'but this whole operation will be carried out as speedily as possible and within hours we should have the pair of them.'

'Wow!' Paul breathed out, leaning back in his chair. 'What an adventurous life you do lead, Jenny Wren!'

Chapter Twenty-two
MALTA

'Déjà vu.' Jenny said, as she followed Paul down the steps of the Boeing A300 and on to the shimmering heat of the tarmac at Luqa Airport.

'It probably does feel like that to you.' Paul said smiling at her over his shoulder. He had not been keen for her to come back, in spite of the assurances given by the Interpol guy. She was far too vulnerable. It only needed one person to recognise her for the news to reach Ben Standish via the theatre and that, of course, meant Gerald Smith. He did not like the situation, but at least he was here with her; he would be her personal bodyguard. It was not as though Paul underestimated her abilities for survival, but he was under no illusions; they were caught up in one hell of a tangled mess. Although he had tried to lessen the potential dangers of the accident with the car, he was still having nightmares of what could have happened. The brakes had definitely been tampered with; he was positive about that. The car had been in for its six-monthly maintenance only two days before he had driven up to Scotland and he had always gone to the same garage and trusted them, knowing something as crucial as a bolt linking the brakes would have been thoroughly checked and tested. Also, that guy; the stalker as Jenny was now describing him, seemed to have made a speedy departure from that Saturday morning although it didn't necessarily mean he had left the neighbourhood.

Paul had only been to Malta a couple of times before; years ago with his parents and he had little real memory of the island. In those days he had only been interested in swimming and learning how to snorkel. Just a kid really; he couldn't even remember the airport and mentioned this to Jenny as they waited at the carousel for their baggage.

'That's probably because you would have been at the old airport,' she explained, 'totally different to this one.'

'How do you know that? I thought you spent all your holidays up in Scotland?'

'I did, but before Caroline and I came out here, I read as much as I could about the island.'

'I should have done that,' Paul said, 'but, hopefully, this will only take a couple of days.'

'Look, Paul,' she touched him on his arm, her beautiful face serious for a moment, 'I know you're not happy about me coming back here, but you can see it is something I feel I must do. For Caroline.' she added sadly. He knew how deeply she was feeling about Caroline's death and he hoped that once this whole business was cleared up, she would learn to come to terms with losing her friend so tragically. He wished he could do more for her, but perhaps by being here would help. He hoped so. Over the days since arriving in Saint Angus he was seeing her quite differently; she was no longer that young girl; optimistically carefree, ridiculously romantic and reaching out for the impossible. She was ten years older and there was an aura of maturity about her now which certainly had not been in evidence back then. He wondered whether recent events had something to do with this.

'Okay, Jenny,' he squeezed her hand, 'I understand.'

'Here's our baggage,' she said, moving quickly forward to grab the strap of the first one, 'they came through quicker than they usually do.' she said walking alongside him, through the Nothing to Declare section and out on to the wide concourse of Arrivals. 'Mr Sanderson said we should go straight through; not to the taxi rank which is on the right-hand side, but out towards the car park where there should be a car waiting for us.' she added.

As soon as they emerged, shading their eyes against the glare of the mid-afternoon sun, a white Mercedes limousine drew up alongside them.

'Miss Graham? Mr Watson?' the uniformed driver asked, climbing quickly from the car and opening the rear door for them. They had been booked into the Hilton and the journey, once they had left the motorway to follow the road through the built-up industrial area around Hamrun and after leaving the Misida roundabout and heading towards the coast, became more picturesque and more as Paul expected it to be; Sliema, Balluta Bay, Saint Julian's, all familiar names to him now, having read Julia's report. He wouldn't be catching up with her until he was back in London; she had already left the island earlier that morning, Robert, having decided that with the way things were developing he should now pick up from where Julia had left off and for them to eventually co-write their story. Paul had no objection to sharing what he had, right from the beginning, always considered to be 'his baby' but he respected Julia Warburton. She was thorough, extremely intelligent and perhaps, above all, and necessary in good investigative journalism, had a feel for when something didn't gel. She had once laughingly told him when he had remarked on how intuitive she had been on one case to which she had been assigned, that he should just call it woman's intuition. But, it was far more than that. She had that rare ability to stand back and take the time not only to listen, but to swiftly sift right through to the core. She was one tough lady and he suspected, although he would never admit it, Robert felt the same.

Thirty-five minutes later, the Mercedes glided to a smooth halt outside the entrance to Malta's Hilton Hotel; the driver saying he would follow them inside with their luggage. They were certainly getting the full treatment Paul admitted. No little back street one-star establishment. This must surely be one of the island's best hotels: the high-ceilinged foyer and the marble pillars; Italian tiled flooring; the quiet subdued elegance of the good life. Not bad, he admitted to himself. Not bad at all.

'Where's James Bond then?' he muttered under his breath.

'It's a bit like that, isn't it?' Jenny smiled, taking out her passport from her bag.

'Surreal!'

'Let's book in, Paul. I know I wanted you to lighten up, but don't overdo it, eh?' but she was still smiling at him as she handed her passport to the straight-from-the-beauty-salon girl behind reception.

'Miss Graham,' the girl said, glancing briefly at Jenny's passport, 'we hope you had a pleasant flight to Malta this afternoon.'

'We did, yes.'

Formalities over; his own passport receiving the same automatic treatment, slim perfectly manicured finger nails much in evidence as she did so. Where do they find these girls he wondered; these especially-cloned hotel receptionists. He had seen dozens who had looked exactly like her: Hong Kong, Singapore, New York, London, the list was endless and, apart from different skin tones, they could very well have emerged from the same mould. He just could not imagine him spending any time with them. In an ordinary place for instance: a steamy little café off the King's Road, drinking espresso from thick china mugs and sitting on hard plastic chairs; rummaging through stuff in Petticoat Lane, hoping to find the bargain of the year; sharing an enormous pizza Margarita at Tony's in Notting Hill or standing in a downpour in Leicester Square waiting for a taxi. These girls were just not in the real world! At least not in his Paul decided, making an effort to return her programmed smile.

'Your bags will be brought up to your suite,' she told him, turning once again to Jenny, 'and Miss Graham,' she went on, 'this letter arrived for you earlier.' handing over a small white envelope.

'Instructions perhaps,' Jenny said as they took the elevator up to the third floor, 'it's all very hush-hush, isn't it?'

'It has to be my love; don't forget that.'

'I won't.' she said, prodding him gently in the ribs.

'They do seem to be giving us the top treatment,' Paul remarked once they were in their suite, Jenny having drawn back the curtains: cherry-red with splashes of vivid green fronds, mirroring the palm trees in the gardens below. In the centre of the room, a long, low, glass-topped table facing the sliding windows, a bowl of fruit: peaches; avocados; grapes and baby bananas, all juggling for space and alongside, nestling in a bed of ice, a bottle of champagne, 'look at this, Jenny,' he added, pointing to the table, 'what are they trying to do to us?'

'I don't know,' she laughed, turning away from the window and throwing herself down on to one of the softly upholstered chairs, 'but don't knock it, Paul!'

'I'm not,' he said quickly, 'but it doesn't seem right somehow.'

'How do you mean?'

'Well,' he started, not quite knowing how to express himself. What he wanted to say was, it was more like a honeymoon suite, but of course he didn't say that. They were on the island for a purpose and to have these frills, because that was how he viewed them, seemed a little bit over the top, 'I don't know,' he said at last, 'but I suppose what I mean is they do seem to be overdoing things rather.'

'True,' she agreed, 'anyway, let's read what this is all about.' opening the envelope.

Watching her, he waited. This was it he thought; this was when this trip became serious. This was when it was going to start. She didn't take long and without saying anything passed the note to him.

'Brief and to the point, eh?' Paul said after he had read it.

'Yes,' Jenny smiled up at him, 'so, they'll be sending a car to the hotel tomorrow morning at ten but nothing else.'

'No hint of where we'll be going; we'll just have to wait.'

'Have you noticed, Paul,' she said, standing up, 'it's addressed to me. They didn't say anything about you.'

'So?'

'Perhaps they only want me to go wherever it is I have to make this phone call.'

'I don't want you out of my sight, Jenny –'

'- but –'

'Jenny,' he interrupted, pulling her gently towards him, 'I really didn't mean to say this so soon, but –'

'- yes?'

'I'm falling in love with you, Jenny Wren,' he sighed, dropping his arms to his sides, 'and I don't want to spoil what I think we could have. You and me.'

'Paul –'

'Don't say anything. Not now, please.' he said, taking both her hands in his and raising them to his lips, 'I've said it now. But, Jenny, let us get through these next few days.'

'Okay.' she said softly; the wide almond-shaped eyes focused on him and with the light streaming into the room he could see himself reflected in their blueness. Who was this guy he thought. Prematurely pouring out his heart to a woman he had only recently, very recently in fact, met again? But, he didn't really feel like that. It was as if he had never seen her before, certainly had never known her before. He was falling in love with her and at that moment, still holding her hands, he wished they were anywhere but on this island with goodness knows what hanging over them. Bad timing, Paul, he concluded, very bad timing.

*

'This is Saint John's Street, Paul,' Jenny said to him, 'where Ben lives.'

'Is it?'

'Yes,' she nodded, 'I noticed the name on the plaque as we turned in to it. Why are we coming here do you think?'

'I don't know, my love,' he said. He was as puzzled as she was and he didn't feel all that comfortable either. There had still been no sign of George Sanderson; it was as if the pair of them were performing in some sort of crazily distorted movie.

Their car, this time a dark navy saloon, drew up outside an apartment block and the driver who had up to then said little, directed them up to the second floor adding that they were expected.

'Honestly,' Paul grumbled as they pushed open the heavy oak door to the building, 'this gets more and more like a John le Carré every minute.'

The number on the door, in gilt lettering, told them it was number 2B and with a feeling of foreboding, Paul pressed the bell. Immediately the door swung open and at last they were face to face with George Sanderson.

'Come in,' he said, 'I apologise for all this secrecy, but it's necessary.'

They followed him along the impersonal hallway to a door at the end. It didn't have the appearance of being an apartment; not a home where someone actually lived, but on the other hand, it didn't resemble an office either. Intrigued, in spite of his concerns, Paul chose not to say anything; as much as he would have liked to. He couldn't rid himself of the feeling that in George Sanderson's opinion he was only here, quite literally, for the ride. The man's whole attention was focused exclusively on Jenny. She had, he noticed, become quite pale since they'd arrived and he could tell by the way she kept biting her lower lip that she was nervous. Why the hell had he agreed for them to go through with this farce? He should have tried to dissuade her; she may have listened to him, but now in this lion's den of a place it was too late. She would have no option now but to go through with it.

'Across the road, Miss Graham,' George Sanderson was saying, leading her over to a chair which had been placed in front of the windows; horizontal blinds positioned in such a way to make it impossible to be overlooked, 'is Ben Standish' apartment.'

'Oh.' was all she said.

High-powered binoculars on a tripod had been set up to the left from where Jenny was sitting. Seeing them, he began to understand; to understand they had rented this apartment for the sole purpose of giving them the vantage point they needed to watch the comings and goings of

Standish. Neat, he thought, once again reminded of a seventies espionage thriller.

'Yes,' George Sanderson said to her, 'he is in there now, Miss Graham, and as far as we are aware he's on his own. A woman, we think she's his housekeeper, left the apartment about ten minutes ago, so,' he continued, 'this is perhaps a good time to telephone him.'

'Okay,' Jenny said quietly, taking a deep breath, 'I'm ready.'

'Good,' he smiled this time, 'I'm not going to tell you what to say; I'm going to leave that up to you. The main object is for him to admit that he is indeed Ben Standish. Once that has been established, it will be up to us; we'll go in there immediately. Mr Watson,' he turned to face Paul for the first time, 'I believe you could help us at this point.'

'Me?'

'Yes, I want you to come down with me. He hasn't seen you since you were in his company in France, but you've seen the photograph we have made up of what he looks like now.'

'Yes.'

'Your presence will assist us in the identification, you understand.'

Did he understand? He probably did; there could be some logic in it, but to Paul as he saw the way Jenny was sitting in what looked an extremely uncomfortable chair; high-backed and without any cushion, he began to wonder why she was being subjected to this ordeal if, as George Sanderson was now suggesting, the arrest of the man could be achieved solely on his own acknowledgement of recognising Standish.

'Of course I'll help.' was all he said, placing a hand on her shoulder which felt cold; the muscles beneath his finger-tips, tense.

'Right, that's settled then,' George Sanderson said quickly, obviously eager now to get on with the job, 'we have the number, Miss Graham,' he said, pushing a phone towards her; the kind of telephone Paul hadn't seen for years. Like a prop; the thought jumping into his brain and this was what this whole business was like. He hadn't been wrong when he had used the word to Jenny the day before. Surreal. It *was* surreal. Was this really happening, but he didn't need any answer to that; it was happening alright. Like, right this minute. From the moment Ben Standish picked up the receiver of his phone in the apartment across the road they were in at the deep end.

Jenny, her hand quite steady and with no hesitation, dialled the number written on the piece of paper George Sanderson had given her. Her eyes didn't waver; she kept looking straight ahead as if, Paul thought, she could see right through into Standish's apartment.

'Ben?' the Sloane drawl exactly right, 'Is that *really* you, Ben?'

'Who is this?' staccato and metallic, the man's voice entered the room, emerging from the apparatus at the other end of the table and from where George Sanderson was now seated, an unreadable expression on his face.

'It's Diana; you remember me?'

'Diana? I don't think I do.' wary, but not suspicious. Diana was a common enough name. He was sounding puzzled, interested even, but he was giving nothing away. Jenny is never going to crack this one Paul thought.

'Oh, come on, Ben, of course you remember me. I am just beginning to feel a teeny bit hurt. I know it's been a long time.'

'How long?' playing for time now.

'Ten years, Ben,' Jenny drawled, 'we had such a great time. Surely you can't have forgotten?'

Jenny's accent was perfect. How did she do it he wondered; her facial expression had not altered. Only her eyes told him what she was thinking; how much she hated every single second talking to the man who may have murdered her best friend.

'When exactly was this – Diana?' the voice crackled across the room, 'you say it was ten years ago?'

'That's right; the south of France. Remember?'

'How did you know I was in Malta?' a change of tack here and Paul's heartbeat quickened.

'Simple, my sweet,' Jenny went on, 'I saw you in Valletta and I recognised you immediately. How could I not; you're still the extraordinarily good-looking man who entertained us so well, especially me, Ben.'

Silence for a couple of seconds. How could Jenny succeed here Paul fretted; the man was a professional and then it began to happen.

'So, where are you staying?' Ben Standish asked her.

'You do remember me then, I thought you would.'

'What about Stephan?'

'He's ancient history. We divorced years ago!'

She's going too far Paul thought, holding his breath, so much his chest began to hurt and willing her to stop, to bring the call to an end, but she didn't.

'When you left Cap d'Ail, Ben, I was so unhappy, but,' Jenny went on relentlessly and he noticed tiny beads of perspiration along her forehead and he longed to take the phone away from her and hold her close, 'then you were very involved with that girl; you had no time for anyone else.'

'Jenny wasn't important, Diana. You should have realised that.'

At that point, George Sanderson could not restrain himself, rising from his seat and mouthing, 'Got him!' and gesturing to Jenny to end the conversation.

'Diana?' the metallic and grating voice reached them, 'Are you still there?'

'I'm here, Ben.'

'You haven't told me the name of your hotel. We could meet, have a drink perhaps.'

'Look, Ben, I have to go now; my boyfriend, no-one special you understand, has just turned up. I'll phone you later. Okay?' and then she put the receiver back on to its black cradle and leaned back against the hard wood of her chair, closing her eyes.

'You were brilliant, Miss Graham.' George Sanderson said, taking the handset from her, the same look of admiration on his face as he had the first time they had met him, 'Just think after fourteen years, it is indeed incredible!   Now, Mr Watson, if you're ready, we'll go down there. Inspector Secluna is already in position; this won't take long.'

'I don't like to leave Jenny here on her own.' Paul said quickly, not liking the look of exhaustion on her face, now paler than ever.

'As I said, Mr Watson, it should not take too much time to complete this part of the exercise.'

'I'll be alright, Paul,' Jenny said to him quietly, 'honestly.'

*

Jenny watched the two men emerge out on to the pavement and make their way across the road where they were immediately joined by a third. Presumably this was Inspector Secluna. Annette had described him well; considerably shorter than both Paul and Mr Sanderson and even from where she had positioned herself by the window and peering through the slatted blind she could see by the way he walked; briskly, striding towards them, he exuded confidence. How was he feeling she thought to herself, watching the brief shaking of hands as Paul was introduced to him, having to relinquish his position to a senior officer from the high echelons of Interpol! He didn't look to her the sort of man who would take second place to anyone.

They were now standing in front of the apartment block and George Sanderson, moving in front of them, leaned over and rang one of the bells to the right of the door. Expecting the door to swing open to allow them access into the building, and realising soon she would be seeing Ben she couldn't help a shiver of apprehension. This was it; after all these years. She didn't want to see him, but something prevented her from moving away from the window and turning her back on what was about to happen down there. A morbid fascination, perhaps. How had Caroline felt that night when she had come face to face with him? She had certainly, according to what she had told David, recognised him.

Nothing was happening; the door remained closed; three, four, five minutes and still no response. What's wrong she thought, the initial feeling of apprehension being replaced by the stronger emotion of disquiet. He *was* in there! He had to be! In the short time between replacing the receiver and to them leaving the apartment, if he had decided to go out, he would have been seen by the police. There could be a door at the rear, but, she tried to rationalise why he would have gone out that way. No reason, the only possible one being he hadn't been fooled by her. What would they do now she wondered. Unless they had a search warrant there was nothing they could do. The three of them moved back from the building, the inspector she noticed going to the edge of the pavement and looking up but all the windows on each floor had the same cream vertical blinds. Paul, shrugging his shoulders, was now walking back across the road. So, that was that; so much for their plan. It looked very much as though Ben had done it again. She had never doubted his cleverness. In France, he had always come across a lot smarter than anyone else and he was, without any doubt, resourceful. But where did this leave her and Paul? Surely there was no need for them to stay in Malta for much longer. She had yet to make the signed statement on Gerald Smith, but after that they would be able to leave. After all, it was no longer her problem anymore. She could get on with the rest of her life and if, as she was rapidly beginning to believe, Ben would be aware the authorities were closing in on him, her life was no longer in any danger. It all made sense, but then how could she be sure? And she waited for Paul to come back.

*

The telephone rang again in Ben Standish's apartment, shortly after he had replaced the receiver. Picking it up, he absently looked across the road towards the apartment block from where two men were coming out. They must be the new tenants he thought idly, having wondered over the past few months how much longer the apartment on the second floor would remain empty. He was about to look away when one of them; some years younger than the other, looked vaguely familiar; he had seen him before somewhere, but it must have been some time ago. He never forgot a face and then, like a physical blow, he remembered.

'Lawrence, are you going to answer or not?'

'No!'

'What's wrong?' Gerald asked, 'Are you alright?'

'No!' he repeated, moving away from the window and sitting down heavily on the chair in front of his desk and dragging the phone towards him. 'Gerald, I've been set up!'

'You're not making sense, Lawrence. Why not calm down and tell me what's happened?'

'My whole world is about to collapse, that's what!'

'What do you mean?'

He then told him about the call he'd had from a woman he had believed was an old friend from his Cap d'Ail days. Diana. He couldn't even remember her surname, but he had recognised her voice instantly. As he was explaining as best he could, trying to keep his voice steady and to stop the terrible nervous trembling in his body, his front door bell rang.

'Did you hear that, Gerald?'

'Yes.'

'That's them.'

'The police, you mean?'

'Yes, although by the look of them not Maltese. Interpol, I expect.'

'Shit!'

'One of them anyway, and do you know who the other one is, Gerald? Not that you ever met him, of course.'

'Who?'

'One of Jenny Graham's friends; Paul Watson. He was with them in France. Also, Alan reported that he joined her in that place in Scotland. Remember?'

As he finished talking, the front door bell rang for the second time. Now he realised without any doubt whatsoever that it had been Jenny on the phone. What an absolute gullible fool he had been.

'How did this Diana person know where to find you?'

'Don't ask me!' furious with himself to be tricked in such a simple way, waiting for the bell to ring again.

'It must have been Jenny.' Gerald said.

'I've just reached the same conclusion.'

'It looks as if it's all up for you, Lawrence.'

'Listen, man, if I go down, you go down with me! Understand?'

Just a minute!'

'No, Gerald, you wait. Somehow, I'm going to get out of this.'

'You can't stay in your apartment for ever, Lawrence. They'll be back.'

'I wish you would stop stating the obvious. I need time to work out something. And believe me, I will. I've done it before and I'll do it again!'

Chapter Twenty-three

He watched Paul Watson walk back across the road to the apartment, noticing the way he looked up at one of the windows and saw a slight movement; a strip of scarlet behind the blinds: Jenny Graham; the woman responsible for reducing him to this state; once again a fugitive on the run.

The other man, the one he'd come out of the apartment with, had stopped to talk to someone. He was Maltese and with his experience had police written all over him. Could be the same person Gerald had told him about; the one who had been to the theatre questioning everyone after the murder. Inspector Secluna; he remembered the name, also how Gerald had labelled him; a smooth operator he'd said. Well, Ben thought grimly, here was another smooth operator!

He would have to move quickly; they would be back and the next time they would have a search warrant. It wouldn't take them long to get one, not that they would find anything incriminating; he was far too smart for that, but now, while he still had time, he had to leave. And fast. Obviously, he couldn't go out the front way and the only other exit was by the fire escape at the rear of the building and trust they didn't have anyone positioned down there.

The pavement was deserted and, without looking back, he walked briskly to the end of the street, turned left and without lessening his pace continued across and into Merchant Street. His bank, was half-way along and the transactions took less than fifteen minutes; drawing out most of the cash from his current account and transferring all the funds from the deposit one to his bank in Switzerland. There was no problem; they knew him well, also that he had other accounts; the business ones, and although he made sure there was never too much of a surplus in them, they still showed healthy balances. There was nothing for the manager to get alarmed about; money was the very least of his problems. He left the bank, acknowledging with a nod as he always did, the armed guard standing inside the doorway.

There was nothing else for him to do in Valletta and he walked back up Merchant Street deciding to stay away from the city centre and on towards the bus station. He had been lucky so far, there was no point in taking any unnecessary risks. It would have been simpler and definitely more comfortable to have taken a taxi, but instead, he crossed diagonally to the stance for Sliema. It was not yet mid-day; mostly the passengers were tourists returning to their hotels after a morning of sightseeing and a few Maltese housewives; their baskets filled with produce from the market. Six minutes later and they were approaching Msida roundabout and he stood up to pull the bell cord and within seconds the driver was drawing up at the stop opposite the marina. Pushing his way through a gaggle of school children waiting on the pavement, he crossed the road.

'Silver Bird', the motor cruiser; the epitome of luxury and undoubtedly the most expensive vessel there, was berthed half-way along the jetty. He had bought her soon after arriving in Malta, more as insurance than anything else. An insurance against the need to make a quick exit, like now, but first there were a number of things he had to do. He had no idea how long he would have. Gerald was the only person he had told about the cruiser, not even Sylvanna; there was no need for her to know in any case. His past belonged to him and he never had any intention of giving her an inkling of what had gone before. Now, everything was changed. His future on the island had been reduced to rubble! He had the remainder of the day and night before he would be able to sail out of the marina and for these hours he would be forced to remain here. In spite of the ban on anyone staying on board overnight, he was going to take the risk. Another one. Like most he had taken, this was a calculated one. 'Silver Bird' was not overlooked by the water authorities and except for passing motorists and any passerby who may have noticed him going on board, they wouldn't know whether he had left the cruiser or not, so, he reckoned, this part of the plan should be foolproof.

He unlocked the built-in safe where he kept all of his private papers; his passports and most importantly, his Beretta; a nine millimetre automatic and one which had served him well. He had thought a number of times of replacing it with something less cumbersome, but had never got round to it. It did not matter all that much now, he decided, slipping it into a drawer next to the instrument panel. The ignition key; he had always kept on him and this also he took out, unclipping it from his key ring and sliding it into place and for a fraction of a second resisting the temptation to turn the key and to get the hell out of here, but commonsense, or more like self-preservation, prevailed, and instead he moved his hand away and walked back along the deck and into the saloon.

The first call he made was to the airport, asking to be put through to Ricardo Mion. They had helped each other over the years; a good relationship where neither of them asked to know too much and both of them gaining. He had helped him with a number of lucrative deals and in return, Ricardo had been forthcoming with information which he had readily extracted from the data on his computer. This time was no exception; within minutes Ricardo confirmed that a Miss Jennifer Graham had arrived on the island the previous afternoon from Heathrow, also there was a Mr Paul Watson on the same flight. Good. That was a start. There was a time when it would have been possible to have learned the name of their hotel, but not anymore. Those days for non-residents to fill in boarding cards had, regrettably, gone.

Ben settled down; a can of lager on the table by the side of him, to think through the next stage; to find out where Jenny was staying and, presumably, Paul Watson would be booked in at the same hotel. Surprisingly, this didn't take long. After the third attempt he had what he wanted; they were both at the Hilton in Saint Julian's and satisfied, he leaned back in his chair, taking a deep sip from the can. So far, so good.

There was nothing else he need do for the present, except to get through the hours until morning. He had already worked out what the next steps would be, having no illusions there was any guarantee they would work, but they had to. This was his last chance and for this, he needed Jenny Graham. Pay-back time, he thought grimly, taking another lager from the fridge. She had now become crucial in getting him out of here. He had no qualms about what he was planning; she meant nothing to him. If he allowed himself to think about her at all, which he tried not to, it was only as a reminder that if it had not been for her presence and her interference he would probably at this moment be winding up at the office and telephoning Sylvanna to arrange where they would meet for their evening meal. Instead, all that was over. No more business, no more Sylvanna and even more important to him, no marrying into a family which he had hoped would bring him into the affluent community for which he craved and then once and for all he would have been able to put his past behind him. But, it was not to be. As for Gerald, it was high time they severed their ties, long overdue in fact. Gerald had become a hindrance. Not that he ever reminded him about what they had been through, at least hardly ever, but what jarred was simply that Gerald was living in the same place as himself.

Chapter Twenty-four
ENGLAND

'And how was Mr Barton today?' Andy asked her, accepting a glossy printed menu from the Chinese waiter. They were in the 'Golden Dragon'; a small Chinese restaurant in Soho and one he had told her had been his favourite ever since he started working in London.

'Quenton was his usual cantankerous self,' Annette said, opening her menu and scanning down the long list of dishes, 'although more so than usual. I think he was a bit miffed I didn't go into the office yesterday.'

'He's not the most sympathetic of bosses.'

'No,' she smiled, 'in one word I would describe him as difficult. Do you know, Andy,' she went on, 'he could have booked me on the Monday flight out; there's very little I'll be able to do over the weekend.'

'Why did you think he did that?'

'Oh, that's easy to understand; Quenton likes to crack the whip and he hasn't quite forgiven me for taking time off; insists on calling it a holiday!'

'Have you ever thought of finding another publishing house?'

'Often,' Annette laughed ruefully, 'but I might be even worse off, although I'm sure there cannot be two Quenton Bartons in London!'

'Annette,' Andy said, 'I've told you a little about my business. It is very much still in its infancy, but we're doing quite well. I would like you to come and work with me.'

'Andy! Do you mean that? I thought you already had a partner.'

'I do, but not for much longer; he's leaving at the end of the summer.'

'Why?'

'He's getting married to an Australian girl; she's in the same business, so he's going over there to set up his own publishing firm.'

'I see,' hesitatingly, 'but, I don't know, Andy –'

'– I don't want you to decide anything right now, Annette. Think about it. We've been deliberating for some months about bringing a woman into the business, more of a balance if you know what I mean and, besides,' he paused, looking at her closely; the eyes so like his mother's, 'I can think of no better person than you. You've been in publishing for a number of years and frankly I think you're wasted working for Quenton Barton. I believe you have a lot more to offer than he is giving you scope for, Annette. That's all.'

'Thank you, Andy. I will think about it and I won't keep you waiting too long. You'll want to make inroads to replace your partner quite soon, I expect.'

'It will give you something to do this weekend.' he grinned.

'Oh, Quenton has already taken care of that,' she said, 'he's given me a bulky manuscript to review. To keep me occupied until Monday morning he said!'

The waiter returned to their table and they ordered; choosing slices of Peking duck in a sweet sauce; prawns in batter; sweet and sour pork and Cantonese rice. What Andy had suggested excited her, but she still needed time to think it through; what it would mean, leaving someone for whom she had worked for so long. In spite of her frequent irritations with Quenton, she did respect him, also she realised how hurt he would be if she were to resign, especially to join Andy's firm: Andy, the man who had turned down an offer to work for him. Quenton would certainly find that a bitter pill to swallow!

They had almost finished their meal when her mobile rang. Quickly, and apologising, she pulled it out from her bag, pressing the on-switch. She had meant to turn it off before they came into the restaurant, but it had slipped her mind.

'Annette! Jenny, here.'

'Jenny! How did it go today?' looking across at Andy.

'In a nutshell, it didn't work.'

'Oh, no! What went wrong?'

'Well, I phoned him exactly as we said I would and we all thought it was going okay, but when they went over to his apartment – the police had taken occupancy of one across the road – he didn't answer his door bell.'

'Do you think he was still inside the apartment?' Annette asked; this was the last thing she had expected to hear. Mr Sanderson had sounded so confident their plan would be successful.

'He must have been, Annette,' Jenny was saying, 'it was only a matter of minutes from when I finished the call and there were already police outside the building; they would have seen him leave. But,' she continued, 'this is the bad news; he's not there now. They went back later with a search warrant and the housekeeper came to the door. All she could tell them was that he'd gone out.'

'So, what happens now? Will you be able to come back home soon?'

'I think so; I'm not sure exactly when, though.'

'Are you worried about this setback, Jenny?'

'Not really. I think Ben's main aim will be to get off the island.'

'I suppose you're right,' Annette agreed, 'you remember I'm leaving for the States tonight, don't you?'

'Yes, I hadn't forgotten and, Annette?'

'Yes?'

'Please don't worry about me. Paul's here and we'll be coming back to London together as soon as we can, but I must get in touch with Moira before then. I feel I owe her an apology; also I have to speak to Adam.'

'They should understand you had no choice.'

'I hope so, but this fraud business is still under wraps, at least for the time being, so I'll have to watch what I say to them both.'

'I see, but be careful love, won't you, and I'll see you when I get back home. It should be by the end of next week, unless Quenton finds something else for me to do while I'm over there.'

'I don't know how you put up with that tyrant!'

'Neither do I,' Annette said, amused by the quizzical expression on

Andy's face, 'I didn't tell you, Jenny, but Quenton was a great admirer of Moira when she was in the West End, so he can't be all that bad!'

'Point taken,' Jenny laughed, 'anyway, Annette, have a safe journey.'

'I'm intrigued,' Andy said when she had switched off, 'I take it the plan failed and Standish is still on the loose?'

'You're right,' she said and relayed the gist of what Jenny had told her.

'I don't think they will be able to keep this news quiet on the island, you know.'

'Don't you?'

'No, it's a small island, my love. People talk; it's only to be expected and speculation will be rife. You can bet someone will come up with something pretty close to the truth.'

*

Andy had driven her to Heathrow and they had enough time for a coffee before she needed to go through to Departures. He was going to miss her. He could not remember feeling so relaxed and comfortable in anyone's presence before. He knew already she was the woman for him and he had waited a long time. A number of affairs; none of which for one reason or another, ever lasted more than at the most six months. But Annette was different from any other woman he had ever met. Not only was she lovely, but she had a quick brain; articulate without losing any of her femininity and he admired that tremendously. He didn't want to rush things; not forgetting they had only met so recently, but each time he was with her, more so now they were back in London, there had been quite a few times when he had almost said the words which could have frightened her off. And only for that reason he had held back. But now, seeing her sitting across the table from him, slowly stirring her coffee, he wished she didn't have to leave. Knowing that it would not be for so very long wasn't much help to him at that moment.

'I'll give Moira a ring, shall I?' he suggested, 'She may have some more up-to-date news for us. If there is, she will be bound to have heard, I'm sure.'

'Good idea,' Annette smiled, 'perhaps she's spoken to Jenny by now.'

Andy dialled the number, sipping his coffee while he waited.

'Moira?'

'Andy, darling! How lovely, I was just thinking about you!'

'I thought I'd find out how you were; I've been meaning to phone you before but it's been a bit hectic her.'

'That's alright,' she said quickly, 'but where on earth are you phoning from? There's a great deal of noise in the background.'

'I'm at Heathrow to see Annette off. She has to go back to the States for a few days.'

'That punishing boss of hers, I suppose. Anyway, give her my love and of course a safe journey.'

'I will,' he promised, 'and what have you been doing?'

'It's not what *I've* been doing,' Moira emphasised, 'it's what everyone else around here is up to! Honestly, Andy, you just would not believe what's been happening here. In fact, it's been one thing after another.'

'Such as?'

'For a start,' she began, 'Gerald has been arrested! At Luqa; he was about to board a flight for Rome! Imagine! Adam telephoned me earlier; he is absolutely furious. The season is in full swing and he is quite literally pulling his hair out!'

'And what's Gerald supposed to have done?'

'They're not saying. It really is so frustrating, Andy!'

'And very dramatic.'

'Yes, it is, but one lovely thing did happen today; I had a call from Jenny. The relief learning she was alright was wonderful. She wasn't able to tell me the reason why she left the island so suddenly; mind you, she had no idea that this had caused such mayhem. In fact, it all sounds very mysterious, darling. All she did say was that her life was being threatened, that was all.'

'No doubt everything will come out in the end,' Andy said, 'the main thing is that she's safe.'

'I know and that is exactly what Edward says, but you know how sanguine he is, always looking on the bright side and he never did believe Jenny had drowned, in spite of all the evidence.'

'You really shouldn't concern yourself so much, Moira,' Andy told her, 'you'll make yourself ill.'

'Oh, I'm fine, darling and,' she went on in the same breath, 'there's another thing!'

'What?'

'You remember the wedding Edward and I were invited to?'

'Yes.'

'Well, apparently it's off! The groom, Lawrence Stanton, has gone!'

'You mean, he's left Malta?'

'I suppose so. Do you know, Andy, I am convinced there is a connection here. Somewhere.' she added, and he could visualise her, facing out towards the bay, a tiny frown of puzzlement on her forehead and tendrils of hair escaping from the clasp she always wore.

'Do you think so?' how he disliked questioning her in this way; pretending he was ignorant of what was happening, but it was the only way to try and find out from her what she had heard, not only at the theatre, but in and around Balluta and Sliema.

'Well, yes, darling, I do as it happens. Although Lawrence has been living here for about ten years or so; has an extremely lucrative finance business on the island, it would now appear that no-one seems to know very much about him.'

'His fiancée, Sylvanna you told us, she can't be too happy about him leaving her in the lurch.'

'Too right,' a dry chuckle at the other end of the line, 'that is putting it mildly; according to what I've been hearing, she is out for his blood!'

'Oh, dear.'

'Is that all you can say, Andy, especially when I have bought the most beautiful outfit for the wedding!'

'Never mind, Moira, perhaps you'll go to another wedding soon and you can wear it then.'

'Andy Henderson! What are you trying to tell me?'

'Nothing, mother, nothing at all.'

As he switched off, he looked at Annette, realising she must have understood exactly what he had meant. She was smiling; her eyes sparkling mischievously and she reminded him of Julia Roberts in 'Notting Hill'; towards the end of the film when she looked as if she would never stop.

Chapter Twenty-five
MALTA

Ben dialled the Hilton number at nine the following morning. His luck was still holding; Paul Watson answered.

'Mr Watson?'

'Yes?'

'You won't know me, Mr Watson,' Ben said, trusting he wouldn't recognise his voice, but it was unlikely; too long ago. 'but I have some information on Ben Standish which you may find interesting.'

'Who is this?'

'You're a reporter, aren't you?' side-stepping the question.

'Yes, that's right, but –'

'– working on a follow-up article on the man you once knew as Ben Standish.' he interrupted.

'Look,' Paul Watson's voice now edged with irritation, 'this is a bit irregular, isn't it; phoning me like this?'

'I don't think we should concern ourselves too much with irregularities, Mr Watson. Let me put it this way; I have something for you, something which would certainly add to your story, once this news hits the headlines.'

'Okay,' Paul said, 'and what do you want? Or should I say how much do you want and before you go any further, I am not personally in a position to pay out. That would be done through my newspaper. So,' he continued, 'I'll need to have your name and address.'

'I see your point,' Ben said, fully expecting this reaction, 'why don't we meet; this morning, in about half an hour?'

'Where?'

'How about Marco's in the Strand?'

'That's in Sliema, isn't it?'

'Yes,' Ben said, 'the large gilt-fronted café next to the stationers; you can't miss it. I'll be sitting at one of the tables outside.'

Ben waited six or seven minutes before phoning the Hilton again; this time asking to speak to Miss Graham.

*

I don't know why I'm doing this, Jenny thought, climbing into the back seat of the taxi outside the hotel, but Ben had been insistent, also his manner; as if he genuinely wanted to see her. 'You know, Jenny,' he had said, sounding quite different from the last time she had spoken to him, 'I'm in a pretty bad spot, but I want to try and explain a few things to you. I am not as black as they are all painting me.' he added, not giving her the opportunity to protest; to mention Caroline's name, but there was something in his voice which had, in spite of any misgivings she may have had, reached out to her. Perhaps, she thought, looking out of the window but without really registering anything: the continual traffic jams as the vehicles waited to join the main road out of Saint Julian's before reaching the coast road; the tourists, apparently without any worries on their minds, strolling in the way only holidaymakers did, along the crowded pavements, she'd been wrong about Ben having anything to do with Caroline's death. Apart from Caroline telling David he had been to her apartment, it wasn't actually conclusive.

By the time her taxi was approaching Msida roundabout she had convinced herself there was no harm in meeting him and hearing what he had to say. It was broad daylight after all. What could happen to her? She wasn't in any danger, but nevertheless, a small, microscopic part of her brain was doing its best to remind her that she didn't really know him. That brief affair was well and truly buried. Of course Ben was guilty of the fraud thing, but a murderer? She paid off the taxi where he had told her to stop; in front of the marina and saw him standing on one of the pontoons at the other side of the low wall. He waved to her and she walked down the couple of steps to meet him.

'Hello, Jenny. It's been a long time.'

'Yes, Ben, it has.'

'If you don't mind, I would rather not stay out here. We'll go aboard, shall we; more comfortable anyway.'

Polite, inconsequential conversation between two virtual strangers and she followed him along the narrow wooden platform, stopping when they reached a royal blue and white motor cruiser; Ben stepping easily and lightly on to the deck and putting out a hand to help her. It was when she felt the slight pressure of his hand, cool in spite of the heat, she had the first twinge of unease. This was not a very bright thing to be doing. She should not be here, but, she couldn't turn back now. There were quite a number of people about; several standing at the bus stop, also a couple of men on the boat berthed next to this one. She would be alright.

'Coffee?'

'No thank you, Ben,' she tried to look at him directly, but it was not easy, 'I can't stay long, but on the phone you sounded as if you wanted to say something to me.'

'I did, yes.' Slowly, taking his time and walking over towards the front of the cruiser and casually leaning against the control panel and for a fleeting moment looking like the Ben she used to know: sophisticated, charming and so very much at ease. 'Why did you do it, Jenny?'

'Do what?'

'Why did you shop me to the police?'

'You are quite wrong; I didn't.'

'Do you expect me to believe that?'

'It happens to be true.'

'Really?'

'Yes, really.'

'And this morning's little performance. Phoning me; pretending to be

Diana. Are you going to tell me that isn't true also?'

'It was me, yes, but I was asked to do that.'

'By the police?'

'Well, yes —'

'– You surprise me, Jenny,' he interrupted, still remaining where he was; 'you used to be a lot brighter.'

'What was it you wanted to tell me, Ben?'

'There are a number of things I would like to tell you,' he said, moving away from the instrument panel; the key she noticed was in the ignition and she watched him opening one of the drawers at the side, 'but all in good time.'

'I don't understand what's going on, Ben, and I think I should go. Nothing is going to be gained by me being here. It was a mistake.' And she turned to leave.

The hand on her bare arm was like a vice, whirling her body around to face him; in his right hand, perfectly steady and pointing directly at her, a gun. This is not happening to me! This is not real! It can't be! She could hear the traffic on the main road, also voices on the pavement above the marina.

'Are you mad?' she whispered; fear, like a thick blanket, stifling and suffocating and all she could look at was that awful black hole in the gun.

'Shut up and listen to me!' his voice totally changed now; all pretence of friendliness gone and she saw for the first time the real Ben Standish: Ben Standish; fraudster, con-man and murderer. Ruthless and, yes, perhaps he was mad, 'You are here for a reason, Jenny. I intend to get away from this island and you are going to help me.'

'How?'

'You can call yourself a hostage,' he said, 'prisoner, even; it's all the same. Take your pick. Shortly,' he continued, the gun held high, aimed at her and she stood there unable to move, 'I'm going to telephone the police; tell them where I am and when they arrive you will be my protection while I do a little deal with them.'

'What sort of deal?' she breathed, 'I don't understand. Whatever it is, Ben, it will never work and if you kill me, what would that achieve?'

'Leave that for me to decide and make no mistake, if I have to, I will.'

Without taking his eyes, dark and unblinking, from her face, with his free hand he took the mobile from his jacket pocket and dialled.

*

It was warm and airless in the interview room of the Rudolph Street police station and Inspector Secluna switched on the overhead fan; the rhythmic movement doing little to bring much relief. George Sanderson was sitting across from Gerald Smith; a dictaphone positioned in the centre of the plain wooden table.

It was eleven on the clock on the wall in front of him and, as if to confirm this, the bells from the church nearby began to chime. They had covered the preliminaries; formalities, the two charges had been read out, complicated by the fact that the one of abduction was a Maltese matter while the other, international.

'You will be confined here, Mr smith,' George Sanderson was saying, 'until such time as you will be escorted back to Britain to face trial for fraud and although of a far more serious concern, does not in any way diminish the one of abduction; abduction with intent. However, there is the possibility that this charge may be waived, but that is up to you and of course whether we have Miss Graham's agreement.'

'How?'

'We require information about Phillip Jackson or Lawrence Stanton as he is known in Malta.'

'I don't think there is anything I can tell you that you don't know already.'

'I doubt it,' George Sanderson said dryly, 'let us start by asking you one question. Alright?'

'Alright.'

'As you learned last evening we already have the airport covered, also the ports and those along the coast of Sicily. All vessels leaving the island have been searched and are continuing to be searched. Have you any idea how he could try to escape? You must have both discussed such a possibility, surely. There was, I would imagine, a contingency plan.'

'He has a boat,' Gerald Smith said at last, 'a motor cruiser.'

'I see. And where does he berth it?'

'I can't remember.'

'Come along, Mr Smith,' George Sanderson said quietly, 'you can do better than that. Who else knew he had this cruiser?'

'As far as I know; no-one.'

'I see,' he repeated, 'and you are not prepared to divulge where this cruiser is kept.'

'I didn't say that.'

'No, you didn't, but,' he added, 'let me remind you that you are in a very tricky situation, facing charges both here and in Britain. I don't think you would enjoy spending an indefinite period in prison on the island awaiting trial, knowing, of course, that you had another one looming.'

'Okay,' Gerald shrugged, running a hand through hair which looked as if he hadn't combed it for a very long time, 'the marina. At Msida.'

'And the name of the cruiser?'

'"Silver Cloud".'

'Thank you.'

The telephone rang at that moment, disturbing the stillness in the room and the chief inspector picked up the receiver.

'It's alright, sergeant, put him through.' pulling his notepad towards him and taking a pen from his shirt pocket, said: 'Yes, Mr Watson?'

Sirens, faint at first, growing louder as the three police cars approached the roundabout; tyres screeching as they swerved round the last bend and coming to an abrupt halt alongside 'Silver Cloud'.

'What the hell! You've stitched me up again, you bitch!' he hissed, swinging her round and pushing her hard against the instrument panel; the pain as her back hit the wood was excruciating, making her catch her breath, 'there is no way they could have got here so quickly; no way! This is a bloody cavalry charge!'

'No-one knew I was here,' Jenny gasped, pressing the palm of her hand on her spine to ease the pain.

'Shut up!' dragging her out on to the deck, the gun this time pressing hard against her spine; the coldness of the metal like ice through the cotton of her tee-shirt, 'you will do exactly as I say; I'm getting out of here and I don't care what it will cost. You are dispensable, Jenny Graham!'

Jenny looked up towards the pavement, her eyes watering in the harsh sunlight and saw George Sanderson walking over to the low wall separating the marina from the road. Armed police were spread out on either side of him; some of them crouched in a firing position. Behind this tabloid, traffic continued to roar along the main road, the bus for which the people must have been waiting, drew up at the stop and across the road, a second bus; this one going in the direction of Sliema, was disgorging its passengers and none of them appeared to notice what was happening. All of this Jenny saw instantly, like a snapshot and one which would no doubt soon be replaced by another one.

'Mr Jackson!' George Sanderson called across.

'I'm sailing out right now!' Ben shouted, pushing her forward in front of him, 'and I want you to get clearance from the harbour master.'

'Release Miss Graham and then we can talk.'

'No! She comes with me! Otherwise, she is dead!'

'If I do contact the harbour master, how do you propose to move out as well as use Miss Graham as your shield? Have you thought how difficult that would be?'

And then he laughed; high-pitched, but without any humour. In all her life, Jenny had never heard a sound like it and for a fraction of a second the gun shifted as he tried to control himself. Then, as though annoyed by his lapse, he cleared his throat and pulled her back towards the centre of the deck. She was glad she couldn't see his face, but she now knew with certainty that Ben Standish was indeed mad. The realisation was terrifying; the knowledge she was never going to be able to break away, suddenly the inevitability of it all was too much.

'Miss Graham will be taking her out, not me!' Ben bellowed, although the distance, ridiculously close, didn't warrant that. Another example of how unhinged he was.

'Be reasonable, Mr Jackson,' George Sanderson said, both hands resting on the wall, 'let Miss Graham go and we can talk rationally; that way, no-one will get hurt.'

All the time he was talking, Ben was forcing her to walk backwards until they were at the controls. He was actually going to try this crazy thing she thought, waiting for him to tell her what she had to do.

'Listen,' his voice harsh, far too close to her; she could feel his breath on the back of her neck, 'I want you to stretch your arm round and turn on the ignition.'

'Ben,' for the first time she was pleading with him, trying to get through to the Ben she had once known and loved so passionately, 'can't you see, this won't work! Why don't you do what he's suggesting?'

'Do it!' he spat out.

'Okay,' she sighed, 'but do you think you could take the gun away from my back; it's going to make it even more difficult for me to twist round.'

Surprisingly, he did as she asked and she half-turned until she could see the instrument panel.

'It's not there.'

'What?'

'The key, Ben, it's not in the ignition!'

He spun round and this was her chance, her only one, and she took it. She pushed him as hard as she could and caught off-balance he fell sideways against the controls. She didn't go towards the pontoon, but instead ran to the other side of the boat and hurled herself over the side, allowing her body to sink below the surface and swimming underwater for as long as her breath would allow before emerging, gasping for air.

'Jenny! Over here!'

At first she thought she was hallucinating. Paul? How could it be? He wasn't here! Nobody knew she was going to the marina, but as she began to breathe more normally, she saw him with a wonderful clarity, leaning over one of the pontoons, his arms stretched out, waiting to haul her out of the water.

'Oh, Paul!' she was crying now, tears streaming down her cheeks, unable to stop.

'Sssh, darling,' he said, holding her tight, 'you're safe now.'

And looking up at him she realised he was crying also. And for a couple of seconds they clung to each other.

'What happened back there?' she asked at last, trying to stop shivering. By now she had become conscious of her saturated state; there was water everywhere and not too fresh either; her jeans felt slimy, the denim clinging to her legs and her hair, a tangled smelly mess.

'They got him, Jenny. You'll hear all about it later, but we must get you back to the hotel.'

He helped her to her feet and they walked towards where the first police car was parked. Immediately a constable came running towards them carrying a blanket and placed it gently around her shoulders.

'Are you alright, Miss?'

'I'm fine.' she managed to smile at him, gratefully pulling the blanket tightly across her chest.

*

The irony is,' George Sanderson said later that afternoon; they had agreed to meet him in the hotel lounge. Jenny had emerged from a deep and recuperative sleep; only a couple of hours, but it had been sufficient. She felt able, although with reluctance, to discuss the recent events with him. The morning now seemed like a nightmare and all she wanted was to leave the island and return to London and forget, more than anything else, about Ben Standish and how he had been in those last desperate moments. 'it would seem that we could have very well been spared most of what has been happening recently.'

'In what way?' she asked him.

'Because,' he explained, 'yesterday a formal complaint, substantiated by a firm of lawyers, was handed into police headquarters in Valletta with very strong evidence that Lawrence Stanton has been involved in a number of dubious dealings. One of his clients had for some time become increasingly concerned about discrepancies in the account he had entrusted to Stanton's firm and he mentioned this to one of his close friends, namely, Marco Giannini.'

'Isn't that Sylvanna's surname,' Jenny put in quickly, 'the girl he was engaged to?' remembering what Annette had told her and how distressed she had been at the time.

'That's right, Miss Graham. You see, Mr Giannini had not been too happy about the impending marriage and he had been employing a private investigator to find out what he could about Stanton and so far he had come up with nothing. He could find absolutely no trace of the man before he arrived on the island, none whatsoever, and when Mr Giannini heard what his friend had to say, he began to put two and two together. What I'm trying to say is; it would not have been very long before Stanton would have been exposed for what he is. Not only an imposter with no credible past, but with apparent criminal tendencies. Need I say anymore?'

'So, really,' Paul said, 'he was carrying on in exactly the same way as he had done before. Conning people and creaming off the money they were investing.'

'Precisely.'

'And, Mr Sanderson,' Jenny said, 'from what everyone is saying, there seems to be no doubt that Ben is a fraudster, but do you believe he is also a murderer?'

'You're thinking about your friend, aren't you?'

'Yes.'

'The evidence is building up,' George Sanderson smiled at her, as though he knew what she was thinking; that she still blamed herself for Caroline's death, but then, although she was gradually coming to terms with it, she knew there would always be a part in her memory which would stay there. She just had to learn to live with it; perhaps for the rest of her life. 'Now Stanton is in custody we've been able to take the investigation further. His fingerprints match those found in Miss Johnson's apartment. We will, of course, need much more than that, even with Mr Grech's evidence and no doubt a good defence lawyer would put forward a sound case on his behalf, but either way, Miss Graham, he's going to spend a considerable length of time locked up.'

'And the other man,' Paul asked, 'Gerald Smith, what will happen to him?'

'He'll face charges along with Stanton for his part in the London fraud. As we speak,' he added, 'both men are on their way back to England. You could say they have had a good run for their money, if you'll excuse the pun! And now, Miss Graham,' he continued, 'I have heard on the

Maltese grapevine they are hoping you will be returning to the theatre.'

'Oh, no, Mr Sanderson,' Jenny answered, scarcely believing what she had heard; was there nothing private on this island? 'I'll be going back to London. With Paul.'

'I rather thought that might be the case,' and for the first time permitted a genuine, although benevolent, smile to cross his thin features, 'and Mr Watson,' he said, turning in his chair to look at Paul, 'you will be returning to your editor with a first-hand account; a scoop in fact, of the winding up of this affair?'

'That's right,' Paul matching his smile and putting an arm around Jenny's shoulders, 'my paper will have its scoop and I will have my girl!'